ART DYGACZ

INSIDE-INSIDE

ISBN: 978-1-5272-2849-8

First published 2018

Cover Design created by Andrea Brajnovic

Typeset by Anton Pshinka

CONTENTS

AUTHOR'S NOTE

The idea of writing a book where the world would be as unpredictable, as unknown to the people living in it as if their lives never happened; where the characters would be so torn apart from inside that they questioned even their own identity, was one of the oldest I ever conceived. In fact, the title for the book was first coined in... Polish, which is my first language, back in late 2007, and put down in one of my original, tattered notebooks that I keep to this day. Even the drafts for the opening chapters were initially created in my mother tongue. I only translated and used them as a "springboard" for the whole plot once I decided to write everything in English.

Many years have passed since my earliest grapples with the title; a lot of things have happened along the way, but what is the most important, some brave new ideas for books have been developing in my mind. Now *INSIDE-INSIDE* is written as a prologue for the entire series that is set in a fictional, imaginary world that bears a probabilistic resemblance to our own, mimicking the reality we experience in our everyday lives. One of the main purposes of the book is to beg the question: Is reality really real? Are we in control of the lives we live or are we just players, shooting stars in a blockbuster movie, the scenario to which someone has written for us and slipped it under our pillows at night while all of us were asleep?

These and other questions may spring to your mind as you go along with the main character in a journey to discover the world, but many of you will certainly be asking yourselves at this point: What is *INSIDE-INSIDE?* What if I tell you that your life is a never-ending journey and a never-ending destination, and the best you can find while exploring the world is how to discover yourself? This is what *INSIDE-INSIDE* is in its primal meaning; it is what lays behind your thoughts and feelings, my friends, hidden in an oblivious land of unconsciousness; it is where something that people may call spirit, soul, or self come from.

Since I have always been curious about the origins of what makes us humane, I couldn't leave the mind out and alone on its own, pretending it has never existed or never had any impact on me. Hence the second meaning of the title — as a state of being inside someone's mind when, for instance, one may have an ability to read other people's minds, and to manipulate the paths they would take through their lives. It's also about whether the mind is a primordial means of control itself, which allowed me to explore a broad concept of "freedom", and what it means to us.

Thirdly, I attempt to go inside of an insight as it happens, try to explain what it is, why it occurs and, more importantly, how it influences our lives. Insight has always been fundamental to me as a source of creativity, inspiration, and progressive thinking; the unavoidability of it happening has been intriguing me ever since I learnt about it. I am convinced that the more aware we become of what we are, the more we understand the forces that rule our days and nights. I also believe that insight taps into a notion of how coincidental our choices are, and how much we are driven by fate or personal calling.

Why? To answer this question, I let my characters lead you through the highs and lows of their lives on the pages of this book.

Last but not least, I would like to acknowledge and express my sincere thanks to Richard McMunn for mentoring me all the way through, and Brian Cross for his fantastic work on proofreading and editing of the book.

INSIDE-INSIDE

1
THE GATES

Movement of the eyelids — every single one — opens and closes the door. We see how the sun rises and sets over the same horizon line, which is everywhere, everywhere we look. We are what our eyes can see; what's beyond them doesn't exist. Reality is an image framed with the horizon line, isolated in a mausoleum underneath a dome of bones. The key flows in your bloodstream. The motion of films that shroud those sole "periscopes of the soul" marks both sunrise and sunset — for day equals night and night equals day — only the shadow divides them. Skeletons are opening and crave for space instantaneously; only their eyesight defies them, constricts them within their means. You can't take any step further if you walk on a well-trodden path, which can be seen, lost and found by virtually anybody. You've got to blaze your own trail.

Metamorphosis — the subtlety of continuous change, the eternal magic of sleepwalking and daydreaming simultaneously in the present, but always moving only along the edge, the very perimeter of some omnipresent, intrinsic gates. You knock on them, but you don't know the password, neither do you have the key — the key is inside of you: it flows in your bloodstream. You're just unable to draw it out. Who are you now, you almighty force who reverses the stars in their orbits? You'd better be off finding your own shining star and taking her (still daydreaming or slowly floundering in consciousness?) among the unfolding gates of the sun, enlightening the entire reality.

She would then ask: 'What is the time now?'

'It's time to beam and time to shine.'

Saying this, he waved his hand towards her, but as smoothly as tingling of the dew beneath your bare feet in the cerulean summer morning. Then he took the camera from its case, intending to take a photo of her whilst she was clad in gleaming, silvery, diamond-like threads of flowing veil, woven by the same creatures who bring about the golden autumn. Who doesn't want to make everlasting impressions of these fleeting moments of pure beauty when the single split of a second seems to be trapped forever between two people? The last thing he managed to capture with his eyes glued to the lens of the camera was the grinning smile of his beloved woman. He slipped on wet grass while stepping backwards, trying to get the best shot.

Before reaching the summit, they had encountered a school trip, which they passed quickly by the waterfall. The excitement of those kids was reverberating in the whole valley, seeming to rise to the high heavens, which were in sight. It appeared as if the morning mist, rising above the mountain peaks, couldn't withstand its own weight, decided to make its way back among the blades of grass, sprinkling everybody's faces with refreshing drops. Slightly wet rocks and stones were sneering contemptuously. Here and there school kids tripped clumsily and faced bare masks of granite. The guide of the school trip spotted the moment of the tragic fall. She reflexively covered the eyes of the girl who was standing closest to her with her own hands and whispered to herself: 'Here is falling a man of marble.'

An old-looking man has just reached the peak of the mountain where the accident happened. Belatedly.

'You walked up so quickly; I'm nearly out of breath!' he said rapidly, still huffing and puffing.

'Where is Nathan?'

'He's down there,' he heard the quiet voice of the woman who sat on the edge of the cliff, 'but he's probably rising up to the sky now.'

'Mary, are you feeling all right? Where's my son?' Saying this, he approached her and bent over her shoulder. He looked down and wobbled towards the precipice. Mary grasped him tightly above the knees and toppled his body onto the grass.

'Please, tell me it's only a dream,' she said in a quiet, squeaky voice, and fell into his arms.

At that, the sister of the moon broke through the clouds and dazzled their faces with a blood-red glare. Alas, it wasn't a dream.

A golden, heart-shaped necklace was dangling listlessly from Mary's chest. Flooded in the sun's glare, it changed its colour into purple-crimson. Mary clenched it as if it had suddenly become an unbearable burden that was drawing her to the ground. She took it off her neck and rested it in her palms. In the middle of the golden shape of the necklace was engraved the exclamation *"I love you"* in curvy, old-fashioned letters. Mary looked at the old man sitting by her side while she was turning it tenderly in her palms.

'He gave it to me for our engagement instead of a ring. He's always been original, just like this pendant — it changes colour depending on the time of the day. Now the sun is rising, but my heart is sinking, it's breaking!'

She started to cry loudly and heavily an ocean of unnumbered tears. Then, suddenly, she stood and ran off towards a small area of undergrowth.

'Mary! Where are you —'

'Marty, leave me alone! I want to be by myself now.'

The old man just stood there, perplexed. The day was lost. He took the necklace from the ground and put it into the back pocket of his trousers. Mary suddenly turned to the old man and accosted him swiftly as if she was drawn by some unseen, magical force.

'Where are you hiding it?!' she shouted.

'Ermm... what?' mumbled Marty, completely taken aback by such a direct demeanour. 'It is still in my pocket,' he added after a pause.

'Give it to me now!'

She took it from Marty's hand in the blink of an eye and threw it into the sky with full force.

* * *

Many years later, the melodic chirrup of some singing birds was heard from beyond the frame of an open window. The wind was blustering into light-green curtains, trying to take them for its own. A small, neatly furnished room was awash with rays of the early summer sun. A young man was sitting at a wooden desk, which looked like an antique that had withstood the test of time. He wasn't paying attention to the strengthening wind; he was studying some papers diligently, turning one page after another every other minute. Suddenly, he pulled his chair back and strode towards the windowsill. When he was back at his desk, he noticed a small white feather quivering lightly next to his pencil box. He stood still momentarily, staring attentively at the newly observed find. Then he stepped forward and drew his hand towards it. At this moment, the feather was lifted above his head, gliding over the airwave, and disappearing from his sight. He began to look around nervously. Finally, he caught sight of it drifting away through the open window. He ran from his room.

'Derick! Dinner is just being served,' said a female voice, which seemed to be emanating from the wall itself. Derick literally flew over the staircase, darted through the long corridor, and vanished behind the large, wooden door, leaving it wide open.

'Oh, here you are!' he said to himself, seeing it land on the bench next to the bus stop.

The feather was lifted off again and flew away, driven by some eldritch, elemental force, even as he was trying to grasp it. Derick resumed the chase immediately. He could always take the right turn as if by the work of some unknown, strange stroke of luck, although the feather was beyond his vision for most of the time spent chasing it. When it landed once again, he took a massive breath, looked left and right, then ran across the road. 'You won't get away this time,' he murmured to himself.

There he stood before large, wooden, run-down porch stairs, reinforced with metal overlays. The feather was resting on top of them, in the middle of the rugged and frayed doormat. Derick climbed on the first and then second step but flinched suddenly as he heard a lock being opened with a key. His eyes wandered up and fixed on a very rusty, white signboard, which was dangling and swinging playfully just above the opening door. Inside the signboard, the word "WATCHMAKER" was written in black, capital letters. A sharp, creaking noise broke through, and a figure of an old, whitebeard man appeared before Derick. He was wearing an old-fashioned frock coat and tattered trousers held up with braces. His face was carved with long grooves of woes and misgivings from bygone days, taken away by the unrelenting flow of time. Huge, round spectacles hung loosely from his nose, while his eyes gleamed with bright, blue sparks.

'Good morning, my boy,' said the old man, softly. 'What errand has brought you over here?' He eyed the young man up and down carefully, but his attention was distracted by an unusual sight.

'Good morning,' answered Derick, very kindly. 'I'm just looking for… what you have under your foot!' The old man didn't say anything. Instead, he nodded his head invitingly and showed Derick the entrance to his house with open hands.

'I bet you are thirsty now,' said the old man once they were through the door. 'Maybe you'd like to drink some tea or try my own pumpkin juice?'

'Sure, thank you,' said Derick.

Everything around looked so archaic, so obsolete as if time had stopped here long, long ago. Clocks of all sorts were hung everywhere on the walls. Even though there was a multitude of them, a bare silence was overwhelming in an immense living room, only to be broken by the acute voice of the old man.

'You have to try my own pumpkin juice!' shouted he, from another room. 'It's just marvellous!'

The old man eventually emerged, carrying a silver salver with two long glasses and a crystal-clear jug on top of it, filled to the rim with orange liquid. He poured the juice into one glass and placed it right before Derick's nose. He filled his own glass, and after taking a few sips, he sat on a black chair close to a round table with a thick, pellucid, glass top, in the middle of a vast space of similar circular shape. He pulled the feather out of his pocket and began to examine it carefully. Derick didn't notice it at first, completely engrossed in staring at all those time-measuring devices.

'Do you like them?' asked the old man.

Derick twitched vibrantly at once as if he had been awakened from a deep, hypnotic slumber; he refocused his attention on the old man's amiable face. 'My feather!' he exclaimed with a cheer and astonishment in his voice.

'Yes, I've found it by the porch door. I thought you may have forgotten about it. Now, it's yours.'

The old man caressed Derick's hair, then he slid his palm down and over his cheek, finally letting it rest on his shoulder. His eyes were squinted so tightly that not even a photon of light could pass through them; they resembled minute clefts embedded deep below the forehead.

'You are very much like your mother,' said the old man after a while, but with such tenderness in his voice that Derick's cheeks blushed scarlet-red with joy.

'Thank you,' said Derick, modestly. 'Do you know my mother?'

'Yes, I know her very well,' said the old man, then he sighed poignantly.

'Where from?' was the immediate question, asked with a sudden fire of expression.

The old man's countenance shifted in the blink of an eye. He looked even more ancient than before: the wrinkles and furrows on his face had deepened, and his brightly-sharp eyes had shed a fathomless path of old memories. He wandered with his insight into distant, old worlds, buried under the shroud of darkness and mystery. He didn't resemble the grey old man anymore; he stood tall and proud as kings of old — his eminence was emitting radiant, wizardly wisdom.

'You are so young and curious about the world,' he began slowly. 'You know — I could have been your grandfather... You'd better go now; your mother won't be waiting with dinner for much longer.'

2
THE NECKLACE

Marty seemed to be a very nice old fellow. For some reason, he treated Derick like his own child. Derick really liked spending time with him. Marty never talked about himself or about his past. 'You are very young,' he would say to him time and time again. 'There is always an appropriate time for everything in life because life is balanced,' he would often say to Derick as if it was some commandment of his or a riddle. It really started to boggle his young mind after some time.

Marty always chatted about his marvellous pumpkin juice and the secrets of its making. He spoke with a resonant and vivid voice, slowly articulating every word to some mysterious, somnambulic tune. He was very thrifty and concise with his vocabulary, sometimes to such an extent that every sentence he pronounced sounded like a puzzle. One of his favourite sayings was: 'Speak a little, say a lot.' When silence fell, he never spoke first to break it. In fact, he never spoke without any utmost need. He liked to look, sometimes everything he did was looking.

One day, when Derick came home after paying a visit to old Marty, he overheard this conversation:

'How dare you still do this to me?! Why do you still wear this necklace?!'

The woman who'd been addressed said nothing. She looked shrivelled, coiled inwards as if she'd just received a hit in the deepest, ever-bleeding wound inside her heart.

'Why are you still doing this!?' growled the tall man who was standing next to the woman, looking older and much angrier than her. His eyes were glowing with wrath. A deathly silence fell. There was a sense of growing tension in the air. It would have taken just one little spark to make the whole room explode with

THE NECKLACE

long-suppressed regrets interwoven with years of torment like an ocean of hot, volcanic lava. But the woman's heart remained silent.

'Listen,' he began, lowering his voice a tone or so, 'I've got a very difficult case to handle tomorrow, so I wouldn't be bothered to speak with you today if only you hadn't been so ostentatious with it. It makes you cry but drives me mad! I can't even focus on what is important to me now. We must put a definite end to this farce — right here, right now!' He paused, looking very much out of breath, too electrified with emotions, with his hair nearly standing on its ends. He took a few puffs of heavy air and continued, 'He's long but gone now; he's never gonna come back — do you understand? You can't forget him, can you? Look at me! Who am I? So many years have passed, but you still come back to those days where there is nothing left but death! Now, there is this old idiot Marty — I forbid you to see him again.'

'So, you're spying on me?' she wailed thinly, and her eyes filled with tears. She threw herself into his arms, thumping her fists against his chest. The necklace was gleaming unobtrusively on her slender body.

'Mary, please, listen to me for once,' said the man, calming down again. 'He would be just a bad influence for Derick, and I forbid my son from seeing him too.'

* * *

Later that day, when Derick was in bed and ready to sleep, his mother came in to his room. She looked so mystifying, her eyes shimmering like wildfires, but the eyelids still twitched nervously. He saw the picture of a worried, persecuted human being who was silent and deep as bottomless depths of an ocean. She was standing over his bed, gazing at the moon speechlessly. She sat down after a while and caressed his hair. Then she took the necklace off and placed it coiled in his hands, which she covered with her hands tightly and lodged them against his heart, pressing lightly.

'Please, my only son,' she began in a whispering voice, 'keep it inside, inside your heart and protect it from your father. May he never see its glimmer again… Please, don't ask any questions now, it's such a burden for me,' she added, somewhat apprehensively. Tears began to surface in the corners of her eyes; her lips were fluttering like the wings of butterflies in the wind — foreboding an imminent storm of feelings pumped from the bottom of her heart, trying to escape, to manifest their very presence, their own right to speak for themselves.

Derick remained silent, silent when she said: 'good night', silent when the rain fell with its magnificent display of lightning, which inundated the whole neighbourhood with series of sudden, short flashes of light, like glimmers of hope that spring to life in a whirlpool of free-flowing thoughts. He felt like running away, like plunging into his very own solitary confinement, a tranquillity base where he could be free from thoughts, feelings, and mind again. Questions, speculations were like dust — invisible to a naked eye, seemingly nonexistent when you were not preoccupied with it; inexorably overwhelming, flooring to the ground when sunken into the mind. People ran to and fro all their lives: worrying, speaking with riddles to one other, meeting dead ends, hanging loose words in some strange places, then letting them loiter on empty streets in complete speechlessness.

Now, he didn't see things any clearer. The more he looked at it, the more details he perceived, yet his mind became number and number in the gloom of incompleteness — as if he was trying to piece together a jigsaw puzzle but never able to find the last missing element. The necklace seemed to change its properties every day: sometimes it was as heavy as lead, sometimes it was as light as a feather; it changed colour depending on Derick's state of mind, the time of the day, the weather. It was golden and heart-shaped on a thin chain of miniature links. Derick bore it with pride, but it was concealed inside him. Before long, it had become precious, near invaluable to him. He was spending increasingly more time with it as days went by, treasuring it, admiring its daily metamorphoses. Something enchanting must have been embedded into its very core, something that was inaccessible and invisible to the eyes. Together, they were one; it had grown into him and he had grown into it. It was like mutual infatuation that wasn't communicating with senses, although he felt like it was whispering something to him in a language he could not comprehend. It constituted an integral part of him; it was like a never-ending tale where amazement turns into awe, where an endeavour brings you hope with a mirage of joy. Craving to discover its past was intensifying in him by the day.

His mother was silent, maundering from nook to nook and filling them with her shadow, which was so impalpable you wouldn't notice it even if it was spread under your very feet like dreams you could tread on. Derick didn't insist, he couldn't. Sometimes she would just lock herself in her bedroom at the end of the corridor and stay there for hours without any sign of life. No one knew what she was doing there; she never spoke about it. Her bedroom was completely empty — four walls and one very wide window with the sill in the middle of one of them, exactly opposite to the door.

* * *

Wandering on a gritty bypath of his thoughts, boiling in the evaporating air of summer, Derick savoured every moment with his treasure. In contrast to steaming hot, vaporous surroundings, it remained barren and as cold as ice this time. He held it in his hands tightly, cooling himself down at the same time. The relief was instant and refreshing; it soothed sweltering heat from the sky in the same way as aloe soothes burns on the skin. He couldn't see any living soul around. Fields full of crops were undulating delicately under a gentle, caressing touch brought by the lightness of the breeze. The world around was turning yellow-green and golden — corn and wheat fields were spread over countless miles, flowing beyond the horizon. Everyone was counting on fruitful yields this year, and some were even calculating their future profits. All the people in the area were consumed by talking about crops, sales, and money. However, no one was to be seen working on cornfields today; there wasn't a sound of heavy machinery to be heard either. Maybe it was because of this heat, Derick thought at first, but he rejected this explanation straight away as he saw farmers working in much harsher conditions. So, why was there no one around? His curiosity didn't have to wait for long to be satisfied…

Just before the turn of the road towards the first village buildings, he went past a very neglected, desolate field, which was flourishing with various kinds of weeds. He saw a dark-skinned, old woman working in the field. She wore a long, thick frock-like dress covered by an even longer black smock, a thin, white lace hood was loosely tied under her chin. It didn't take him long time to recognize her. They'd often been meeting each other in this very place. Mrs Dauntwraith, who was always hunched, absorbed by her own few acres, wouldn't have taken any notice of him if he hadn't spoken to her first.

'Good afternoon, Mrs Dauntwraith.'

'Good afternoon, Derick,' said the elderly woman, warmly. She raised her eyes, and the fleeting smile emerged on her face.

'Why is no one working in the fields today?' he asked without delay.

'No one?!' Mrs Dauntwraith answered with a mixture of irritation and surprise. She looked firmly bewildered by Derick's question, then cast a few piercing, inquisitive glances at him, simultaneously frowning as if she was weighing up various possibilities of riposting.

'Today is the special service in the church where all farming equipment is being hallowed to bring a successful harvest. It's an unmissable ceremony for anybody who owns farmland.'

'So, why are you working today?'

Mrs Dauntwraith shot him an even fiercer glance, gazing from far above as if he'd got caught trying to get away with a theft of her uttermost secrets. Derick was simply astounded seeing her with her back fully straightened. She had grown to a mighty stature: her thick, sombre eyebrows were nearly touching each other so that sparks of an electric current could be charged between them; the wrinkles on her forehead were overlapping one another in one massive glower so the forehead appeared warped all over. He noticed that the sky had turned black, and unforeseen darkness fell from nowhere. He couldn't turn his sight away from Mrs Dauntwraith, although he was really striving to do it at all costs.

'You'd better go home now. Your mother must be worrying about you,' said Mrs Dauntwraith after a long while.

Having parted from Mrs Dauntwraith, Derick left the field and resumed walking — he was back on the road home. It was getting late already, the sun was tilting westwards, being pulled down by a derisive horizon. The air stood still and lifeless, bereft of breath; it was suffocating in hazy decorations of the summer. It looked like another sultry evening. His home was on the other side of the village, so he had to pick up the pace to get there before dusk. Total silence was soon abruptly disrupted by some strange noises coming out of nowhere, getting closer and closer. He turned around a few times, but no one was to be seen. Then, three figures on bicycles loomed up in the byway that was dividing a huge cornfield into two parts. Once they spotted him, they swerved sharply and began pedalling ferociously as if they were chased by someone or something that scared them to death. They were yelling at him, one trying to outshout the other: 'Derick the Slayer! Derick the Slayer!! Derick the Slayer!!!' Derick couldn't move a muscle, limiting himself to looking only; there was no point in running away anyway. When they were going past him, one of them threw a corncob at his face. They disappeared into the distance even as they appeared, yet he could still pick out their wicked chants from afar. There was nothing he could do about it; there was a grain of truth in their words after all — his father was a judge.

3
THE EMISSARY

Fire was smouldering playfully in the hearth, giving off waves of cosy warmth, which permeated a large room with the scent of comfort. Several sizeable photographs framed in golden wood stood on the mantelpiece. Each of them depicted a family of three: two adults and a child. Faces of parents — always smiling gently, were changing only slightly from photo to photo, but their offspring was growing up, taking more and more space, marking his very presence ever so bluntly, blatantly shifting others to the background, yet he was still unable to spread his wings at full stretch.

A figure of a short and stout elderly woman was bustling about at the lavishly set table; by the look of her clothing, she was a housemaid. When a dark-haired, tall man wearing well-tailored, black trousers, white shirt, and a black waistcoat entered the room, she bowed so deep before him that she could touch her knees with her chin. 'Good evening, Mr McCrafty,' said she. The man did not motion to her at all, neither did he reply. He just strolled along the red carpet that was shimmering in the reflections of a multitude of bright bulbs peering down from the golden chandelier. He stopped by the windowsill, over which he leaned, crossing his legs and looking into the murky distance through the closed window. The rain was bombarding heavily, completely obscuring the world ahead. Trees and shrubs were kneeling beggarly under the burdensome barrage of wet, sticky drops. The man looked rather concerned; his head proudly aloof was stuck to the glass; a sense of urgent inquisition was creeping onto his face. Only the eyes were unmoved, firmly fixed at some dusky point somewhere outside.

'Where has he gone for so long this time?!' he shouted out, loudly, without warning, banging his fist against the windowsill. 'He lets himself off far too much; he has his head in the clouds all the time, instead of being here, down to earth. I'm gonna cut this idyll short and take him right down from his seventh heaven. It's mere disregard of... me!'

Even as he was talking to himself, a woman entered the room with vernal grace. She was clad in a light, white dress, identical to one of the photographs on the mantelpiece. A fragrance of the first spring dew on the meadows diffused into the room as she walked in, soon reaching even the furthest corners. She trod through the red carpet with feathery elegance; inserting her fingers between those bent ones belonging to her man, she kissed him once on his cheek and whispered softly in his ear: 'Derick will come on time, he is a strong and prudent man.'

'I know, he's my son!' said the man, haughtily.

The couple walked away from the window and sat on the thick sofa finished with polished, beige oak wood. The housemaid, who seemed to anticipate full well what was going to happen, dished out an elegant black, leather photo album and put it swiftly down on the short crystal table beside a large bottle of cognac with a thick, red bow tied around its neck. The housemaid drifted away into the shade of the room after bending down to the floor. Upon leaving the room, she cast a slinking eye on the couple, blissfully submerged in perpetual memories, then she laid her eyes on the drops of rain still thumping angrily against the windows. Even as she left, a mighty lightning struck nearby; the immense front door, covered heavily with carvings was opening slowly inside, bringing in a backdraft of suspension, disturbing the intoxicating aura of equilibrium, bringing down the invisible barrier between two separate worlds. Then a deathly hush fell. Only the soft clatter of crockery coming out from the kitchen stirred it. Both parents were sitting still with their faces pasted into the album. The mother lifted her body reflexively as she heard the sharp sound of thunder but was stopped halfway by the hand of the man who pulled her down gently. Then he poured himself a glass.

'You are late,' said the man with a deep, bass voice.

'I'm sorry, Father,' his son replied, humbly, then he sat on the sofa beside his mother.

The housemaid, Mrs Deeprow, emerged from the kitchen,

pushing a large dish table on wheels. She gave the impression of being on autopilot as she placed the food on the luxuriantly set table so mechanically and carefreely that one could think she was just an unreal image of imagination moving effortlessly through space-time. Then she would invite you to the table with the softest, quietest voice in the world, and your slumberous bubble bursts like a balloon being pierced by a needle.

Her white as a ghost visage was constant, making it impossible to read her emotions. Reality seemed to be like water off a duck's back to her. Her very signs of inner feelings appeared to be washed away by the water or blown away by the wind. Her eyes twinkled with a barely visible, lightly green fire that was wrapped around by the ocean of lava turned into granite. The McCraftys hardly spoke to her; Mary was the only one who was making rare exceptions. If she wanted to talk, she would take her to her "hermitage" at the end of the long corridor in the loft. Mrs Deeprow had always been apprehensive and resistant to go there with Mary, but she never refused. It was the only time when her emotions could be clearly read, the only time when her effortless, mechanical movement through the air gave way to flounder and grope. When looking at Mary, she always kept her wits about her, hardly ever allowing herself to blink, as though she always feared that Mary could disappear at any time. Mary never spoke much but gesticulated a lot instead; exchanging long gazes was her favourite mean of communication. It was like love that does not communicate with senses.

On that day — on the eve of another wedding anniversary of Mr and Mrs McCrafty, the sun shone bright, but the evening came crimson; dense extents of ominous clouds were looming over the horizon. The soft breeze had been overturned by volatile blasts of the wind, which frazzled hardly audible whispers of mutual conversation. Words cut into pieces were whirling around, muddling with the noisy rustle of restless leaves and the whizz of darting air. The dialogue between the two was short and quiet on the outside, fiery and tense it was inside: a whole diverse palette of facial expressions, gestures, and impressions came into play. Mary was holding Mrs Deeprow's hand tautly with the look from her eyes as if she was talking to the living oracle. The elderly woman was answering laconically but not casually, looking invariantly deep into Mary's eyes.

Having sensed the imminent change in the weather, Mrs Deeprow decided to shut the window. Mary was standing still in the middle of the emptiness of her private room, wavering. In the end, she came close to Mrs Deeprow and whispered into her ear: 'Do you think it's the right time to tell him now?' The housemaid turned her gaze away from Mary's face and let her sight loose to venture beyond the closed window, piercing through the curdling air like lightning through the clouds. She focused it on one tiny dot, as small as the head of a match. There, far away, Derick was just coming back from Marty's. 'I daresay he already knows,' said Mrs Deeprow, stolidly, turning back towards Mary. Her face was as cold as ice, perfectly immune to words and circumstances.

She was peering through the kitchen door at Derick consuming late dinner with exactly the same expression. Her eyes though, they were like glaring torches, like highly sensitive gauges that weighed up emotions, perceiving even the slightest movements of his chest, counting down every loose spark that could kindle the fuse, the length of which she was acutely aware of.

Mr and Mrs McCrafty sat at the table, both looking heavenly relaxed. Total silence dominated the dining room, stifling itself more and more until it became unsettling. Mr McCrafty was busy eating and drinking, looking even haughtier than when he spoke last time. Proud as a peacock he was, sitting high on his throne of gold, looking at everything from above. He didn't even cast a single glance at his son, neither did he utter a single word to him. Mary began to swing her head around nervously, but Mrs Deeprow was nowhere to be seen. She finally rested her eyes on Derick. Her heart was in her mouth when she was looking at him, although she couldn't see his face clearly because he had it dived into the soup. She only saw his raven black, spiky hair that was growing in all directions. When he raised his head, darting a couple of shrewd glances at his parents, Mary shed a few tears, which run over her pale cheeks and dropped into her platter. Derick took after someone she knew like no one else. He resembled him more and more as he grew up. Mary had no courage to say anything; she twisted herself around, hoping to see the familiar pair of glimmering eyes, but even her shadow was now invisible. At last, she overcame herself and said to his son:

'Derick, my son, I see that something is gnawing you.'

A long silence fell before he spoke. The storm was in full force, wreaking havoc outside. Here, inside, it started to rain now. Mr McCrafty has just finished his meal. Having swallowed the last bites of food, he took a massive breath, then he opened his mouth at an obtuse angle as if he was about to give a speech or something, but Derick had forestalled him.

'Soon there will be no more space for our family photographs on the mantelpiece,' he said, loudly, without looking at anyone, just as if he was talking to himself.

Sharp, bright light was lit in the kitchen. Mrs Deeprow had her hands full with the washing-up. From time to time, clattering and pattering noises were heard. Mrs Deeprow stopped doing her duties even as Derick spoke. She understood very well these unspeakable words, fuelled with suppressed emotions on the spur of the moment. She came close to the kitchen door, which she opened slightly. Mr McCrafty frowned badly when he heard Derick's words but spoke nothing. Mary, who couldn't be kept guessing anymore what her son meant, rushed with a response, seeing growing irritation on of her husband's face.

'New family photographs can go on the top of the liquor cabinet. It's very long. What do you think about it, Bruce?'

'Yes, of course,' muttered Mr McCrafty, quite indifferently, and turned himself towards Derick.

'Derick, my son, tell me where you have been for so long today.'

'I bet you know.'

Derick hauled the chair away and stormed to his room after uttering a vanquished 'thank you' for the dinner. Later, a few hesitant knocks to his room's door were made. Soon, they were both sitting side by side, gazing into each other's glaring eyes. Derick had already known the secrets of his "heart".

24

THE EMISSARY

Earlier that day, he left the house in a hurry, leaving unfinished breakfast on the table. He took his bicycle and was gone to see his friend who lived on the other side of the village, with whom he was planning to revise for an upcoming law exam. He also took his old fishing rod, which he buckled the last time when he was fishing in the lake, for a repair. On his way back, he passed the old Marty's place. Why not pop in? he thought. I'm curious what he's up to this weekend.

He knocked, but the door opened instantly with a familiar creak even as he touched it. In "the room of thousand clocks" — as this was the name Derick coined for Marty's living room, no one was to be seen. After looking around thoroughly and calling Marty's name a few times, Derick took the stairs and went up in silence. All doors were closed, except for the one at the end of the corridor. There he saw Marty, literally stirring still on the old couch, hunched over a very old, dingy photo album, which he was staring at with his head clamped between his hands. He didn't notice Derick, who was looking at him inquisitively, for quite some time.

'Hello Marty,' said Derick, as calmly as he could, trying not to scare him with his sudden appearance. He levelled his head with Marty's, then rested his hand on his shoulder. When Marty saw him, he didn't show any signs of surprise: he only raised his eyes with a great deal of resistance as though he was grappling with an unseen, magnetic force that was toppling him to the ground every time he wanted to break free. His eyes suddenly glistened with a powerful, lustrous flash, like two exploding stars. At the same time, his body was thrust away from Derick's as if it was smitten by an invisible shockwave that blanched his face. Derick's necklace was dangling from his neck on a thread-thin, silver chain right before his eyes, swinging involuntarily back and forth. Two rivulets appeared on

Marty's cheeks, running free from their springs. Tears, as big as green beans, dropped free on the surface of the photographs. It put Derick out of countenance at first, but his desire to find out what was happening with Marty was too overpowering. Regaining his poise, he sat next to him. Even as he did it, Marty got up, closed the photo album with a bang, and much to Derick's astonishment, who was under the impression that everything was happening in the blink of an eye as if all time-space was frozen in this very moment, he said with all too familiar composure: 'Come down with me to the living room.'

Before long, they were standing next to each other in front of the large, round table, the countertop of which was made of the thick slab of crystal. Marty put his hand on Derick's shoulder, softly, without him noticing it, and looked at him in silence. Derick had spent long hours in this place where Marty had his workshop set up and did most of his watchmaker craft. He meticulously examined every single one, and there were hundreds of them in the room, virtually everywhere, except for the floor. Every time he looked at them, they gave him the same sense of hypnotic wonder so that he couldn't do anything but stare in awe at them for ages. Even now, he was rooted to the spot and turned to stone, slowly moving his head as if it was a big scanner that was fitted on the top of the spine. Marty focused all his attention on Derick's face, of which he couldn't take his eyes off. He was silent and waiting, waiting patiently. Studying this great assemblage of clocks and watches had become some sort of an obsessive passion for Derick over time. He would compare every feature he could find they had in common. Sometimes he would bring a notebook and write things down in it. He tried to do it discretely to keep it secret from Marty, but the shrewd old man had seen everything, although he always remained silent. After some time, Derick had discovered some relations between all the time-keeping devices. This riddle had been boggling his mind ever since. This time he decided to speak.

'Marty —' he started timidly, 'a lot of your clocks are set for different times; some of them repeat a lot. What's the reason you set them like this?'

'You see, every moment in life has its own event that belongs only to that particular moment. For example, the moment you are born, the moment you lose your first tooth, the moment you go to school for the very first time. Everything in life has its own distinctive place and the event that belongs solely to that place in time.'

'So, what happened at half past eleven?'

This was exactly the time that repeated itself the most on the faces of mechanical clocks and watches in "the room of thousand clocks". This "repetitiveness of times" — as Derick called it himself, had been intriguing him ever since he'd detected it. Marty clawed his hand into his arm so powerfully that traces of tears tided ashore of the young man's eyes and told him to sit in the armchair. As soon as Derick was settled down, Marty asked to give him his necklace. Derick handed it to Marty very reluctantly, which resulted in a grimace of jealousy overcasting his face even as Marty grabbed it from him. Suddenly, Derick felt intoxicating spurts of abhorrence for the very first time towards someone whom he loved dearly.

Marty's words, although spoken with the utmost certitude, were coming out of this mouth strangled and fainted as if they were subdued to some inconceivable will that was breaking them apart in the air. He was sweating profusely from the forehead; salty trickles were oozing down both of his cheeks until they joined forces right below the beardy chin before finally falling into his hands that were tenderly holding and turning "the heart". His consciousness seemed to be trapped in a wormhole, gone space travelling to unknown places caught in a time-wrap, even so, on the bottom of his semi-closed hands, the shape of which resembled a heart, a small pond of sweat was forming.

'This necklace was given to your mother by my son for their engagement.'

For Derick, that afternoon had turned out to be a thunderstorm with lightning battering the earth, and a wuthering wind beating high mountains down. He'd learnt the story of his "heart" entwined in the fates of two people. He sat there and hearkened in complete stillness like one who was paralysed from head to toe. Marty depicted his son and Mary as two lovebirds, singing nightingales bathing in the summer rain under the warm rays of the sun. His voice broke abruptly when he got to the point when he with his son and Mary went hiking in the mountains one bright, summer morning.

'Your mum used to be a completely different person,' he said and sighed longingly. 'She used to have so much energy; you could bestow it upon a battalion of troops freely, and she would still have it left in abundance.'

Returning to his story, he depicted a panorama of high mountain gills, in which stars could see their luminous faces, bare granite ridges, long slopes still withholding remnants of wintry snow, shadowy pinnacles reigning over the area crowned in clouds.

'Your mother loved mountains; it was her element. She was like a chamois in the mountains. On that day, we were trekking through the narrow pass and had to walk slowly in single file. We would have been going much faster, but I suddenly started limping on one leg. God knows why. Reaching the crossroad before the summit, we encountered a school trip, which we passed quickly by the waterfall. The excitement of those kids was reverberating in the whole valley, seeming to rise to the high heavens, which were in sight. It appeared as if the morning mist, rising above the mountain peaks, couldn't withstand its own weight, decided to make its way back among the blades of grass, sprinkling everybody's faces with refreshing drops. Slightly wet rocks and stones were smiling unforgivingly. When Mary and Nathan reached the peak, long before I did it, he decided to take a photo of her whilst she was clad in gleaming, silvery diamond-like threads of flowing veil woven by the same creatures who bring about the golden autumn. Who doesn't want to make everlasting impressions of those fleeting moments of pure beauty when the single split of a second seems to be trapped forever between two people? The last thing he managed to capture with his eyes glued to the lens of the camera was the grinning smile of his beloved woman. The slipperiness of the crag took his life…'

*   *   *

Upon leaving, Derick glanced over at Marty's old bicycle. 'I bet some of its parts remember the time of war,' he said to himself. 'Everything here is so archaic.' He smacked the hard, wooden saddle with his hand, stirring up a dust cloud into the air. He got on his own bike and rode away. As he left Marty's, he remembered that he forgot to take the revision notes with him from his friend. He veered sharply on the narrow rubble road and began pedalling vigorously without even looking around as he knew these parts like the back of his hand. It suddenly started getting dark; Derick looked up and spotted a thick band of dark clouds rushing towards him from beyond the horizon line. He stopped, looked around, and to his bewilderment, he saw Mrs Dauntwraith's field on his right. Then he realized he'd travelled too far.

'What made me go so far out?' he asked himself. He propped his bike clumsily against the short fence of decaying wooden planks, painted light green. Not knowing why, he whizzed through the grass in the front of Mrs Dauntwraith's house and knocked on the door vehemently. His heart was running wild, his lungs could barely cope with inhaling and exhaling the air as if they were sobbing. Suddenly, something else attracted his senses. Behind him stood a tall man with beetroot-red cheeks, holding his large, lurching body up against the fence, which started to tremble like an aspen in the wind under his weight.

'What are you doing over there, Derick? Hey, I'm talking to you! Come over here now!'

Just as he noticed the familiar face of old Mr Smith, the closest neighbour of Mrs Dauntwraith, he was pulled out of the state of dreamy, emotional trance he was in. Heavy drops of sweat on his forehead made him starkly aware of the passage of time. His face developed a stern look as he went to meet Mr Smith who was brandishing his hand, which resembled more a bough of a tree than a human limb.

'What are you doing here? Mrs Dauntwraith isn't home and probably she won't be for a long time.'

'What are you talking about?'

'No one has told you what's happened to Mr Dauntwraith?!'

4
THE CAVE

Clarksdowne was like a big hollow, forsaken long ago, bereft of its identity that had been squandered away by the eternal movement of coincidental passersby trying their luck, who nowadays bypassed it with a damning sense of unfulfillment. Mothers were feeding their offspring with some antediluvian pabulum of indigenous plebeians. Plastic fog was lurking by the window shutters, descrying its prey with a basilisk, lupine glance. All windows were shining spotless. Living here was like going down the cave — as if you were a stranded drop of morning dew falling from a blade of grass into the fathomless blackness of the earthy, thick as tar night, into which you were gone like an atom of oxygen into the bloodstream.

'I wonder how you can go crazy mad only because you've been losing someone you love...' Derick said to himself whilst being fixedly sunken in a stare at the lacunar ceiling of his student room. 'Mrs Dauntwraith has always been as solid as a rock in my eyes.' Then he felt that biting, repulsive feeling of smog coming through his throat. He jumped on his feet quickly and leaning forward with his left hand propped against the radiator, he intended to close the window with his right hand, but he found himself opening it even wider and sticking his bust outside. 'She may now be maundering about somewhere in the woods, brooding, clad only in hair.'

Thumping, resonant knocks on the door dispersed around the room with a resounding bustle like a swarm of hungry locusts so suddenly that made Derick jump like one that was made to walk on burning coals. He nearly leapt out through the window in surprise. 'Who the hell... at this time?!' he wondered whilst turning away from the window, but very recalcitrantly, against his will. It was like forcing a clock to go anticlockwise to measure the passage of time. Then the knocking turned into a hostile, barbarous pounding. It sounded like a hunter trying to flush their prey out of the hiding place.

'Derick, open the door right now! I know you're there!'

Derick was in a state of shock when he heard the voice of Mrs Fluffery, the caretaker of his student house. It just boggled his mind even to think what force must have been conjured up to made her leave her cosy office on the ground floor and go all the way to his room on the very last floor. He only managed to unlock the door when he saw her hurtling like a storm around his place. There she stood before him in the middle of the room, the very menace of the house, inspecting everything with her flaring, hyaline detectors, then fixating them ominously on his stature.

'Your father is calling upon you. He is waiting for you downstairs,' she said with great difficulty as if every phoneme she was uttering was like a sharp shard of glass.

* * *

'Do you not think you should be with your mother right now? She is dying.'

'Don't ask unnecessary questions, just get in the car. We have no time to lose. Everyone knows she is still alive only thanks to me!'

When they got into the long, black limousine, the mechanical sound of the door being locked drew Derick's attention. They sat on the sofa at the back of the car, which by its touch and smell was made of a mixture of plastic and leather. The lights went out even as they sat down. Then they heard the low and monotone voice coming from the seats on the other side of the car. Derick couldn't quite make out who that voice belonged to as he could only see a silhouette of the person sitting deep in darkness. The windows were as dark as night too, so nothing could be seen through them. Derick knew they were moving but rather slowly. He looked at

Bruce's face, and to his surprise, he saw him struggling to hold his nerves. His boastful confidence was hanging by a thread. He looked timid and tamed. It was the first time in Derick's life he saw him in this position.

'I'm glad you brought your son with you, Bruce. Derick, we have something to talk about.'

'May I ask whom I have the pleasure of speaking with and why are you sitting there in the dark?' asked Derick, without even thinking why someone he might have never seen or met before was calling him by his name.

Then the lights went on, and Derick saw the oblong face of an almost grey-haired man who was sitting in a reclined position with his legs fully extended, rested on the hassock. The fingers of both his hands were touching each other in near perfect alignment at the height of his head so that he couldn't see the details of his face clearly. He was making a tapping noise with both his index fingers.

'My name is Simon Redeldrag.'

Bruce quickly broke in even as Simon was pronouncing his name: 'He is the head of the High Court in Clarksdowne,' he said, carefully measuring the tone of every word, turning his head towards Derick, who looked at Simon with newly found curiosity, then an image sprang to his mind.

'I may be mistaken, but I think I saw you at the university campus before.'

'Simon goes there from time to time to give a speech or a lecture to law students,' said Bruce, hurriedly, before Simon even managed to open his mouth. Derick found it quite peculiar how Bruce spoke for Simon, but when looking at Simon's face, he noticed that he was undisturbed at all by this occurrence, so he pursued with his thoughts.

'I am pretty sure I saw you together with biotechnology PhD students.'

'You must have mistaken him for someone else,' said Bruce. 'Simon has more interesting things to do than hanging out with some random students.' Now Bruce's behaviour really began to get on Derick's nerves. He was just about to tell him not to intrude when the lights went out again, and he heard Simon clapping his hands steadily, at regular intervals.

'Clever man you are, Derick. Just like your father…'

'Indeed,' said Bruce, putting airs and graces on his face. The blood started to boil in Derick's veins upon seeing his puffed cheeks. He gave him a thunderous look into his fawny, crawling eyes of a confounded hypocrite. Then, Simon asked: 'Do you know any biotech PhD students?'

'Personally, no, but I've heard of James Niggle.'

Simon's eyes glistened in the dark for a second after Derick has recalled James's name.

'Good, very good,' said Simon, very casually. 'Now I want to ask you, my young man, what do you know about Mrs Dauntwraith's disappearance?'

Derick's heart began to pound wildly when he heard Mrs Dauntwraith's name. Lights went on again at this time, and he saw Simon's small as slits, sharp eyes piercing him inside out. He looked as if he'd known him very well all his life, but he'd always stayed incognito, obscured and hidden in the shadows. Derick felt suddenly naked and exposed to his ravenous hunger for information. Thoughts began to flutter in his mind; they began to go past his consciousness like a train that passes by a station it doesn't need to stop at, one by one. He felt more and more uncomfortable in this situation; eagerness to run away was surfacing alarmingly. He looked at the window by his side, hoping to find a route for escape, but it was all dark. Then he felt Bruce's elbow prodding him in the ribs. He realized that he was on the spot, and his answer was long overdue.

'I saw her on that day…' he started, completely bereft of confidence, 'when everybody went out to churches to hallow their farming machinery, for the last time.'

'What did Mr Smith tell you?' asked Simon. It surprised Derick that he knew about this, but he figured very quickly that Mr Smith must have already told him that he saw him and that it was something bigger than he thought.

'Nothing special,' said Derick, as calmly as he could. 'He just said that Mr Dauntwraith got busted.'

'Is that it? Then what have you been doing on the very doorstep of Dauntwraith's house at that time?'

'Ermm… I've got lost,' Derick answered in a hurry.

'You've got lost around your own village?! Oh, poor you! Do you think I'm gonna believe in all that nonsense?'

'I mean — I was just coming back from Ma…' Derick stopped there as he felt unexpectedly impulsive misgivings that he shouldn't tell Simon about Marty. What if he queried about him? he thought. Moreover, Bruce was here too. Then he looked at his face and realized it was too late, seeing his jaw dropping, and his eyes rushing to jump out of their orbits.

'Did you see Marty on that day?!' asked Bruce, angrily, still half-stupefied. Derick felt like the shadow of confrontation that loomed in the air was getting heavier and heavier, that the outburst of a conflict was nothing but imminent. He didn't want the greatest family secret to be divulged before a complete stranger unless he…

'Bruce, did you mean old Marty Deeprow?!' Simon burst out, but with such strong surprise and curiosity that nearly made him stand up.

'Yes,' said Bruce, then he sighed.

When Derick heard Marty's second name for the very first time, something suddenly flashed inside of his head like a surge of flashback coming out of nowhere. Then Bruce's cell phone rang. By the sound of his answers, he was asked to attend the Greenfields hospital where his mother was lying on her deathbed, but Simon told him to stay. The car stopped, and Derick was ordered to leave immediately. His head was so heavy-loaded with emotions and strange memories that he didn't even notice he was walking through the wide avenue made of smooth, square slabs of concrete that was leading to the main square of the university campus. He somehow managed to shrug off the feeling of overthinking about what just happened, which rendered his eyes fixed to the pavement; he looked up and let his eyesight wander far and wide. Even though the resit exams session was over nearly a week ago, there were still lots of students around. Then he noticed that someone was waving at him from afar. 'They must have already recognized me,' he said under his nose, but could see scarcely a thing as the sunlight was directly in his eyes. When he came closer, the figures of two people loomed out of the dazzling sunshine that was reflected on the surface of the lake, the banks of which they were standing by. Derick thought he knew one of them, at least from the posters — it was James Niggle himself who was waving at him.

'How on earth does he know me? I've never met him,' he said to himself. He was there with a woman he had never seen before at the uni campus. She was holding a recording device in her hand, so Derick thought they might have been doing an interview about his project or something. When he approached them, James shook his hand and introduced himself.

'Hi, I'm James Niggle, but everyone calls me Niggle.' Before Derick could say a word back to him, the woman who was next to him started talking.

'Hi, I'm Natalie Maine, but everyone calls me Natalie.' The way she introduced herself struck Derick because she shook his hand in exactly the same way as James did: first squeezing and smothering his hand, which was definitely bigger than hers, with hers and then shaking it so vigorously that it made his whole arm swing back and forth like it was a spindly twig of a tree that was trying to withstand the vehemence of a hurricane-force wind. They both looked so alike too: both about six feet tall, blonde-haired, dark blue-eyed, with small, hooked noses and elongated canine teeth that gave them a little bit of a "vampirish smile".

'Are you twins?' Derick asked, mesmerised to the bone by their mutual resemblance to each other.

'Oh, no, we're just good friends,' said James. They looked at each other, then burst into loud laughter. They even laughed in the same way, Derick thought, feeling a bit embarrassed. When they gracefully stopped, he turned to James and asked: 'How do you know me by the way? I can't recall we ever met.'

'We? No, we've never met; it's our first time, but you must have met my twin before!' chuckled James and then they started laughing again. Derick felt really stupid now. They were just having a ball at his expense, taking the mick out of him and he, being poor, had only those glistening, small eyes of Simon Redeldrag trespassing on his mind. He began to call up all the recent memories with newly found vividness, completely forgetting about what was happening around him. They were not even paying attention to him anymore, lost in their wild surge of cackling. James looked all too merry for a person who had recently been elected a new Students' Head of Department of Biological Sciences. What may such a successful student like him want from Derick? The image of Simon's gleaming eyes when he called James's name in the car intruded on his consciousness again. What kind of riddles is he hiding beyond his "take it easy", outgoing front? Natalie was following his suit in almost every move. Maybe she was his secret twin or a clone indeed? When looking at her, Derick felt this strange sensation of having butterflies in his stomach all at once. His heart began to throb jerkingly as if it was signalling its desire to be released from the bondage of being imprisoned deep inside his ribcage. Driblets of sweat rushed to the surface of his skin, and before long his face was covered with these salty mines all over. A cool breeze from the lake was his only relief.

'What are you gawping at like that?!'

'Errmmm... what? Me? Nothing, I was ammm... just wondering if your sound recorder or something that you're holding is still registering our voices?'

'And why do you think I've brought it for? You're gonna be a sensation of the month!' Then she guffawed sinisterly, and turning to James, she poked him frolicly, saying: 'What's wrong with that guy? He's as stiff as my clipboard! Who have you brought over here, a madman or a lunatic?'

'Take it easy, Derick; she's always like that when she sees someone new. She's a journalist and works for a local paper. We've known each other for years. She used to study here too. We've just been doing a little interview about my recent project.'

'Blah! Blah! Blah!' Natalie barged in. 'And what are you up to now? Telling him my biography? He knows my name now; he can read the rest on the internet if he's interested, can't he?'

James's aspect got a bit sterner, and he gave her a grouchy look. Natalie, however, seemed to be rather unimpressed by James's mimicry and just went on.

'Why so serious? Turn that frown upside down right now!' she cried out, pointing her index finger at James so close to his face that she could pluck his eyes with it. 'We have no sympathy for bad jokes here, have we, Derick?' James just gave up on it at this point; he flicked his hand languishingly and, turning to Derick, he said: 'I read your biochem stuff, and I think it's awesome. Keep it up, man. I thought you might be interested in joining my own, exclusive project and add your two cents in.' Saying this, he produced a card from his pocket and handed it to Derick. It read: "Sombrero Tree Project" written in large, red font. Underneath the name of the project was written its slogan: "When science meets evolution". What is this supposed to mean? Derick thought. James was described as "lead scientist". The logo of the project was rather special. It depicted a plant resembling a coiling vine or ivy that was twisting and turning its numerous branches all over the free space on the card. Its fruits were little, colourful sombreros seen from the top. Due to their projection, showing only top view orientation, they looked more like archery targets than sombreros.

As Derick was exploring details of the card, he suddenly felt someone's heavy hand landing on his shoulder, then squeezing it like a lemon fruit. The force applied on his body made him lunge forward a bit, but then he saw the shadow of a person who was behind him as he was dipping in the air, distracted from examining the card. He raised his eyes only to see both James and Natalie standing completely still, rooted to the spot like two pillars of salt. Their faces showed a state of shock and bewilderment, to say the least. Derick turned his head and then he saw Simon's glistening eyes again. He'd appeared out of nowhere as if he was a magician or similar sort. Tilting his head like a snake, he signalled to James and Natalie to keep a safe distance from them by moving his exceedingly dilated pupils from one corner of the eye to another, very tellingly. Then looping his gangling neck around Derick, he hissed into his ear: 'Tell me — young blood, is it Marty's new trickery that has been playing on your mind?' His vicious words were like poison hurtling down his bloodstream straight into the heart, which he felt was squeezing itself sharply in a valiant act of resistance. Derick raised his head and stared into the eyes of a snake that never blinked and never cried. Then he quickly turned away from his face, afraid to know what lay behind the stare.

'I — I really don't know what you're talking about, Mr Redeldrag,' he replied in a tattered, subdued voice.

'Oh, don't you?' he jeered. 'Not to worry, not to worry at all. I guess this may help,' he said, pointing at the card Derick had just received from James. Then, twisting and tilting his serpent-like head, he drilled his slur into his other ear.

'You'll join James's project, and we shall forget about what has come to light today. I know you gave up on law long ago. You don't want your father to find out about it, do you? He would be really upset if he knew...'

Derick's heart sunk even lower now. He felt like he'd got all his life on a plate as if it was a piece of yarn or a movie reel, which he could unroll at will, cut into pieces, and then inspect each one of them under his microscope.

'Who are you?!' asked Derick after a pause, with flames in his eyes, finally putting the scraps of courage together to face his pair of cold as steel, greyish blue, fathomless voids.

'I am many things, Derick, but above all else, I am your friend.' He loosened his grip on Derick's shoulder, then he turned to James and Natalie who were still standing as if they were paralyzed.

'What a magnificent coincidence I found you two together!' he roared, throwing his open arms in the air.

'Indeed, Mr Redeldrag!' James replied.

Simon approached them swiftly and said to James, very quietly: 'I will see you at the usual time.' Then he was gone in a flash even as he appeared as if by magic — he vanished into the shadows. No sooner James and Natalie came near Derick than he started throwing questions in his face, quite spasmodically, as though he was having a fit.

'Do you know Simon?! What were you talking about? Did he mention my project to you? I saw him pointing at my card.'

'We just met,' Derick answered, very casually, 'and as far as your project is concerned, I guess I'm bound to be in now.'

'Oh, that's... that's great! You'd love it, I can tell you!' he crowed with exultation.

'I'm very sorry, but I've got to go now. I have some things to check up on. It was really nice to meet you two.'

'Hang on a minute!' Natalie cut in. 'What do you mean, you're bound to be in now?'

'I think, we are all gonna find out in time,' Derick replied, all the more vapidly, without even trying to make eye contact, still staring at these fancy sombreros hanging off its twiggy, coiled stem, looking like flashing targets as the sun's rays fell on them. 'I don't even know what I'm doing here,' he added after a short pause. 'I think I'm gonna get a taxi.'

After Derick parted from them, James and Natalie stood still and puzzled for a while.

'I don't know what Simon told him, but it has changed him for sure,' muttered James. 'Would you please keep an eye on him for me?' he asked, gazing deep into Natalie's dark blue eyes. 'I want to know what he's really up to.'

'Yeah, sure. I'm a journalist after all,' she said, briskly, '— the best in town! I will stay close to him,' she assured James and gave him a blink.

* * *

When Derick reached home, he noticed that every window and door was wide open, even the front door. He walked in and found the place to be deserted. Mrs Deeprow has never done such a thing before, he thought. Then he saw something so unusual that completely reassured him that something very odd and uncanny must have been going on here. Bruce's office door, which was closed and carefully locked at all times, was opened too, and he wasn't in. He would normally come out of his den at this time and have a puff of a cigar downstairs by the fire or on the balcony if the weather was nice. Then an irresistible idea to explore Bruce's very own formidable fortress came to pester Derick's mind so suddenly and ruthlessly that he couldn't do anything else but give in, forgetting all about the strangeness of the situation. This may be my only chance, he thought and sneaked in very furtively. The office was in an intact order, very neat and organised. Nothing seemed to be out of the ordinary, but only for one thing. In the middle of his dark and thick oaken desk a small book of files or a dossier laid open, and there were many single sheets strewn over its surface. Derick bent over the files, and to his bewilderment, every sheet he had in his sight was blank. He took up the opened book and leafed through it. None of the sheets had anything written on them. He turned the book over and at last, he found something. The covering page read: "The case of Mr Dauntwraith (Confidentiality classification: 5)".

'Mr McCrafty? Is that you over there?'

Derick dropped the files in a reflection of the fear of being caught completely flat-footed, but then he realized that it was Mrs Deeprow's sweet voice, and a smile appeared on his face, his heart filled with joy.

'No, it's me, Derick,' he replied and leaned out of the door frame, showing only his face.

'Thank God it's you, Derick! What a relief, believe me! I feared that this dreadful, miserable creature of a man was still here! He... he just appeared in the front door, trespassed in and made me open every window in the house. He said it stinks here like at a fish bazaar. Would you believe it?! To say something like that to me? Such an insolence! He exasperated me like a ruffian in a dark alley who is trying to pinch my handbag! Then he rushed straight to your father's office. I don't know where he's got the key from. The gate was open too. I was unflinching, dauntless, I tell you, in the peril of his menacing presence. I felt like smacking him in the head with something from behind when he was busy in the office, but then the phone rang, and I ran downstairs to take the call, but it hung up on me as soon as I took the handset to my ear. I felt like calling the police at that point as that man walking out of the thin air as if into his own property and rummaging your father's office stank to high heavens to me, but I wavered and walked back upstairs instead, and lo and behold, it was you in the office! You must have just missed him, and I must have just missed you! Good gracious, what a day!'

Derick was so amused how she could tattle about someone's breaking into the house like she was selling gossip at the marketplace. However, he didn't have the heart to interrupt her. He looked at her beetroot cheeks and shiny, silvery hair with a new fondness. Why had she never told him through all these years? Why was it only now that he was discovering everything at once as if by coincidence? Then he felt the strong urge to see Marty — not knowing why; he looked at the staircase with this desirous hope as if it was his only way to escape and find the answers to all his riddles, but his right hand, which was holding the "unreadable" files of the case of Mr Dauntwraith, squeezed them in a retaliating impulse that made him feel like he'd just grabbed a cable under high voltage, indicating what was the more pressing matter. When Mrs Deeprow had finished spilling the beans, he felt he could finally say something.

'Mrs Deeprow —' he started, carefully.

'Yes, my dear.'

'How did that man look like?'

'Oh, he looked just horrible. He moved so stealthily like an adder, and he resembled one, I tell you. He's even taller than you, and you're not a midget, but he was inhumanly humped and twisted; his very long neck and those icy cold, grey-blue eyes sent shivers down my spine every time he stared at me. He could pierce anyone through with them like with the sharp head of a spear.'

Then Derick saw Simon's glistening eyes yet again today. He really began to resent him now. Simon was already becoming a personification of wickedness to him. He looked at Mrs Deeprow's reddened cheeks and felt so overwhelmed with emotions that his tongue started going numb and dry from the tip. She was struggling for breath as if she hasn't talked that much for a very long time. He never knew she was such a chatterbox, but perhaps it was only the spur of the moment.

'Mrs Deeprow,' he carried on, 'can I call you grandma?'

Now she was staring at him as if she was trying to pierce him through. She didn't look surprised by his remark, though, not even in the slightest. She let her stare go and brood over the multitude of kaleidoscopic patterns of the vast, Persian rug, then she asked with a ponderous sigh: 'So, he's told you now, hasn't he?'

'Who? Marty? I mean, your... No, he hasn't told me this; I haven't seen him for ages. It was the man who was in Bruce's office. I just met him not so long ago. I think Bruce had given him the keys to the gates and to his office.'

'Oh, you should have told me you met that man today.'

'I tried, but it was hard to get through the cannonade of your words. By the way, why are you and Marty not together anymore?' asked Derick, utterly overpowered by curiosity.

'Not together anymore?' Mrs Deeprow repeated his words, looking rather dismayed. 'You see, nothing constrains a human being more than another human being, but we've never departed from each other completely. My Marty was the master of his life once. One day he told me he had to go when he felt he was being mastered by his life. Now he's back after all those years, and he's found his grandson. You're only now finding out that there isn't such a thing as normal life, there's only life...'

Saying this, she wept, not being able to suppress the tears any longer. Derick approached and embraced her in a compassionate bear hug. When her sobbing eased off a bit, he leaned backwards and, gazing into her bright, cyan eyes, he said: 'He hasn't found me. I've found him, purely by accident. I don't think he's been searching for me anyway.' She looked at him with a spark of wonder in the eyes as her tears had suddenly withdrawn to their sources. 'The gift of foresight runs strong in our family. Your father had it, and you have it too.'

'Marty has taught me how to read between the lines.

Otherwise, he's always so secretive, so hard to get into. I know you're very close to my mum. Tell me, please, how has she paid for my studies?'

'She paints,' Mrs Deeprow answered.

'Oh, does she? I've always wondered what she gets up to when she's locked for hours in that room at the end of the corridor.'

'She loves you for the world, Derick. She never tells you certain things because she wants nothing but happiness for you. She somehow knows that you must go out, get lost and find yourself again to be content with yourself. She knows your very nature inside-out as you're just like your grandfather.'

'She's never told me who my real father was,' Derick snapped at her.

'Let me tell you something, my darling,' said Mrs Deeprow, softly, giving his upper lips a gentle touch with her index finger. 'I know you have little sympathy for Bruce, but you must understand that he couldn't have anyone else, but you. His only desire was to raise you as his only son. He hasn't always been so stern and cold with you and your mother. After Nathan had died, your mother fell into deep depression. She's become desperately catatonic, crying speechlessly without shedding a single tear, without moving a single muscle she had been wailing for her lost love. That was the time when she started to paint. She was about to die from hunger and thirst when miraculously Bruce appeared in her life and reviewed her; however, I don't think she's fully recovered from it to this day. He was a rising star in the lawsuits scene at that time and helped her to stand on her own legs. He and Marty used to be great friends. Everything started going downhill when they met that man called... Maarten Burdent was his name I think. He was one of Marty's closest comrades, apparently helping him hugely to get his coveted doctorate in microbiology, which was rare back in the day. Then I saw Bruce getting swollen-headed by the day, intoxicated with a false sense of power he's gained, and my poor Marty falling into wane of his prowess and demise. About that time your mum and Bruce began to grow apart. You were just a few years old then, you're not gonna remember.'

Mrs Deeprow suddenly stopped there; her voice cracked, and she gave Derick this very frightful look coming from her eyes, which opened so wide as if they craved to absorb all the light for themselves. She clenched him with both hands just above the elbow with such vehemence that he felt like he was having a straitjacket put on him.

'Do you remember that man's name? Did he tell you his name?' she asked, very nervously, expecting a quick response. For the first time in his life, Derick saw fear in her eyes in its purest form — as white as the light from an exploding star, coming from the primeval Pandora's box, nested in the deepest, darkest regions of her most suppressed, unwanted memories.

'Yes, I do,' Derick answered, quite staggered by the immobilizing strength of her grip. 'His name is Simon Redeldrag. What's the big deal with it?'

All the clouds of gloom and fright had disappeared from Mrs Deeprow's face even as he called Simon's name. She tilted her head towards her shoulder, puffed the opposite cheek, which looked like a bulging horseradish now, and gazed at the ceiling thoughtfully.

'Redeldrag?' she said in a tone signifying both irritation and surprise. 'What an odd name! God be my witness, as long as I live I have never heard of anyone called Redeldrag. That's weird, but anyway, it's a weight off my old, frail shoulders he's not Maarten Burdent, but he looked so much like him, I tell you, he was like his ghostly double but way older. How many years have passed since I saw his obnoxious face for the last time? Let me think — twenty-four? Or even more? I can't remember clearly now, it was so long ago.'

Derick looked flummoxed as if he was struck by lightning, listening to Mrs Deeprow's new monologue. Then he decided to chime in, feeling the burning desire to see Marty even today.

'Granny, are you sure about this?'

'Yes, yes, I am. I was a super-recognizer back in my youth. A lot of unrelated people may look like twins, it's natural to occur. By the way, what's that you're holding in your hand so tightly?'

'Oh, these? These are just notes for a uni project called "Sombrero Tree" or something,' he lied.

'"Sombrero Tree"? Ah, another bizarre name goes to my dictionary today. So, are you staying at uni for the rest of the summer?'

'Perhaps, yes. I haven't decided yet.'

'Are you staying for dinner?'

'No, I don't think so. I've got to see Dorian today. Where's Mum?'

'She's gone to Greenfields Hospital. It's Bruce's mother.'

'Oh, I'm so sorry.'

'Alas… You should talk to her. I noticed her depression has returned recently with an intensity I haven't seen since…'

'Since when? Gran, why are you still speaking with riddles to me?'

'Since Marty's downfall. He and your mum have always been very close. He treated her like his own daughter,' said Mrs Deeprow, somehow bitterly, 'so maybe it's psychic.'

Derick felt absolutely overloaded by surprises, riddles, and unearthed facts as for one day, but he really wanted to see Marty by the end of it. He squeezed the files in his hands again and made for the stairs.

5
BLUE FEAR

'Why did you not tell me he's come back?!'

'I'm really sorry, Mr Redeldrag. No one knew he's back. He's changed a lot. Moreover, he wears a disguise now. His wife somehow recognized him, though. I have no idea how she's done that. I would have never guessed it was him. I don't think he had it planned to be recognized.'

'He's been in disguise all his miserable life,' sneered Simon. 'Perhaps, it may interest you to know that your housemaid worked for police forces before she came to clean dust from your dirty files.'

'Did she?!' screeched Bruce, very much surprised. 'As who?'

'As someone who has the ability to recognize people in disguise, for example,' grumbled Simon. 'I bet your lovely wife doesn't know it either.'

'I have no idea,' mumbled Bruce. 'I've checked her files thoroughly, and nothing like that ever came up.'

'You'd better check your memory right now and tell me when it happened!' growled Simon, very impatiently.

'About two months ago, at Willowood's marketplace' stammered Bruce, then winced quietly under the fierceness of Simon's face.

'About two months ago... Well, well, well,' drawled Simon, 'you may live to pay a price for your insubordination, Mr McCrafty.'

'My grovelling apologies, Mr Redeldrag. I didn't know you'd be still interested in his persona,' said Bruce, apologetically, then he added: 'He's not been seen anywhere since.'

'Of course, he won't be,' scoffed Simon, 'he's the most elusive man I've ever met.' Saying that, he gazed through the black-dimmed window of his limousine and gave a prolonged, reflective sigh.

'So are you,' said Bruce, dubiously, after a while of uncomfortable silence.

'You don't understand, Bruce. We're like twins in a way that we are at opposites poles of the spectrum. Our differences are so mutual that they cancel each other out, and then everything gets blurred.'

Bruce made no reply. He just knitted his brows with exertion to decipher what on earth Simon meant by that.

'Marty hasn't told you everything about himself, has he?' asked Simon after a while. 'Heh, so typical of his secretive character — always full of riddles. Now his secrets might just be turning against him…'

'So,' resumed Simon, getting even closer to Bruce's face, 'two months is the very least. I really thought he was dead by now. He's lulled us all into thinking he's no more, shifty old man. Do you think Marty would have risked showing his duplicitous face up only to let his grandson know who his real father was?'

'I don't think so,' said Bruce. 'I think they must have met by coincidence.'

'Coincidence, you say? Funny little thing this coincidence — you may be thinking something happens just like that, without any underlying reason, then you dig in and find out that the reason lies hidden and buried. Coincidence doesn't just happen; it flows like a river of variables into which many other, smaller rivers fall as it turns and swerves towards a destination. It always ends flowing when it meets a bigger water, but at the same time, it still flows in that water. Marty's the same, he's walking coincidence. Everything around him seems to be chaotic and accidental, but is it? Did you see Derick's face, how he looked at you when you called him your son?'

'No, I wouldn't expect he will have found out by then,' replied Bruce.

'He's more cunning than you might have thought. Don't forget he's Marty's grandson.'

'How has Marty found out?'

'I don't know this. He's had enough time to dig something out. Marty is a very old man. He might as well be older than we all think he is. He's certainly old enough to have known Walter Dauntwraith even before you met him or perhaps, even me.'

'That's why he tries to skulk about, knotty creep. He wants to make a contact, doesn't he?

'Who knows what's on his mind. One thing is certain, either way, Marty wants to have his cake and eat it at the same time.'

'What do you mean?'

'No matter who's found who, Marty's aiming to use Derick as his own pawn, a personal dogsbody. He'll slowly but surely creep into his mind by singing his devious lies to the beat of truthfulness. It's a dangerous time for this young man now; he's just gone out his front door onto the road of discoveries and without him even watching to keep his feet, he's being drawn between the hammer and the anvil. Marty will be thinking it's both fate and a golden opportunity; he's so assured in his foolishness that Derick is his own reincarnation as if he was already dead, and I presume he is but even more powerful than him. Poor old Marty is playing with fire without even knowing it, and we're having yet another ace up our sleeve...' Simon paused after finishing the sentence and put a crooked smile on his face. Then he continued, 'Marty had already lost both his sons, he'll be desperate to hang on to Derick now.'

'Did you say "both"?' asked Bruce, clearly astounded by Simon's new revelations.

'Yes, there's another Deeprow, and there's the rub — he's kept locked up at Windchain. In fact, he's been rotting there for the past twenty years or so.'

'How do you know he's Marty's son?!' asked Bruce, completely stunned.

'I know many things, Bruce. I told you, me and Marty, we're like twins. I wonder if Maggie recognizes his husband's second son if she sees him.' After saying so, he burst into wild and sinister laughter. He didn't stop laughing even when Bruce's phone rang.

'You'd better take this call; it may be something very important for you,' said Simon, choking on his own cachinnation.

As Bruce finished talking, Simon muted his laugh and squinted his slitty, slithery eyes at him, looking very bemused. Bruce then went on shifting his thumbs one on the top of the other in a nervy, rolling movement, waiting for Simon to say something. Simon's joy of stillness gradually elevated both corners of his lips, bringing a shade of ludic yet baleful smile. Bruce gave up in the end, sighed and said in a restrained, monotone voice: 'Mary phoned from Greenfields. She thought I was having a party when my mother —' Before Bruce could finish his sentence, Simon brandished his arm in full extension with his palm opened before his face and looked at him scornfully.

'If you must go there, my driver will give you a lift,' said he. 'I have to get off here. I've got a few things to catch up on, and it's well past lunchtime now.' Then the car stopped, and Simon opened the door. Rays of sunlight completely dazzled Bruce so that he didn't notice when Simon came around his side until the door was open and he saw Simon leaning down with his face hovering above his ear.

'You might as well know,' Simon said in the softest, silkiest voice ever imagined, 'Derick gave up on law years ago. Ask him how many.' Then the doors whammed shut, and Bruce's body landed on the other side of the couch, blown away by a tumultuous bluster of wind. He stared at the black sunroof of the limousine in utter darkness, dazed and disoriented when he heard a violent screech of the wheels and found himself sandwiched between two black, plasticky-leathern slabs of the couch like a nail that is being hammered into a too hard piece of wood.

* * *

It was well past dinnertime when Derick met up with Dorian. They both rushed through the university campus, caring only sparingly about their unobtrusiveness.

'"Sombrero Tree"?! What a funny name!' cried Dorian.

'Oh, tell me about it,' replied Derick, 'only a nutcase whose head's screwed loose must have given their own project such a name.'

'Or a visionary who likes riddles,' added Dorian, quite enigmatically. He was turning the card over, rotating it around its own axis under different angles and putting it in various positions versus his body. It looked as though he was trying to catch a butterfly in a net and then dancing around with it. 'These little "sombreros" look like some sort of targets, and they turn luminous when put under the sun.'

Derick started clapping his hands with approbation and gave Dorian a few nods of his head before saying: 'Hmm... I think you've just reinvented the wheel there. Congratulations! And the grand prize in whimsical investigation goes to... Dorian Rose! Applause, applause! You'd better stop fooling about with this card; otherwise, every lost soul in this place will want to investigate us.'

'When you draw lines between all those "sombreros", they form an octagon, don't you know,' said Dorian, still with all his attention planted into the intricacy of the card.

'What are you waffling on about over there?' asked Derick, not very much focused on what Dorian was saying, looking for something in his pockets quite fervently. Then he suddenly stopped, gave Dorian a snappy look and went on: 'What did you just say?! Give me that card back!' Then he snatched the card from Dorian's hand and plumped his ardent attention on it.

'Dorian, you're a genius!' hailed Derick, emphatically. 'Now I can tell you without a shadow of a doubt that you should have gone to study geometry, not biochemistry.'

'I must admit, I am somehow quite good with shapes and patterns, and I tell you, there's more to this card than meets the eye. When you look at these sombreros under the sunlight and squint your eyes a lot, you may be able to discern that they're not completely round and seem to be made of many uniform shapes.'

'Damn, it's just got cloudy! I can't see any shapes or patterns, for goodness sake. Don't keep an idiot in suspense, just spit it out you eagle eye!'

'Fractals my friend, fractals. I've got to shove it under a strong magnifying glass or even a microscope to see whether I'm right.'

'I'm sure you'll be spoilt for choice when we get to the lab,' said Derick. 'Now, let's speed up.'

They went along in silence through the back door into the monumental leviathan of a building of rooms, theatres, and chambers interconnected by a Daedalian maze of gangways and corridors, all inundated under an impenetrable mass of deafblind concrete. When Derick finally found the right key in his endless bunch, they entered a dark room, which still bore a smell of mixed compounds that was residing in a form of hazy veil levitating in the air just above their heads. The lights went on, and the mysterious vapour was no more, it ceased to exist like a morning mist under the rising sun; down it went, into the world of the unthinkable. The lab was all in white: the floor, the ceiling, the walls, the furniture, and the equipment, most of which was placed on or underneath a large, rectangle table that was taking a lot of space in the middle of the room. The floor felt very spongy and soft as it was made of a special material that prevented stuff from breaking into pieces when something hit the ground.

Derick got busy using the ultraviolet light scanner for his files right away, while Dorian, who after a quick search found a few magnifying appliances and a small microscope, got on his venture to reveal the hidden secrets of Derick's newly acquired card. Dorian was a sturdy young man. By the look of his face, he seemed to be younger than Derick by a year or two. He was well built, about five feet eleven inches tall and having broad shoulders he looked properly mesomorphic. Derick was getting increasingly agitated as he flicked through the pages of his clear as crystal files under ultraviolet light. Every single page stayed as blank as it was so far. He began pointing his eyes at Dorian who was completely absorbed in eyeballing the card. Then he turned the scanner off, closed the files, and rolled it into the cylinder.

'Have you got anything?' asked Derick, leaning over Dorian's wide shoulder.

'Indeed,' replied Dorian, still stuck into the surface of the magnifier, 'have a look at this.' He swung his head back and let Derick see through the glass.

'Beautiful, aren't they?' asked Dorian. 'They look exactly the same when you change the magnification.' When Derick took his eyes off the glass, they found themselves staring into each other's eyes enquiringly. For a moment, it looked as though they came across the same question, which they were unable to find the answer for. Then Derick broke the silence.

'You were absolutely right! Not only you're an eagle eye, but also a brain box!' said Derick, with amusement in his voice. 'I wonder why someone made such an effort to make a card as elaborative as this one.'

'It's a riddle. Either someone is trying to say something that is unknown to the reader or play mind games. One thing is certain, this card is a masterpiece. You said you got it from James Niggle, didn't you?'

'Yes.'

'He's gone up in the world recently, hasn't he? I didn't know he's your acquaintance.'

'No, I made his acquaintance just today. It's so weird, I have this strange feeling that my life is being played from a playback even as it unfolds itself under my very feet like I was a mere spectator of it. I'm finding out things — like today my... father has introduced me to this man who seems to be his big boss, and then I'm finding out he's probably the founder of this project. You probably know him by sight, his name is Simon Redeldrag.'

'Never heard that name before,' said Dorian, 'it sounds queer to me, but I can call my father and ask him about it. You know my father, he's got one of the biggest broadcasting companies in Clarksdowne; he knows people. Just give me a second, and I will find something out for you.'

When Dorian was busy calling his father, Derick sat down on one of the white chairs in a severely hunched position as if he was too worn-out to keep himself erect or even reclined. He stared at the opaqueness of the floor aimlessly, brooding deeply in his own thoughts when he heard the unrhythmical clop typical of somebody walking too fast in too unfit high heel shoes drawing closer to him by the step. He slowly protruded the tip of his head beyond the frame of the scarcely open door when he felt a few gentle pats on the back of his head. He twisted his noddle and saw one of his newly made acquaintances.

'Oh, hi! And what are you up to this late in the afternoon, all alone? Whoops, I didn't see that one!' said Natalie after she's had a quick peep into the lab.

'Well, you tell me,' replied Derick, who stood up to her and faced the gaze of her almond-shaped, dark blue eyes.

'I don't know about you, but I was just walking home from an interview,' said Natalie, straight in Derick's face as she looked even closer into his dark brown eyes. She was nearly as tall as him, maybe shorter by an inch or two. Dorian, who was still chatting over the phone, took it off his ear and gazed at those two, whose faces were so close to touching point as though they were about to kiss.

'Why is this man gaping at us like that?' asked Natalie, with her index finger pointed at Dorian, whose fixated stare she decided to pick on this time. 'Who the hell are you, and why are you looking at us like we were plotting how to kidnap your father?' she carried on.

'He's my best friend and his name is Dorian,' said Derick, and grabbing Natalie by her hand, he pulled her in. She rampantly released herself from his grasp and accosted Dorian with startling confidence.

'Look, look!' she called to Derick, 'he's shorter than me, but he looks like an overgrown thug, not like a best friend of one of the most promising students in the department,' said Natalie, measuring up to Dorian.

'Only a tiny bit,' Derick returned, 'and I am not a student anymore. You're doing nothing but interviews all day long, aren't you, Natalie?'

'Well, yes. Me and James —'

'So, you're Niggle's girl?' Dorian broke in.

'No, you silly man. He's the dullest stuffed shirt I've ever met.

Yuck!' exclaimed Natalie, giggling. 'I'm just writing an article about his project. I couldn't quite understand their chemical jargon, but they must be on the verge of a breakthrough or something. Even their director, Mr Redeldrag was there. What a charming man he is, and I thought he's just another big-headed asshole.'

Derick and Dorian looked at each other with wonderment upon this coincidence that was unveiling itself into their ears.

'And what are you two looking for in the biochem lab at this time of the day?'

'We were studying this!' said Dorian and waved the card in front of Natalie's nose.

'Isn't that the card you got from James today?!' asked Natalie, quite pompously.

'Indeed,' answered Derick.

'It looks really slick, right, but what is there to study about it?'

'Nothing you may be interested in,' Derick retorted.

'Oh — you know, I think you and Simon will make good friends; you both have this annoying, slippery look to your faces.' Saying this, Natalie crouched down to reach for her shoe, fiddled with it a bit, and while trying to stand up again, she lost her balance, which she regained by splatting her hand on Derick's thigh. 'Do what you want; I will see you soon,' said she, smiling cheekily. Then she turned back and left the lab.

'Did you see that?' remarked Dorian, suddenly aroused.

'See what?' replied Derick.

'She blinked at you! I think she likes you.'

'Oh man, you know, it's been one of the weirdest if not the weirdest day of the year so far for me that I don't think I would bother my swollen head about a woman blinking at me for whatever reason, and it's not even evening yet.'

'We can talk about it later. I'm going on holiday with my family and Jamila in two days. My father said to stay away from him when I told him his name. I don't know what he meant, he didn't want to tell me, but he knows something for sure. I'll find out for you. You just got to be careful.'

'I don't think that anything can surprise me now,' replied

Derick, quite indifferently, 'but thanks, I will stay vigilant. You should tell me instead how it is going between you two. Are you planning anything?'

'Quite right, but please don't tell anybody. I'm gonna propose to her during the holidays. I've already set everything up and will send you the stuff I'm planning to do on your webmail; it's too much talking to explain.'

'That's cracking news, my friend! Very best of luck to you! I bet she's gonna say "yes" with no hesitation. You're the wittiest loser I've ever met in my entire life.'

'Oh thanks, you wisecracker. This is what they all wait for, but I'm still curious about this card and this... slogan.'

'Yeah, you're right, it's a compelling puzzle, but I guess I'm about to plunge all out into it. That Redeldrag just blackjacked me to join Niggle's project today. I've been thinking about such a move or a similar one for a while, but it now feels like getting out of check if you know what I mean. I got tired of mixing those shitty compounds just on my own.'

'I see what you mean,' said Dorian, thoughtfully, 'but you're quite unorthodox when it comes to creating new stuff, you know, as though you had a sixth sense to do it or something. But anyway, what did he say to you?'

'He told me he'll grass me up to Bruce, I mean — my father about law if I don't join James's "geek squad".'

'What are you saying?!'

'Yep. I hope they at least have a UV light scanner with better wavelength spectrum. That one is just crap.'

'So, you didn't find anything?'

'Not a single mark.'

'This whole thing just smells fishy to me. My father sounded taken aback after I'd mentioned the name "Redeldrag" to him. You'd better keep your feet, especially now when they think you know something about Dauntwraith.'

'So, you heard of the burning of Mowhaken library?'

'Yeah, from my father. It's strange there's been a complete hush in the media about it. My father would like to exploit it if only he could get hold of Walter.'

'I didn't really know him. It was only his wife I liked to chat with. I was just in the wrong place at the wrong time, and this podgy Smith is a stinking rat.'

* * *

The weather had already gone bad when they came out of the building; they were welcomed by vicious, trenchant blasts of northerly wind and small pieces of biting hail, hurtling down from the stormy sky. Dorian offered to give Derick a lift, but he refused.

'Say "hello" to Jamila from me. I wanna see a beautiful ring on her finger when you're back.'

'Certainly, you will. We're gonna catch up in a couple of weeks. Now you take care of yourself, my friend.'

'Thanks, and you too.'

When Dorian drove away, Derick waited only a few minutes for his taxi. He never liked to use buses or trams very much. He'd got his preferred taxi drivers, though, and one of his ultimate favourites was Jim, captain Jim as Derick called him — out of respect and fondness towards this soft-tongued, gentle giant of a man who had witnessed so many withering springs and scorching summers fading into everlasting nights that it was no mean feat to gauge his age correctly from his parched, fuscous physiognomy, the crown of which was still dusted with barely conspicuous, small patches of curled, grey hair. He was a former sailor who had seen the seven seas, and with more than forty years spent on the frothy waves of immeasurable oceans, sometimes without seeing dry soil for many months, he'd always had some adventure tales to tell.

This time he was talking about dramatic events that occurred more than two decades ago in his own country — Zambu, or the "Land of Darkness", as Jim dubbed it because it was all rivers and rainforest according to him. He claimed there wasn't even electricity in his hometown when he was born. Upon his first return to the homeland after the years of hiatus, he'd found the whole country engulfed in a revolution brought about by a "diamond craze", which exploded only a few years after his departure from the homeland. All that unrest had been allegedly created by franchisees from rich, overseas mining companies, whose representatives lobbied for a "low tax rate" on diamonds by bribing and corrupting the current government with the aim to overthrow it and supplant it with their own "theatre of puppets". He went on to tell how he'd rescued and transported his family to a safe place and ended in his own typical fashion — with a tagline. With a soaking soreness in his voice, he illustrated how his greedy best mate of back in the day got shot dead by his half-brother, having been mistaken for a trespasser when he wanted to pinch some more looted diamonds for himself.

'Poor old Giova — he's gone a carat too far in his exploits,' said Jim, with sorrowful poignancy.

'Hey, Derick, are you even listening? What's biting you, my young brother?' asked Jim, seeing Derick biting his nails affectionately. 'You don't wanna talk? Oh, don't worry, it's one of those days, isn't it? You just need to sleep on it, and by the way, what is the place you're heading to?'

'Just turn the next right and stop on the right after three hundred yards, please,' requested Derick, very formally.

'Okie-dokie. Here we go. It was a good call you phoned me — no public transport would have taken you there, and this weather — look at it, it's dreadful out there.'

'Yeah… all this day is going to end up in a new low,' replied Derick, sombrely, opening the door with a gentle push.

'Listen, Derick, sit back down, and let me tell you something,' said Jim, sounding very commanding, then he nudged him back on the seat. 'I'm old, very old now, but on the other hand, I'm glad I have already seen the most of my life through, and by no means I envy you, the current young generation, for living in this peaceful time of comforts of modern society. Let me put it into perspective for you: I grew up in the "third world" country, shattered by coups and rebellions, ruled by ruthless, callous authoritarian governments or dictators, but we all knew point-blank what we were up against, and who's been selling the wealth of my country to whom, and we have fought united against far much greater power than we had, and we died valiantly because we had a purpose — a purpose to fight for a better future for our children. Here, your "tomorrow" had come and gone, you've got everything that you wanted for granted: advanced civilization and society, liberty, all kinds of freedoms, equal rights for everyone, and above else, your crown jewel — democracy, but let me ask you a question: Are you feeling free?'

'I — I don't know,' answered Derick, 'it's been a very long day for me, and it's that uni thing that is doing my head in now. They're asking me to stay on.'

'I see —' said Jim, looking into Derick's eyes with consideration. 'You did mention that you're pondering about moving on. Listen, you're young and well educated, enjoy your life a bit more. Don't get lost in society, it's a black hole; you're just playing a lead role in a cage in it. I wish you'd known how it feels to be a bit-part in the war… You're doomed to die, but you feel free to do so.'

'Thanks, Jim. Your stories are always so telling,' said Derick, 'and I'm sorry for being a sulk.'

'No worries, my friend. Just remember, the more advanced you are, the more isolated within yourself you become. Let yourself be free with your tempo.'

'I will. Thanks for a ride, Jim.'

'No probs. I hope you have an umbrella in that cylinder.'

'I don't like umbrellas,' said Derick and got off the cab. He waved at Jim as he was driving off, then he started walking briskly, very much against the wind. When he reached Marty's small house, he noticed that everything was cleared out of the front porch and from the side. Marty's dangling signboard was no more too. 'I think I am out here for another surprise,' Derick said to himself as he climbed the rugged stairs. He was just about to reach for the bell when he spotted the black drapes on his left moving slightly to the side. Then the door opened suddenly, Marty's face loomed out of the gloom, and before he knew it, he was pegged to the wall in the room with no lights by an invisible force.

'Have you been followed?' asked the voice.

'What?! No, I don't think so. Marty, for crying out loud, put me down, please. What is all this creepy "hide-and-seek" show about?'

'Who knows you were coming here?!'

'Jim Loyd, the taxi driver, my friend Dorian Rose, and... your wife I suppose. Now just let me off, please. What's happened to you?'

'I just didn't expect you to come so late in this kind of weather,' said Marty, releasing Derick on the ground. 'Did you just say, "my wife?"'

Marty turned the light on, and before Derick's eyes the room appeared completely bare and empty. It resembled in no way "the room of thousand clocks", except for its round walls, slanted slightly inwards, and painted grey. It looked as though someone was trying to leave this place in great haste, yet in an unobtrusive manner, keeping their grace and poise intact at all cost. It was so typical of Marty, the hastiest, the most meticulous plodder around. The better Derick got to know him, the more aware he became of his futile lunacy of always wanting to be one step ahead of life and the future. It seemed like Marty had the freakiest ability to hear the voiceless, to read from the mouthless, to see behind stars and under hills; he was always more interested in feeling the water and the earth or smelling the air than in what was being said to him. He would have appeared as plainly dumb and egotistic to Derick, if not for the fact that the vast majority of his crazy preposterous at times forebodings had actually happened. Thus, seeing the unexpected scenery right out of the crime movie, he began to wonder what new plots of mischief he'd seen in the dregs of his afternoon coffee.

'Yes, I did,' said Derick.

'Mmmmmm, I wonder if your surprise visit has anything to do with her,' replied Marty in his usual, full of stoic curiosity way, 'and with that thing you're holding in your hand. You're coming to me in the hour of need, riding on the storm without even knowing that you're the storm bearer.'

'You know, you never stop fascinating me with your insightfulness,' said Derick. 'You always speak with riddles, but I think I am just like you — a walking riddle with a cloud of question marks always lingering above my head.'

'A nice try, but you still have a lot to learn when it comes to riddles, my boy,' said Marty. 'I am terribly sorry we have nothing to sit on, but I am just waiting for my contact to arrive, and I will be off to Clarksdowne. You see, it's all insight to you, but for me, it's mere detection of causality now. Remember how we first met in this place? You found me, but you only did it because I was here in the first place, and I heard you climbing my creaky doorstep because I was in exactly the same spot where I am now, and you only found yourself there because you've been chasing the flying feather so relentlessly as if your whole life depended on it. I must admit, I didn't mean to find you, but you found me instead, quite expectedly. Is it not a perfect coincidence? Or maybe it's just an odd fluke of causality? What do you think, my smarty face?'

'Both,' was Derick's answer; however, he said it in such a hollow and dull way that surprised even him. He cast Marty a wary, feline glance, thinking if he'd just come across as rude, but he found the old man smiling at him candidly, with his eagle eyes arching away and beyond the frame of his thick glasses.

'Now, let me have a look at the thing you brought in that cylinder. May I?' asked Marty, stretching out his arm. 'Thank you,' said the old man and opened the cylinder. 'By the way, my apologies for behaving so unpleasantly suspicious, but I must remain highly vigilant, and this time I did not expect you to come, in earnest,' Marty carried on, pulling his glasses onto the top of his nose with his index finger as he skimmed through the first few pages of the file. Then he closed it softly, rolled it up, and handed it to Derick saying: 'I know now how taxing and extraordinary day you had, but since you came here with the file of the case of Mr Walter Dauntwraith, which is completely blank, except for the very first page, which you have found not because it was a "lucky coincidence" but because someone wanted you to find it, and I bet that this someone is a certain Simon Redeldrag, whom you most probably just met today and who told you my surname, which caused you distress for all the flashbacks you had today because of so-called "Proust effect", and the overwhelming feeling that since you've found me, your life was turning upside down, but let me tell you this — Walter Dauntwraith is the real cause I have returned to Willowood, but now they think you might have something to do with it because they have seen you loitering around his house, and Simon knows who you are better than you can imagine yourself.'

Derick's jaw dropped upon hearing Marty's strikingly accurate deduction. He stood there, in the middle of "the room of thousand clocks", of which none was left now, in the same awe as he was when he first entered this room a long while ago. He nearly dropped his cylinder, feeling all his muscles relaxing involuntarily one by one, turning him into a soft lump of jelly — he looked down and saw how his legs were shaking and bending in the knees. One more second, and he'll be a mere blob of flesh and bones scraped over too much floor.

'Derick, look at me!' Marty rumbled in a voice resembling a firing cannon. 'Don't you even try to give in within yourself now when your destiny has come to your very doorstep, when it had been banging on your memory-locked door with a sharp blade of its scythe for a long time. I need you now, and I need you more than you need me. Without overwhelming your tired mind anymore, tell me only one thing: How did Simon react when he heard my name?'

'He was certainly angry and looked very astonished. He told me to get out of his car straight away after Bruce had confirmed your name. I don't know why, but I'm getting this weird impression that you speak a little bit like him, although it seems to me he's your complete opposite.'

A sense of long-awaited victorious relief brought a cheeky smile to Marty's face. His poise relaxed considerably; suddenly he opened the front door and was gone for a few minutes. When he reappeared on the threshold, he was really soaked and holding a large, unwieldy gramophone which had rust all over its obtuse horn that was now sprinkling on Marty's black vest, turning it black and smeary orange. He put the gramophone down on the floor, in the middle of the room, and then he produced a dusty, dry, cardboard-like case, from which he pulled a dark as night vinyl that landed straight on the turntable. Marty stepped back and withdrew against the wall, pulling the curtains slightly to the right. He submersed his gaze under the hailing rain, letting his fingers tap gently against the windowsill as the accords of music began to flow through the croaky horn of the gramophone. Derick, who sat on the staircase with his arms crossed on his hips, just above the knees, tilted his head. He witnessed that enchanting, perfectly synchronized dance of Marty's fingers with the rain to the beat of the sound reverberating in the house. When the music stopped, Marty pulled the draperies carefully, and turning to Derick, he asked: 'Did you enjoy it?'

'Ermmm… yes, I did,' replied Derick in a low, dreamy voice as if he'd just been pulled out of a hypnosis by the click of Marty's fingers.

'It's called *"Blue Fear"*, and it is one of my favourite classics of my youth,' explained Marty. 'When I first played it to your father, he was only a young lad. He told me that music was just mathematics. Then I asked him whether he thought that love was just mathematics too, and he turned to me, saying, "indeed", with a glance full of certitude. A few years later, he'd fallen in love with your mother, losing his head completely to her, nearly dropping out of his dream studies. I remember that one day, he stormed to the house like a tempest of fire, running through the stairs like a wild boar; he flounced into my room without knocking, and seeing me at my desk, focused on my own paperwork, he smashed his thesis right in front of my nose saying, "music is just mathematics". The title of his work was: "The predictability of musical chords as forms of mathematical sequences". Strangely enough, I was just listening to exactly the same composition I just played to you when I read that. A few months later, he was no more. He would have made a great mathematician if he was to stay longer with us; he lived for the idea, the idea of proving everybody wrong but himself. He lived just too short to understand that life is not just maths, neither is music,' ended Marty, with a heavy-hearted bitterness in his voice.

Derick didn't say anything. He liked to listen to his grandfather's stories from his past. Somehow, he knew he would try to teach him a vital lesson once a conversation broke between them. Something had always been dragging him to Marty's captivating personality — full of contradictions yet unified within. Therefore, he was mute and still, patiently waiting for Marty's move.

'There is another reason I played you this particular work,' continued Marty, putting his arm around Derick's shoulders and gazing into his eyes. 'You see, you can't let life go through you, like your father... You have to let yourself go through life. Life is not to be stared at from a safe distance but to be plunged into. This composition was such a thing for the composers who created it. It was their first big hit, then fast forward twenty odd years, they were legends in their own right because they've put their heart in everything they've done in their entire lives, making thousands of people feel happy and excited because they've been doing it for them, not for themselves; yet little did they know where their life was gonna take them to when they first released this composition, but they've never shied away from any challenges on the road, although they knew nothing about where they might be swept off to next. Do you know why? — Because they always knew that music was not just mathematics, and they've never tried to prove it to anybody — they just lived it.'

'Oh, I see now,' Derick burst out, as though he'd just had a flash of an insight illuminating within his mind. Then he felt like his hand wandered off his thigh involuntarily, against his will, towards his pocket before tucking itself into it and getting the feel of James's card. Suddenly, he'd got the recurring image of Simon's glistening eyes appearing right before him as a shady, obscure phantom looming out of the gloom. He winced and shuddered with an unknown, omnidirectional fear that seemed to be oozing from within, shrouding him in a trembling veil of premonitions. He took the deepest breath he possibly could, his eyes opened so wide that one could see near the entirety of his eyeballs, then he saw Marty's head that was inches away from his left cheek as if through the mist, with his lips moving, trying to convey words towards him, which he couldn't conceive clearly.

'...a favour, please. I know that Walter is kept locked at Windchain prison. I cannot go there myself, even in disguise, but you could try. I need to know what happened at Mowhaken that night when it went ablaze, and why he was there when he should have been on holiday with his wife.'

'I will do my best, Grandpa. I won't disappoint you, I promise, but tell me, please who Simon Redeldrag is before you go. Dorian's father said to stay away from him at all cost,' said Derick, putting an even stronger hold on his card as if he was growing increasingly aware it may get stolen or taken away from him.

'And I say the same to you,' said Marty in an irritably commanding voice. 'Mr Rose is a wise man, and you should avoid Simon at all cost. Now, you tell me what you've got in your pocket. You keep on twisting and shifting your hand in it as if you were afraid that something may fall from it.'

Derick's eyes reddened and glowed with sudden misgiving; he squinted them at Marty with suspicion but took his hand from his pocket quickly, yet instead of the card, he was holding his old embroidered handkerchief that he'd got from Mrs Deeprow.

'It's only my old handkerchief,' he said through his teeth, waving it before Marty's face, which was getting subdued by a confounding frown that was now giving way to a grinning smile when he saw his wife's own work appearing over his head. He put his hand into Derick's flourishing mane of hair, and it went missing in a flash, completely smothered by the black mass before looming out of it in a whirl of gentle, shaking strokes that made Derick's tense, flexed facial muscles relax from the point of compulsive twitching to a blissful state of approval and self-assurance. Then the buzzer rang a good few times in a sound resembling an odd, merry melody of the past, creating a rhythm that might as well be a type of password or code. Marty whirred towards the window, leaving Derick's hair in a dire mess, and before long he was standing by the front door, just managing to hold his awkward gramophone in both hands.

'Come on then, we must leave now,' urged Marty. Derick was still sitting on the staircase, taken aghast a bit by Marty's sudden, swishing swiftness through the air. He hardly lifted his hand to tame his wayward hair when Marty forcefully abducted it, then he felt like he was being picked up.

'I can only drop you at the Vanguard's Square, but we must take a little detour first,' said Marty. 'Now, can you open the door for me, please? The keys are in my…' then he wavered, looked above and around, finally fixating his stare on the windowsill, 'still on that bloody windowsill. Damn it, Derick, can you take them and lock the doors after me, please?'

Derick obeyed in silence, and soon they were both out in the shackles of the copious rain. Marty shoved the gramophone to the back of the black van and gave the driver a signal to reverse a bit more so that he could attach the trailer to the towing ball.

'Grandpa, you still didn't tell me about Simon,' asked Derick, pressingly, as Marty was opening the back door of the van, which he closed immediately upon hearing Derick's recurring request.

'Listen, my boy,' started Marty, with a usual softness in his voice, which was somehow missing for the large part of today, now sounding eerie and foreboding, 'Simon is an evil creature, and I am still one of a very few whom he's still afraid of. You will have to make your own mind about him, but beware, whatever you find in this file, do not believe anything in it. In fact, you might as well burn it in your hearth as soon as you walk in to your house as you know now that he'd set it up for you. He's an absolute grand master of mind games and riddles and will do anything to lure you into believing that all his lies are true, thus provoking you to have an upside-down judgement.'

Derick and Marty hadn't exchanged a single word whilst being driven in the van. They were both brooding deep in their thoughts, both boding about the future events, seeking answers in their own quests, confined within their own worlds of bubbles — Marty was peeping out with an intent at the patchy sky with thinning clouds at first, then withdrawing to the back of the seat, pretending to be asleep, whilst Derick's face was portraying increasing relief that the day's end was closing in. He glanced at Marty every now and again, feeling that an answer to the questions he felt bound to ask laid hidden within him, yet his run-down body was showing signs of such tiredness that even his earnest desire to go on was burning out now, making his mind benumbed and unreceptive.

When the van stopped at the Vanguard Square after about ten minutes ride, a fleeting smile appeared on Derick's countenance. Keenly he looked at Marty, who was indeed asleep, snoring mildly, then he kissed his cheek, whispering sounds of goodbye into his ears and pulling his old, squared frock coat over his torso. When he got off, it wasn't raining anymore. Narrow stretches of starry sky were right above him, but he felt the blusters of the wind on his back growing in strength with every blow he was smitten by, his own shadow vanquishing out of sight with every strike of lightning just behind him as he was walking home, which was a good ten minutes of pacey stride from the square.

When he arrived at his final destination of the day as he thought, mighty lightning struck nearby as he was pushing inwards the immense front door, covered heavily with carvings, which illuminated sinisterly as silhouettes of unworldly beasts, guarding the entrance to the lair of the most formidable of them all, the looming shadow of which he could momently discern as the lightning struck. A sudden draught of cold air snuffed out the glow of barely smouldering coals in the fireplace. A black darkness fell, even so, he could tell that something just wasn't right with the view to an even higher degree than the last time he came in through this door. He felt the sheer presence of something gross and formless right in front of him, although he couldn't tell what was lurking behind the shroud of the night. Then the lights went on and his whole life loomed out of the gloom; it appeared as a shapeless, warped pile of everything he ever felt attached to. His thoughts had gone astray in all directions as a herd of fear-stricken sheep, running wild into their doom upon hearing the ominous howling of many cohorts of hungry wolves. He was struggling to pull himself together from the initial shock and emotional dispersion when he heard a loud, dull clapping of hands just behind him, the sort of clapping he'd heard once today. His head twisted on the neck while the rest of his body remained motionless, rooted to the ground, to see Bruce's smiling face, who just came to greet him with open hands.

'Congratulations, my son!' he yelled in a triumphant voice of a traducent lackey, opening his hands as wide as they could span. 'It's your greatest day of freedom! Twenty-odd years is breathing down your neck, and your only lifetime achievement is to get kicked out of my house!'

Upon hearing these words, gurgling tears of wrath began to lustre the rim of Derick's bloodshot eyes; the plastic cylinder was being crushed by the brutal force of his clenching fists while Bruce accosted him with an irritably pretentious, guileful gait as if he was indeed celebrating his own birthday prematurely.

'You have it until tomorrow to take all that crap away, or else it burns! It will be chucked out to the shed in the morning,' whispered Bruce in a slanderous tone, slinking and slithering around the motionless statue of his stepson in his twisted danse macabre. Suddenly he ducked, swerving and tilting his upper body outwards, turning his back to Derick, then he bounced off his hip and pressed Derick to the starting newel of the oaken, winding staircase forcefully, manacling him with the powerful grip of both his hands right above Derick's elbow.

'Do you think you're so clever, eh?!' growled Bruce, right in Derick's face, splattering his spit all over it. 'You nasty, egregious liar! You think you're master of your life and all your choices, don't you?! Then let me tell you this — you're not even a blip, not even a fart in the machine's grand ass; you're not even a loose, expendable screw in the machinery you've been enslaved by from the day you were born. I've worked my bloody, haemorrhoid ass off only to become the fifth wheel, and you're just strolling along into my house, announcing to the whole world that you're about to conquer it with a bunch of your outright bullshit! Who do you think you are!?' shouted Bruce, savaging Derick's body back and forth, banging his back against the newel and rending his shirt until the top buttons had enough and burst out, falling on the carpet silently. All of a sudden, his grip loosened, and Derick plummeted down the stairs, just managing to catch balance by grasping the handrail blindly with both his arms extended on both sides of his body at a largely obtuse angle. Bruce was taken aback, confusticated momentarily by the unexpected force that had come to light. Derick peered down at his half-bare chest to find out what had drawn all Bruce's attention and seemingly, his strength. It was the necklace, cold and still, stuck to his flesh, hanging off his neck on the thinnest silver chain, bestowed by his mother one grey, rainy evening.

'What, what the fuck is this on your chest!?' bellowed Bruce, in a berserk outburst of madness. 'You're not only a liar but also a traitor! You've already fabricated your life, now you're fabricating your past?!' Saying this, he wrested the necklace from Derick's chest with one fierce, wrenching thrust of his arm, which forced Derick off balance, and cast it away onto the top of the heap of Derick's belongings.

'I've done it, you fool,' said the voice from behind. There, at the peak of Derick's life, stood Maggie Deeprow, tall and proud, holding his necklace in her hands. Then she slid down to the bottom in a sleek manner, full of glee as if a spirit of youth had blown a breath of a new life down her bloodstream, giving her the exuberant vigour of days gone by. She came up to the base of the staircase and glared up at Bruce's immovable stature. 'You're just your bosses' bitch! Look at yourself —' she hailed thunderously, flourishing her arm as if she was wielding a sword, moving it slowly anticlockwise round her own axis, 'you pitiful man; you're so hollow that all you've got is money. If he goes, I shall follow the suit!'

'So be it,' was Bruce's curt retort.

'I've done it all with love for Derick, by the will and bidding of his own mother,' said Mrs Deeprow. Behind her appeared the shadowy figure of his mum — lost and petrified. Just when it couldn't get worse, it got worse. The day was lost on a new low, even as Derick thought a few hours ago. Even so, his cheeks posed playfully purple on that deathly exhausted aspect of his — he'd just got reminded how a certain old man told him, not very long ago, that it could always get worse when you thought that it just couldn't.

6
THE CASE OF MR DAUNTWRAITH

Derick stormed out of that house of lustrous corruption right into the thick of the thickest, the stickiest stormy rainfall he'd ever experienced. It was an absolute deluge, and he didn't even have an umbrella. In fact, he didn't need it — the whole point of possessing such an essential as an umbrella, especially at that crucial moment when all the sky was falling down on his head, seemed to him just obsolete and redundant. He didn't have to think about it because he simply didn't have it — the shadow of the imminent feeling of frustration when you cannot get what you want to possess, and the even more tragic sensation of getting it, has passed like rain in the mountains, like wind in the meadows. It has gone into the distant land of remoteness, beyond the horizon line. He felt as light as a feather, being freed from all those things that constituted his life, living proof to the whole world that he'd been alive since his birth, now turned into a formless rummage. Did it mean that he had ceased to exist as a person who owned his life through the prism of his assets? He felt every single droplet of the rain falling on his bare face, every stroke of the wind dabbing his body with a newly found wonder of curiosity. He was alive — more than he'd ever been! Suddenly, he understood that all his belongings owned him more than he owned them. When he'd rendered them unneeded, they'd vanished from his mind like morning mist vanishes from the pastures. Instead of thinking what else he needed, he'd realized what else he could live without. That spontaneous insight made him, for a moment, acutely aware that all boundaries, limits, borders within the society he lived in were mere assumptions based on imaginary paradigms.

Now he was free to be the self-proclaimed, first citizen of the World, the citizen of the Universe. His world was where his feet were — grounded to the solid earth. He felt shapeless and carefree: it didn't matter what taxi he took and what the driver looked like; it didn't matter how he shouted at him not to move a muscle because he would soak all the backseats of his cab; it didn't matter he didn't ask for the change when he dumped him in the middle of the enormous, multi-levelled crossroad in the centre of the city of Clarksdowne, which was absolutely desolate, save a few lonely ladies walking aimlessly in fancy, shiny miniskirts. Derick started walking towards Doorway Street where most of the city's entertainments were amassed. Without any whim, without any purpose, he passed by doorstep after doorstep, illumination after illumination he followed with his eyes, all the crafty decorations of the night becoming all the more tempting, the more he spent staring at them.

Then, just so unexpectedly, he thought he was hearing that too familiar voice again. Maybe he was dreaming or was just so exhausted, maybe his mind was playing up with him now, but there, diagonally across the wide six lanes of tarmac, he saw her, tussling and wrangling in the arms of an unknown male. Derick rushed for the nearest crossing, yet at this precise moment the gates of the closest cinema to his left popped wide open, and a veritable swarm of human bodies hurtled right in front of his nose, almost taking his run-down bones on the tail of the wild current of the air that created a wind tunnel to the very spot where the traffic lights were, now occupied by that rowdy mob, forced to stop abruptly by the unspeakable shift of the lights, which initiated a swirling, mind-slaking cacophony of mechanical sounds. Derick quickly peered across the road again, hoping to catch even the faintest of glimpses of her, but the view was supplanted by a train of cars and taxis, speeding through to their destinations. He felt bamboozled by that rampant orchestra of engines and horns; he drifted his attention from them and fixed it on the crowd, whose resentment seemed to be reaching the zenith, bulging with every passing second spent motionless in the bondage of the unrelenting redness of the light. Then the magic happened and "green" was showing — a moment of great tumult and uproar, then silence — pristine and clear like a mountain spring; all the people having dispersed in all directions of the world, save one lost soul, who was sitting on the stairs on the corner of the street before the large gate to the cinema, staring at Derick as if she saw an otherworldly apparition. Maybe he looked like one hell of a phantom now, having gone from the longest day of his life into the endlessness of the night like one who does not need anything to live on, just the air to breathe. He stepped off the curb and sat down beside her. Giving her a warming cuddle, he wrapped his hooded sweatshirt, which he didn't really need anymore, around her back and gazed deep into her almond-shaped eyes.

'Long time not seen, ehh?' said Derick, somehow sarcastically.

She gazed at him keenly with her cunning dark blue eyes as if he was a loony or something, then without replying, she arose and began waving and shouting for a taxi, walking unsteadily towards the rounded curb in the same too small, too high, red heels he saw her last time. It wasn't raining anymore; a few shady bodies were popping up here and there. Derick didn't even notice when it stopped raining, but it didn't matter. Natalie looked really nervous searching through her baggy handbag, which she let hang loose on her wrist after turning everything in it upside down.

'Bollocks! I haven't got any money with me!' she shouted, kicking the kerb of the round corner of the street so clumsily that she lost her balance, nearly falling over, drawing the attention of a few close passersby. 'It was supposed to be a romantic evening, but look where that prick has taken me out!' she said, very pretentiously, turning towards Derick with her hand raised above her head. 'All men are just the same!'

'It sounds like your ex-date had a bad taste when it comes to movies,' Derick replied, with an even greater dose of sarcasm.

'He had shit, not a taste! Just look over your shoulder! Ahh, why do I always have to come across twats and wankers?!' she kept on moaning.

Derick stood up and looked at the posters behind the glass of the cinema's gates, and to his amusement, they all showed bodies of half or completely naked females and males in lewd poses, with their naughty bits out and blurred, all to remain "customer friendly".

'Ahhh, I have to correct myself now — I think he's got great taste! And look at these cheesy, saucy titles!' Derick burst out, then turned towards Natalie, chuckling under his nose.

'Oh, fuck off, Derick! What on earth are you even doing here?! It was only the second date, but I had to dump him because he took me to the bloody porn cinema! He couldn't even understand why I dumped him, cheeky bastard, he thought I'm easy-sleazy, eh?'

'Ermm… I don't know, I think you're not,' Derick replied, hastily, 'but speaking of the dumped, I've just been ditched out from my stepfather's house for good, and the only thing I've got left for being alive for over twenty-six years is the wallet full of ID's and credit cards, so I think I could get you a fare home if you want one.'

'What?!' she snapped. 'What stepfather? Are you serious?! Then I don't wanna be rude but Clarksdowne is a very poorly chosen place if you're looking for a shelter. Over a million heads live here, but I could name you just a few who might give you a roof over your head. It's a breeding ground for snakes and rats, mark my word for it, I'm a journalist after all.'

'So where do you live then, miss journalist?' asked Derick, giving her a straightforward smile.

'Hillbarrow, you cheeky bugger!'

'Oh, spooky!'

'There may be a few supposedly haunted old houses around, but I don't give a damn what people say. I love it because it's tranquil and close to nature. Anyway, I know the atmospheric cellar bar a few cross streets from here. They have good vibes over there. We may sit down, and you'll tell me the story of your life.'

'Sounds like an invitation for an interview, but I just wouldn't have the heart to reject your cuteness.'

'Oh, stop being so cheesy, or else you'll be ditched twice in one day,' said Natalie, giggling away.

'Should we take a taxi then?' asked Derick, quite seriously.

'Nah, it's a bit off the main avenue, close to the Old Market;

paths are cobbled and quite narrow there, so we'll walk if you don't mind, of course.'

'No, not at all. Besides, it's not raining anymore,' Derick stated the obvious.

'It's all right to walk then, ain't it?' said Natalie, but so jovially that it left him startled speechless by this swift change of heart; then she slid her hand tastily between his left arm and ribcage, and winding it around his side, she pronged him slightly to start walking. They walked off Doorway Street and made a good few hundred yards when the paving turned cobbled, the path itself was narrowing by the foot, the streetlights were scarce, giving off dim, meagre illumination, barely enough to light their own vintage, wiggly posts, allowing nocturnal shadows to grow senseless and surrounding in an obscure circle of phantoms. Derick had to keep squinting his eyes tightly to see his next step; it was getting cold and really hazy, the noise of the River Brook that was flowing through the nearby channels was drowning out every thought that came to mind. Natalie was clinging close to his arm, trembling, even though she still had his sweatshirt around her neck. Derick had goosebumps all over his hands too, but it didn't matter.

'You know, I've come to the realization that you're the most honest and truthful to yourself when you don't give a damn about your life anymore.'

'You're so long-winded,' replied Natalie and returned him a smug, half-sarcastic grin of the Cheshire Cat, showing all her snow-white, bare teeth. Then her eyes bulged out suddenly as the eyelids ebbed away, her mouth opened obtuse, leaving the lower jaw on her chest, quivering fearfully. No sooner had he noticed her expression changing rapidly than he felt someone's freezing cold hand stifling his mouth from behind and was pushed and dragged back abruptly into the shadows of a dark, gloomy backstreet. Derick felt the icy roughness of the brick wall of an old tenement house on his back as some invisible, brutal force shoved and pressed his body straight into it as if it was a plank. He was almost choked to death when his mouth could breathe. He couldn't speak or shout, even if he really wanted, as his lungs were overwhelmed by the rapacious uptake of oxygen, making him almost feel high for a moment. Then there was a click and a flash — a bright, tall flame sprang out of the handy gas lighter, dazzling him so acutely he had to close his eyes for a long while and rub off the pain with his fists. When he opened them again, he saw the face of Mrs Kitty Dauntwraith — frightened and persecuted, probably outlawed too. Then he was distracted by the imminent feeling of déjà vu as Natalie looked really nervous searching through her baggy handbag, exactly the same scene he saw less than an hour ago. She finally produced a black box with a strap that looked like a personal alarm from her bag.

'A personal alarm!' Derick's whole body contracted alarmingly as if he was having a seizure, yet he managed to burst his mind out: 'Natalie, no! Stop it! I know her!'

She looked at them, flabbergast to the bone, then she exclaimed: 'What!?' letting her handbag hang loose on her wrist.

'Derick, my dear, you are a godsend in the hour of need!' said Mrs Dauntwraith. Derick tried his best to hide the complete surprise of the situation, but as he was coming back to his senses after the initial shock, he realized that he was not surprised at all; maybe he was too concentrated or too exhausted to be surprised or maybe... he was only dreaming.

'Listen to me now, please. Take this from me and give it to your grandfather,' she requested with a grave and earnest seriousness on her haggard face and produced a dingy, rugged scroll of a large format, tied meticulously with a thick sash. Derick listened carefully to everything she was saying; in all honesty, he had neither strength nor willpower left to say anything. He took the scroll from her and held it in his hand whilst she kept on talking. She looked terrible, a mere shadow of herself.

'He's the only person who'll know what to do with it. We've got no time; they all over me!'

Even as she spoke her last word, they could catch the faint yet sharp noises of the sirens of several police cars, coming from many directions. A moment later, they heard a sound resembling dogs' howling and barking, much closer to them. 'You've got to run for your life now!' urged Mrs Dauntwraith. Derick looked at her, then at Natalie. They were all lost and horrified to death.

'Fire stairs! Let's take the fire stairs!' cried Natalie, pointing up at the winding metal stairs and rushed towards Derick.

'Give me your alarm now!' commanded Mrs Dauntwraith, but seeing hesitation on Natalie's face, she just wrested the handbag off her wrist ferociously and, finding the alarm, she thrust it out into the air, quickly removing the trigger before letting it fly. They had never seen such a strong and violent throw in their lives. The alarm must have travelled a good hundred yards before landing somewhere as they couldn't hear any sound of impact nor beeping. Or perhaps, it plunged into the river channel, which was about a hundred yards from here.

'That should distract them for a while!' said Mrs Dauntwraith, firmly content with herself. 'Now, up you climb you two. I'll give you a piggyback.'

'What about you? Where are you gonna hide?' asked Derick, worriedly, feeling his heart's wild palpitations.

'Don't worry, I'll manage. Natalie, look after him please!'

'I don't know where Marty lives now. He's just moved out,' Derick said from the first level of the stairs, but Mrs Dauntwraith was no more; he could only hear a short sound of the plastic lid being slammed somewhere beneath him in pitch black darkness.

'What are we doing now? We're perching like two sitting ducks in here. It was your plan to climb here, miss clever! They will find us easily.'

'Ah, stop moaning for once! Climb silently two levels up and quietly give three, then two and then one sharp knock to the window on your left,' whispered Natalie.

'What? Are you crazy?'

'No less crazy than you are, my lovely. Now fucking go!' she ordered and kissed him on the cheek.

Derick clambered up as stealingly as he could, almost stumbling over the slippery stairs along the way. 'Damn, why must it rain just now?!' he swore silently. He reached the window on his left with great difficulty; spreading his limbs to their breaking point like condor's wings, he performed the tapping sequence as directed, but then nothing — no response whatsoever. Natalie's tremulous face just emerged next to him; she was roosting there like a wet hen on a perch. 'Do it again!' she said with a sweet, insisting indulgence in her voice. Derick looked at her trembling wet lips as she spoke, but let his arm stretch out to the window as if by reflex, and without losing eye contact with her he tapped out the secret formula, but sharper.

Below them all hell was breaking loose — dogs were yapping, people were yelling, whistles were yammering, and the rays of spotlight torches were cleaving and slashing the blackness of the air from all directions, in a madhouse rummage, ever so close to them, their beams crossing one another in the sky, making it a delightfully theatrical spectacle. For a moment they'd forgotten where they were; the night was endless, and they were crazy, they were young, the lights were always shining — they just lived for fun. Their palms met and interlocked, their lips touched, their fates entwined. They were taken away into the night of pouring rain, riding the wild wind on the lid of the bulging Pandora's box.

Unfortunately, as all moments made of pure, heavenly delight, they don't last forever. No sooner were they as one for a split second than the window above them opened in a whizz, and a small mop of dark, curly hair protruded, starting to explore the environment by shaking the head with a nerdy inquisition. They were quickly taken up and safe, for now. The lights were out, the drapes were pulled down to the floor and stretched carefully so that no light could go through. Floundering about for a few seconds, trying to find his bearings, Derick somehow located a piece of furniture to sit on in this tar black darkness and threw his flesh on it immediately. Straightaway he noticed that there was something odd about that place. The air was so stuffy as if a squadron of troops was jampacked there, hiding and breathing heavily. The smell was funky, to say the least, and these shrilling noises — they were all around him — chirps, tweets, and whatnot; he felt like he was inside of an aviary of some sort. Then a small lantern was lit, giving off just a flicker of tiny light. The person holding the lantern looked like a Satanist or a member of an occult sect at first glance in this dim light. Shabby black jeans and a black T-shirt, all not very well tailored, hanging on a shady, malnourished body of a shaggy middle-aged male with a far too long beard; tattoos all over his arms and a multitude of crappy wristbands above both of his palms. He lifted his old-school lantern up to his face, then Derick saw these clunky spectacles on his nose with huge glasses, taken probably from binoculars. He flicked the lantern unsteadily right before Natalie's nose and then spoke with a rough voice of an unhealthy drunkard.

'Aargh, it's you again! What new hornet's nest have you stirred up this time?' asked he, nodding his mane towards the window.

'Believe me or not, it wasn't me this time!' rejoined Natalie.

'Hmmm, of course, you're just an innocent victim of raging cruelty and terror of this world, as always. So, what devil has brought you here then?'

'That devil!' replied Natalie, blatantly pointing her finger at Derick.

'Well, not your usual sort I must say; looks rather too dweeby for your liking, but good enough for a one-night stand as any.'

'Shut your face, Randall!' cried Natalie, now looking really butthurt.

'Ouch! So it runs deeper this time, eh? Don't wanna talk about it anymore? Fine. And yes, you can take my bedroom for tonight. I just need to move a few cages from there.'

'Oh, bless you, Randy!' Natalie burst out, then threw herself at him with open arms. 'You're one of the finest men still living in this city of venom.'

'Now you're talking,' replied Randy. 'I'm not sure whether to take it as a compliment, though. Anyway, maybe you shall introduce me to your new acquisition? I mean, an acquaintance,' corrected Randy, bobbing his furry head at Derick and smiling mischievously.

'Oh, yeah, sure,' said Natalie. 'Derick, it is Randy. Randy is a professional canary breeder, one of the best in the country. Randy, it is Derick. Derick is ermmmm… he works at East Point University — I think,' muttered Natalie, looking dubiously at him.

'At least you seem to know his name,' said Randy and

gave Derick one of those smugly sly smiles of his. 'Well, that's perfectly enough for a start, ain't it, love?' he said to Natalie, then disappeared deeper into the darkness of his flat. He left his lantern in the room that looked like the living room, but to Derick, it was a zoo.

'I didn't know she knows you, how come?' Derick questioned Natalie, coming back from a reclined position to talk about Mrs Dauntwraith's mysterious appearance out of the dark.

'Oh, her!' began Natalie after a short moment of silence. 'That woman, wow, it was bloody scary! I don't know her really; I interviewed her husband back in the day; she must have still remembered my name. And you what, playing curious, eh? Maybe wanna interview me now?' she went on, and playful, gamy notes in her voice had taken the upper hand again. She was like water; she just couldn't stay in one place or a state for long. She simply flew through the time of her life like a migratory bird, like a white cloud that is ever riding on the westerly belt.

'Not now, please. You'll interview each other later,' said the voice in the dark. Then Randy's lanky body loomed out of the blackness of the corridor with the same cynical, knavish smile planted on his scrawny face. He was carrying a number of birds' cages with one of his selectively bred species inside.

'Would you please help me to hang them all on that silver railing that runs above your heads, guys?'

They took to the task not very eagerly at all, having been snuggled up on his cosy sofa under a warm blanket. It was no mean feat to get them cages hung up on the railing because the ceiling was just ridiculously high up in this place by any stretch of the imagination. Randy had some handy stools at his disposal, though, and soon they were standing like utility poles on them, but maybe only just a tiny bit shakier.

'How come she knows you?' asked Natalie.

'How come?!' Derick paraphrased, 'I've known her all my life, not very well, though, but she's been living on the opposite side of Willowood ever since I remember. I've just discovered that my grandfather and her husband used to be some sort of friends.'

'Your grandfather?! What do you mean, you've just discovered? I've just met you, and you're like a walking riddle to me, always springing out of nowhere, always up to something, and things just seem to happen everywhere you go.'

'Maybe you've just happened to meet me at the wrong time of my life.'

'I don't know what you two are talking about,' Randy chiselled in, 'but I bet it must have something to do with all those police units downstairs.'

'Randy, shush, please. It wasn't really us, we were just on our way to *"Twelve Barrels"* when it ensued. We got scared and sought shelter at yours,' explained Natalie.

'Hmmm, let's assume it was as you said indeed,' replied Randy, not quite convinced by Natalie's story. 'It's not the first time you've landed here in similar circumstances,' he murmured.

'I know, and I'm sorry,' answered Natalie, 'hard is the job of a journalist. What would I have done without you, my dear?'

Randy didn't say anything but gave Derick the last cage to attach to the railing. It was the most awkward one, as the only available space left was just above the window through which they got into the house. Derick didn't really fancy tripping over and flying through the same window yet again, this time in the opposite direction, basically handing his head to all those cops, still wandering about, on a plate. That would have been a really "bad trip"… When he'd managed to get that shitty cage dangling up there at last, he nodded his dozy head down and saw that Natalie was gone somewhere. Now Derick was left with this loon, birds keeper Randy, all alone. The situation turned really sticky and uncomfortable when their eyes met. Derick had absolutely no clue how to spark a conversation with him; words just stuck in his throat; his body froze, and he felt this strange uneasiness down in his stomach. Randy wasn't making it any easier by being annoyingly sparing with his words, staring at Derick in dead silence. In fact, Derick wasn't quite sure whether he was observing him or his birds; it was all too blurry for his dropsical, drooping eyes. Then he felt his legs giving out, and his body slumped down on the sofa. Half-conscious, he turned his head, tilted badly backwards, on the side and saw this small, little bird cringing in the corner of its cage. It was of sooty-black colour, making itself hardly discernible in this dusky lighting. Derick raised his head and saw Randy's huge, golf ball-like eyes staring at him narrowly.

'Are you OK? I thought you blacked out.'

'Yes, I'm fine, thanks. I'm just so tired — had a hell of a day. I bet you never experience boredom with all your flock,' said Derick, trying to change the topic, and successfully so, as Randy's face frowned on, his cheeks puffed up.

'Boredom is a gateway to depression,' he snapped at Derick.

'Oh... I didn't... Are you depressed?' Derick spluttered, without taking much heed, amazed by Randy's surprising answer.

'No, you fool!' Randy rapped on, looking more irked than before. 'It's just uncertainty, the most certain thing in today's world. If you don't do a damn thing in your life, you start to feel it creeping into your mind with every thought you conceive. You see it penetrating, permeating through your walls, feel it so real like the cold kiss of a naked barrel of a revolver, cylinder full of bullets, except for one slot, your only lifeline. Then you look at the face of the maniac who is about to play a roulette with your life, scared to death, and it makes you twitch... Click! Tick! Off the rails you go... You're pegged down to a landfill like this place — a promised land! As a garbage, unneeded, used up, spewed off the screwed up societal bitch tits like a puss you're forced to drink from your tap every day with your afternoon tea. Would you risk experiencing boredom then? I tell you what — boredom kills; it kills you silently, yet it does need no silencer, it leaves no traces.'

'Randy! Where's my emergency bacon, for God's sake?!' Natalie cried out from really far away, breaking Randy's gruesome account.

'I think I've given it to my cats!' Randy shouted back.

'You must be out of your mind!' yelled Natalie, this time from a much closer distance. Then she appeared in the door's frame, holding a piece of toast with some melting butter on the top. 'What am I gonna eat now?! I'm starving, and all you've got is pet food and some toastie bread!'

'I'm sorry; I was just too busy with my new breed, I couldn't see I'm running out of food for my cats,' explained Randy, apologetically. 'You see, it's hatching period, they're all over me now!'

'You've got till next morning to fetch me some emergency bacon back!' said Natalie. 'I hope you haven't scared him too much with your horror stories. He needs to get some sleep tonight,' she carried on, then she sat next to Derick, caressing his hair. 'Oh, you look so pale, what has he done to you?' she asked in an annoyingly patronizing voice.

'Sure, he's gonna get a lot of sleep with you aboard, captain,' smirked Randy.

'He's so weird, isn't he?' said Natalie. 'He wanted to be a detective when he was young, but they didn't want to take him on because he was too much into birds as they claimed, a band of morons, they said he was too much of a cuckoo to be admitted. They sent him to Taitam instead, and he's returned even more cuckoo. He knows lots of bloodcurdling stories, though.' When she finished piercing the veil of secrecy behind Randy's all too direct demeanour, she took Derick's flaccid hand and dragged him along to the bedroom. 'Night, Randy!' she screamed before shutting the door.

'You're probably dying to hear my stories now,' said Derick, sitting on the edge of the bed, feeling neither dead nor alive.

'I think we'll have more interesting things to do,' said Natalie, then she kissed Derick tenderly on the lips, gave his body a gentle push by pressing her warm palm against his chest, exactly in the spot where the heart was. His drowsy head landed softly on the fluffiest pillow he'd ever felt, his senses had gone into a land of dreams and fantasy...

* * *

The next morning, the sun was bright and had risen far above the horizon line when Derick felt the almighty smell of bacon. Randy was hustling and bustling in the kitchen, singing something in bird language to his canaries. Natalie was with him.

'He'll cost you more pain and misery than you can imagine. Beware, please.'

'Who do you think you are, Randy?! A freaking oracle on two legs, speaking canarian?'

'I'm Randall Wharton, the forgotten hero of this city!' replied Randy, inflating himself with pride. 'A puzzle breaker, a mind cracker who knits only with one needle with random precision these days!'

'I know you're Mr Inquisitive, Randy, but you won't be giving me lessons on how to live my own life. I'm too old for that now!' said Natalie, then she left the kitchen.

'Ah, you're still studying this plan?' said she, upon entering the room. She put down a bacon sandwich on Derick's lap and sat down right beside him. 'Please, don't go to Mowhaken alone. I have a bad feeling about this.'

Derick gazed into her deep, blue eyes and saw them pulsating with profound care. He had no idea what was going on with this woman; he thought she might just be going mad.

'We can go there together if you wanna go today, but after I've finished my job,' said Natalie, softly.

'I think you must be already late to work,' replied Derick, peering at the screen of his cell phone.

'Oh, don't you worry about it, I'm always ahead of the curve with my work,' said Natalie, perkily.

'I don't know what to do, to be honest,' Derick expressed his doubts. 'I think I have to go to uni and turn them down or bargain something out from them. Jim was right; I need to take time off everything. You know, ever since I met Marty, my life has been turning upside down like I've been driven forward in the front passenger seat, but ass-backwardly, in a wayward direction. I wasn't paying attention to anything like it was not my life, not my problems, but I can see like the shadows grow longer and darker around me with each passing day, every passing face, they seem like such a blur. I feel like I'm being watched with every step I take; it's so weird. I've been getting these really eerie flashbacks from my childhood ever since I met him as if it had triggered something hidden deep inside of me. The more I get to know him, the less known he becomes. Sometimes it feels like he's many personas at the same time.'

'Maybe you just have to stop pushing the envelope too hard and leave it all behind for now,' said Natalie, with growing concern in her voice.

'You may be right, so is Jim, but I can't — he's my grandfather. He's the only person I've felt attached to for a very long time. My stepfather hates me, I have no relationship with my mother, and the housemaid who's turned out to be my gran is probably gone away by now. I have no one to turn to. I think you've hit a really wrong person.'

'The more wrong it feels, the better,' said Natalie and snogged Derick affectionately. They started to kiss in the door frame of Randy's bedroom, who was just feeding his hatchlings. Even he, for a moment, had forgotten all the love he had for them, neglecting his duty of care, he gaped at them with open mouth as at aliens, spilling the feed all over his lap, which was now dribbling from it onto the floor. Derick's phone fell from his pocket too and hit the floor with a ding. He was about to call Jim for a taxi, but it turned out that he too had gone on holiday.

'Why do people always go on holiday when they are needed the most?' said Derick, throwing the phone on the bed.

Natalie looked at him, then, quite bluffly she suggested that he could use the attic at hers to flock all the stuff he still deemed needed or worthy. She didn't like Derick's lack of willingness for that mundane task at all, not a single bit of it. Derick thought he had to overcome his obstinate reluctance to do it just because he didn't want to be seen as an asshole when someone he barely knew suddenly offered him the keys to her house and a car to move around. She just might be out of her mind, he thought, but it didn't matter. He took things as they came.

'It's thirty-five Hardlay Street. I live with my poorly mum there. She's partially paralyzed, so I'm looking after her, but mind you, she's a devil in her new electric wheelchair.'

'Are you gonna trust me just like that?' asked Derick, still not quite believing his ears.

'I'm really good with people,' answered Natalie, 'and don't worry about my mum, she's not gonna call the cops on you. I will let her know about you.'

'That's life-affirming,' replied Derick. 'I really don't know how I'm gonna return a favour.'

'I bet you do,' said Natalie, leaning her body over his, poking and flicking his nose playfully with her index finger, 'more than you can guess.'

They left Randy's somewhat late in the morning. Natalie rushed to work, and Derick took a taxi to Hillbarrow. It was well past lunchtime; he was about to set out on the second run to Natalie's house with his garbage when he received that strange text message from an unknown number, inviting him to a meeting of the "Sombrero Tree Project". Strangely enough, James Niggle's name was signed under the invitation, to whom he hadn't given his private number. 'What now!?' he blurted but soon concluded that it didn't matter; he was just taking things as they were coming. He called Natalie straight away to find out whether she hadn't given him his number by chance. She told him that it wasn't James's number and James just left her office after he'd popped in to find out something about his interview transcript, that he wasn't using his mobile at all whilst being with her. Derick thought it was really weird now but quickly decided not to boggle his mind over that matter. He concluded he just had to get used to strange things happening around him on a daily basis. On the other hand, he wanted to come over to talk with the university officials about them extending his summer break anyway, so he might as well pop in and see what they were up to. At least, he wouldn't have to deal with Simon's potential press-gang taunts anymore if he happened to be there because he'd already been kicked out of Bruce's house, and now it'd become his alibi. Quickly he dumped the last crapload of his belongings at Natalie's attic and was off to the East Point University.

When he arrived at the entrance to the Department of Biological Sciences, very late in the afternoon, his card wouldn't swipe for some odd reason, so he called the reception, but no one answered. He peered through the glass doors to see if there was anyone sitting around, but there was not a living soul inside. He felt like the wind of oddities was blowing in his face. He turned around a couple of times, waited, but no one appeared to save his day. He looked up at the sky where massive, dark clouds were gathering right above his head, then he felt the first droplets of rain falling down on him, yet out of the corner of his eye he managed to catch a glimpse of a human bust jutting out of the window on the very last floor of the building. For a moment, Derick thought that he was having hallucinations; this feeling darted through his mind with the speed of light, for that person's head disappeared as abruptly as it appeared. In the end, he wasn't sure what he saw.

The front automatic doors started opening slowly but seamlessly, immediately after that ghostly figure was gone from his sight. No doubt he was spotted, but he stepped forward with marked hesitancy as it was getting really late now to be admitted. As soon as he poked his nose out to the atrium, he heard a tink on his left, then the lift door opened. To his outward astonishment, he saw the surreal physique of Mrs Fluffery, staring at him with unusual intention. She was wearing a black, furry trench coat that was at least two numbers too large for her, and a broad, felted top hat, all making her look like she was wider than she was tall, actually being about five feet four and quite plump. Without saying anything, she pulled Derick by the shirt and shoved to the elevator as soon she saw him, even before he could move a muscle or let his brain figure and deal with sudden waves of oddness hitting him right in the face. The lights were dimmed everywhere, even inside the lift. Mrs Fluffery pressed the button indicating that they were about to go up, right to the last floor. Derick had never been to that floor before; he didn't know what to expect. She was smiling at him warmly, trying to break the ice, seeing astonishment muddled with puzzlement on his face, clearly knowing that he'd never seen her outside the student residence halls of Warwick House. Once the lift door closed, she broke the silence.

'How are you feeling Derick, my dear?' asked she, with dignified compassion in her voice.

Hearing her voice hit him with the unmistakable realization that this feeling of unreality was more than real, it just came crushing through his walls. He felt cold sweat on his brow, wiped it off with his hand, noticing he was having pins and needles all over his forearm — he felt his senses sharpening, coming back to reality.

'I'm absolutely fine, thanks. Can we stop on the fourth floor, please?!' he burst out vigorously, sensing a tremendous upsurge of energy. It must have been the food he had in the car, he thought in an instant. 'I've got to go to the dean's offices now.'

'It's too late for it,' Mrs Fluffery explained with stoic calmness, 'everyone is expecting you.'

Derick was completely distracted by that remark; his eyes opened wide, and he felt like he was getting off track again, seeing the light switching from "four" to "five" on the lift's control panel. Who was "everybody", he thought, and why was she dressed like another ice age was just around the corner? What was on the very last floor of the main departmental building? Engulfed in a fever of curiosity, he'd lost all sense of reason and had no sense of danger. He just felt like talking.

'Why are you wearing all these thick clothes now?' he asked. 'Summer's not over yet. Who is expecting me, by the way?'

'Oh, it's really cold up there,' she replied, phlegmatically. 'Have you got the invitation?'

'Yeaa...' drawled Derick. 'How do you know about it?'

'I am the caretaker,' said Mrs Flufferey, very humbly. 'Everyone is doing their bit for the common cause,' she ended, quite mysteriously.

'What's the common cause?' Derick asked.

'Freedom, my dear,' said she, in a stifled voice, then got off the lift when it stopped on the top floor. Derick followed Mrs Fluffery's steps carefully through the long corridor because it was partially dark out there. She was right; it got really cold once they got off the lift, but the air was so stuffy as if this place hadn't been ventilated for ages. Mrs Fluffery was treading so fast that Derick was nearly out of breath after a while of tracking her trail. He would never have guessed she could move her chubby body so quickly. It was difficult to keep up with her, especially when he'd lost his bearings for good. It felt like he was navigated through a maze; they'd gone through countless doors, but he couldn't really focus on what was around him, trying his hardest to keep the pace. He had only this weird feeling that the distances between subsequent doors they were passing through were getting longer and longer, somehow systematically. There were only dark rooms on his left and right; every time they were through the door it looked just the same, only the number of rooms passed by was increasing. It was like going through the compartments on a train. They were heading only straight and forward, but he was falling under this bizarre impression that they were going in circles and downwards, steadily but downwards. Suddenly, Mrs Fluffery's race was brought to a halt before yet another door to pass through, as it seemed. Derick bumped into her, completely unexpecting her to stop in a million miles.

'Derick, be careful, please,' she said with true indifference. 'We cannot pass through this door, it's closed.' Even as she said this, a silhouette of a man emerged out of the gloom. He wore very similar clothes to Mrs Fluffery's, but the real surprise struck Derick in the head when he moved his head out of the shadow of his resting place. It was none other than Mr Smith, the closest neighbour of Mrs Dauntwraith. He was smiling warmly at him, exactly in the same compassionate fashion as Mrs Fluffery, although Derick barely knew him. Before he could say anything, Mrs Fluffery began to talk.

'Meet Mr Smith, our keymaster. He's got the keys to every door here, and he's the one to decide whether to let you through — or not.'

'Have you got the invitation, my son?' Mr Smith requested in a deep, bass voice.

'Yes, yes, I've got it,' Derick replied and handed him his phone.

'Mmmm, very well, very well. He is free to go if he wishes so,' said he, very formally, eying Mrs Fluffery and giving the phone back to Derick, who was really disorientated right now and looked at Mrs Fluffery as if she was his last lighthouse.

'Are you going in with me?' asked Derick.

'I can't. I'm not allowed,' said Mrs Fluffery, with stolid tranquillity in her voice. 'I don't know what lays behind this door. This is where my role ends.'

'What do you mean?' asked Derick, plainly surprised. 'Are you not curious to find out?'

'We only know as much as we need to know to fulfil our roles, and it's for the better of the cause if it stays like that' said Mr Smith, in a low-pitched voice, smiling warmly at him. 'It's your last chance. Are you proceeding?' asked he, showing Derick the door with his hand.

'What are you two blathering about?!' Derick burst out suddenly, unleashing his suppressed resentment for this whole bizarre situation. 'You're just standing here like hands-on lackeys, sipping idyllic cliches of so-called "common cause" into my ears. It's nonsensical! And you, fawny squealer, why did you grass me up?!' Derick snarled at Mr Smith, wrathfully.

Even as he was inflamed in a fury of words, Mr Smith produced an endless chain full of unnumbered keys that looked like they were all exact copies of one another. Without any hesitation, he thrust one of them into the keyhole, then the door disappeared into the wall, and Derick was sucked up into the rabbit hole by a sheer magnitude of the pressure created when the door opened. It closed behind him as swiftly and unexpectedly as it opened. On the other side, it was even colder, stuffier, and dimmer. Derick felt his jaw shuddering almost involuntarily. He couldn't see or hear Mr Smith or Mrs Fluffery through the door. It felt really plasticky to the touch but gave off a clearly metallic sound when it was punched. To his bewilderment, he noticed it hadn't got a handle. He didn't think he saw any door handles on that floor at all. He would have probably wasted himself away lashing at this door if he hadn't heard that eery, unsound murmuring at some point, resembling many stifled voices that have just learned to talk. Mesmerised as if by the voices of the Sirens he followed the waves of sound till murmuring turned into a loud shriek of approval, followed by fanatic clapping and the airless breeze that ensued, hitting him in the face, causing vertigo.

He was standing on the edge of the dais, his hands hanging behind the bar, looking at the large auditorium through the glass, seeing the sea of faces, all of them wearing large, dark sunglasses. Below the auditorium, there was a stage, three people on it — none of whom Derick could recognize, and a huge, flat screen behind them. Two of them were showing the results of what looked like a chemistry experiment to the audience. The other one seemed to be talking about the paper on the screen. This was when it struck him. He was clearly in possession of Derick's own, yet unpublished study; he could recognize the notes, the structural formula, and the reaction with stark precision. It felt like Derick was inside his own laboratory, but it wasn't him doing the experiment. When some members of the audience took off their sunglasses, he could recognize Simon Redeldrag's face in the front row. He was absolutely unrecognizable in those glasses, not in this sort of nocturnal, shadowed light.

Derick slapped the glass a few times forcefully, shouting Simon's name, but no one behind it seemed to notice him or pay any attention to what he was doing, even when the lights brightened up above their heads. Then he noticed he wasn't alone on the other side of the glass. He was so immersed in a logic-defying wonder of seeing such a large theatre on the last floor, as it seemed, and all the curiosity happening before his eyes that he didn't even spot yet another silhouette of a man sitting at the small desk, over there, a few steps below him, in near complete darkness. Derick stepped down to meet him, but when he looked close up at his face, he felt cold shivers shooting up and down his spine. It was yet another familiar face — this one belonged to Mr Whitaker, a local beekeeper who sold honey every Saturday at Willowood market. Once he saw Derick, he took the earphones off his ears and looked at him intently through his half-glasses.

'Hello, Derick. I'm glad you've made thus far,' said he, with all too familiar warm compassion in his voice. He was clad in a warm duffle coat, and a black top hat was on his head. 'Now pardon me, please, but I have to carry on with my job. I must not miss a single word,' gloated he as his eyes glowed in the dark. The earphones were stuffed back deep into his ears, his hands landed heavily on the keyboard of an old, jamming typewriter that looked as though it was out of the ark a long, long time ago. Then his hands stood up, ramrod straight, and let their fingers dance over the keys in an enigmatic waltz of hops, leaps, and prances, which mesmerised Derick so much that it caused a sudden dizziness to his body. His head fluttered in the air over Mr Whitaker's shoulders, trying to keep up with his tempo in a dreamy, melodic trance of the beats being tapped out of the keyboard with shrewd mastery. When he finished a page, the sheet of paper from the typewriter landed straight into the hole in the desk that was right behind the writing machine. Derick looked down underneath the desk, and to his sheer befuddlement, he witnessed how the whole sheet was being shredded into micro pieces! He felt like all his legs and back muscles were stiffening sharply, then his whole body sprang at attention like a metal ruler that was set free into motion after it had been bent too much. Derick towered over the small, hunched stature of Mr Whitaker, glaring at him with his thunderbolt eyes, but he was unmoved, still banging out the keys of his machine. Then he unplugged his left ear and began talking without even making any effort to look at Derick.

'This is called the ephemeral copy that I am making,' said he, with this annoying indifference in his voice as the rest of them. 'I am the scribe and therefore I create the ephemeral copies of every document,' he carried on without stopping.

'Copy of what?! You've just shredded it!' Derick rumbled.

'Of the proceedings on the other side, obviously,' said Mr Whitaker. 'Yes, you're doing a fantastic job for the common cause. Everyone here does admire your efforts,' he said, even before Derick could close his wide-open mouth, still without trying to make eye contact with him, engulfed in spasms of creation.

THE CASE OF MR DAUNTWRAITH

Upon hearing that, Derick felt like his head took a tumble on his neck and was spinning over its rim effortlessly, without his word or will. His eyes galloped deep into the vastness of space of the chamber he was locked in; he grew increasingly frightened to see what else may be lying hidden beyond the shadows, yet he couldn't help the crazy feeling of digging and plunging into the unknown. He was a trailblazer, pushing the boundaries of discovery; a root seeker, pioneering new paths of reality. Suddenly, he stumbled upon something. Deep down to his left from where he was standing next to Mr Whitaker's desk, he saw a long column of benches rising in height towards the back wall, full of people, all of them wearing strangely shaped black glasses, which were covering most of their faces, sitting in total silence a good few feet below him, on a submerged level, as it seemed. He thought that they must have been the people whose voices he heard when he was pushed through the door by Mr Smith. Where did they come from? What were they doing there, and why on earth were their faces covered with those black devices resembling ridiculously thick, convex glasses?

'Who the heck are all those people down there?!' Derick barked at Mr Whitaker, who was clearly in his element orchestrating all his tiny, twiggy fingers to dance to his mysterious tune. Again, without seemingly paying even the slightest attention to what Derick just said, he pulled the earphone out of his left ear and began talking in an overly formal, monotone fashion, still not giving him any eye contact.

'The people who are sitting below us on the bench are the witnesses of the proceedings on the other side. They read exactly what I'm writing here from the built-in screens in their special glasses.'

Now, it was all far too much for Derick. It was time to put a definite end to all this circus of dreams and put their poise to a test. It was all just a fantasy, meticulously contrived to blind and then trap his mind inside of it to make him lose his way. But he knew better how to tell a snake from its skin because he'd been prewarned. But what about the other people around? Oh, nevermind now, he thought. Without further overthinking, he snatched Mr Whitaker's earphones by pulling them off from him with all the wiring and smashing them against the window with brute force. It made a terribly loud, scratchy sound, but it was far too light to break the glass. His reaction, though — it absolutely shocked Derick. Mr Whitaker just stood up, closed the typewriter, pulled the chair underneath the surface of the desk carefully, buttoned himself up and walked off towards where Derick came from without even looking at him once as if nothing happened, as if he just expected Derick to do exactly that, as if he was just set up to do certain things at certain times in response to certain stimuli, as if he... wasn't there.

As he turned the corner, all the people on the benches who were sitting motionless in grave silence so far, all of a sudden, left their places at once and began to run around at random, screaming and shouting something in an incomprehensible, unspeakable language like a horde of lunatic maniacs that had just managed to escape beyond the reaches of an asylum. Their shrill, razor-sharp voices were just unbearable; Derick's ears were pierced by dozens of cutting pins concurrently. They dispersed in all directions but were running in circles as if they were blinded by the glasses they were wearing — unable to take them off, feeling the caustic pain of their faces being burnt alive. Amazingly enough, none of them crashed into one another; they too seemed to be programmed by some mysterious force that was steering them from above like lifeless puppets, now set to motion by a ruthless unperson of a master.

Derick didn't know what to do; he had to get out of there somehow. He felt he was left with only one solution. Mr Whitaker's typewriter was still on the desk, now "smiling" at him invitingly. He grabbed it with all his strength and pulled, but it didn't move an inch. It was glued dead to the desk, which in turn was screwed down to the floor. Seriously frustrated, he seized the chair with both hands and pulled it with full force, which nearly put him off balance as it was so heavy it weighed maybe half a ton. He swung it behind his back and was about to throw it against the window when he felt this overpowering downward pressure, which abruptly pulled him to the ground. He was toppled down as he lost the chair, which was now smashed on the floor, swayed his body around in fear, still on the floor — he looked up and into Simon's glistening eyes yet again.

'Get out of my sight you fool!' hissed he and pushed Derick back forcefully a good few yards until his body was slammed against the wall, which gave way immediately and he was thrown into a black hole to sit there forever in utter darkness, without anything to eat or drink, without anyone to hear his cries for help. He only noticed he was shoved into a lift when the whole place started moving up. When the door opened again, he found himself exactly at the starting point of his journey through the building he thought he knew inside out. The hall in front of the reception was as badly lit as it was when he came here first a time ago. The glacial silence was sinisterly disconcerting. He ran outside only to see the sun hanging just above the horizon line. The lapse of time was much greater than he thought when he was inside as a good few hours must have passed since he was taken through the intricate meanders of the heart of the Department of Biological Sciences.

He had a quick gander at his phone, which was just about to die, and discovered countless miscalls from Natalie. He'd completely forgotten he still had her car with him. Now the phone was buzzing again, and it was her — again! He couldn't talk right now; he had to go somewhere quiet to collect the thoughts from all the events of recent days and try to make something intelligible out of it; he strongly felt like he must get his act together right here, right now before even weirder things happened. He had no clue if anyone would believe in what he saw today, but the first person he wanted to confront was James Niggle. He pulled his phone out again, but then — damn it, it just died! Natalie must be properly angry with me now, he thought. He put the phone back into his pocket, but he pulled something else out of it in turn. It was the card he had from James. He didn't even notice it was still there until now. Not knowing why, holding the card reminded him of Mowhaken. He knew he shouldn't act on impulse, but it was stronger than him; moreover, where could he find more peace and tranquillity than in the library? He thought it should be open to the public now. After all, only the oldest part of it had been badly affected by the fire. It was such a monumental place.

That was when it all clicked inside Derick's mind, out of the blue as it seemed. Wasn't it Marty who asked him to seek Walter Dauntwraith to find out what happened there when it all went terribly wrong for him? Wasn't it Walter's wife who gave him that strange, old plan yesterday? Wasn't it Simon who questioned him about her disappearance? Well, it seemed like all roads led to Mowhaken... He couldn't go there straight away, though; he just remembered he'd left the plan at Natalie's.

'What a stupid bum I am!' he said to himself. 'Ah well, nevermind — traffic shouldn't be too bad now. I hope Natalie isn't home yet; I bet she would love to go there with me.'

He quickly got in the car and shot for Clarksdowne's northern beltway. He was at hers in no time, mainly thanks to her overachieving turbocharged engine. Luckily she wasn't at home, neither was her mum, but he wasn't bothered. He dumped his phone on the top of the pile of some randoms of his, just to have an alibi, and eagerly rummaged through the rest of it to find what he came for. When he noticed it, it was laid down next to the cylinder, inside of which he had the file of the case of Mr Dauntwraith. He took both of them, just in case. He wondered why Marty wasn't even slightly interested in the file as he came through the doors of Natalie's house, which he shut and locked carefully. Maybe somehow he knew that it could have been Simon's clever artifice. After all, he told him not to believe in anything that was inside. 'Yeah, right. Nice one, Grandad — if only you had known that in fact there is absolutely nothing inside...'

The trip to Mowhaken was brief as it was situated on the north-western outskirts of Clarksdowne, just a few miles from the city's beltway. Even as Derick guessed — it was open to the public; only the ruins of the old part were still cut off by the police barrier tape after the conflagration. From what he could read from the map, a hidden subterranean floor was located exactly below the ground level of the part that had gone up in flames. He took a closer look at it to seek some clues, but the plan showed only an overhead view of the hidden floor and a little cross-section view in the right top corner of the old part, which was no more now, showing that the floor must be precisely underneath the old part. He rotated the map in his hands a few times, then he turned it over on its blank side, laid it flat on the large rectangle-shaped table and funnelled all the light from the lamp, the brightness of which was amped to the max now, on it. Still nothing, not even the slightest clue. He didn't entertain the idea of sneaking beneath the barricade tape into the old, wasted part of Mowhaken without even knowing what to look for. The whole place must have been rigged with hidden surveillance cameras and movement detectors anyway.

He took the plan off the table with one dashing swing of the left arm and walked off, holding it clumsily by the corner, filled with frustration that it might as well be the end of adventures for the day. He pulled it up by the collateral corner with an intention of rolling it up when he noticed that he might have picked something out with the corner of his eye. It was just below his left thumb, written in the faintest, the most unintelligible fashion with a blunt, wet pencil. The letters were so tiny and dim that no wonder he couldn't see anything under the very bright light. It was plain that someone added them to the plan by hand, probably not very long ago. He rushed back to the table, fetched a handy magnifying glass from the custodian office and began deciphering the letters slowly, one by one. The whole sentence when finally decoded read something along these lines: "PULL THE EVOLUTION OF SCIENCE OUT AND PRESS THE OCTAGON ONTO THE WALL". He read it silently a few times yet had no clue what to make out of it, but at least he'd got wind of something that looked to him as a plausible lead he could hang on to now. He thought that there may be something more to find around this section of the plan and quickly found out that he wasn't wrong. When he folded the plan a bit by the corner, next to which the message was written, he noticed a small arrow pointing to the borderline of the plan of the hidden floor, scribbled exactly in the same fashion as the message on the other side, but even thinner and fainter. The arrow was pointed towards the north-eastern wall of the library, which was all occupied by the old history and archaeology manuscripts. He had never been to those parts, although he'd got to know Mowhaken like a book over the years as he'd become a regular here.

'Still, who on earth would have placed a book about science and evolution together with old history manuscripts?!' He had to find that bugger now. All the science books were just by the reading room, which couldn't have been on the plan as it was nearly on the other side of the library. Whatever it was, it must have been misplaced on purpose.

Derick strolled quietly through the vast spaces of the athenaeum before he finally stood by the grand, high door to the archaeological and historical books section and archive. He had to obtain permission from the custodian to enter through this door, but he had no problems with that since he knew almost everybody here. He was only advised to take a long ladder with him, which made him wonder why until he got there.

Upon entering the unchartered, deep waters of the premises where seemingly only the books about times gone by were stored, he was met with a strong whiff of decaying wood and paper that was sedentary in one place for ages, probably since ancient times. All around him there were coffin-like sarcophaguses with slabs of hard glass on the top of each one of them strewn evenly over the whole area of the floor. All over the sides of the perfectly rectangular chamber, the immense columns of wooden bookcases were situated like mighty blocks sculpted into the wall, side by side. They were at least twenty-five feet tall, and he could be only foolishly hopeful that the one book he was after wasn't on the top shelf. According to the arrow on the plan, the shelf with the book he was looking for should be nearly exactly opposite where he was standing now, still by the door. Indeed, he could just discern from his standpoint that there was a narrow gap between two blocks of bookcases parallel to where the door was, right in front of him.

THE CASE OF MR DAUNTWRAITH

He thought that this could well be a good benchmark where he could start his search from, strode through that sombre graveyard of manuscripts for a good fifty yards before stopping by the face of the formidable bookshelf.

It was all made of hard oaken wood, very thick and solid, painted in an opaque, dark brown colour. Derick skimmed through the titles of the books that were at the height of his eyesight and found out that all the titles he saw began with the letter "F". At this point, he knew he had to climb. The only question was: "how high?" His mind filled with inexplicable dread when he tilted his head awkwardly backwards to see where the top of the column was. He placed the foldable, metallic ladder along the centerline of the shelf, then began the scramble upwards. And upwards it was, right to the very top. Luckily, the book he sought was to his left and within reach of the hand without having to dismount the ladder and moving it from the bottom. He pulled the thick hardback out of the shelf, but nothing happened. He waited for a few moments in bare silence, carefully looking around for any sign of some oddity happening, but couldn't notice anything out of the ordinary. Then he remembered about "pressing the octagon onto the wall" bit. That was the hard part — absolutely nothing was springing to his mind; it felt like it was filled with nothing but cumbersome void. He thought he couldn't just perch here all evening long like a dead duck, on the top of the ladder, nearly thirty feet above the ground, in the most forgotten place of the whole library that no one wanted to visit anymore, trying to crack the greatest riddle in the world. He looked just ridiculous, to say the least.

Then, all of a sudden, a breakthrough happened! Derick's mind was filled with flashing light as if when the first electric bulb was lit to enlight the dark of the world, as if some mystical universal force had come down to his aid and whispered into his ear: 'Let there be light,' and there was light...

'Dorian, you're a genius!' he roared with joy; his hand landed in the back pocket of his jeans, then the very card he got from James Niggle was produced from it. He nearly completely forgot he still had it with him until now. 'It's been there since I got it,' he said, peering and smiling at it. He thought that it was a bit like his necklace now, for some reason. Being at full stretch, he pressed the card to the wall, but the only odd thing that ensued was that it clipped to the wall like a magnet. He took it off the wall with ease after a bit of examination and tucked it back in. Resigned yet still vigilant, he stepped back down from the ladder.

On the ground, he rotated the card a few times in his hands, thinking that the next clue to the solution of his riddle must lay within it. He stepped forward towards the narrow strip of the wall that was sandwiched between two blocks of oaken bookcases with an intention to see if it clipped to its surface when he saw it. A very dim, thin outline in a shape of an... octagon appeared on the wall, more or less at the height of his waist, illuminating light orange. He was automatically drawn to it like a moth to a flame. No sooner had he touched the outline with his hand than the floor under his feet collapsed. He didn't know how deep underground he slid through that tube, but when he came out on the other side, he was in a different world.

It was plain to him after the first glance that the blaze of Mowhaken was most probably an arson that started there. Nearly everything around was scorched to the dust, except for some machinery, which looked miraculously untouched and in intact condition as if it was brought there after the fire had been snuffed out. He drew the card from his back pocket and noticed that one of the "sombreros" was flashing like a target. 'Dorian was right, there was definitely more to this piece of... something than meets the eye,' he said to himself. He wished Dorian had been there with him now. He would have given the world to know what he would have made out of this sight. The room he was in was clearly conditioned as the air was cool and refreshing down here, the backup lighting was on from what he could see. He felt he suddenly found himself inside of some top secret, yet quite an obsolete laboratory. He could recognize some of the equipment, or rather the debris of it, but it really racked his tiresome brain why this bloody "sombrero" on his card was flashing and not the others, who and for what reason had brought all that new, hi-tech stuff there like that — UV light scanner?!

A sight of the cutting-edge UV light scanner in a ruined, partly forsaken site that looked like a bio lab was outright phenomenal, near on the verge of absurdity, but, oddly enough, it was the one thing Derick really needed right now. Without any fear or hesitation, he took the file of the case of Mr Dauntwraith out of its case, placed it on the desktop of the scanner and began fiddling with it, trying to figure out how to operate it. When it was finally turned on, at least it gave a bit of brightness around the place, which was rather badly lit since only the emergency lights were on.

He took a curious, intent new look at the site when he thought he spotted something beyond any scale of oddity. It seemed to him that one of the many sheets of paper scattered haphazardly on the table behind him bore his own name on it. With the blood curdling in all his veins, he quickly found it out to be the truth. Among the virtual mishmash of subjects, there was indeed the excerpt of the results of one of his not very recent and not very finest studies, for which he'd been smashed, slashed, and slain like a dog by so-called peers or pals. It was quite erroneous at the time of publication as it turned out, but he would have never thought that someone else could have made an effort to take it out for a further study. He really thought it was all bollocks in the end. He quickly noticed that major amendments had been made to it, which encapsulated all his attention in a flash as there was a chemistry he was looking at that was unheard of, half of which at least was far beyond his own comprehension, although it was not all too unfamiliar.

Suddenly, he heard someone's steps coming as though... from a little above his head, then the loud yet slow clapping of hands was to be distinguished. His heart was throbbing compulsively as if it was right in his mouth, which dried out completely at this precise moment; the air got stuck in his throat — he wasn't there alone...

'Well, well, well,' said the unseen voice, from behind the wall, 'who's there that was bold enough to stir the serene waters of this lonely place?' Then a small figure of a really old, shrivelled, stoop-shouldered man emerged out of the gloom from around the corner. He looked so much like a caricature with his spidery arms, petite legs, and exaggerated head, nodding and protruding a way forward from the line of his body as if it was just but dangling from its neck. He accosted Derick promptly with a resolute yet shuffling gait. When his head moved slowly upwards, Derick noticed these steely, greyish blue eyes of his, the pair of which he thought he saw somewhere else before, but these ones were twinkling with a distant, lacklustre, dying radiance.

'You're the youngest lad I've seen in these parts for a very long time,' said the stranger, without ceasing to give Derick that wearisome gaze. 'How did you find this place?' asked he, still maintaining his relentless fixated stare but moving slowly around Derick, examining him like he was his newly discovered artifact. Derick was rooted to the spot, speechless, and sweating like a dripping icicle. The old man just carried on talking, quite comfortably. 'I see you don't wanna talk to me... Your mother must have taught you well not to talk to strangers, so let me quickly introduce myself. My name is Maarten Burdent, and I am a scientist, a very old hat of a scientist, lingering far behind the times, but when I look at your young, daring blood, I see all but red mist overshadowing my world and think to myself with resentment why I'm not you and you're not me, Derick.'

'I — I don't think I can understand you, Mr Burdent, but how do you know my name?'

'I think you know the answer to this question too,' said Maarten, slowly nodding his overgrown head towards the table on Derick's left where he noticed the extract of his study. 'You might as well be more known than you may have thought or wanted to be, but it is never in your hands to decide how you are perceived and whom you are befriended to.'

'I still don't quite understand the point you're trying to make,' Derick replied, half stupefied by this old man's relaxed but stingingly direct manner of talking.

'Do you have friends? Of course, you do; it's completely normal at your age to seek friendships. Now let me tell you something about those people — they are only there for you as long as you have something to offer they secretly desire from you; they are only there for you as long as you're high enough on their priority list. You know, they're never gonna tell you this, they're never gonna ask you if you feel the same. I used to have lots of friends, virtual swarms of them, but with time I learnt that they've been killing me just a little bit every day. I learnt that the only truth about friends is that they're just the first class of victims.'

Derick didn't know what to say to those austere statements. He thought he would just listen to whatever he'd got to say and then move on from there. After all, he'd seen and heard more than enough strange accounts over the last few days.

'You see, my boy, the greatest thing about life is that it doesn't matter. It is only when you've come to this realization that you can set yourself completely free, above everyone and everything else.' He paused at this moment, noticing that his latest declaration had captured Derick's attention.

'I think I may know how it feels like a bit,' Derick replied, carefully putting his words together.

'Certainly, you not only may but you do. It is only the society you're born into that thwarts you in your pursuit of freedom by making you believe that you've already got all the freedoms of life given to you for granted, but secretively you are shackled by it, harnessed like a working horse even before you're born to this world. You are told that you, likewise the others, must bear the cross of public debt, which you couldn't even have had a chance to contribute towards, towards its creation and further existence at any point since you were not in existence yourself at all. But it doesn't matter to the society — since you're alive you belong to them, and whatever is with them, real or unreal, belongs to you.' He paused here again, looking intently at Derick, whose mind was too preoccupied with his harsh, crude breakdown of life, especially when he'd already heard quite similar stories recently.

'The only tangible thing the society gives you to experience and experiment with is the pain of mere existence,' he went on, seeing no response from Derick, 'but what if I tell you that all this pain could be taken away from you forever?' he finished, then brandished the sheet of paper with Derick's own experiments on it right before his very nose.

'Sorry, Mr Burdent, but I think I've lost you again. Was it you who made those amendments?' asked Derick, focusing on the writings.

'Indeed. Do you like them? Come, let me show you something,' said he, then he placed the paper on the surface of the UV light scanner that was right behind Derick, next to the file of the case of Mr Dauntwraith.

'I see you've brought your detective work with you here,' noticed Maarten, glancing over the cover of the file. 'Very well.' He turned the page over, then ducked down suddenly and was nearly completely gone beneath the scanner, fiddling with its control panel. Derick peered down attentively at both documents, searching for any visible changes on them, but he noticed quickly that all his attention was slowly but surely swaying towards the blank pages of the file of the case of Mr Dauntwraith. Then the lighting started to change. It went from dim, light violet, through shades of purple violet, to acutely dazzling, vividly bright violet mixed with indigo before darkening to near completely black, dark violet. This was when the magic happened. The letters suddenly appeared on the pages of the file of the case of Mr Dauntwraith. The first line read: *"Pain is only a bridge. Pain is only an intermittent and transient feeling that is doomed to die..."*

7
CURIOSITIES

The sun was still hanging just above the horizon line when Natalie arrived at East Point University. She got off the bus quickly and was confronted by no other than James Niggle, who stood outside of the entrance to the Department of Biological Sciences building, smoking a cigar.

'Hey, Natalie! Over here, it's me — James!' shouted he, taking the butt out of his mouth.

'James?!' stammered Natalie, stupefied by the sight of a cloud of smoke hovering around his head. 'I never knew you smoke, couldn't recognize you!'

'Oh, only once in a blue moon; only when I'm really stressed,' admitted James, and put out the butt into the ashtray. 'I think we're gonna go far today. Anyway, what are you doing here?'

'I'm looking for Derick,' replied Natalie. 'Haven't you seen him?'

'No, I haven't. I've just arrived. Why?'

'He doesn't answer my calls, and now he's out of reach or his phone is dead.'

'Do you not think you're getting all too sympathetic with your new role, Natalie?' asked James, looking intently at her face, going red like a brick, blushing all over. It wasn't Natalie he'd known since the school days that he was looking at — so fearless, limitless, and free — she just looked like she had everything to lose now. He pulled the cigar tin out of his back pocket after a long sigh, but it was all empty inside.

'Oh, crap! Nothing's left! I've got to borrow some from Simon now,' he noted, chuckling under his nose, then he gazed into her pulsating, flickering blue eyes. It was so unusual of her to remain stone silent for that long during a conversation.

'You look like you've got everything to lose, Natalie,' said he.

'I'm getting old,' said she after the longest pause ever. 'Long gone are the days when we were two young souls at college — I've been part of the woodwork for so long now, and he's the most tantalising, the most wayward guy I've met for months.'

'In other words, you're falling for him,' said James, now being quite unable to hide his surprise for such an "unexpected" turn of the state of affairs as Natalie really looked like her cat had just jumped out of the window; the eyes of the woman couldn't lie, though. 'He's a bit off the rails, but still he's one of the most talented biochemists around. No wonder they admitted him without the PhD.'

'Was it really you who sent him this message earlier on then?' asked Natalie, with pressing urgency.

'Yes, I've already told you so! I sent it out just before coming to your office. It must have reached him with a delay, that's it. Those things sometimes happen. He was asked to come early as he needed to catch up with some things if he wanted to get on right off.'

'Where is he now then?'

'Don't know. He must be somewhere around. Let's go and find him, shall we?'

When they turn around, they saw Simon Redeldrag just coming through the door. He too had a cigar in his mouth, but it wasn't alight yet.

'Oh, there you are!' said he, peering at James. 'I've been looking for you everywhere, thinking you'll be late… Oh, surprise, surprise! Look who the wild winds have brought over here — our "caretaker,"' said Simon, looking at Natalie. 'How is she getting on?' asked he, now turning to James.

'I think she's doing exceptionally well, Mr Redeldrag,' answered James, who gave Natalie a short glance but couldn't quite prevent himself from laughing.

'I see Derick is becoming nearer and dearer to you by the day, my lovely,' said Simon, then a fleeting smugness appeared on his face. 'Unfortunately, he's gone somewhere; didn't want to tell me where, curious, young fellow that he is. I like him, I really do,' added he, after a short pause.

'How long ago has he left?' asked Natalie.

'Hmmmmm… Maybe fifteen minutes?' replied Simon, then he made a step forward towards Natalie, rested his right arm on her left shoulder and carried on, gazing deep into her eyes, leaning over her ear. 'Curiosity is the second most potent human drive. It sits right next to sex drive. So, please go home now, and he'll come to you, sooner rather than later.'

'Come with me, my friend,' Simon said to James, taking his eyes off Natalie, 'we are already late.'

They parted without saying anything to Natalie, only James eventually managed to give her a slight wave goodbye with his right hand, from afar.

*   *   *

When Natalie arrived home in the evening, Derick wasn't in yet. Only her poor, crippled mother was hustling and bustling in the kitchen with some grocery shopping, struggling to harness the new power of her electric wheelchair. The attic was full of Derick's belongings, strewn haphazardly across the floor. She found his black mobile phone with ease, though, left on the small, pink pouffe of hers as if by "accident" — it was out of charge. The only one thing she was unable to find was the one she really wanted to find there. After a good fifteen minutes of thorough search, she'd given up and slouched down on the pouffe with a groan. The plan of Mowhanken was nowhere to be found.

'Curious, young fellow, isn't he?' she said aloud. 'I will teach him…'

'Maybe he's right, and I'm stepping into his life at the wrong time,' she carried on her monologue after a long silence, 'but I can't help it! I think it's fate.' Then she felt like a single, warm tear burst into life from the geyser of her heart, travelled through her rosy cheek and dropped down on her icy cold hands. She peered down at her shaking, open hands, then she aroused all at once and left the room in a hurry as if she'd got burned.

'Mum, Mum!' cried Natalie as she was running down the stairs, as noisily as an elephant, 'I really need to talk with you!'

There was no answer from below, but when Natalie stormed down from the staircase, her mother was driving forward and backwards with a bowl of yellow, glazy mass in her left hand, fluttering in the air unsteadily. A disaster was just about to happen when she saw her daughter and brought herself to a halt.

'What's the matter, my love?' asked Natalie's mother. She was tiny, very slim, wearing a pink, loose tank top and black, skinny jeans. A rainbow-coloured "peace sign" necklace was hanging freely from her chest on a brown piece of leathern strap. A pair of thin glasses, shaped like rock stars was barely holding on to her nose. Her long silvery-grey hair was tied in a ponytail. Her weedy stature was quite unlike Natalie's who was almost six feet tall and rather athletically built. 'I'm just tryin' to put together a lovely pound cake but haven't quite figured out how to drive this devilish thing! Think I'm gonna give up now.'

'Let me help you, Mum,' offered Natalie, then she took the bowl from her hand and put it down on the kitchen table.

'Couldn't you shout louder by any chance, luv?' reproved Natalie's mum. 'Soon all Hillbarrow will be talkin' our house is haunted too!'

'Sorry, Mum,' mumbled Natalie.

'Am I mistaken, or do we have a very elusive, new lodger here? Is that what you wanna be talkin' about?'

'Elusive and slippery,' added Natalie, feeling like she's blushing again.

'So put the kettle on, please and make some tea! Then we can talk, my luv,' said Natalie's mum and rolled out from the kitchen into the living room where she quickly got hold of a remote control of her massive telly that was hung on the wall in a white frame, just like a painting. When Natalie entered the room with two cups of tea, she sat down next to her mother in a deep armchair, but only on the very edge of it and in an acutely inclined position, with her legs crossed.

'You're lookin' feverish, love,' said Natalie's mum, touching her forehead with her palm. 'I think you're fallin' ill of a very contagious disease…'

Their teacups were about half empty when the doorbell tinkled.

'I'll get that; I'll get that!' Natalie's mum cried her lungs out, then she reversed awkwardly into the tea table, spilling some brew. 'I told you this thing lives its own life,' said Natalie's mum when she'd finally found the right gear.

'Maybe it's haunted like the rest of our house now,' smirked Natalie.

Her mum whizzed past the short corridor and through the enclosed front porch to open the doors for a mystery guest. It was a daunting ghost of Derick who came to haunt them. When Natalie's mum wasn't coming back after a minute or so, Natalie grew fidgety sitting in the armchair and was about to move up when they both came out of the woodwork.

'Speaking of the devil, and behold — the devil has appeared,' said Natalie's mum, pointing her hands at Derick like he was some sort of lost treasure trove. 'Just look at him — hormones are buzzin' and frothin' in his blood, but he's a bit smelly. You'd better shower him first, and maybe I'll get this bloody cake done by tomorrow!'

'Are you sure you're talking about the same guy, Mum?' asked Natalie. 'He's looking so pale as if he's been chased by all the restless spirits of the Hillbarrow Cemetery all the way up here.'

'Just give him a break, you hothead,' retorted Natalie's mum. 'Take him upstairs and sort out his… hair, and by the way, he's already introduced himself.'

There was no need to repeat this twice to Natalie; she literally grabbed Derick by the scruff of his neck and was gone. The only words Derick managed to utter before disappearing into the stairway were 'see you soon'.

'Soon — yeah, right. I might as well bake a quarter pound

cake instead,' murmured Natalie's mum.

Upstairs, the very first thing Derick felt after being trailed along to her bedroom was Natalie's bare mouthful on his cheek as she gave him a hairdryer. 'Why did you go to Mowhaken alone?! I asked you to wait for me!'

'I'm sorry, OK,' repented Derick, 'but if I tell you what happened to me today, you're not gonna believe me!'

'Oh shut your scruffy face now!' returned Natalie. 'When I see you in such a state it sends me shivers up and down my spine. Please, don't leave me, love me.'

The windows were opened wide that night, and very starry it was on the night of a new moon when the clouds were none. The starlit look of the sky was all the more magnificent because Natalie's house was one of the last houses in the village of Hillbarrow, situated at the top of the northern hill, right before the gates of the old Forest of Elmhawk where the trees grew to be so dark and thick that the sun was entirely blocked from the forest floor in many places. It was very warm too — the summer, huffing and puffing on its last legs, gave off its last waves of warmth generously. However, the nights were still short, too short for some.

* * *

The far-reaching scent of a newly baked pound cake and freshly grounded coffee woke up Derick's and Natalie's hungry souls the next morning. They rushed downstairs like two arrows shot from a bow, took full plates, and were back up again.

'I just can't believe you didn't take the plan back with you!' grunted Natalie, having her mouth full of food.

'I'm sorry, I just forgot, but I can't believe you don't wanna believe in my story!' moaned Derick, yawning wide.

'Because it's bonkers! We've got to go back there and take the plan back,' asserted Natalie, 'I bet we'll quickly find someone who'll be prepared to pay a lot of money for this piece of information.'

'Are you crazy?!' reacted Derick, 'we're not telling anyone about it; besides, we don't need that plan now. I've got a better idea and the point to prove to you now.'

'What do you mean?'

'It's Saturday, and that means it's market day in Willowood,' replied Derick, looking at the screen of his phone. 'I will take you to Mr Whitaker's stall and then we shall talk.'

'Don't you think it's a bit late to get there for the market?' asked Natalie, peeking at the wall clock above her head.

'Not if we go out like now,' said Derick, standing up from the bed. The next moment he was out of the bedroom.

'Where are you going?' asked Natalie.

'Attic! Got to change as my other clothes are soiled!'

*   *   *

Before long, they were walking hand in hand along the wide path of the main alley of Willowood market, passing by lots and lots of stalls and booths on each side. It was unusually crowded so late in the morning, though. It could be that many people had just rushed to sell their summer goods before it moved on and colder days came along. Natalie was clinging ardently to Derick's side as if he really was a lost and found treasure trove. When they reached Mr Whitaker's stall, there were still a few people looking and jostling one another around the place. Others were bustling around their booths, trying to dismantle their structures. One of them was Mrs Fluffery.

'Now I'm gonna kill two birds with one stone,' muttered Derick.

'You what?' asked Natalie.

'Just watch,' he replied, then made a step forward. 'Good-day, Mr Whitaker! How is the honey business turning over today? Are your bees buzzing loud enough?' asked Derick, glancing over Mrs Fluffery's beetroot face.

'Oh, good morning to you, my boy! Sold nearly all my honey as you can see,' answered Mr Whitaker when he saw Derick. 'Haven't seen you for a good while! How is your mother keeping? Haven't seen her for a bit too.'

This remark had really balled him up; it was not the answer he expected. He kept his poise though, trying to carry on with the conversation.

'I don't know for sure; I haven't been home for a couple of days, but I think she's well.'

'I see someone is keeping you busy,' Mrs Fluffery chipped in, giving Natalie the evils.

'Oh, that's a shame!' said Mr Whitaker. 'Tell your mum that I hope to see her next week. That delicious honey will not last forever! Would you like to get some for her?'

'Maybe another time, Mr Whitaker,' replied Derick, completely ignoring Mrs Fluffery. 'I just popped in to ask what you two were doing at East Point University yesterday. What was all that scene about?'

Mr Whitaker gave Mrs Fluffery a properly dubious look. It was matched by her facial expression that resembled a "question mark". Then they both glared at Derick as if it was them who were expecting the answers to their burning questions.

'Derick, what are you talking about!? What scene?!' fired Mrs Fluffery.

'I was at my farm, preparing the honey for today, so couldn't be anywhere else,' explained Mr Whitaker.

'I saw you two at the Department of Biological Sciences yesterday! Mr Smith was there too. You were all wearing winter clothes and talking about the "common cause" or something,' Derick pressed on.

Mr Whitaker and Mrs Fluffey looked at each other as if Derick was just coming at them one wave short of a shipwreck. They were simply astounded by his fey revelations, which left them speechless and rooted to the spot for a while. Even Natalie peeked at him nervously as his countenance was frowning more and more with each passing moment.

'Honestly, I don't really know what you're talking about, son,' began Mrs Fluffeery, with grave seriousness in her voice, 'but talking about scenes — it is you who are making a scene now! Are you feeling alright? Are you distressed about something? Have your exams not turned out the way you wanted?'

'Ah, shut up, you!' growled Derick. 'I've always hated law; never really studied it,' he boasted in a triumphant voice.

Now all eyes had turned on him. Even the people who were busy taking apart their stands stopped at once and lifted their heads at alert. Everyone was expecting all hell to break loose at any moment, but it was the calming voice of Natalie that spoke.

'I'm really sorry for him; I think that some sort of misunderstanding must have occurred, right?'

'Misunderstanding!?' Derick broke in. 'I saw their faces as real as I do now. How dare you two deny everything right in my face, you glaring liars!?'

Even as Derick finished his sentence, he was violently pushed aside from the back. Next moment, he was facing Natalie, whose eyes were glowing red.

'The fact no one believes in your "out of this world" stories is a foolproof sign that they are just trumped up, don't you think? But at the same time, it's not a reason you should be throwing all your toys out of the pram, my dear,' rebuked Natalie. 'A lot of people know me here. My dead father was from Willowood.'

'Oh, I'm sorry. I didn't know…' replied Derick, in a muffled voice.

'Come on then, we're going back home,' said Natalie.

Before long, they were walking hand in hand along the same, wide path of the main alley of Willowood market, now looking a pretty desolate place to be, but without speaking a word to each other.

* * *

The rest of the day and the next day passed without any signs of stranger things happening to Derick. Natalie stayed close at hand to him, bending over backwards, making sure he had everything out of his mind and didn't get distracted by anything or anyone. She was taking care she was his only distraction for the time being. She had a calming effect on Derick's shattered nerves; it seemed like the occurrences of the passing week were nothing but a dream. This delightful idyll didn't last long, though.

The postman came early to this northernmost part of Hillbarrow on Monday morning. Natalie looked as though she was getting ready to work, hanging over the phone to someone. The next minute, she was back to the bedroom where Derick was just stretching his bones in bed, still half-asleep, half-awoken, and announced that she was having a day off from work.

'I wanna stay with you just a little bit longer,' said she. Then the doorbell buzzed, and she was back down as swiftly as she was up from the bed this morning.

'A true whirlwind she is,' Derick said to himself when she was gone. No sooner had she disappeared from his sight than she emerged in a doorframe again, this time holding an envelope in her hand.

'I think someone's got a love letter from a secret admirer,' trumpeted she, in a dashing voice, then thrust the envelope in the air, which landed on a duvet in between Derick's legs. He stared at it for a while — puzzled, unable to tell whether he was still daydreaming or floundering in consciousness.

'Come on then! Are you gonna open this letter today, or do you need to be sent an extra invitation?' nagged Natalie. 'It's definitely your name on it.'

Derick swung his body onto the edge of the bed, put his legs firmly on the floor, and tore the top of the envelope off, leaning on his hips. He pulled out a single sheet of paper from it. It looked like an official letter. He peered at it keenly; his eyes were rolling, devouring the text with rapacity. Then both of his hands started twitching and shaking profoundly. All of a sudden, his grip over the letter loosened, letting it slip through his fingers and flutter down towards the floor. Derick lifted his head with stark reluctance, making it look like he was really struggling to keep it up on his neck. A picture of fright and disbelief was painted on his face when his and Natalie's eyes met halfway.

'What?! Why are you looking at me like that?' asked Natalie, aroused by Derick's curious behaviour. 'What's in it?'

'See it for yourself,' was Derick's hollow answer.

Natalie stepped in and grabbed the letter from the floor.

'Crikey! You didn't tell me you were to see the uni officials on Friday,' she spluttered in dismay.

'I wasn't.'

'They're just saying they've agreed to extend your summer break! It's all right for some, ain't it? — What did you just say?!'

'That I can't remember seeing anyone from uni on Friday,' replied Derick's sunken voice.

It was a wake-up call that it might not have been a dream at all. Natalie's loving eyes were laced with the first marks of fear since the day she met him. She cast Derick a dull glance, not quite believing her ears, and sat down right next to him, on the "razor" edge of the bed.

'Look,' said Natalie, opening up the letter in front of their eyes, 'it says that they concur with YOUR request. It's dated Friday, last week; it's got the seal of the dean of YOUR department and my home address with YOUR name. It's only you of all the people in the whole world who could have given them my home address as yours, my lovely,' stated Natalie, then a smile returned to her face.

'That's why I just can't believe what I'm seeing now. It just wasn't them whom I saw on Friday.'

'So be my guest and fucking call them!' Natalie burst out, then she grabbed her phone and smacked it on his lap.

'No, you do it. I know clearly where I was and what I did!' Derick retaliated.

'Fine!' said Natalie, then pinched her phone back and browsed for the number.

'They're saying that the dean is on hols for the next three weeks, and his secretary is off too,' said Natalie, hanging on the phone.

'So typical. It's like all the people in the world always seem to be on holidays when they are needed the most,' sneered Derick.

'But they have your name in their records book, and it says that you were admitted on Friday at quarter to five,' Natalie went on.

Derick said nothing. He was just gawping at Natalie, dumbfounded. Then he got up and made his way out of the bedroom, walking towards the staircase.

'Are you gonna say something?!' shouted Natalie.

'I think I really need to find Marty before I go completely mad!' he shouted back, moving up the stairs.

'I think you're already really mad if you ask me,' giggled Natalie, then went out of the bedroom, chasing after him.

'Marty?!' asked Natalie once she found him changing his clothes in the attic. 'Your grandfather? You talk about him literally every day. I think he has a bad influence on you.'

'You know what? You're talking just like Bruce,' was Derick's curt response.

'Who's Bruce?' asked Natalie. 'Oh, hang on! Is he not your stepfather who's kicked you out?'

'Yeaaaa… Thanks a lot for reminding me.'

'That's fine. Anytime, luv! Don't you think you'd best go out and seek your mother?' asked Natalie.

'You know, I've tried to call her, but she doesn't answer. The landline is dead quiet too.'

'I know you've been thrown out, but maybe you should go to see if she's still there,' Natalie pursued.

'Yeah, it wouldn't go amiss to give it a go,' Derick agreed. 'I was going to do that today anyway.'

'Don't be there all day, though,' warned Natalie, 'I wanna go out somewhere with you later. I didn't take today off for nothing, my lovely.'

'You don't wanna go with me?' asked Derick.

'I would but need to help my mum with her weekly shopping. She always likes to do them on Monday, but I'm usually at work, so it would be nice if I could help her today,' responded Natalie.

'I see. If only Dorian were here with me…'

'Dorian? That short guy who was with you in the lab on Thursday?'

'Short?!' repeated Derick, surprised by Natalie's remark. 'He's not that short; only you're a bit overgrown.'

'Do you think he's jealous of that?' flared Natalie.

'Heheheh,' Derick laughed. 'I really don't think so. Dorian is the most logical, the most level-headed person I've met for the whole twenty-six years of my life.'

'What's his surname?' asked Natalie.

'Rose.'

'Rose, Rose — is he not the son of…?' asked Natalie.

'Yass.'

'Holy cow! I've always wanted to work for his company. It's the biggest name in broadcasting business around!' exulted Natalie.

'It may be; I don't know,' replied Derick. 'I'm still not quite sure why Dorian bothers with studying masters in biochem while it's plain he'll take over from his father sooner or later as he is his only child. Anyway, I'll have to go now if you expect me to be back in the afternoon as I presume you're gonna take the car.'

'Yes,' answered Natalie, 'and you should get one for yourself too.'

'I'll think about it later,' replied Derick, very casually. 'I think that there are more pressing matters to sort out now than my car.'

'Like your head, for example.'

'Oh, get lost, you!'

'Oh, no! You get lost!'

Even as she said or wished, Derick was lost and gone — back to Willowood to seek his mum, and only God knows what else.

'I just love this guy!' crowed Natalie. 'He just might be out of his mind, but he's into something.'

* * *

It seemed like Natalie's joke has turned against her when there was no sign of Derick coming back by midafternoon. She must have tempted all the fates in the world by simply saying it…

'I don't even wanna try to guess what happened to him this time,' croaked Natalie. 'I promise I wouldn't be surprised if he just turns up and says that he's stepped into a time warp by accident and has been chasing mammoths with an assault rifle in his hand.'

'Or has been chased by a sabre-toothed tiger,' mocked Natalie's mum.

'It's not funny, Mum,' grumbled Natalie. 'I really wanted to go for a long walk along the path that encircles Elmhawk Forest with him tonight. It's so eerie and enchanting over there. He would have been in his element. Instead, it's pissing down with bloody rain now! How charming is that?'

Natalie's mum eyes glazed over the blackened surfaces of the windows, now studded with a sticky mixture of hail and rain when they caught sight of a shady silhouette of a man creeping in by the front porch. Then the doorbell rang loud and continuously, without stopping. It only ceased to make this annoying high-pitched sound when Natalie made haste to open the door. It was Derick's soaking wet shadow that loomed out of the gloominess of the storm. He really looked like he'd been haunted by a pack of hounds.

'What on earth has happened to you this time?! Where have you been for so long?!' Natalie got hysterical when she saw Derick in a state of deplorable misery again.

'Oh, don't even ask,' was Derick's response.

'Why are you being so miserable?'

'Because I am miserable!' Derick snapped. 'This weather has been doing my head in recently. It's blasting out there like it was a twister coming on.'

'We have no twisters around these parts,' said Natalie's mum. 'They're much further away to the northwest.'

'Look Mum! It's what's left of him after he's been away for half a day,' Natalie lamented. 'You'd better run upstairs and get changed before we hear about your latest fantastic adventures, meanwhile, I'll make some tea,' she said to Derick, who didn't hang about even for a second but was gone again.

'Just don't read the news over there, boy!' shouted Natalie's mum.

'He's such a pain in the neck, isn't he?' asked Natalie. Her mum said nothing, only made one telling grimace of stark approval. Soon they were all sitting around the table, listening to Derick's adventure tale.

'We, I mean them — they never had dogs. They had cats but dogs? Never before.'

'Were there any signs warning against the dogs on or near the gate?' asked Natalie's mum.

'No, there weren't,' answered Derick. 'The gate was shut, but I knew the secret passage through. What was really weird, they only attacked me when I was close by the front door as if I've been watched for all that time and those dogs were only unleashed when I least expected them.'

'It all sounds to me that someone knew that you're gonna come back sooner or later but didn't really want to welcome you back in,' said Natalie's mum.

'It's a shame you didn't get hold of your mother or your gran,' said Natalie, pressing a moistened cotton pad gently against his red, scratched arm.

'Ouch!' bawled Derick. 'What's that?! It freaking hurts!'

'Oh, shut it, you baby boy!' riposted Natalie. 'It's only hydrogen peroxide; it won't do you any harm.'

'It burns like it rather was a hydrochloric acid!' cried Derick.

'Whatever, you silly,' returned Natalie, 'you do biochem, not me.'

Weather conditions only exacerbated through the evening, and there wasn't even the slightest chance they could poke the tips of their noses outside tonight. Natalie's siding house was virtually shaking to its foundations as if a tornado was around for real. It was no fun to hear that cacophony of shrill, sharp noises made by the constantly raging gusts of wind. Even the television, turned up to the maximum volume, wasn't enough to turn off the world around them.

'Oh, I've had enough of them muppets for the day,' whimpered Natalie, shutting the TV down.

'What else you wanna do?' asked Derick. 'It's still early.'

'I've got an excellent idea!' exclaimed Natalie. 'Tonight, you'll tell me everything about yourself.'

'I would, but you never wanna listen. You always have "more interesting things to do".'

'I promise, this time I'll do my best not to doze off,' said she, then put her cardigan back on. 'I'm just gonna go down and grab some coffee. Do you want some?'

'Nah, I prefer without,' replied Derick, then put his tongue out at her.

*　　*　　*

The weather had aggravated even further the next morning. As it turned out, the Clarksdowne area and its surroundings had been affected by the storm that had been forecasted to bypass it until only very recently when the "sudden" swerve in wind direction changed everything. Even Natalie, a dedicated journalist, was told to stay in and work from home if she could until further notice. She took the message very seriously, as it seemed, and spent the entire day stuck to the many screens of her personal computer, apparently searching and researching things. Derick and her mum, especially her mum, had been taken by surprise by Natalie's steadfast stance. One could get the impression of her as a secret agent on a mission, or a knight on a crusade to the Holy Land. Derick, perhaps feeling a bit like an ostracized outcast, was busy making the attic his new home.

'Psst, Derick, come here for a second,' whispered Natalie's mum when she saw him taking the mugs from Natalie's bedroom/office. 'What did you do to my daughter yesterday? Just take a look at her — she's been like that for at least ten hours straight. She's turned from a carefree, light-hearted fairy into a stern, hardcore sergeant major.'

'I think she just needs to catch up on some important work,' replied Derick, taking a quick gander at her concentrated face, shrugging his shoulders, 'or she's got wind of something.'

'What do you mean?'

'That she is an absolutely top, top journalist,' said Derick.

'Ah, keep your little secrets to yourself then,' purred Natalie's mum. 'Would you be so nice and help me to take some flowers out from the back porch, hun since she's temporarily unavailable? I reckon we haven't seen the best of this mad storm yet.'

'Certainly, Mrs Maine,' said Derick.

They'd left Natalie with her mystery quest thing and made their way downstairs. The winds had turned into a proper hurricane through the evening, shaking the flimsy structure of the house as if it were a wooden boat in the sea amidst the frothing waves of a violent storm. The conditions only deteriorated for the next couple of days. The first rays of the sun were not seen until Thursday morning. In spite of the destruction and devastation the storm had wreaked on everything around, making the streets practically impassable, Natalie still received the call urging her to come back to work. Naturally, she'd refused, saying that "she's ahead of the game anyway". Instead, she and Derick went to East Point University for a "pivotal" meeting of the members of the "Sombrero Tree Project". This time Derick was invited by Simon Redeldrag himself as a "special guest". They went out immediately upon receiving the invitation from Simon, knowing that most probably there would be no viable transport there, and they would have to manage on foot at least till they had reached the boundaries of Clarksdowne.

Although they left the house way early, they still ran late for the meeting, but understandably so, as the road to Clarksdowne was wracked with lots of rubble and debris lying around. Both Derick and Natalie were absolutely mind boggled by the reception they received when they came in. He was treated as some sort of a hero of the day, a saviour of the nation, a redeemer of fates as everyone around, whom neither Derick nor Natalie knew, queued to speak with him and shake his hand. On paper, it all looked unbelievably enthralling and captivating: an "accidental" error that slipped in to one of Derick's forgotten studies had inexorably yet indirectly brought about a new, breathtaking yet quite unexpected advancement in the development of a new, unique generation of painkillers, which would have the ability to "prevent" the pain from reoccurring. What was the most striking for Derick was not the fact how many people had used his paper to date, but the impetus with which everyone was swarming to be as close to the proximity of his personal space as possible; everyone except one person. That person was Simon Redeldrag. James Niggle was nowhere to be seen this time. Both Derik and Natalie were relieved when it was all over. They couldn't reach Simon throughout the course of the meeting at all, no matter how hard they tried. The only person of contact had always remained invitingly out of reach.

'Had absolutely no idea you're so popular and revered among your… peers I suppose, just wow!' gasped Natalie when they stopped after managing to slip through the back door. 'Now this one was quite different from the one you described to me last week, wasn't it?'

'You know, me neither. I've told you I've always had the impression that it's someone else out there who's been living my life for me. Since meeting my grandfather, all have started to go down the rabbit hole into a new, strange wonderland.'

'Strange indeed,' admitted Natalie, 'but I've already sensed something, like an aura of oddity around this whole "Sombrero Tree" thing. While Simon's name seems to appear here, there, and everywhere, I couldn't find anything meaningful about your grandad, and absolutely nothing in relation to Simon!'

'So this was why you were like a ghostly shadow of yourself lately, was it?' asked Derick.

'Listen, Derick, I've known James Niggle nearly all my life. We're best friends. He would have never lied to me in a million years, but last time when I saw him smoking a cigar for the first time, he said he does only it when he's really stressed. As far as I know, and I know him very well, most of his life had been stress-ridden, without going too much into details. Now, he just texted me he couldn't come in because his house has been hit badly by the storm. Rather an unusual excuse from him if you ask me. All his life revolves around studying and projects; that's all he's got. Then it was that thing with the text you allegedly received from him, inviting you to the previous meeting.'

'Where are you heading to with all of this?' asked Derick, clearly absorbed by now.

'I just think he says all the truth to me. But it is only what appears as the truth to him because he has been made to believe it is the truth. I know from experience that a lie is like a brick in the wall. When you take one brick out of that wall, it appears minute and insignificant by itself. However, one lie always hides another lie, which at first glance may appear as meaningless and unrelated to anything else as the first one, but once you begin to disassemble the whole wall of bricks, you find out that it is there only to conceal the light of the truth that is hidden behind it. The danger is — when you get digging deep into the realm of lies, dedicate your whole life, every single inch of your vital energy into breaking that wall into small pieces, brick by brick, you may find out, without even realizing it that the same wall is being now built around you, concealing the truth from you, brick by brick, the lie becomes the only truth known to you.'

Derick's eyes rolled up and down upon hearing Natalie's remarkable account. She wore her round reading glasses, embedded in an extra thin, black frame. In fact, they had been a permanent fixture on her nose for the last couple of days. Only now when she was dressed very formally, her long blonde hair, normally messy and breaking free, now tied neatly in a ponytail, the glasses gave her the look of a dame with a professorship in logic and philosophy.

'What do you think is happening with him then?' asked Derick.

'If you tell a lie a long enough, it becomes the truth,' answered Natalie. Then, with marked bleakness in her subdued voice, she added: 'I began to think — with an uprising horror in my soul, that he had been manipulated, and believe me, it would have taken quite a someone to wrap James around their little finger. Nevertheless, he's a dreamer with a very idealistic underbelly, so perhaps if a carrot of a heaven on earth had been dangled in front of his starry-eyed face for long enough, he's fallen for it. It just worries me because James is very introvert. What you saw of him is just a front; you have no idea what he's been through in his life. It takes a tremendous effort to get inside of him.'

'I think I might have heard that before,' said Derick, in a contemplative manner. 'I saw him only once anyway, and indeed, he rather made an impression of an extrovert on me.'

'He's always into projects that would turn this planet into a paradise. I got involved in this one only to make a simple outline of a report, highlighting what they're up to, and since I've known James inside out, I thought it's gonna be easy-peasy. Next thing I know, I'm up to my eyeballs in it, and now it is you…'

'What do you mean? What me?'

'You're a man of courage, I know, but I don't think you're telling me everything,' Natalie responded.

'Wow wow wow!' exclaimed Derick. 'Are you really on the top of your work as you're claiming or have you just been turning yourself into a self-declared hole digger of a snoop?'

'No, I'm not,' confessed Natalie. 'My bosses will probably tear me apart when I turn up to work tomorrow. By the way, where did you get such a scathing tongue from?'

'It's always been like that if you haven't noticed,' returned Derick.

'Mmmm, I like that answer,' pipped Natalie. 'I'm gonna suck that tongue off your mouth now, slice it into the smallest possible bits, and then scatter them to the four winds.'

'Well, catch me if you can then!' blustered Derick, whilst opening the door to an unknown place and wiggling his index finger invitingly before Natalie's very nose. Then he disappeared into a dark space that turned out to be a pantry to the nearest students' candy shop after the lights went on.

'You know, since I've met you, my life took rather an unexpected turn,' began Natalie, leaning on Derick's body, whose balance was hanging by a thread, or by a few boxes of crisps to be precise, against which he propped himself, with both of his hands firmly behind his back. 'I think I'm slowly but surely getting to understand your position and what bothers you so much, my lovely.'

'What position?' asked Derick.

'Relax and I show you what,' she whispered in the sweetest, the most enamouring voice. Then he felt like her fervent body jiggled down below his knees, yet somehow strange it was — this feeling as if the whole world was going down with him. It was the box of crisps that was collapsing under his arms.

*   *   *

Friday. Summer was back, back in full bloom. Hot, tropical winds that ensued after the storm had gone far north had surprised everyone, including the weather itself, with their full-blown aroma of fresh, spicy coffee. Local people were busy wondering whether to start growing mangoes instead of corn. All available hydrants were undone by thirsty kids, those big and those small — every single one of them was mobbing and dancing around them with an excitement of a toddler who's just discovered how fun the mere act of walking is. Fun it was, but not for all, especially those trapped in plastic, glassy-glossy, air-conditioned offices on the high floors of the city's skyscrapers, surrounded by all imaginable comforts and commodities of modern civilization. One of them happened to be a drinking water from synthetic dispensers, which... had run out in Natalie's office, who was stuck there until the early evening, working after hours as a journalist of great diligence. Derick's day was fully captivated by Dorian, who chose this late hour to appear on the desktop of his computer, bearing a stack of ill news with himself.

'As much as I'd like to be back in the country by the end of the week, it's now impossible. They've suspended all weekend flights in the morning, but now pretty much all of them are cancelled, including ours,' complained Dorian, dejected and angry.

'That's such a shame, man!' replied Drick. 'I haven't even

watched any news lately, no time for that as you can imagine, but has there been any info released as to when they plan to resume the flights?'

'It looks all really bleak now. That bloody mountain is reeking and spewing fumes all over the place even as we speak,' Dorian ranted on. 'I have no clue when I'll be back home, but this is not the only thing I wanted to talk about. My dad has got something important to tell you too.'

'Your dad!?' squalled Derick, nearly falling off his chair.

'Yes, indeed, me,' Dorian's dad joined in. 'Hi Derick, how are you doing?'

'I'm, I'm very well. Well, as much... as well as Dorian told you I am now anyway,' faltered Derick. 'It's a pleasure.'

'Thank you. Listen, Derick,' said Dorian's dad, 'I do not wish to air your dirty linen in public by any means, but what I've dug out might be of high importance and personal interest to you. Dorian told me about your latest "encounters" and personally asked me for help.'

'To be frank, Dorian is the only person alive I know I can trust for sure,' Derick declared. 'He's your only son, so I trust you all the more.'

'Very well,' said Dorian's dad, whose complexion seemed to darken and harden at once. 'You may first close that door behind you since we're not gonna be talking about fairies or nymphs here.'

'Ah, please don't worry, Mr Rose. Only Natalie's mum is around at the moment. She can't come here anyway because she's disabled, and Natalie isn't home yet. I presume she has to do a few odd overtimes now,' said Derick, chuckling lightly.

'I would have never thought you two would get on together so quickly,' said Dorian. 'Congrats, my friend!'

'Thanks, but it's rather worrying that even you have failed to predict such a turn of events,' joked Derick. 'It must be something really strange in every possible way then!'

'Strange or not, it's actually a stroke of fortune you've got her onboard. She's a very clever journalist, despite her young age,' said Dorian's dad.

'If I tell her what you just said, she'll be like a dog with two tails,' said Derick. 'When I told her that Dorian is your son, Mr Rose, she went berserk, rattling how much she would love to work for you.'

'Well, she's yet to come along and ask. I suppose I could squeeze her in somehow,' said Mr Rose. 'I would say she's quite diligent — sedulous in getting to the bottom of the matters that concern her a lot. Once she scents an aura of intricacy around something, she would go by leaps and bounds to be the first one who gets a sniff of a rotten, decaying truth on the bottom of the barrel.'

'Is she that good?' asked Derick.

'Well, you're her man, not me, so you should know by now,' answered Mr Rose, bursting into laughter again.

'Hehe, that was a good one, wasn't it, Derick? Anyway, how do you know her, Dad?'

'Been around the block long enough to come to grips with everybody whose interests overlap with mine to any degree,' replied Mr Rose, whose laconically enigmatic answer painted a puzzlement on Dorian's and Derick's faces.

'I bet she's been losing a lot of sleep over the matter or the "common cause", I should say,' Mr Rose continued. '"Sombrero Tree" has been causing a few eyebrows to raise for quite some time now.'

'I think she might have had other reasons for losing some sleep lately,' said Dorian.

'Oh, please, don't start stating the obvious all over again, my son,' returned Mr Rose. 'The matter is really serious. I think that you're a critical missing element to her muddy puzzle in which she's been sitting up to her ears.'

'"Common cause, common cause..."' mediated Derick as if he was losing the awareness about what Mr Rose was saying to him, 'I think I might have heard this before.' His pupils were dilating as the head went level with the computer screen, occupied by arduous expressions of Mr Rose and his son.

'What are you babbling about over there?' asked Dorian.

'Derick, can you tell me where and when did you hear this before?' asked Mr Rose.

'I'm not quite sure now, but I think I overheard like some people at Willowood market were talking about it,' replied Derick, in a wavering voice.

'What people?'

'Mr Whitaker, the local beekeeper — don't know if you know him, and Mrs Fluffery.'

'That old rag from Warwick House?!' burst Dorian.

'Yes.'

'Are you sure about this?' asked Mr Rose, in an ever more pressing tone.

'I'm not, but I think they were,' faltered Derick, pretty unconvinced these were his own words he was uttering.

'Has anything else you would have considered unusual or strange happened to you of late apart from stumbling upon the paths of Simon Redeldrag and Kitty Dauntwraith, being chucked away from your house and seeing your grandfather disappearing into the unknown like the most wanted man in the world?' asked Mr Rose.

'I don't think so; I've spent the last week in Natalie's bosom, literally,' said Derick, regaining his conviction. 'She's clung to me like crap to a shovel. There was no getting rid of her even to take a piss.'

'I can only hope you're right about this, Derick,' replied Mr Rose. 'I've known Simon for a long time since my background is business law. He's both a snake and a shark at the same time, but what's the most strange about him is that everyone who deals with him has a completely different opinion of him than people from outside of his ring of interest. It's remarkably true that this man has an otherworldly ability to contrive different, warped, make-believe realities and then to convince all his audience that it is the only truth in existence. I've met lots and lots of creative and powerful people of success during my broadcasting career, but he's above and beyond all of them brought together because of his unreal skills that make his own very existence straddle over a verge of a dream. He's got one weakness, though — he's lustful,' finished Mr Rose, then he sighed portentously.

'Dad, how are you so sure about this?' asked Dorian.

'I've nearly walked into one of his traps once upon a time,' responded Mr Rose, then a smudge of bitterness appeared on his forehead. 'It's an old, old story, which we shan't be delving into now.'

'Why are you shaking like this, Dad?' asked Dorian, seeing his dad being seized by waves of convulsive spasms. 'Are you all right? Would you like some water?'

'Yes, please. Thanks a lot! Hope it's not yellow fever.'

'Do you remember being bitten by a mosquito?' asked Dorian.

'No, I do not. Ahh, I feel better now. Thanks, my son,' said Mr Rose. 'I think, it's this hot, tropical weather getting under my skin. Sorry, Derick. Where was I? Ah, OK, I know. Listen, Derick, he'll make you believe he's a villain who wants to rule the world and all that kind of nonsensical stuff, someone who's hated and persecuted by anyone for anything, while he's the only righteous man on the planet, a philanthropist in his own right who wants to release the humankind from bondage of... whatever. He'll do it only to evoke the feelings of compassion and pity for him to make you be immune to what he does to you, which is selling you a myth of life wrapped in silver and gold, twisted and turned upside down and warped in his fingers. In the end, you wind up building an impenetrable wall of lies around your own life, which becomes so real to you, you'll be in denial to absolutely anything in opposition to your new truth, finding with an ever-growing wrath and spite that the whole world becomes your enemy — enemy, you'll have an unstoppable urge to cure with any available medications to you, like a good witch doctor who desires only to save terminally ill patients from a certain death, while resorting to anything under the sun for, after all, their very survival is at stake. The real danger is that he might as well provide you with the "medication" you need or worse — use you to get one that he needs.'

Derick's head swelled like a helium balloon that was about to fly away and burst upon hearing this news. Suddenly, his mind ignited inside as if all neural highways in his brain met and crashed together at one unimaginably small point of junction, enlighting it with such an outburst of brightness that could be rivalled only by an explosion of a supernova. Then the very image of Simon presented by Dorian's father came into existence in a form of a stream of lucid memories of him portrayed to Derick by his grandad. They were both so strikingly alike as if they both came from one person. Instantly, he remembered what Natalie said yesterday, what memories of him had been invoked by his own feelings. In a heartbeat, all of those images converged into one vivid vision, a personification of the man persecuted and paralyzed, who's got all the hatred of all living creatures against him, the one who eludes everybody but is eluded by no one. Why was he so loathed by everyone Derick knew? Weren't these nothing but other people's opinions that made him think this way? What if the opposite were true? The desire to finally find out who was Simon Redeldrag was growing inside of him like a virus planted to supplant all his thoughts with an incurable, obsessive fascination with his persona.

'Why don't you try to do something about it if you know so much, Dad?' asked Dorian.

'It's much easier said than done,' returned Mr Rose, but in an irksome manner as if his own son's inquisitiveness was prickling him in the ribs.

'So you've already tried, haven't' you?' Dorian pressed on.

'It's not the matter to chew over now,' answered Mr Rose, yet the words he uttered had hardly made it through his teeth as if he was properly struggling to keep at bay all the unpleasant, undesirable memories that they had awoken.

'But we ought to help Derick if Simon is after him, oughtn't we?'

'He's after nobody. He wants everybody to be after him. That's what we're doing now, my son, we're trying to help, help Derick — and everybody.'

'What are you trying to say, Dad?' asked Dorian, curious more than ever.

CURIOSITIES

'You'll see. Derick, I want to ask you something,' said Mr Rose, again turning his attention to Derick, whose cloudy presence indicated an absence, a lack of response to what was happening around him. Only upon hearing his name from thousands of miles afar, his body jerked irregularly like it has been taken from a state of trance with a click of a hypnotist's fingers.

'After I've found out about the seemingly mutual abhorrence between your grandad and Simon, something that must have run deep through the years, I've searched far and wide for the clues and causes of it. To my great, great disbelief, I've only managed to find out that Simon's name seems to appear here, there, and everywhere, but I couldn't find anything meaningful about your grandad, and absolutely nothing in relation to Simon! It all looks to me highly suspicious yet unbelieving because I get an impression that your grandad's very existence, both in the real and virtual world is strictly confidential, prohibited, I would say. Even his peculiar behaviour indicates it. I think he may hold the key to Simon's very doorstep, yet it looks as though both him and Simon are painstakingly unwilling to get rid of it as if they both had something to hide inside of them that links their lives irrevocably. Do you know anything of interest about your grandad's past? I am sorry to be so nosy, but when you'll later hear about what I've actually managed to dig out, you'll comprehend why I'm asking this question.'

'It's all good, Mr Rose. I really appreciate your and Dorian's insight into finding out what links Simon and my grandad. It's been eating me alive since I met him, believe me. I know it might sound harsh and crazy, but sometimes I just wish I'd never met him and carried on living delightfully unaware of my very existence outside of my little world if you know what I mean. Sometimes I feel like an awareness of perception of the world, or the lack of it would have been a blessing. But alas! I can't just jump into a "time machine" and go back in time to where I wanted to be — all my past memories erased, sitting comfortably numb, sunken in my favourite armchair, in front of virtual reality on the TV screen, clenching to the remote control as if it was the most precious thing in life, waiting for an angel of death to come for me, feeling like all my life passes through me painlessly, without a whisker of breath. But I feel it, I feel it with my every nerve, the pain of not being alive for nearly all my life, the life which he had breathed into my dead body for the very first time. Now I see, I see that the reality is far much stranger than I would have ever thought, for which, believe me or not, I'm grateful to him.'

'I fully understand you, Derick. I grew up as an orphan myself; I've never known my biological parents, let alone my grandparents,' Mr Rose replied pensively.

'Dad!?' exclaimed Dorian, but he shut his mouth quickly seeing as his father raised his hand high and open it in a flash.

'But I don't really know much about his past, unfortunately,' Derick carried on. 'Pretty much nothing, apart from the fact that he was with my mum and his son, who is my real father, in the mountains on the day of his premature death before I was born. He never mentioned his past, never wanted to talk about it really, which is strange, but I've never pressed him too much because of the great respect I have for him.'

Having said that, Derick stopped. His head, the weight of which he had to support with his hand, dropped significantly. He gave the impression of one being deep in his thoughts.

'I think there is just one more thing,' Derick went on after a pause. 'On Thursday, last week, when I had a chat with Mrs Deeprow, funny enough, this was when I'd figured she's been my nan, she said that Marty had a doctorate in microbiology, so I presume he must have been an academic in his past. She also mentioned something about Marty's downfall about the time when my mum and Bruce started to grow apart.'

'Oh, really?!' reacted Mr Rose, clearly aroused by Derick's story. 'Did she mention when it all happened or any other names?'

'She only said that I was only a few years old and too young to remember it. She didn't mention any other names, though. She wasn't really specific about what happened to my grandad and why. She just said that he fell.'

'I see, I see,' said Mr Rose. 'Thanks, Derick. Now listen,

please. It happened only yesterday when all this volcano farce started to unravel. I stumbled upon something that thrilled me to the marrow. Having found absolutely nothing about your grandad across any media or data platforms known to me, I came up with quite a desperate idea to search for his name in other languages that I know, and I know a few... One of them happens to be Xuvan.

'When I put your grandad's name into their domestic search engine and browsed through images, I fell upon something really mysterious. I came across the photo of a cut from a local newspaper, dated more than twenty-three years ago, still all in black and white, you know. The snapshot was dim and very blurry. Well, what would you be expecting from cameras of so much back in the day, especially in the country like Xuva, but anyway — it took me to a very dodgy website when I clicked on it, all in Xuvan of course, about a top-secret training facility for Xuvan soldiers. I've been to Xuva as a correspondent many times during the so-called "Old War" when the Xuvan expansionists' madcap plans to usurp vast chunks of the land of the neighbouring countries were very much underway, but I couldn't really recognize the place where the photo was taken. The quality of it certainly didn't avail me. My wild guess is that it was taken somewhere in the Alati Mountains because you can see the mountain range far in the background. The photo depicts three men wrapped in wintry, mountain clothes, in front of the gates to some sort of a base, I would say. Lots of snow around, everything surrounded by tall, thick spruce and fir trees, a terrain ideal for such an... enterprise. The names of the people in that photo go as follows: Marty Deeprow on the left, Alexander Kubla in the middle, and Maarten Burdent on the right. I'm sending you the link now. Take a look at it yourself. My question to you would be, do the other two names ring a bell?'

Derick's eyes rolled and glowed momentarily when Mr Rose mentioned Maarten's name. He looked fazed when his eyes met with a smiling face of a much younger version of his grandad, wearing a white, furry trapper hat.

'Wow, just wow!' Derick panted. 'It's been over a quarter of a century of my life to finally get a sight of my grandad's past for the very first time. I'm sorry, I think I'm gonna cry now.' His eye ducts rapidly filled with limpid buds of watery crystals that oozed along the borderlines of the lower eyelids, held from overflooding the cheeks by Derick's sheer resistance against showing how tremendously moved he felt inside. It looked as though he was about to weep, but instead, he burst into laughter.

'Life just doesn't stop surprising you when you're about to believe you've already seen it all, does it?' asked Derick, guffawing wildly. 'No, I have no idea who those other two mystery guys are, but this site looks one click short of a memory to me, a distant and forlorn memory, as it's merely one lonely page with some bits pasted at random in it as if someone tried to delete the whole content in a hurry, but simply missed or forgot about this one. It might as well be fabricated.'

'Or left on purpose,' said Dorian.

'Very good points, guys,' acknowledged Mr Rose, 'but I do not think it's fabricated at all, and here's why. Let me now translate to you what's written in this cut from the article. It's about the sudden and mysterious disappearance of Mr Maarten Burdent who apparently has never made back to the country after the scientific project he'd been working on with your grandad and this Alexander Kubla has been abruptly aborted and abandoned some twenty-three years ago. It doesn't say anything about what had happened and why, but it later goes on to indicate that there had been a growing misunderstanding as to where the project should be leading to. I can only decipher that they have been trying to figure out how to increase the stamina in soldiers and their resistance to… "a feeling of being hurt". Literally, this is how it's written here. The info under the photo says that it's the last time he was photographed alive there.'

'What are you making out of it all, Dad?' asked Dorian, curious as always.

'I am not sure as of yet, that's why I wanted to ask Derick if his grandad has ever mentioned those names to him because it's a definite clue for us. However, I would give a lot to find out what they've really been up to over there, hidden deep in the high mountain valley.

'How is this supposed to link my grandad and Simon?' asked Derick.

'I certainly heard of Mr Burdent, very long ago, a time before this photo was taken,' began Mr Rose. 'He was one of the first people I was interested in approaching to do an interview with for my new broadcasting initiative, which was very much a "work in progress" at that time. He was known to hold degrees across quite a staggering number of disciplines but has never been renowned as an "expert" in any of them. He really epitomized the saying: "If you're good at everything, then you're good at nothing". However, it was his startling skill to synthesise approaches from many disciplines of his interest at will, as it seemed, into one completely different and distinctive approach that made him so successful as a multidisciplinary scientist. It was exactly that unique ability of his that I wanted to touch upon but never managed to make contact with him because he had been repelled from his various posts at universities, seemingly about the time when I got really interested in his persona. I remember that then I just couldn't get hold of him, no matter how hard I tried, and lost my interest as a result. The fact that he might have gone to Xuva about that time could explain his complete elusiveness. But what really struck me when I found and read the content of this snapshot was the time it was dated — twenty-three years ago. You might find it absolutely unbelievable, but I just could barely find anything plausible about Simon from before that time. He looks like a man in his early sixties I would say, but as far as I remember, he's just come out of nowhere into the scene and taken the world by storm since then. Back in the day, the access to information wasn't so widespread and easy as it is now, so no one, certainly not me, questioned his identity until now.'

'What do you mean by all this, Dad?'

'That Simon has got everything to do with Mr Burdent's abstruse vanishing,' Mr Rose replied emphatically. 'This may very well explain why Simon's and your grandad's mutual loathing is so apparent.'

'But how?' asked Derick.

'I don't know,' said Mr Rose. 'I thought you'll be able to shed some light on the matter, but you seem to be as bewildered as myself if not even more.'

'What about the man in the middle?' asked Dorian. 'He looks considerably older than the others, especially Maarten who looks to be the youngest one.'

'Ah, Alexander Kubla,' sighed Mr Rose. 'If you think I know not a great deal about Maarten and Marty put together, then my knowledge about him is next to nonexistent. Never heard of him during my numerous stays in Xuva, which is odd; heard his name only but once, later on, from the source I would have considered dodgy at any time of the day — the government press officials. Moreover, it was a stack of nonsensical bullshit, I deemed at the time. Now, the more I look at this old cut from the paper, the more conviction I get that my conclusions might have been simply wrong. Apparently, he is or was, as I believe he's dead by now, one of the Xuvan's brightest brains. "Crazy Alexander" was his nickname, and he's been believed to be captured by Xuvan intelligence and forced to work for the army on projects to make soldiers indestructible. Well, even if it is the truth in every sense of this word, he must have failed badly since Xuva lost the war in the end. The only worrying thing is that it is your grandad standing next to him.'

'It sounds like another hell of a reason to find him, doesn't it?' asked Derick.

'Given that what my father has found is not a hoax,' said Dorian, in a calming voice.

'Why would it be?' asked Mr Rose, moved by his son's reasoning. 'It was so long ago, but the dates seem to match well to link Simon with Marteen, which in turn would explain why Simon and Derick's grandad detest each other.'

'You may be right, but what if you are wrong and the truth is even weirder than we can imagine?'

'Like what!?' asked Mr Rose, now clearly irritated by his son's challenging stance.

'I don't know. I have no idea what to make out of that, I really don't.'

'So, please stop your what-iffing if you may, and let us focus on something more concrete, would you?'

'Yes. Sorry, Dad.'

'No problem, I know you're trying your best, but I don't think it's the best place and time to test how iffy your guesswork is.'

'What do you think about it, Derick?' asked Mr Rose. 'Heard that the area had been hit by a derecho, by the way. How bad was it?'

'Ahh, yes,' snorted Derick, 'yet another one this summer, but that one was stronger than previous. However, I don't think you'd have much to worry about, to be honest, because you live in a mansion.'

'I'd rather call it a castle or a maze,' sneered Dorian.

'It's not the house I'm concerned about but my orchard, especially my hazelnut trees. I haven't strengthened them for such an eventuality. Didn't expect another blasting derecho to pop in. They all might be flattened now, darn it!'

'It was at its worst to the north of Clarksdowne, so maybe it hasn't touched your place so badly,' explained Derick. 'Coming back to your former question, I wouldn't know how to answer it until after I've seen my grandad again. The problem is — he can be anywhere around the world, but I think I might just know how to narrow the possibilities.'

'Can you speak more clearly what's on your mind, Derick?' asked Mr Rose.

'I truly believe,' Derick began, carefully putting words together, 'that our best bet is to ask Walter Dauntwraith himself.'

'Are you insane!?' Dorian and his father screamed at the same time.

'As far as I know,' said Mr Rose, 'he's locked down at Windchain — one of the best guarded, the most notorious prisons in the country. All kinds of obnoxious, ignoble creatures... and Walter are put to rot there forever. Have his circumstances changed? Has he been miraculously released?'

'I don't think so,' replied Derick, timidly.

'So what do you think you can do if he's still there?' Mr Rose ploughed on. 'Knock on their door and ask politely for an attendance? It's like sticking your head into a lion's mouth; Windchain is dragons' den, it's worms' liar.'

'I don't know, I will have to think about it,' replied Derick.

'It's madness, it's suicide even to consider it!' Mr Rose thundered.

'At least it's probably the least anyone would have expected me to do,' answered Derick, but with such a cold resolve that made Mr Rose shoot thunderbolts from his eyes.

'I bet you've already got some ingenious plan in place,' said Dorian. 'Why would you otherwise mention going to such a dangerous place as Windchain? Or maybe you wanna send someone else?'

'No, nothing of that kind,' said Derick. 'I really don't have any plan. I simply wanted to share my thoughts with you.'

'It's quite noble of you to be so open with us, Derick,' said Mr Rose, 'but let me tell you this — if the shit hits the fan, you will take the brunt of it, so be careful, be very careful.'

'Thanks, Mr Rose, I will. I really appreciate your involvement. I will stay in touch with you two. I bet Jamila is the happiest girl in the world now, isn't she?'

'Oh, she's over the moon,' replied Dorian. 'Not even the sooty fumes from that confounded volcano could take the smile off her face.'

'Say "hi" from me, please. Hope to see you soon and safe on the other side, guys,' said Derick.

'Thanks, my friend. See you in a couple of days, I hope. Meanwhile, don't do anything stupid, please.'

'Don't worry. I've got two girls looking after me now. Take care guys.'

'Thanks, and you too. Bye!'

'Bye now,' said Mr Rose.

'Bye!'

When Dorian and his father disconnected with Derick, he got

off his rickety desk chair, stood up erect as an arrow and looked down at his bed in silence for a long while with hands crossed over his chest. Then he sat down on the edge of it, took the cylindrical case that he stared at for so long, and took the long scroll out of it, which he rolled out with his palms evenly over the surface of the bed. It was the object he knew he's gonna need; it was his trading card, the only trading card he had — the plan of the hidden, underground floor of Mowhaken library had proven to be an extremely valuable asset. He cast a last, melancholic glance at it, then in it went, back to the cylindric vessel, the same that used to hold the case of Mr Dauntwraith. He grabbed it, threw it over the shoulder and made way towards the door, tightening the string around his chest. The door suddenly opened inwards, even as he got hold of the knob. It was Natalie who went flying through it with two cups of coffee, one of which landed on the floor, but the unfortunate touchdown of the second one happened to be on Derick's body.

'Oh, my God!' cried Natalie. 'Are you all right?! I'm so sorry. I was… just opening the door when it opened at me, and I've lost my balance.'

'You know, I noticed that first-hand,' Derick sniffed back at Natalie. 'Look, it's even on my case!'

'Let me take care of this and your clothes,' said Natalie, urgently. 'Come on now, take'em off, quick!'

'Easy tiger!' replied Derick. 'Soon I'll be only in my trunks, and you're still in your work outfit. It's not fair!'

'Stop whining and carry on!' cautioned Natalie. 'What's in that case anyway?'

'Ermmm… here? Nothing really, but I think I need to talk with you now,' said Derick, struggling to pull yet another dingy sweatshirt up and through his neck.

'But aren't we talking now?'

'Yes, but there is something important you need to know.'

'Well, I'm all ears now,' said Natalie.

'I'm travelling to Windchain tonight,' was Derick's crude confession, which really sounded like a lacklustre announcement of a death warrant by some callous bigwig.

'You what?!' Natalie cried out even before the message had hit home properly. She pierced him with her fearsome eyes, leaving the impression as if she was confronted by a war-hungry, militant maniac who rode only three wheels around his own boot camp. 'Have you completely lost your ways?!' she rapped at him when the realization of his intentions had finally struck the home turf.

'Why?'

'Maybe because I'm slightly blinded, maybe because it's the only way forward,' was Derick's straight up, cold-blooded response that was thrust through Natalie's throat like a neat shot of whisky that nearly knocked her off her feet, leaving her intoxicated, barely standing ground, staring at him with new eyes.

'Were you just about to leave then?' she asked in a trembling voice. 'But how? How can you expect to just turn up there and be admitted? It's impossible! Or maybe you…' she stopped suddenly, gazing at the leathern case, the surface of which still hosted droplets of spilled coffee, with a scared face. 'Is there what I think it is inside of that case?' asked she, pointing her finger at it.

'Yes,' Derick answered quickly as if he fully expected that question.

'You're mad! When did you retrieve it?'

'Today.'

'How come? How did they get you to trade something that has most probably been hard-earned for pure uncertainty?'

'They've already conferred the admission,' said Derick.

Natalie's face looked as if a series of violent storms were passing right through it — the expression of disbelief mixed up with consternation was a dominant scenery.

'Has it ever occurred to you that it may be a trap? Do you think they would have granted you permission to see Walter just like that if their conscience wasn't filled with blackness and treachery?'

'It has,' Derick admitted, 'and I think you're absolutely right about them. Nevertheless, I feel like I've got to do it, no matter how absurd and insane a move it is because it is the only move that allures any prospect of success.'

'What do you mean by "success"? What are you expecting to achieve?'

'I just want to find my grandad,' replied Derick.

'I fear for you, but I don't think I can go there with you because I have to go to work tomorrow in the afternoon and maybe on Sunday. I'm so behind!'

'I have to register in person before the twenty-hour period prior to the admission,' explained Derick, 'so I've got to leave soon because I'm due to be admitted on Sunday morning.'

'So were you actually leaving just now without even intending to let me know?'

'I was,' said Derick.

Just a fraction of a second after he'd uttered these words he saw something whizz through the air in the blink of an eye. Then slap! Bang! He found himself back in bed — with one of his cheeks swelling playfully purple.

'Ow, that hurt! Why did you just whack me in the face?!'

'Because I feel like I love you, and you were about to slip away through the back door under my very nose!' exclaimed Natalie, with a thunder of emotions. Pearls of hot tears shimmered in her eyes, then she collapsed next to him, crying solemnly into his already bedraggled sweatshirt. Derick, being half-naked, half-dumbstricken, put his arms around her and kissed her forehead tenderly.

'I know. I promise I'll come back to you soon,' he whispered into her ears. They sat there for about half an eternity: motionless, speechless, embraced in a girdle of love. They would have spent another half in exactly the same state — when one single moment was trapped forever between them if Derick hadn't started to tremble like the wind among the reeds.

'I also wanna tell you something else,' said Derick, breaking the silence. 'I spoke to Dorian today. They're stuck in Barracuda Island because of that horrific volcano explosion. All the flights had been cancelled, and no one has a clue about anything. A complete chaos. But it's not the volcano thing I wanna tell you about. His father was around when I was talking with him, and he joined the conversation. When he found out that I live in your house now, and we… you know, he's like praising you to the skies. Finally, he told me he would have loved to have you in, but you've never come out and asked, you silly goon.'

Natalie answered nothing. A mixture of joy and confusion emanated from her heart. She cast a few penetrating glances at Derick as if she was trying to find an answer to the questions she felt bound but was too afraid to ask.

'You're not excited or surprised?' asked Derick, feeling a bit thrown off, seeing a shadow of indecision on Natalie's face.

'Oh, no, I am,' Natalie defended her stance. 'I was just… ermm — not expecting you're gonna tell me that, but I guess I've got to see Mr Rose now whilst you're away.'

'Given they'll be back soon,' said Derick.

'I'll give him time till Monday. Otherwise, I'll slap my resignation on his desk!' said Natalie with a sudden outbreak of perkiness and enthusiasm, and giving Derick a delicate spank on his bum, she carried on, 'Off you trot to the bathroom then! You don't wanna appear before the magistrate as filthy as this, do you?'

'Filthy? The courtesy of who, your majesty?' replied Derick, then was out of her sight again.

She pulled the blanket over her lap and wept noiselessly under her breath.

* * *

Saturday. Natalie was back, back at Willowood market. Walking hand in hand with the dancing mischief of western winds, which spelled an imminent change of the weather, she was strolling aimlessly along the alleys full of people whose faces — comfortably snug in a numb epiphany of acquiring possessions — she could barely recognize. She saw her reflection in a window and didn't know her own face, the face that was being pulled to the ground off her head by some burgeoning weight inside of her. Her gait was heavy and burdensome; she was looking for something desperately without knowing what it was. She was making the rounds around the block without even realizing it. The number of unanswerable questions on her mind was rising with each passing thought. She only realized that she'd been following her own trail when she spotted that the space she thought was previously empty, now was occupied by an unusual yet charmingly quaint sight.

Paintings of all sorts, most of which were picturesque landscapes but for one, next to which a middle-aged woman sat on a rustic high stool, were displayed all over the area of a good few square metres. The woman looked tall but slender, aloof but down to earth, proud but aggrieved, engaged so deeply in an emotional conversation with a man that Natalie's approach went completely unnoticed. She stared in wonderment at the odd painting that was exhibited on the thin, wooden stand beside the woman — whose world was encapsulated in that vibrant discussion — now turning into a violent argument, ostensibly, about the price of that painting, which showed the image of the human heart turned upside down so that the downside that was now up, was entangled in flames, but the upper side that was now down, was being stabbed from the bottom by a dagger, through its centerline. Only hilt, quillons, and the bottom part of the blade were visible. The heart was breaking from the stabbed side, the fractures ran deep into its core; it was blackened from the bottom, but the colours turned brighter and brighter towards the part that was aflame, going from pitch black, through deep purple and light indigo, into a mixture of bright red and yellow near the top. The heart was fluttering over the serene surface of a deep blue ocean. Right underneath its overturned centre, a concave crater-like dip was made on the surface of the ocean, with one single drop of water suspended in the air right above it, making the impression as if the invisible tears were falling from both sides of the heart into this place, which was encircled by all but vanishing, faint ripples that were being vanquished by the imposing subtlety of the waves. The heart itself seemed to be diving over the surface of the ocean.

It was a sight so surreal, it had woken a burning desire that had sprung like a light from the shadows inside of Natalie's heart to find more out about it. Suddenly, the woman burst into tears and ran away from the man, taking shelter at the back of the stall. The man melted away into the crowd, shrugging and swinging his hands in dismissal, taking no notice of Natalie. Instantly, she was confronted by a pair of light green, blazing fires, railing thunders at her from close range. These two sudden flames belonged to a shorter, stockier, and older woman than the one who sat there just a moment ago.

'Do you think it is appropriate to harass a lady when she's made it clear to you that this painting is not for sale?!' scolded the older woman, pointing her finger at the painting Natalie was so mesmerised by.

'I'm sorry?' spluttered Natalie, quite disoriented by the whole situation.

'Feel like playing dumb, do you?' the other woman carried on blasting Natalie's head off. 'Do you really think you could outfox the old fox, you niggard?'

'Maggie, who are you talking to?! It wasn't her, it was a man,' said the woman who was in tears, now drying her eyes with a white, embroidered handkerchief.

'Oh —' said the other woman, then to Natalie, 'I'm deeply sorry for that. I mistook you for someone else! Ah, silly old me! My apologies. How... can I help you?'

Natalie, who couldn't make any clear sense of what had been unfolding in front of her eyes had just one thing in mind. 'What did he say to make you cry like that?' she asked the woman with the handkerchief.

'Because this painting reminds her of her only son, she feels she's lost; she just couldn't sell it now,' the other woman explained in a strangled voice, seeing her compatriot's eyes lustrous with tears again.

'What was his name, may I ask?' queried Natalie.

'Derick. Derick was his name,' the oldest woman said with a sigh.

Natalie's heart sunk into her stomach, skipping beat by beat.

The glare in her eyes withered away, only to burst into life a moment later. She was like a shooting star, sparkling diamonds across the sky, stealing the attention of no other than Mrs Deeprow and Mary like a comet in the night.

'Do you know Derick?! Do you know my son?!' cried Mary, seeing Natalie's unmistkably open body language. She ran up to her and shook her like a tree, the fruits from which you want to have in your basket; her face was flooded with tears.

'Yes,' she said, 'yes, I know him, yes, he's my... he's my boyfriend.'

'Mary! Please stop squeezing her throat or else she's gonna faint into your arms,' said Mrs Deeprow.

'Good gracious! Are you OK?' asked Mr Deeprow.

'Yes, I think so, I am, just a bit... beyond words,' gasped Natalie.

Releasing Natalie from her grip, Mary fell to the ground listlessly, sobbing next to the painting, which stood tall, speechless, and unmoved — a silent spectator of the world's miseries, put into the frame of lasting memories.

'I think Derick may be in grave danger!' said Natalie when her and Mrs Deeprow's eyes met again, sparking an inexplicably harmonious line of communication.

'Tell me now! Tell me everything you know,' said Mrs Deeprow, then showing Natalie the way into the small room, 'Would you take this painting inside, please? I'm gonna take care of Mary.'

'Come on, Mary, stand up now,' urged Mrs Deeprow, 'finally, there is light at the end of the tunnel.'

Even as they were speaking revelations to each other in the course of this unexpected yet fortunate and fate-binding encounter, hundreds of miles away, Derick arrived in the far and remote village of Windchain. Quiet, slumbery, and oddly picturesque settlement it was, with perfectly flat, curving, zigzagging roads, full of freestanding or semi-detached cottage houses, all covered with ash-grey thatched roofs. Sometimes, if you were lucky, you could spot a few people of an advanced age, strolling patiently along the streets, armed with their sticks and walkers on wheels. It would have been with horror and dismay for any visitor to find out that such a delectably innocent place could contain "the worm of the devil" — as the people in the know were affectionately calling Windchain maximum security prison — partially due to the fact that most of it was actually hidden underground and the whole complex looked like a wiggling earthworm from a bird's-eye view, within its boundaries. It was guarding the northernmost frontier of the whole province as a "gateway" outpost to the Central Highlands, a cold and largely desolate region where a few hardy people lived in small villages and hamlets, still probably out of their own obstinateness towards the cosiness and luxuries the cities of the modern world had to offer.

His enchantment with the village quickly burst like a bubble when he caught sight of the impregnable watchtowers of the prison, tall as mountains, black as the darkness of the night. He was ordered to check in to the small, solitary building that looked like a sheriff hut of some sort, on the left side of the road. It was a sight rather queer to see this small, lone, shack-like structure right before the formidable front gates of the prison. After registering, he'd found out that it was the place where he was supposed to spend the last twenty-four hours prior to being admitted for the seeing. Underneath this peculiar "station of a building" was the intricate web of corridors, each of them leading to the room at the very end of them, with only one small elevator going back and forth to the ground level. Even though it hadn't got the amenities of a five-star hotel, it was well lit and considerably warm, given that the whole place was dug and hidden deep underground like an obsolete coal mine that was adapted as a dwelling for humans.

About twenty-four hours later, Derick was walking into a much darker place, badly lit and cold, striding anxiously on the black, opaque floor tiles, feeling like it was going to be the last mile of steps in his life. He was allowed to wear black trousers and black shirt, black boots but no socks, all of them given to him to wear on the spot before entering the life-long, endless passage that would lead him to Walter's cell. The clothes were too short and scanty, making him shiver senseless in this frosty, hostile environment. He was not allowed to take any of his possessions but himself; goosebumps were all over his body like a swarm of locusts on freshly yielding crops after he'd made just a few yards forward. All but silence was heard around the place as if nobody was ever kept in those cells, which were deep and dark so that absolutely nothing was distinguishable in this total lack of light and brightness. As he carried on walking, he was falling increasingly under the impression that he could hear voiceless cries, mutters, and murmurs fluttering wingless all around him and biting his skin like a band of blood-thirsty, toothless mosquitoes. He was told he must stop by the cell "thousand and one A".

When he reached his destination, he stopped by the bars and peered in. The cell looked as empty, as bare, as impenetrable as any he passed by. The guard who'd been following him unseen all the time like a shadow of the night was now standing next to him, wearing his huge, mascarade helmet that guaranteed unrecognizability, maintaining his firm, assigned namelessness of an everyman. The man with no name was Derick's best friend at this dire moment in time. Suddenly, he pushed his half-open right palm, with his fingers folded in half as if he wanted to emulate some martial arts punch in a flashy, quick thrust so that the bottom side of his palm just touched the wall. Next thing Derick saw was the bottom half of the bars that were barring his entrance to the cell disappearing into the floor and the cold blackness of the cell pouring out, blasting him in the face. The guard turned around his own axis and stood at attention, parallel to the wall, perfectly erect, keeping his lofty, war-like helmet tantalizingly aloof. Derick looked lost, unsure what his next move was going to be. He gazed deep into jet black darkness with the utmost reservation yet with a face more and more captivated by curiosity.

'Come inside and sit on the bunk that is on your right,' said a calm, soft but clear voice belonging to no one.

Derick wavered at first, but the overpowering desire to pierce through the veil of darkness has prevailed in the end. He stepped into the cell, which didn't shut behind him, much to his befuddlement; he floundered about for a while before finding the edge of the bunk, which he sat on immediately, still not able to discern anything or anyone. The light bulb that was directly above his head lit up just as he rested his body, then he saw him — sitting patiently with his hands on his lap, joined in palms, his leg crossed in near ideal "lotus flower" position. He was smiling at him candidly with his bright blue eyes on a face that belonged to someone who didn't seem to be so much older than Derick.

'I expected to see someone who would look way older than you,' remarked Derick, staring in awe into the eyes of a newly met stranger.

8
LOST SOULS

Derick was in awe and shock of what he saw. The face of this man was so amicable, so polished and pale as if it hadn't been touched by strokes of wind or filled with beams of light for millennia — he knew right away it wasn't Walter Dauntraith he was looking at as Mrs Dauntwraith's husband was chubbier, older, and had definitely much darker skin complexion. From what he could recall, he was almost like her male twin. Who was this man he was looking at then? There was something odd about him; he wasn't giving him any signs of indifference or apprehension that he normally linked with strangers. He appeared as one who was far from it — his bright blue, sparky eyes were filled with some sort of understanding and coherence as if they belonged to someone else, but above all else, they were smiling at him. Was it yet another "stranger" who knew him better than himself?

Derick looked lost and hopeless, feeling like he was letting his grandad down. He raised his head and looked again into his eyes — they definitely belonged to someone else; they were so cool and poised, radiating a mellow, airy selflessness. Derick knew this man was there for a reason, he also knew that he was concerned about how he felt inside. Derick could sense he was reading him with ease like a Sunday morning newspaper. On the other hand, his motionless, formless appearance wasn't oozing any hints of emotions, a watery shapelessness was what he was — he could be anything, anyone, anytime. Oddly enough, Derick didn't feel any discomfort, any misgivings towards him, he only felt he had to say something but had no idea how to begin. Then the man spoke instead.

'I know what has brought you to this place,' he began in a flat, placid voice, 'but the person you hoped to find here was taken away more than a week ago.'

After he had spoken, Derick felt like an enormous weight had been lifted off his mind. Still, he had no idea what to say, he knew only that one thing led to another.

'How do you feel about it?' asked the stranger.

Derick didn't expect such a direct question so early, but the more he kept hesitating with an answer, the more exposed he felt he was to this void aspect of his that was absorbing every single piece of him, one after another, with every passing moment. The best he could do was to speak from his heart.

'I feel like I'm letting someone down,' said Derick, then looked at him with all intent; he had to see what reaction his words would bring about, but there was none — he remained in a state of nothingness all the same. Derick couldn't read anything from him, his eyes urged him to speak, but words just couldn't stick together in Derick's mouth; nothing meaningful was coming out of the gloom of confusion inside his brain.

'Speak,' he insisted. 'Have you gone so far only to stare into the eyes of a stranger?'

'No, but your eyes — they remind me of someone.'

'I know,' he said.

'How do you know?'

'I know the person you're so desperate to find much better than you.'

'Who are you?'

'Have you not figured it yet?'

'You must be his brother.'

'No, I'm his son.'

Derick felt like he was about to melt down, turn into an invisible vapour and vanish from his sight at this precise moment, but he couldn't. He had to face another revelation on the road of discoveries, but this time they couldn't get stranger than that.

'How do you feel about this?' he asked again, still moving only his mouth.

'I don't know what to say.'

'If you don't then ask. I don't need to do anything. I don't even need to be here.'

'You wouldn't be here if you didn't want to.'

'Now, you're talking more like him. Marty's got too much trust in you. It was his own trust in himself and in other people that ultimately cost him everything. He's always believed to live with a trust in something imperishable within himself, like a flame that has always been hidden from him deep inside the chasms of his soul, permanently concealed from his conscious mind. You're exactly the same, a living copy of him... from inside.

'What do you mean?'

'He's always had that eerie aura of creativity about him, like a black storm cloud with lightning and thunderbolts hovering above his head and following him everywhere. He's let his creations live lives of their own, then he's lost control over them, unable to decide which reality he's been living in. I remember one day he would start questioning whether your father was really his child since he looked quite unlike him or his wife. It was about the time when you just started to toddle.'

'So you know everything about me, don't you? May I know your name, please?'

'It's not a picnic, Derick. You've got half an hour only, so choose your words wisely, but be quick.'

'How can I find him?'

'Come closer and prick up your ears.'

Derick pulled his body along towards him and sat a bit askew, tilting the side of his head to the right. Then he felt like the subtle, ethereal whispers of his began to tickle the bottom of his ear with some strange sounds of names and places. When he finished, Derick backed off and looked at him again; he was staring at him with the same sincere, smiling eyes, ready to speak. His overly friendly demeanour didn't do justice to how comforting his rarefied presence was to Derick. Suddenly, life had brought him before his close relative, the existence of whose he'd been completely oblivious of throughout his entire life.

'My name is Shean, by the way.'

'How can I believe what you just said is the truth, Shean?'

'You'll have to find it out for yourself and make up your own mind about it.'

'Why are you being locked down in such a nasty place like this?'

'It was a sacrifice.'

'Sacrifice?'

'Look, the person who you hoped to meet will probably be dead within a month or so. He's got to be rid of because he knows too much so he's being tried for a very serious offence.'

'How do you know all these things?'

'I've been outside of a "free world" for the last twenty years, so I had time to check up on things, believe me.'

'How old are you?'

'It doesn't matter. Besides, I think someone else will be better equipped to tell you my age.'

'Marty?'

'Perhaps. We may not meet ever again.'

'Do you know Simon Redeldrag?'

'Yes… and no.'

'Your sacrifice?'

'Yes.'

'Oh, how much time have I got left?'

'Relax please, I'm measuring your breath.'

'What?'

'This place is a "time trap". Time does stand still here, only life passes. Nearly half of your time has gone now. How do you feel about it?'

'Already?!' Derick uttered with surprise. He didn't know whether to run away with what he knew or try to delve deeper into the unknown. Difficult as it was, the situation didn't matter in the end because what he knew he was searching was already inside of him. Perhaps, he was a never-ending journey and never-ending destination for himself. Shean was just another learning curve for him, an obstacle he had to permeate to pass through. He had a feeling that going through difficulties was the best and the only desirable state of being because it brought the excitement of learning. The rest was only a matter of calculation.

'You didn't answer my question,' said Shean.

'I feel like nothing matters now, apart from us being here, now.' Shean's lips smiled for the very first time upon hearing these words, but he said nothing as if he anticipated Derick wanted to go on. 'Why is there so much mutual hatred between Marty and Simon? Are you the reason why they abhor each other so greatly?'

'I'm here because I love my father. I haven't seen him for all that time I've spent here, but you're the living proof he's never given up.'

'Given up? Given up what?'

'To stop Simon. He's the only man who knows him like his own shadow. Marty once told me that he and Simon are like twins. I am not so certain what he meant to this day; he's always been a bit of a riddle, even to himself. Simon is a great illusionist. He's a salesman who trades the truth about life for people's lives.'

'And you seem to be another person who loathes him with all you've got. Tell me at least what he does to deserve it. Everybody I know talks the same thing about him. I wanna know whether it's true. That's why I need to find Marty.'

He smiled at Derick for the second time, then he opened his mouth and began to talk.

'He tells lies and sells them as the only truth in existence. He does miracles with opposing forces. He would tell you that left is right and right is left, and you would believe him merely on his merits. He would denounce the ever so important act of checking as something obsolete, loathsome in its essence, something you would get rid of forever as if by evolution. Then when the differences between oppositions disappear for a mere "fact" or "truth" that they haven't existed in the first place, that everything is the same and everybody is the same, people would be able to feel and unfeel anything at will — or so he would reassure them of.'

'That is the most alarming, the most nightmarish account of him I've heard so far, but — how can you prove that what you're saying is true?'

'I don't know that anything said about Simon is true,

unfortunately, so you've got to make up your own mind about it. It seems like only Marty knows what he's really up to, but I think Simon would kill him with cold blood if only he...'

'What? Why did you stop?'

'Quiet. Relax, please. I'm seeing your breath — your time is passing.'

'What?'

'If only he could find him. I don't know why, but Simon was more than happy to take me instead of Marty twenty years ago, even so he knew very well I lent him my own fingerprints on that day when he failed to be done with him, once and for all. I remember that night very well, oh yes, I do — when he came back, and he was frightened. I thought it was him who was dead, then he said that he just couldn't do it because it was like "trying to kill the perfect image of himself". I knew then that he'd failed; his downfall was the most tragic moment of my entire life. I couldn't do anything else but give him my own. I knew what was coming next. He disappeared once he told me that, leaving absolutely everything behind. It was the last time I saw him. I found out that day that only Simon knows the one thing Marty is so badly afraid of.'

'What is it?'

'I don't know. You have to find out.'

Even as he said this, his eyesight wandered off from being fixated on Derick's face to a distance above it for the very first time since he showed up inside his cell. It must have been something profound to distract someone as sedate as him. Derick turned around, seeing that his eyes had found a new point to focus on. It was a tall, grim stature of the guard who came to tear them apart like a dark angel of death. Derick's time had come, he knew he had to go, leave Shean behind and face the truth. He cast the last fleeting glance at him and smiled — he knew his eyes belonged to someone else.

'Farewell, Derick.'

He gave no reply. Somehow he knew it, somehow he felt it wasn't going to be the last time when their paths would cross. He gazed at the abominable, inexpressible statue in front of him, then made two giant, bold leaps outside the cell. The bars shut behind him in one swift and seamless move that barely made a sound. After walking another long mile through the black corridor, he was set free again — he let the air to take care of him, his only friend was the wind now. 'It's going to rain anytime,' he noted as grey, heavy clouds were hanging low above his head. He took a frightful and ponderous look towards the hills of Central Highlands, looming ominously in the distance. His next destination was far to the north, beyond them.

9
LOTUS FLOWERS

They sat around the small, wooden tripod table when they came in. The double doors of the stall were carefully closed by Mrs Deeprow, who then put the red plate signifying the closure of the business on both of them, just in case. Natalie propped Mary's painting up against the old, ashen sideboard and sat beside the painter herself after making sure her work of art was secure. Mrs Deeprow got on preparing the tea. Soon the refreshing, revitalizing scent of jasmine pervaded the room. Mary went on talking about her newest creation with blooming passion once she felt comfortable inside. She called it *"Conception of the lotus flower"*. According to her, what was the most beautiful and lasting in nature was the universal birth from the seeds that work in silent tandem to make something out of nothing — when pleasure becomes pain and pain becomes pleasure. It was conceived in her imagination only last week and made whole all at once in one wild stroke of inspiration.

After Mrs Deeprow had entered the room, holding the sterling salver full of tableware and served the tea with some treats, Derick was the talk of the hour. There they met — three divas of separate generations, coming together from different eras of the world, brought into one place by a fluke of heart — each one of them singing the song on their own about the one that got away. Mrs Deeprow took Mary, whose state was a constant rollercoaster of discontent between the voice of her inner will and dissonance of depressive moods, to the pilgrimage town of Kirkwood, no more than twenty-five miles to the north-west from Hillbarrow, where her younger sister lived. Mary had always lived off selling her paintings; it was one of the two sources of passion that still kept her alive, the latter of them was her only son, whom she'd lost now. Since that day, painting had grown to be more of a serious matter, almost life or death matter after she'd been cast away and cut off from her usual habitat, having been accused of being an ill-spirited witch who'd developed the art of concealing the truth to the ranks of apt mastery. Yet to anyone who could catch even the slightest glimmer of light coming from her eyes, she was a sight of someone with stuttering mind, pinned down by the haunting sound of melancholy. Natalie was a true godsend in her eyes, even as Derick was for Mrs Dauntwraith not so long ago. She was brimming with joy to find out about her and Derick, but when she learnt about Simon, Marty, and what Derick had just set out for, her heart collapsed and life shrivelled inside of her like an early spring flower that fades — out in the cold.

Natalie's relief for being able to share her doubts and misgivings about someone who became close to her heart almost overnight with someone who was even closer to him was salvific. She felt like the rush came every moment his name was pronounced, but a creeping breathlessness was more and more evident on her face as she carried on speaking like someone possessed by the spirit of the person she was talking about.

'Are you all right, my lovely?' asked Mrs Deeprow, seeing that Natalie's breath was struggling to keep up with the stream of words flowing out from her mouth.

'I'm just a little bit fatigued — I think I've already made enough steps today, and I've still got to go to bloody work, but I feel suddenly sleepy, I don't know why.'

'Night is as its darkest underneath the eyelids, my lovely,' said Mrs Deeprow, 'but sometimes we need it to overcast our minds with it to reflect and look inside more clearly. Let's go outside now and repose.'

'Thank you, Maggie. You're an angel,' said Natalie, then she stood up and made her way out.

'You're very welcome, my love,' replied Mrs Deeprow, then she said quietly into her ear: 'He will come back to you but not until he finds him.'

Mary gave the impression of one being entirely absent from the conversation after her early exaltation. She was switched off completely from the world outside. She was staring at her painting without even giving a single blink of the eye. She was like a statue of herself, her mind was basking in blissful contemplation. When she came back to reality, her face was silently smiling at Natalie who instinctively returned the smile.

'Pardon her, please,' said Mrs Deeprow. 'It's not the best day for her. She's shaken and getting stone-rigid. Her catatonia is coming back with a force not seen for a very, very long time.'

'I'm so sorry,' said Natalie. 'Derick mentioned something about it, but he didn't seem to be very sure of it.'

'Mary has always been painfully careful not to show him any signs of her condition. She's a very proud and highly, highly intuitive person. Just take a look at her latest work. I'm not an expert by any means, and I'm not into symbolism either, but I can clearly sense the double meaning of that painting. Do you?'

Natalie nodded her head but said nothing. They left the room, leaving Mary inside. Almost all the merchants had been gone by now. The sun was climbing heavenly azure stairs higher and higher, the summer was not ready to move on — it was going nowhere, not yet, not today.

'Isn't it a beautiful place to be when it's so quiet and everything is bathing in the sun?'

'Yes, it's completely different scenery now, different feel, different vibes,' said Natalie.

'Mary always produced the most beautiful, the most captivating paintings when her depression was at its deepest. I don't even think she's fully aware of how psychic she gets when she's agonizing, brooding, completely motionless beyond the horizon line of her conscious mind. Then suddenly she grabs her gear and paint, without eating or drinking, without saying a single word until she's done. Somehow she knows what has been happening with those closest to her heart, and she senses what is still to come. I think that the painting says it all — she loves my Marty too because he's always reminded her of Nathan.'

She paused and sighed deeply. Then she gazed keenly into Natalie's blue eyes and immersed herself in them like a drop of rain in an ocean. After a while — she carried on.

'Your eyes, they're like periscopes to your soul; I can read a lot from them. You're so in love with Derick, aren't you?'

Natalie didn't respond; she blushed bright red instead, her eyes were filled with tears, they couldn't lie.

'Let me tell you something, my lovely. Derick is exactly the same as Marty, he's like a living, younger copy of him. Marty had been a riddle to me all my life; I could never fully comprehend him, neither could he, I deem. When he comes back to you, take good care of him and bring him to Kirkwood. You know the address now, don't you? Mary would be simply over the moon if she could see his son again.'

'Don't worry, I will bring him in one piece and pampered as a newborn baby.'

'I admire your enthusiasm, and I'd like to share it with you, but please, be careful, very careful. My Marty has been like a ghost for the last twenty-odd years of my life. I really don't want you to feel the pain that I feel.'

'I promise, I'll do my best. I'm a journalist after all,' answered Natalie, and a cheeky smile appeared on her face.

'I love your sense of humour.'

'Thank you, Maggie. Thank you for everything.'

'No, I thank you,' replied Mrs Deeprow. 'Without you coming here today, we wouldn't know what is happening with Derick.'

'Oh, my God, I think I'm gonna be late for work again!' Natalie cried out, suddenly, seeing the screen of her mobile. 'Honestly, I have no idea what's been going on with me lately! Normally, I'm pinpoint with my timekeeping.'

Mrs Deeprow gave Natalie a deeply compassionate, comely smile. A thread of intangible mutual understanding had formed between them, meeting and joining their hearts in one unfading, transcendent bond that went beyond sensual experience — suddenly finding two soulmates in one of the most unlikely places, where Natalie's mum used to get away with his father in the days of her youth to admire the sunset over the valley of River Leyron from the green hills to the north of the market where they could immerse themselves in the serenity of the rustling willow groves that grew abundant from the bottom of the hills right to the river bank. The soft noise of the trees was always accompanied by the reverberating, soaring hums of the rapids of River Brook which met River Leyron in the feet of the valley to join its flow towards the sea.

Natalie's conviction in the truthfulness of Mrs Deprow's thoughts was one that surpassed basic concept of human comprehension — their hearts were intuned to the same melody of love, gliding on the long waves of harmonious beats. When the time of parting came, they couldn't take their eyes off each other until it was humanly impossible to keep them up. As Natalie wandered off from the marketplace, leaving Mrs Deeprow and Mary behind, a mixture of sadness and joy was a predominant scenery on her face, just like in Mary's painting. Somehow she felt she knew deep inside that nothing bad could happen to her loved one, that no ill fate could touch him right now, not now when she was in the sate when his mere presence by her side was everything she needed. She was deaf to all the voices other than those of her heart. She'd been falling badly behind at work, but there was no coming back for her now — when the music of love was pouring out of her heart in every possible way. The only thing that still kept her afloat was her cheeky, gutsy self-confidence and belief that she could turn everything around anytime, anywhere at will. Not everybody around her shared the same levels of mirth and optimism, but 'ah well,' she kept saying to herself, 'I'm not gonna be falling for all that negativity. I don't need anything of that.'

She knew it was futile to try to call or email Derick as days passed by in grave silence, but she kept coming back to grab her mobile or the handset, even though she knew it was of no avail. She couldn't help it, though — the desire to hear even the slightest sound of the signal, even the thinnest call of his voice was so intoxicating that it overpowered any sense of rationality. She felt she had no sense of danger, she could go through chasms and then she could smile at strangers, but it wasn't until past midweek when the noise of a familiar buzz of her phone made her jump out of bed before she had to go work. It was only a message, though, only a message. It was sent from an unknown number, but it was more than enough to make her day because Derick's name was written underneath it. She had proof now, although an illusory one, that he was still out there, thinking about her. She tucked the flowers into her hair and was off to work.

The same day, Dorian, who'd finally managed to escape from Baracuda Archipelago and return to the country, had got in touch with her after his failure to get any response from Derick. She's been invited to meet with him at his dad's house or "castle" as Dorian liked to call it, situated in the south-east corner of the outskirts of Clarksdowne, near to the end of the city's built-up area. She went there straight after work. Dorian was waiting for her at the outside gate to his estate. When they came in, they entered the enormous, round room that looked like a hybrid between an atrium and a lounge because of its open roof, but in reality, it was a home library, with dozens of shelves that contained hundreds of books, everywhere she could look. They sat by the fireplace that was now unused for months and months because warm oceanic winds from the south-east were still prevailing over the currents from the north. Dorian's father met and greeted them there; then they sat down and began their conversation after the refreshments had been served by a young couple, chosen from the sheer army of servants employed by Dorian's dad to keep his property in one piece.

It had become clear very early on in their discussion that Derick has withheld a lot of information, but they were uncertain why he'd hidden so much from them. They were unsure whether his lies were a product of cold-blooded, dry calculation or an error caused by misinformation and confusion. Whatever was the cause or causes, one thing they all agreed on was that it must have been quite a lot that has been concealed inside of him for the reasons only known to himself. Both Dorian and his dad couldn't hide their surprise to find out that Natalie had overheard the whole conversation between them and Derick last week.

'So, you've overheard everything last week, haven't you?'

asked Dorian.

'Yes, I have,' was Natalie's short reply.

'That's great!' exclaimed Dorian's father. 'I mean, it's not great that you have eavesdropped on your boyfriend, but you did a great job of not showing him any emotions that you have.'

'It just hurt me so much that he's lied to me on purpose.'

'It hurt us too,' said Dorian's dad, 'but we can only guess what else he's not told us. What did he say to you when he came back from Mowhaken?'

'Not a lot really,' said Natalie. 'He just said that he hasn't found anything because the whole place was rigged with police surveillance gear, so I believed him.'

'He told you the truth about the cameras but not about the rest,' said Dorian's dad in a grim voice, then, turning to Dorian, 'My son…'

'Yes,' Dorian continued. 'Do you remember that day when you met me and Derick in the biochem lab?'

'Yes,' answered Natalie.

'Did he tell you why we went there?' asked Dorian.

'No. Shit! I've never questioned him about it. I thought you were just helping him with his studies. That's it.'

'That's fair enough,' said Dorian, 'but did he ever mention "the file of the case of Mr Dauntwraith" to you?'

'What?!' screamed Natalie, completely taken by surprise. 'He never told me that he was in possession of such a file.'

Dorian gave his father one drawn, telling glance, then he carried on. 'Derick told me that on that day after he'd just met you and James, he went home and found his housemaid petrified and shocked to the core. She explained to him that someone had broken into his stepfather's office. When Derick went there, he found the file of the case of Mr Dauntwraith on the desk, but it was all blank inside. We went to the lab to try to see if it became readable under UV light, but it didn't. It was the last time I saw him. He only told that he really needed to see his grandfather, but I didn't ask him why because I didn't want to be too nosy at the time.'

'Oh, my God! What's happened then?' asked Natalie, feeling

both thrilled and terrified at the same time.

'You know the rest of the story,' said Dorian's dad, 'but what we think is that the file has been left there on purpose by no other than Simon Redeldrag himself only for Derick to find it. His housemaid described him very well when Derick found her at home after the intrusion had happened. I have no idea why Simon did that, but what Derick found at Mowhaken on that day he went there is the key to our riddle.'

'And I thought he's quite a nice, old guy — that Redeldrag,' said Natalie.

'He is evil recreated,' seethed Dorian.

'So that's maybe why Derick is so desperate to find his grandad now! That would all make sense now,' said Natalie.

'Not quite,' said Dorian's dad. 'I would give heaps of gold to find out how he's managed to dodge the security of one the most tightly guarded public crime scenes in the country. After all, it's not every day that someone tries to burn down a place like Mowhaken.'

'I've inspected that map thoroughly, and by God, there was nothing interesting there,' admitted Natalie. 'Certainly, I couldn't see any clues as for how to find the entrance to that floor.'

'Maybe there is something else,' murmured Dorian as if to himself, engrossed deep in his own thoughts. His father and Natalie looked at him curiously, clearly aroused by his words. Then he spoke again, this time aloud, 'I remember how he showed me that strange card he told me he'd got from James Niggle, who gave it to him when they met. A very peculiar thing if you ask me. I took it under the magnifying glass and then under the microscope when he was busy with the case, and found out that it's made of fractals. Then there are those little, colourful sombreros, they form an octagon when a line is drawn right through them to join them all up. I told Derick that there must be more to that card than meets the eye, but he wasn't particularly interested in it. I wasn't surprised why because he's got so much more on his mind at a time. Do you know what I'm talking about, Natalie? Have you seen that card with him or similar ones anywhere else?'

'Oh yes, I remember now!' said Natalie with the exhilaration of a school child. 'I saw James give it to Derick, but I've never seen it since, neither do I remember seeing similar things anywhere else.'

'Even as I thought,' said Dorian. 'Something tells me that this card of his may be an important piece of the puzzle. If you could do me a favour, please, and ask James if he's got more of them to spare.'

'Oh, my God, of course! Easy-peasy! You should have been a detective or a journalist like me with your brain,' said Natalie, 'and I thought you're just a thug the first time I saw you.'

Dorian and his dad looked at each other, perplexed, then they both burst into laughter at the same time.

'Is she always so flamboyant?' asked Dorian's dad, pretending he's whispering to his son, covering his mouth with an open hand.

'From what I've gathered about her, it's just the beginning,' muttered Dorian, even more quietly than his dad.

'What are you on about guys?! This is the way I am, don't you know,' said Natalie, whose face was blushing here and there. 'Would you please stop being silly, you two?'

'I told you so,' whispered Dorian towards his father, but then he stopped laughing at once as his face turned serious.

'Sorry about this, but I just couldn't help myself,' he apologised.

'That's fine,' said Natalie. 'It's your playground, so you play by your rules.'

'Thanks a lot, Natalie! I admire your sense of humour, but there's one thing about Derick that keeps eating me alive,' he proceeded with his deduction. 'It seems to me that he's lying about different things to different people. It's like either he's got some absolutely ingenious purpose to deceive us all at the same time but by different means, which I really doubt, or he's not fully aware that he's lying as it happens.'

As he said that, a dead silence fell in the room. His father gave him an utterly dubious look, shrugging his shoulders. He was of no help this time. Natalie suddenly winced and wizened within herself, trying to avoid the look from Dorian's eyes. She already had her own doubts but felt the stubborn reluctance to express her heart fully in front of two near strangers, especially when it concerned her newly found love, the man who took her heart by storm, the man about whom her heart was giving her more and more misgivings as days went by. She didn't tell them about the letter from his university and the conversation she had with him about it — she knew it would have brought even more confusion to the matter that was already confused enough, but upon hearing Dorian's words, her heart sunk to a new low. She was worried inside, but her feelings took the upper hand, blurring her judgement. She felt a very strong urge to say something to Dorian, but she managed to pinch her tongue at the last moment when she heard his father speaking.

'You may be telling the truth, son, but it really makes me wonder how brazen one has to be to go to the place like Windchain. If only I'd known his intentions back then, I would have knocked them out of his head. Now, he's gone off our radars.'

'Yes, it's hardly believable he's done that,' said Dorian, 'especially when he said it straight in our faces that it was just a "thought". I tried to contact him as soon as I put my feet on the home soil, but his phone was off all the time.' Then turning to Natalie, who'd gone as quiet as a mouse, 'Have you heard anything from Derick yet?'

'Ermm... yes. Today,' said Natalie in a low, hesitant voice. 'I received a text from him in the morning.' Then she took her mobile out of her handbag and showed them the message she got from Derick. It read: *"I'm on my way to Xuva. Lots of love! Derick."*

10
MARTY'S PAST

In Targhau lived Alexander Kubla. The country of Xuva it was: where sunless days were scarce and all the waterfalls, which numbered seventeen, ran into the bottomless, inland lake of Arkhel, which was of dimensions beating down many seas combined into one. Partially salty it was, drying up and dying a slow and sordid death since the urbanization kicked in for good in the country. Ilets of trash were drifting like ghost ships close to the shore where the salinity was at insane levels so that probably an elephant would glide with ease over its lurid, serene surface, which allowed to keep everything afloat, except for water life, which was only sustainable much further away from the coastline and only at certain depths where the saltiness wasn't so toxic. The lake owed its fetid, sulphury-yellowish glare to the gasses leaking and evaporating from the crevices at its bottom; shoals of dead fish were concentrated and trapped in murky, grimy patches that shone vividly sallow in the sun, swimming motionless to and fro alongside shallow coastal waters like menacing beads that formed one ghastly adornment of formidable size over the ever-shrinking brim of the lake, guarding ever so effectively from any unwanted entrances, which could stir up that oasis of peace and tranquility.

Sailing was virtually impossible due to the atrocious lack of winds since the country was crumpled up a good few thousand miles into the continent, sandwiched between mighty, high ranges of Alati Mountains from the north, north-east and north-west. Even then, the lake was indispensable for the transport around the country because of its central position and the size, which accounted for almost one-third of the land occupied by Xuvans. Its rectangle shape from north to south favoured the use of maritime transport, but that, in turn, was of no avail for its rapidly diminishing fauna and flora, yet no one seemed to care about it even slightly anymore: swarms of engine powered ships, boats, and other vessels were at sea since it was quite hard to fathom that Arkhel was a lake, burning fuel cheerfully and disposing of its waste products recklessly into the water.

Most of the towns and cities in the country were situated by the coastline. It was no different for Targhau, which in old Xuvan means *"Pirates' stash"*. Indeed, it was a major city of corsairs back in the day when the lake was flexing its muscles over a much larger area, and marine shipment of goods was the only viable option for traders and rulers because it was snuggled nicely into the near ideally circular bay, with a beautiful lagoon inside of it, which served as a perfect hideaway for all sort of sharpies, dare-devils, and buccaneers. It had been turned into a sandbank as the water of the lake regressed over the centuries, and nowadays used as a filthy landfill site. Derick felt that dry, putrid stench of the lake, similar to that of rotten eggs left sandwiched between two bricks in the wall that has been subsequently plastered over, as he was walking along the quay, admiring dead fish bodies that looked as though they were already fossilized, with thrill and horror on his face as if it was a major tourist attraction. He wasn't sure where he was going; he wasn't convinced that the place his feet had swept him off to was the one he really wanted to be. All he knew was that he had the pavement made of modern, neatly cut sett stones under his feet and the address to that man — from his uncle.

It wasn't the first time he was abroad all alone, no it wasn't, but he'd never been to the distant land of Xuva before in his life. Fortunately, he knew the language a bit from his extracurricular language club at his university, which now helped him a lot with navigation around the city. The streets were largely wide and clean in the city centre and around the public communication, but as he plunged deeper and deeper into Old Port, the oldest part of the city where old Alexander Kubla lived, the one original pirates' settlement, which still retained some of its nocturnal mystique and the elements of architecture that remembered the times of their notorious activity, such as those regularly round, black cobblestones he was walking on carefully, shaped like cannonballs, he felt more and more intimidated as if he was drawing nigh to the heart of terror. Filth and ruggedness were coming out of the gutters of every building he was passing by; he felt like walking on sea rocks and rugs. The wind was dead in those parts and it hadn't been raining for weeks, nonetheless, he could watch the spectacles performed by massive dust balls running after one other in front of his eyes as if no one ever bothered to clear those narrow alleys of all that mixture of sand and dirt, which he thought came from the process of the crumbling and parching of the lake bottom exposed to the sun as the water kept on deserting it.

Evening hour was drawing near when he lost sight of the Lake Arkhel, the surface of which was glaring vividly gleety in the setting sun as if it was a cauldron of boiling acid instead. He felt like he was on another planet momentarily, where the atmosphere was as clear as mud, dense, and hanging low, just above the tip of his head. Twilight was all but over when he came into sight of a large, open area that looked to him like a plaza from colonial times because he could catch a glimpse of the bell tower belonging to the local church before it went completely dark. There were four mighty yew trees growing in its centre, each one of them inside of their own circular enclosure; they were situated in perfect opposition at the ending points of a diagonal of a square, each one of them about five yards apart from the other. There were four low, wide, black benches between them, all of them facing its mirror image in perfect parallel too. On the one side of the plaza, to the right where he came from, there was something odd, though, something that didn't belong to such a vintage place as this, something that must have been a recent but not a modern addition. A grey, grandiloquent block of flats appeared in front of him. It looked like one horrid slab of cold concrete, with balconies sticking out here and there at regular distances from one another — a true monolith! Derick came closer to the floodlit object that looked as some sort of a "welcome sign". To his astonishment, the name and the purpose of that building were written there in many languages, including his own. It was… an old people's home. It was hardly believable as it looked like an ordinary yet quite "out of the ark" residential home, but this was what was written there, so he went ahead to check it.

He found the intercom very quickly, but he could only call the reception, which he did immediately. A female voice was heard on the other side after a short wait. It asked him for his name and who he was going to visit in his own language, although with a strong foreign accent. When Derick answered her shortly, she returned, 'What's the purpose of your visit?' He paused — and paused; he didn't know what to say, he wasn't prepared to share his secrets with strangers, so he waited. He felt like the sweat was covering his brow, but it wasn't the fear because he wanted to go on, but he didn't know how. Then he heard that voice from the intercom again, 'I understand. Please, come on in. Wait in the anteroom for someone to come for you.' Then the intercom went silent, but the door opened.

Derick found himself in an empty room with only a few high chairs at his disposal, but the smell of that place — it was just horrible! It stank like a crematorium or a mortuary. Admittingly, he'd never been to an old people's home before, but this was what that smell provoked in his thoughts. Suddenly, he heard the female voice from the tannoy; it was the same voice that he heard through the intercom. With a very strong Xuvan accent, she spoke: 'Doctor Davis, Doctor Blair, Doctor Davis, Doctor Blair.' Then the tannoy went silent. He was so surprised to hear so familiarly sounding surnames. Just a moment after that announcement was made, a woman entered the room. She was young and attractive, in a skimpy, slick uniform of a nurse, looking far from being foreign. 'Hi, I'm Doctor Jay,' she said in a soft, resounding voice with a full-on smile and presented Derick with her tender, exquisite right hand. He shook it reflexively with his but wasn't sure whether he should have kissed it instead; his face was flaring red like a brick. 'I will take you to Mr Kubla,' she said as if nothing happened. 'Please, follow me now.' Then she turned her back on him and left the room, leaving the door open. Derick followed her immediately.

He asked her where she was from, but when she ignored his

question, he understood that it was just another formality for her: she was there only to do her usual, automatic "meet, greet, be gone, repeat". Nevertheless, he couldn't take his eyes off her, and followed her up and up through the concrete staircase, heaving his cumbersome body on each of the countless, concrete steps like a blind one — that was how irresistibly captivating and beguiling her backside was. Only when she finally stopped on just another floor, as it seemed, Derick noticed that all the doors were painted snow white, but he thought he hadn't seen any numbers or letters on any of them. There were three doors on each storey inside that particular stairwell: one in the middle, one on the left, and one on the right. They stopped by the one on the left. She expressed her reluctance to allow Derick to see Mr Kubla at this time of the day by saying that it was very unusual that someone turned up for a visit so late, but then she permitted him to stay, turned her well-rounded back on him again, and made way downstairs after wishing him 'a pleasant stay'.

As soon as she vanished from his sight, Derick heard that hard yet exotic voice from the tannoy once again: 'Doctor Davis, Doctor Blair, Doctor Davis, Doctor Blair,' she repeated urgently, then all went silent again. Derick gave the door one odd, shy knock, but then he had a second look at it and wavered. A sudden foreboding pierced his head right through the middle. He was rooted to the spot momently, dithering — feeling drops of sweat on his brow. He knew he could still turn back, come home and live life. He swung his arm to wipe the wet drops from it, but suddenly it swerved. Then he heard the wham of his fist against the door, but nothing happened. Absolute silence. He felt soothing relief mastering his thoughts; his body relaxed, his limbs flopped happily on its sides, his eyelids were on a slide, lazily putting today to bed — he was ready to go home, but at this moment something quite extraordinary happened — the door disappeared into the wall in a split of a second in a way he thought he saw somewhere else once upon a time, even before his body could muster its levels of alertness to a respectable state of stately readiness, and afore he knew, a breathing space of a lengthy corridor was gaping at him with its mouth wide open.

Instantly, he was blown away by a pungent scent of gingerbread coming from inside, even though no one appeared in the frame for a while. He hesitated at first, but then a familiar lure of some tasty, baked concoctions with a clearly distinctive, zesty citrus twist acted as a bait and encouraged him to step in. After all, he was really hungry, having had hardly anything in his mouth all day. He walked in, carefully crossing the threshold of something that, at first sight, looked like a small apartment. Quite vintage it was, that abode: the visage, the atmosphere, the furniture; everything was pleasantly retro but not passé. Even an old, cathode ray tube TV in a wooden frame that he saw on the right when he stuck his head into the lounge after a few steps, inside of which the news was being broadcasted in Xuvan, belonged there exquisitely, and he felt that if it was moved even by an inch, lost resonance or got distuned, the universal ambience of this place would have come crashing down on him like thunder from the sky.

He didn't even notice when the door closed. It must have happened so quickly and quietly that he missed it or... Then he saw him — as he twisted his body and swung his head back, facing the door again, his profile slipped past his visual field. He was there, in the kitchen that was situated opposite the living room, but just a tiny bit deeper into the corridor, towards the outside door. He was absorbed by taking care of his baked goods which must have just come out of the oven, neatly moving each one along the hot surface of the baking tray, still wearing the thick kitchen gloves. He wasn't paying Derick any attention as if he didn't exist at all. Derick felt pellucid and light like the air for a moment, but at the same time he was incandescent too because it was so hot inside, maybe because of that oven, which was still open wide. Derick gave him a few timid waves of his right hand in an attempt to get noticed, but it didn't work — he put his gingerbreads away to cool on the kitchen countertop and whizzed past Derick on his cosmic wheelchair, nearly running him over. As he stopped in the living room, Derick couldn't tell whether that man really knew about his presence but prefered to ignore him, or what he saw was only a finely crafted illusion, a four-dimensional hologram — but suddenly the man spoke, and all his doubts melted away like snow in the spring. Derick knew he was spoken to because it was in his own language, with a nearly perfect accent.

'I'm surprised they let you in at this time,' said the strange looking old man, still without even attempting to raise his head and look at Derick. 'They usually prefer to have total peace and quiet and just watch.'

Derick didn't answer anything. He wasn't even sure he was looking at the right person. It looked as though he just met with yet another "stranger" who might know more about him than he could have ever suspected. His relaxing stance was rather intriguing to Derick, who gaped at him with ever-growing wonderment. On the other hand, his face was so furrowed, his hoary look so timeworn, as old as the hills, that he might as well not have given a damn about anything anymore and just taken things as they came along, without all the hassle, scurry, and hurry, so typical to those much younger than him. It looked like a surprise and the excitement of life had long but packed their bags and gone away to warmer lands on the other side where the sun shone brighter and the grass was greener; he was just giving the impression of one deprived of life, bereft of love, from whom all the light had faded away. Yet despite his drawn and droopy semblance, he was an exemplification of composure and contentedness as if his fate was all but sealed, his days were numbered, and he knew it all in a silent pact of acceptance that had always been within him. Without turning a hair and still without making eye contact with Derick, he continued with his speech, peering resolutely at the TV screen.

'What is your name, young man?'

'Derick McCrafty, sir.'

'Never heard of him. Hmmm, strange and foreign name it is,' he said in a manner resembling self-talk. 'Mmmm, my gingerbread must be ready now.'

As he said that he shot off from the living room, leaving the telly on; he jetted past Derick like a rocket, making him twirl like a spinning top. His supercharged wheelchair was an absolute monster; it could rival racing cars with its speed of acceleration, yet it was operated in a superbly smooth and effortless manner by those weedy, flagging hands of his, which turned on quite an impressive display of dexterity once hands-on on joysticks that were protruding modestly on the top of the armrests on each side of the seat. He got busy again with his aromatic gingerbreads, fervently shovelling them off the baking pan onto a humongous plate or a tray that looked like a bottom of a flying saucer, using a scraper. After all, he wasn't as lifeless as he looked from his face of a man who was doomed to eternal condemnation. The more Derick beheld him, the more he was falling under the impression that he must be somehow related to Marty: his appearance and eccentric manners reminded Derick of him so much he began to think that he must have just met another "forgotten" relative. Even the clothes he wore, they were so similar to those worn by Marty: an old-fashioned frock, underneath of which was a waistcoat made of tweed and a long-sleeved flannel shirt, tattered woollen trousers on suspenders were covering his legs.

'I'm Marty Deeprow's grandson,' said Derick, coming into the kitchen.

'What do you want?' was the question, spoken with acrid vehemence as soon as Derick mentioned his grandad's name.

'The truth,' answered Derick.

That was when their eyes met for the first time. Alexander Kubla beheld the grandson of his friend of old whom he mentored for many years before Derick was born. He gazed into Derick's deep brown eyes with profound poignancy, he knew straight away that this young fellow was going nowhere. There was a sense of belonging and the purpose radiating from Derick's face as if he had an inner feeling he was in the right place, at the right time at last. Without replying, he took the plate full of gingerbread and, after giving Derick a little nod, he buzzed off from the kitchen, then through the corridor and into the living room.

'Has he sent you here?' asked Mr Kubla when Derick came into sight.

'No, I came here on my own volition,' answered Derick.

'Are you entirely sure about this?' asked Mr Kubla, and his eyes glistened.

'Absolutely.'

'Sit down then, please,' said Mr Kubla with sudden calmness in his voice, 'and help yourself to some gingerbread. I know you're very hungry. I saw how you looked at them. I'm gonna make some tea.'

On his way back to the kitchen, Mr Kubla switched off his antique telly, which was still showing the news, the presenter babbling something in Xuvan — a language that was yappy and clattery, slightly harsh to the ear. While Mr Kubla was gone sorting out the refreshments, Derick took a new "task" of eating up as much gingerbread as possible very seriously. He tucked in with sheer enthusiasm. Before Mr Kubla returned, nearly half of the plate had disappeared in mysterious circumstances. When he looked at Derick's puffed and stuffed mouth, a smile appeared on his face. He looked rather comical in this situation — being in Xuva for the first time in his life, inside the strangest looking old people's home ever seen, in the apartment of the man he knew only by his name and from the one photo he'd got from Dorian's father, without even being sure that the old man next to him was the one he was after, scoffing his gingerbread as if it was his favourite grandma's cake with a carefree passion of a five years old having a lolly. Old Mr Kubla couldn't help remarking that Derick's grandad was exactly the same — the greatest "sweet tooth" he'd ever seen in his life who had that remarkable ability to "devour sweet foods with his eyes". Then he went on to describe Marty as a simply genial person and phenomenal scientist who couldn't quite handle his potent skills.

Derick had quite a ball listening to old Mr Kubla talking his ears off because he could just carry on gobbling up his gingerbreads, which were so unusually exotic and tasty that he just couldn't restrain himself and felt like eating them all at once. Mr Kubla turned out to be a fairly good chatterbox for someone in such a reverent age as his — even if he was deep into his eighties. It saved Derick having to waste his saliva on figuring out whether he was really the person in that photo of him and his grandad, which he now put on the table for Mr Kubla to see. He had a quick, sparing look at it before getting on praising Marty for his courage and brazen ingenuity for what he'd done. Surprisingly for Derick, Mr Kubla had no idea of his own existence until now, even so he was set on course to tell him more about his grandfather tonight than he'd heard from Marty himself throughout the entire summer. Mr Kubla guessed very quickly what Derick came for after the way he pronounced his grandad's name — with pride, mystery, and a pinch of horror; the name he hadn't heard for so many years now, the name which made such a recondite mark on his life and beyond. Mr Kubla's tale painted before Derick's eyes a completely different picture of Marty to that he was so accustomed to: a strange yet profound thinker, elusive, taciturn yet assertive as a spring, a true saucerful of secrets. Instead, he saw an unfulfilled dad and a lover, a man of courtesy and madness whose ungratified desires consumed his soul with time — a man lost in the ecstatic paradise of himself. More and more he was falling under a hypnotic realisation that all of his life was a myth of a real life, a mere fantasy. Derick's mind was riding on the wild wave of light radiating from inside as Mr Kubla's tongue was unwinding: he wasn't hungry anymore, he was listening with an eagerness and ardency of a staunch, hearty, unrefined bigot. Then Mr Kubla suddenly stopped and took the last, slowly drying piece of gingerbread from the deep tray, which looked like sweet sorcery when it was full, now lying bare and flaunting its emptiness.

'And how is he now?' asked Mr Kubla, still chomping the last bits of today's delicacies in his mouth. All his teeth were as shiny as pearls, flawless, glowing with immaculate whiteness as if he took care of its look with a compulsive obsession of a glamorous celebrity whose only desire was to appear on the front pages of glossy magazines.

'He's still hiding all the time,' answered Derick.

'Ahmm — yes,' mumbled Mr Kubla, staring at the grey void of his TV with an unusual level of arousal as if he had a sudden, foudroyant vision from the past.

'Have you met that man?' asked Mr Kubla, pointing at Maarten Burdent's face in the photo.

Derick had one long and broodingly apprehensive look at the printed snapshot of the photo from the website Dorian's father has recently found, depicting his grandad, Mr Kubla, and Maarten Burdent. He faltered, then he nodded with neurotic uneasiness.

'Tell me, what did you see?' asked Mr Kubla with stampeding fervency. He was one of the very few, perhaps only two people who knew Maarten Burdent's true colours: who he was, and more crucially, what was inside of him. The other person who held the secrets of his persona was Derick's grandad, but he was unceasingly afraid to even mention his name, and Mr Kubla knew exactly why. In fact, he was the only person alive who could still tell the truth about Derick's grandad's past and the events that had changed everything that had come to pass since then. Derick was truly in the right place at the right moment with the only right person who was more than thrice as old as him.

Mr Kubla, whose eyes had seen too many winters, whose soul was already knocking on heaven's door, wasn't showing Derick any signs that his spirit was nearly spent and his body was wasting away with every breath. Even in the very last hour of the twilight of his life when everything was waning, when all his vital strengths were ebbing away from him, he was still smiling at Derick, letting nothing that would divulge the deplorableness of his state out; absolutely nothing in this world had the power to blight his days by darkness. He was a "happiness within", and all the valours and virtues of his heart were independent of what was happening outside of him. His stolid and impassive stance allowed him to take in his stride everything that Derick was telling him, and honest he was, brutally honest — that young man who was speaking with such an inspiration as if his entire life was straddling over the razor-sharp tip of the blade of a sword, ever so hesitant, ever so frightened to lose its balance and fall over the edge or being cleft in two. He wasn't going to forget about anything, even the most minute and delicate of details, he was microscopic and shamelessly meticulous with recalling all the events from the time he glanced into the eyes of his grandad, the day that has changed his life forever. He was saying things as he saw them, as they were, with all his heart and soul.

Mr Kubla wasn't giving away any impressions of being surprised by Derick's astonishing account. He was unmoved, stone silent yet attentive and alert as a solitary soldier at his last briefing before a suicidal mission. He seemed to be like a falling leaf from an autumn tree, guided to whatever end, but in truth, he was hotting up inside like a volcano that was about to explode with all its devastating force, turning everything in its path to dust and rubble. Derick only saw like he was clenching his fists every time he heard Simon's or Maarten's names, for the reasons he was yet unaware of, but old and wise Mr Kubla could read from Derick's mouth with ease about what was coming, what kind of menace had been hanging in the air since the days Marty was in Xuva for the last time, some twenty-three years ago. He saw how his worst nightmares were unveiling themselves in front of his eyes. He saw how much Derick took after his grandad, he was a living copy of him: the same blood flowed in his veins, the same creative mind rushed him forward — headlong, fearless, and unstoppable, yet the same weakness had been marring his spirit from inside, and Mr Kubla saw it as plainly as the nose on his face, he saw it with such lucidity that made his hair stand on its end as Derick's story was drawing near to the present. Nevertheless, he'd shown nothing of his internal emotions and what upheavals his mind had been going through, other than occasionally grappling both armrests of his wheelchair. He knew all too well that he couldn't do anything to stop whatever had been brewing in that hot cauldron of fire from coming to a boil, and even more so to prevent Derick from being in the thick of it as it boiled over. He'd never had the power to command human hearts, especially those that were hungry still. He couldn't redirect Derick from the path of life that had spread itself under his feet, yet he comprehended now very clearly that he wouldn't be done in this world until Derick was sent back to finish what he'd started. His last song hadn't been sung yet.

Derick was like a burning candle right now; he was ready to absorb anything that was thrown at him in the way a black hole devours all the light that gets caught by its gravitational tentacles. For Mr Kubla, it was his moment to seize and own it; it was the time to sing his swan song, then freeze it and hold it — inside Derick's mind — until it turned golden, but he was fearful, fearful that his candle was burning brightest now for it was about to go out. He knew what was laying ahead of him. Now it was only in his hands to pave the way for him. He felt like the impalpable arm of fate was upon himself; he could feel the cold breath of the angel of death on his cheek without looking over his shoulder, he saw the shadow of an axe being wielded over his head, ready to swing back down at him anytime, yet he felt he was untouchable, that he couldn't be defeated, not before his task was over. He poised himself, set his seat to a reclined position and reposed before speaking, peering at him with his mellow, half-open hazel-orange eyes.

'We've managed to scarf down those gingerbreads well quick,' Mr Kubla remarked, slowly but kindly, glancing over the empty tray, then at Derick.

'There are some chocolates in the cabinet, just above the TV. You will need a key to open it. It's inside that silver stoup on the shelf, right above the cabinet,' added he when Derick didn't say anything.

'I know you're still hungry for sweet food, just like your grandad was,' Mr Kubla segued. 'He's never had enough of it; he's always been on the lookout for them like a hungry wolf, and you're the same... you're exactly the same.'

'Do you really think so?' asked Derick, savouring sweet mouthfuls — curious, unrestrained.

'It's clear as day to me,' Mr Kubla asserted. 'You see, when your grandad came to Xuva, it was in the time of great turmoil and uproar, but he could experiment there under a veil of secrecy. The ignobleness and notoriety of the "Old War" had given him the perfect opportunity to have full freedom of expression, far too much as it has turned out. He's always liked to be rather unexpected of character and appearance, working in places where those not very favourably oriented towards him would least expect him to be, that is under their very nose. He didn't like the Xuvan government at all; far from it — he despised it with every inch of his being, and mind you, he was quite conspicuous with it, even blatant I daresay. Yet no one was bothered by it all as long as everything was going according to their plan. They thought they had a bird in their hand, but he had his own designs in mind; he's always wanted to do something grand, something that would have changed the tides of that "stupid war" as he called it, and made a difference to people's lives around the world at the same time. You know, he's been one of those people who simply love to be pushed against the walls only to allow themselves to go through them in the end. But it was my own idea to invite him to come here; I was under the umbrella of the Xuvans' radicals at a time, and that gave me all kind of freedoms and the sense of omnipotence, an aura of indestructibility, and it was exactly what we studied — we've been simply asked to find how to make soldiers indestructible, how to increase their stamina, but what they were especially interested in was the resistance to… "a feeling of being hurt" as it was explained to us, neatly and cleverly, you see. I knew it from the start that it was something that was running deeper than the ocean trench that we've been asked to work on; something that had been clandestinely buttoned up, concealed, and crooked as a dog's hind leg.

'You must be now wondering how I know your grandad so well,' Mr Kubla diverted. 'I thought it was quite plain that he'd been lured here by the prospect of having no restraints on his mind, desperate to wander far and wide, feeling no shackles trammelling his stride, just the cool breeze of the mountain wind, like a bee to a flower blossoming with nectar. But it was a decoy of his, an absolutely ingenious one. As long as he was outright contemptuous of what Xuvans had been doing at the time, he knew that only a provocative outrage could provoke an attraction that could be used as a traction in a long run if you know what I mean. He nearly tricked the trickster, nearly outfoxed the trap by allowing himself to be trapped and feeling trapped, nearly.

'Believe me, he was like a wounded oyster there: rampant as a lion, curious as a magpie, stubborn as a mule; he'd gone far blazing through time — unrefrained, undone, unmade but failed to see that moth of death coming after him, fluttering and hovering around his head like a phantom until it was too late. Curiously enough, I had absolutely no idea of the existence of Maarten Burdent before I saw him with your grandad. He was such a grey area to me, a walking question mark, a dark wanderer of some sort I thought he was; he didn't belong anywhere, but he's been everywhere as far as the science goes. Truly strange specimen! He seemed to have knowledge about virtually everything, but not to a great extent in anything he knew about, which would have made him really useless if only he hadn't had that remarkable skill to join everything up into one big patchwork. It would have been madness, lunacy to operate in such an unseen and extraordinary fashion, except for it all made perfect sense it the end. It was all the same for him, as he's always been saying.

'I had a really hard time guessing what his original field was — if he had one in the first place, but I gave up after a short while, he's been such a hard nut to crack. I thought it would be any of biological science since he's funded and helped immensely with your grandad's coveted PhD in microbiology, but he was nowhere near as insightful as Marty, so it just kept me guessing, but I was the one to discover your grandad's talent. I bet Marty hasn't told you this, poor old man — he must have had so little time, but he didn't join in any university until he was well into his twenties, nearly the age you're at now because he was so poor, he had no money. He had to work hard to take care of his poorly parents and severely disabled older brother who died in the year your grandad decided to risk it all and pour all his prowess and strengths into science. Mind you, there were times when no public or academic funds were available for students, even for those best ones like your grandfather, who's raised a few eyebrows upon completion of his phenomenally difficult five-year degree as bio-science was in just three years, which was a feat completely unheard of at the time. The country was young, rising from the ruins and licking its wounds from the worst economic crisis ever seen in its history that left everyone and everything in limbo, rocking and hanging precariously on the slippery ledge over the jaws of an abysmal precipice, into which many greats of its time had fallen, dropping down one by one like a lifeless lump, with a silent thump, but it was not the case with your grandad; it was rather the opposite. He was the man of great resilience, and thus he found that he was at his best when the world around him was at its absolute worst. It nudged him a bit, but only slightly at first, that strange "relationship" he had with his surroundings, but he had no time to think about it as he had no money to carry on with his research. His parents were in an appalling state of being, suffering from unnumbered diseases, the names of which I can't even remember now, but there was something else, something that kept his head spinning and his mind distracted from the studies that he'd nearly forsaken it for good.

'He was on the brink of his own crisis, hardly making both ends meet when I heard of him for the first time. I'd already worked for the Xuvan government before the coup and the outbreak of the "Old War". I was a kind of a science attaché, doing my utmost to bring out the best brains in the continent and put them all together in one place. Tying the bonds in the area of science and education between our countries was of special prominence and was always very high on the agenda for the Xuvans. Probably you must be getting a picture why that was the case, given what has ensued in following years. That whole coup thing was just a one meticulously contrived hoax; it was a pure farce designed to draw international attention away from what they'd been really up to — that was a preparation for a war, a war that was unlike any other wars that preceded it, war that was waged under the political tables and inside of human minds rather than on a battlefield, but it is a completely new realm of reality, completely different story for another day, which we haven't the comfort of having now.'

As he finished the sentence, he sighed deeply and his body was submerged in an avalanche of heart-wrenching, gnawing pangs. He shrunk and coiled inwards in the way a hedgehog does when it senses danger, twinging in the seat of his wheelchair, turning upside down with the agility of a monkey, then overturning again with one spasmatic, twisting thrust, this time with both of his hands clinging to his chest, just below the throat as if he was about to choke. He just managed to point at the large, metallic, ponderous set of drawers that was standing tall and alone between the door frame of the living room and the wall unit. It was the one and only piece of furniture that didn't match with the rest of the interior. It was too modern, and it looked like a cheap-jack, plastic filing cabinet. When Derick looked inside, he found that it was full of papers indeed. He thought that it must have been his old academic stuff of some sort, but he couldn't see anything else apart from heaps over heaps of paper inside of each one of them. When he got to the bottom one and found nothing, he looked over his shoulder, scared to the bone, and saw Mr Kubla laying motionless in his wheelchair like a lizard basking in the sun, with his tongue playfully poked out at him. His left hand was still thrown above his head, with the index finger pointing up.

Suddenly, Derick sprang up in the air, rocketed up like grass after the rain, erect as an arrow he was standing on the tips of his toes, just being able to peer over the top of the cabinet where he spotted a small wooden stacker full of tiny ampoules laid flat like bottles of good wine. Quickly he grabbed one of them with one deft swoop of his hand and was back with old Mr Kubla in no time. Without thinking once, he poured the whole content into his mouth and waited, holding his pale, cold head in his arms. He put the empty ampoule on the table, next to the empty baking tray. When Mr Kubla began to choke, showing first signs of revival, and turning his head frantically before all his muscles regained sensation, Derick breathed out a sigh of relief. His spirit had been lifted from the gloom, his eyes were smiling, and he pricked his perky ears eagerly, ready to listen again.

Surprisingly, the first thing Mr Kubla uttered after being rallied was to urge Derick to put away the ampoule where it came from, on its original resting place.

'Thank you, son,' said Mr Kubla, laughing softly, 'you've just managed to extend my life for another few hours. Those little miracles keep my heartbeat up when it wants to come to a standstill. Normally, one of them nurses come here at specific

times and administers one of them to me. No one came because
you were here. They're not used to seeing me having guests really;
no one has visited me for so many years, I've completely forgotten
who it was. My dead sister, I think... I don't know. They always
keep those medications up there. I think they don't want me to live
forever, you see. I just forgot to tell you.'

Derick was standing with his rear side to Mr Kubla by that
back-stretching chest of drawers, pushing each of the eight fat
blocks back to the wall while Mr Kubla's big mouth burst with a
hail of words again. When Derick got to the last one, he decided
to have a cheeky look at some of the papers inside, just out of
curiosity. To his astonishment, each one he checked out bore the
titles of Mr Kubla and his grandfather, but Maarten Burdent's name
was nowhere to be found on any of them. He felt the impelling urge
to get down again and inspect the rest of the now-closed drawers,
but he slammed the top one forcefully instead so that it met the
wall with a clacking bang. Inevitably, his attention was drawn to
the segment of the wall unit that was right next to him. One of
the bottom drawers was slightly open, but what was sticking out
a bit from it wasn't clothes but pieces of paper. When Derick bent
forward over the drawer and peered down, he found it to be packed
perfectly with them to its very brim. As he straightened his back
again, he looked around with rekindled snoopiness. The walls had
a dazzling multitude of certificates, commendations, and other
honours mounted and pegged to their surface. Everything was in
snow white, uniform frames that were blending impeccably with
the sanitary colour of the wall. Derick was in shock not to have
spotted them before.

Mr Kubla was chatting away as if absolutely nothing happened.
He'd already forgotten that he'd nearly died, but may it be that
when one dances with death every day, a matter of life and death
becomes such a triviality as having meals at set times — after all
those years of avarous consumption. Derick was stunned how
quickly his body was rejuvenated after taking that medicine. He
had quite a challenge to make sense of all that what was coming
through and out of Mr Kubla's mouth: a pure, sincere stream of

words, ideas racing one another in patchy bandwagons in a train of thought, flying like magic saucers created from a hotchpotch of delirious mind. Even then he thought he could listen to him all night long.

He would have done so, perhaps without even saying a single word, but when Mr Kubla's voice began to falter and stumbled upon his own words before cracking completely, he knew it was his turn to speak.

'But what — what was I talking about before? I can't remember now. What did I stop on? I think... I've forgotten now,' Mr Kubla stuttered, looking perplexed at Derick.

'I think you were saying something about the outbreak of the "Old War" and that my grandad was distracted by something else,' Derick recalled.

'Oh, yes, yes!' screamed Mr Kubla when he'd finally got the gist and managed to establish a vital link between the stories.

'Something or rather someone, I should have said,' Mr Kubla stared anew. 'When I heard during one of the many diplomatic visits to your country at that time that one of the most promising talents had to give up further study due to "personal circumstances", especially when his area of interest was significantly overlapping with mine, I had to get to the bottom of it. I must admit that upon the first time we met it wasn't your grandad who captured my attention, but the person who he was with. You know who I'm talking about now, right? Your grandma, of course. We recognized each other straight away. I knew her through her father who was a high-rank police commissioner in the country and a great advocate and ambassador of education on a more personal level. He was a despot too; he kept her daughter very tight but took care of the business. Your grandma was in an elite police academy of Vernon just at the age of nineteen when her dad introduced her to me at some sort of "pseudo-charity event" for snobs. She was amongst the cream of the crop in the country, people destined for the upper crust. She was already known for her unreal abilities to recognize people and read their minds or something. I don't know, but I was absolutely shocked when I saw her face inside of that claustrophobic, dingy, cold place with a small baby boy in her arms. It was your father, Derick.

'I could only guess how those two must have met; neither of them ever told me how it happened. Long story short, it was a little bit more than a year from that moment when I saw her shining with pure innocence, stealing the show with her pearly hair and unadulterated genuineness, free from any concerns, young and naive, to seeing her expelled from the academy, disinherited, sorrowful, bent but in love; all because she'd fallen for the wrong man. It was a definition of mésalliance, their relationship, but a wrong way around, you see. They really had only each other and their baby boy, nothing else. Your grandfather was so mistrustful and reserved towards me at first, he thought I found them only to take away Maggie and her son from him. He was this way until I showed him my academic background and proved my pedigree was science for science's sake, not the politics of science. Then I did something I should have never done but still, I don't regret it. I saw him working eagerly overnights on his follow-ups like a restless soul, like an abandoned dog who is never ready to give up, no matter how many kicks he receives from his beloved owner. I took great pity on them; I just wanted them to succeed and let them prove everyone wrong. I gave your grandad the full access to my own academic world and beyond, then using my government funds and links, little by little I provided for his studies.

'We've become almost like a family in a very short time. I'd nearly seen through all of Marty's second tier degree when the news of that "bloody" coup stormed through the world. I'd become a public enemy in your country almost overnight. When the "good" old Xuvan government was overthrown, and their alleged lies had been exposed by those young power-thirsty radicals who were in fact just muppets, I'd been branded a spy from a dignitary in an instant. They would have probably locked me up for good and tried for treason or similar nonsense if it wasn't for your grandma who'd bravely stolen some documents from her dad's offices and smuggled me through the border seamlessly. Thank God everything was so chaotic back in the day. To pull off such an audacious, insolent escape would have been a mission impossible nowadays.

'When I was back to Xuva, I was thrown into the underground world of political escapists with others who'd been branded "enemies of the state" before being captured by the extremists who took the power in the country only to be allowed to work on everything I'd been doing so far, with the only difference being the utmost secrecy and total seclusion from the world, which was provided by the mighty Altai Mountains. I was part of the "roots" of "The tree under the mountain" as those formerly in power, now cast out and ostracised called themselves, working on projects supporting and supplying the new political fractionists with means to win the war that ensued.'

'"The tree?!"' asked Derick, whose mind was shining with an insight as the name rang a bell.

'Yes, "The tree,"' Mr Kubla repeated, 'but you must understand that I worked for the same people who hired me once before, although officially I was in the hands of the new establishment. It was all a finely crafted imposture. In reality, all those raging bulls up there were just an army of pawns, bred and kept at bay only for that one moment in time when they were released to wreak havoc on the surface like a deadly, incurable disease to give the time for the "oldies" to go off the radar into the underground, or more specifically, under the mountains from where it all has been steered from then on — after all the rooks and queens had been safely castled.

'Those events marked the beginning of an over a quarter of a century hiatus when I've been cut off from the world and your grandad. We've not seen each other for over twenty-five years, believe me or not, until he came to Xuva himself. They wanted Marty, they wanted him so bad, I couldn't comprehend it; it made me even jealous sometimes, but when it was made clear to them that we had a common history, they used me as bait to get him around here. I felt wanted and important again, and I could fulfil the promise I made to him before I had to leave your country or be removed by force or at worst, be captured and imprisoned, that one day we would join forces to undertake a grandeur scientific project.

'He must have put the resources I supplied him with to very good use because when he arrived, his renown was undisputed, he was untouchable. Of course, neither him nor myself mentioned that we'd been drawing from the common source. As far as microbiology was concerned, he was world class in his own right. I'd been making a switch from my original fields of molecular biology and nanochemistry in favour of fledgeling science of biogenetics or bioevolution — as I preferred to call it, that was already on a rampage at that time, but we quickly found a common language, and your grandad took to new ways of science with a nimbleness and ardour of an ant building an anthill. I couldn't say the same about his buddy or a "friend" he brought with himself, out of the fog, as it seemed. Mr Burdent had Xuvan's government warrant, though, so I couldn't really say anything. He was just loafing about all days, filling the corners, not really talking to anyone, just peeking at everything with marked nonchalance as if all the innovations and excitements surrounding him, teeming with pioneering novelties was a small matter for him, a mere blop in the sky, a vague blip from out of space. He was making an impression of one always unsurprised by anything and anyone, as though he was either so ignorant and self-righteous or… knew it all already. I didn't know, I was just a fish in the bowl there, but what was really annoying about him was his total lack of acknowledgement, resembling a pure contempt and bare, obnoxious reservation, although it was his lumping, maundering freedom of movement as if he belonged nowhere that was vexing me beyond everything else.

'Marty liked him, though. He revealed to me how he'd been an invaluable help and ally in getting his PhD done and dusted, especially on the material side. He's always talked about him as if he was my silent understudy whom I'd passed the torch of support and protection over your grandad's fate to, even if he knew it clearly that we'd never met prior to his arrival in Xuva. Their relationship was an intricate and puzzling one to me because they were both like brothers in arms really, nearly like twins, although of completely different hearts and souls, and I wanted to find out what it was that made them tick so well at all costs.

'Maarten Burdent's incessant and growing interest in Marty was an obscure and indiscernible one at first when we were all so rapt, engrossed, and bound blinded in the yokes of our scientific venture. He and Marty believed that evolution wasn't governed by any intelligent design, except a chance; a simple probability was what ruled the whole aspect of it. We thought that by altering probability we could alter evolution. This was when the multidisciplinary insight of Maarten Burdent and the pure genius of your grandad came to interplay, and it was revealed to me that they complemented each other perfectly like two pieces of the puzzle to make a jigsaw complete as one. They'd been making each other whole again, but it was about the time when your grandad started to talk about the death of your dad, some months, maybe even the whole year after he'd landed in Xuva when I noticed a shift in his behaviour. He became secretive, dwarfy, and surreptitious in his endeavours, he began to treat our shared and common enterprise in the name of science as his own crusade, a challenge of his intent and intellect as if he had something to prove to himself and the whole world. He'd thrown himself into the deep water with a passion for creation like a rutty, horny rabbit. Steam was gushing out from his ears as though his brain was a red, hot locomotive engine. Maybe it was his chance to shine, he might have been thinking at the time, the one he'd been waiting for all his life, and now he had the whole world under his feet — he wanted to use it all: his knowledge and abilities he had to create a universal cure — I know he had only good intentions in this mind, he really had, for all the woes and agonies one have to suffer throughout their lifetime. He wanted simply to eradicate it: the pain and anguish you feel when you're alive, he wanted to make everyone feel alive without the necessity of being conscious of the pain of being alive — that was his dream.'

'But why did you say his behaviour started to change when he told you about my dad?' asked Derick, touched by the mentioning of his father.

'It was already changed,' answered Mr Kubla, 'and had been changing as the days spent under the mountains turned into weeks and weeks turned into months. I don't think he originally planned to stay there for that long. Maybe it was a trap for him, and I truly think it was, but I couldn't just see through those impenetrable, dense brows of that Maarteen Burdent what he was really up to.'

'What do you mean? I still don't think I fully understand you. What kind of secrets was Maarten Burdent hiding from you?'

'Let me just continue, and you will touch the truth as it spreads under your very feet,' said Mr Kubla with his usual calmness. 'It's very important, believe me.'

'I know it is,' replied Derick, 'I can see it in your face.'

'I know you can,' said Mr Kubla, and smiled at Derick. 'Your grandad could feel certain things before they happened too, but he would only tell me nibbles of his past after we'd been reunited, and only spontaneously — as if he wasn't truly himself when he was talking about his inner feelings and doubts. He seemed to be doing it from another person's perspective — just like his own problems and fears belonged to someone else. It was only after I'd found out how deeply insecure he was, which was in the end cruelly exploited by the one he trusted beyond measure, I could apprehend with a new stark insight how much under Maarten Burdent's influence he was.'

'But why? How?'

'Because Maarten was everything Marty wasn't: caustic, crude, contemptuous, slimy, and rotten to the marrow, but at the same time efficient, effective, and highly, highly addictive. Yet he had one big flaw — he wasn't very good at hiding his true colours, which was in the end compensated by your grandad who's become pretty closed off and hard to get to, even more so than many years ago when I first met him. They were both like fire and ice, completely different, poles apart. That may be the reason why they worked together so well as if they were merged into one, like a couple in an old, good marriage, except it wasn't old, neither was it good. It was just jealousy and false, fruitless admiration your grandad had for Marteen and his deepening sense of mythic paranoia he was falling into as he was trying his absolute, inventive best to find the way to become like him without losing his own identity, and tried to attain it in his usual way — by being creative.

'I can see your face now, Derick,' Mr Kubla broke out, 'it's a plain of cold winds of frown and confusion before the arrival of a whirlwind, but you must know that Marty was a severe mythomaniac, although he might have never been fully aware of the scale of his condition until it was fully exploited by his "doppelganger".'

'Maarten?'

Mr Kubla just nodded his head slightly down and carried on in a murmuring, stifled voice, 'I was too blind to see what was brewing under my very nose because I felt uncomfortable that Marty had been stealing my show by his pure doggedness and perseverance in his endeavour of finding a remedy to save the whole world from the feeling of pain, but as I often say that it takes a fool to be a genius, he had his dark side, and we're yet to pay the full price for his mistakes. I only regret that it was far too late when I managed to doze off from my slumber of awe and envy, and only due to the mistakes made by myself and someone who was responsible for assigning the right people to their tasks.

'I remember that day very well since it was in the middle of the winter, probably the worst I've ever seen. Everything froze off and everyone was walking wrapped up so thick that it was nearly impossible to talk face to face. Almost all the equipment, which was then considered a cutting-edge, had gone out of order — only walkie-talkies were available. It was shocking, shockingly cold, at least minus seven hundred I reckon. I remember when I heard that voice for the first time because it left me peculiarly surprised, the situation that was just resultant of the fluky concatenation of events, a pure coincidence, I must tell you.'

'Coincidence?' murmured Derick.

'We were a solid and organised unit down there, under the mountains, like an ant colony: we didn't know one another very well, but we were well aware of our roles and had a tremendous sense of belongingness as a whole, and not often, very rarely someone from the outside world was allowed. It was just your grandad and Maarten that came to join us after the formation of the "Tree" until I heard that unfamiliar voice through the walkie-talkie on that day, telling me that I was supposed to work with a group of people I was unrelated to, led by a man called... Simon who was on the course to join us later, in the zone I wasn't responsible for.'

'What?!' asked Derick.

'She didn't even bother to reveal her name when asked,' Mr Kubla rambled on. '"What an insolent wench she was", I thought at the time but ignored her call, thinking it might have been a silly mistake or a bad joke, you know, but when she pestered me again in an hour or so, reminding me not to be late, I flew out of my office like an avalanche, forgetting even to put the goggles on my nose, which got frostbitten and hard like a stone by the end of the day. I only remember the pain now. I was about to call Marty about her as to hear someone sounding so unfamiliar and flaunting was disturbing for me and my highly organized world, but I completely forgot to realize that all lines had been shut off due to the extreme cold — this was how much that voice on the radio began to nag me when I heard her again and left my office to find out what was going on.

'She turned out to be a distant relative of the old Xuvan vice chancellor, only very lately appointed as a "first-class scheduler", basically the one who was responsible for setting up and organizing all the "high importance" operations, but I had no idea that it was your grandad who was behind all that disarray, in the eye of the storm. I simply confused the corridors to the zones when I rushed out of my office, my nose started to tickle and get red instantly from that sub-zero temperature, and that walkie-talkie — the signal was so harsh I had to keep it at the distance of a foot from my ear just to avoid getting a headache. I think I jumbled up the numbers she was rattling through the radio to me; I just wanted to know her name really. I didn't pay much attention to anything else as far as I remember.

'I dashed through a mile-long tube that we called "worm tubes" because they were all exactly the same, drilled by some monstrous earthworm inside and under the mountains. They were straight corridors linking up perfectly spherical, enormous chambers that we called "halls" because they were the main cells of the whole unit. Each chamber had offices, labs, and other amenities that were linked to it by small "mini tubes". Everything was either spherical or slightly elliptic. Each chamber with its surroundings constituted a single zone, and there were thirty-four of them in total, so you can imagine that this whole "mountain nest" wasn't built overnight, but it had its very purpose rooted in the minds of people who were operating it from the mountain roots.

'When I emerged out of "the tube", the first thing I saw was the big black and white, large screen, resembling today's jumbotrons, mounted on the man-made, granite stalactite, with the zone number and operations taking place in surrounding labs on it and people's names assigned to their tasks. You would see it as one colossal, blurry, unintelligible spreadsheet nowadays, but it was just nothing but a big schedule and the space below the screen was often a point of meetings. Every zone had a scheduler assigned to it. You could usually find one hustling and bustling in the space underneath the screen, telling people where to go and amending things remotely if necessary. I had no clue I was in the wrong zone because my attention was drawn to the ceiling which was more than a hundred yards above my head as I looked up at the screen. All the tubes and pipes were frosted over, they looked sinister but spectacular at the same time. It was a white sensation that was growing by the hour from above as if the coldness was permeating even through the hard granite of mountain rock. The icicles that had formed were horizontal, not vertical that you normally see tapering from the roofs of the houses. Everything had tubular or spherical shapes, just like it was a miniature model of our base laid down horizontally. It looked just magnificent; I was mesmerised by it, but then my walkie-talkie buzzed yet again, and I felt like all that cohesive, dense ice cap was coming down crashing through the walls of my brain.

'"Dr Kubla? Is it you over there?" she asked, ostentatiously. "I see you're late for your appointment."

'The funniest thing at the time was the feeling as if I heard her twice as she spoke. When I took my eyes off the screen, I noticed the figure of a very short woman, swaddled in a thick, long shawl, wearing pink goggles, pink fluffy winter earmuffs and rambling on some meaningless string of numbers into her walkie-talkie that I could hear through my own receiver. It turned out to be my assignment number at length when I looked up again at the table above my head. Then I realized I found myself in the wrong zone. Without hanging up, I approached her so quickly that she wouldn't even notice me.

'"Dr Kubla, are you listening to me? I repeat, did you hear me?" she asked repeatedly.

'"I'm Doctor Alexander Kubla," I announced with grandiloquence, as though I was the king of the world and pressed the button to hang up. She turned her peachy face to me and smiled innocently, blushing all over. She was beautifully sweet like a cherry in the summer, her skin was silky and smooth like the finest china porcelain. I was stunned by the sight of someone so young and cute here as she looked no more than twenty years old, clearly out of place like she was a ripe apple that had fallen off the sun-pampered tree into the cold ground of its own shade. I knew my cheeks were growing rosy immediately but felt like the aching, glowing redness of my nose was overshadowing everything and carried on, "What is your name, my dear? I don't think I've seen you before?"

'"Mir... Mirandelle, sir," answered she, but not without an effort, tapering both her hands on her lap, joining legs at her knees and blinking at me confidingly. I noticed she had a slight speech impediment right away but didn't ask about it at once, feeling rather curious to see such a young soul trapped inside of that "last outpost of progress" for the entire humanity. Later on, I found out that her tongue had naturally grown too short, which was rather an odd occurrence, but made her occasionally bumbling and quacking with words sounding limp and obtuse.

'"Tell me, Mirandelle," I carried on, "what kind of shambles is our scheduling system in today?"

'She looked at me with a rookie-face, full of muddiness, but answered with an acrid candour, "I cannot see you signing in to the zone thirty-four in my register. Have you got lost?"

'"Nothing of that kind," I denied. "Who said I've got to be there anyway? It's miles away."

'"Simon said," she replied, as frankly as a bride-to-be.

'I squinted my eyes and looked hard at her fair yet resolute face, now without being foolishly courteous. Then, I picked out a solitary character passing us by at close range, rambling very unsteadily, taking no heed of us, neither of the vast space of the hall and nearly colliding with us. I saw him strolling along with a bottle of spirit in his hand, supposedly to fight off the ultracold air, but what brought my mind at attention as he was performing his near miss was his badge, specifically its number, which I caught a glimpse of out of the corner of my eye. I used my semi-photographic memory to figure that exactly the same badge number belonged to someone who was purportedly assigned to the zone thirty-four with me at this precise moment. I turned my head towards Mirandelle, who was now peering at me with an earnest curiosity of her comely, bountiful aspect and asked, "Who's Simon?"

'"So you don't know?!" she exclaimed, frowning at me as though it was me who's just arrived.

'"He's one of the lead researchers there, and he says that one day his work will contribute to saving people from hurting."

'Just as she said that, Marty's face appeared in my mind. Her brief description described him perfectly — his attributes and ambitions. But that name? At this point, I remembered I was going to see Marty today, what I'd completely forgotten about, such an ill-fated frozen off day it was, and my nose was already bony and frail. I took the glove off my right hand and peeped at my watch, which was completely frozen too since it was still showing eight in the morning; then I got the time from the big screen, and it was already past the time we were supposed to meet. Thankfully, his office was only one zone ahead of where I was, so I made my way without delay.

'"Where are you going?" asked Mirandelle.

'"Come with me, please. I'm going to introduce you to a man who is all about saving the world."

'We disappeared into the "worm tube" and before long we were at the very doorstep of Marty's office. It was past midday, and the temperature was plummeting even more with each passing moment. Every waking hour was dreadfully painful for my face, yet I had no heart to ask for even a second of relief by imploring Mirandelle to lend me her goggles, even when all my conscious mind had succumbed to that imperious, petulant urge. I simply couldn't afford to let the frost spoil her impeccable, velvety complexion. I just had to fool myself into thinking that I'm impervious to cold — somehow.

'Marty shared his office with Maarten as the couples did, you know, but your grandad's compatriot was nowhere to be seen that day. He'd just evaporated into thin air. When we reached the door of Marty's office, I gave it a few hefty, rapping knocks, but quickly noticed something strange, like an aura of oddity about the situation. Normally it would have taken ages for your grandad to answer any calls: be it his wife, his bosses, or even God almighty — he was notoriously sluggish and stubbornly reluctant to attend to anything or anyone when he was in a state of escape into his own world of fantasies — I mean studies, and ten out of ten times he was, making him a painfully hazy and moony person, extremely difficult to catch adrift, but not this time. As soon as I took my hand off the door, his dreamy and usually dogmatic voice sounded invitingly "swishy-swashy" as you youngsters would say, and he was saying something along those lines: "Come on me darlin', you're bein' a way late for a whole lot of schooling. Come in here, I need some cooling."

'I stuck my frozen, frostbitten face through the door, feeling really mesmerised by those words, but what I saw struck me right in the head: the whiff of hot air and pungent, musky perfumes came out winding and coiling around me like trailing ivy, climbing and enslaving me, intoxicating my body through the nostrils and mouth — I felt my cold face hardened like steel and then breaking into pieces, but I was too benumbed by the sight of Marty wearing that meretriciously flattering hawaiian shirt and holding a glass of cocktail to cringe in pain I felt so deep and sharp. I was too benumbed and enthralled.

"'Marty?!" said I, forgetting I had that pretty, short girl peeking from behind me on her toes, for a moment. When he saw my face, his drink dropped, the glass shattered, the bass sounded low — the novelty had worn off. In came gravity, snapping him back to reality, turning air to stone, frozen solid and cold. Starkness was in his eyes, he was staring beyond me — she made a step in front of me, and I saw her face naked and hard. "Why is he calling you Marty? Do you know him at all?" asked she, feeling shaken but not stirred. Marty was speechless, now trembling from cold, I turned the radio off, the party was over, yet the dice were rolling still even now the tryst was shot off — the birds were knocked off their perch, grounded but still staying upright. I was so confused about the situation, feeling like the whole day was seriously going out of my hands; my whole face was suffering badly. I stepped in and shouted in her poor face Marty's name, position and all the important facts from his life, leaving her in no doubts that either she came for the wrong guy or there was something I was still unaware of. She got the shakes from my outburst, but she was a true handful, she vented on Marty instead of paying me attention before shaking the dust or, in her case, ice off her feet.

"'You confounding, blithering liar!" she screamed like a bat. "Who do you think you are to spit all that bullshit straight in my throat?! Better back to your country before you choke on your own self, you alien! I really thought you're different, but you're like everyone else. What a sucking looser!"

'I didn't even try to stop her as she bombed through the door, slamming it back against the book cabinet, making some of them fall from their shelves into the puddle of glass and booze. I just stared at Marty who was having a meltdown right here, right now, astounded and stupefied. I wanted answers, all I cared about at that moment was a hint of credibility, a pinch of warming plausibility, so I sat Marty back on his chair and rolled it back to the wall, next to the electric heater that was already working overtime.

"'What sort of cheek must you have to tell that poor girl all those flimsy fibs about yourself?" I asked, still keeping calm, despite Marty's inaptitude to render anything even remotely resembling logic or reason. "Did you know she's a relative of old Malachi, the former vice chancellor of Xuva?" I kept on asking. When Marty, at last, decided to open his mouth, I was shocked even more by what he said than by anything else that happened before on that day. It was the first time I sighted him falling into lunacy. It's strange to see how so many exceptionally gifted people must pay the price for their blessing with a curse. If you were immortal, for instance, you would have lasted through eons to yearn for the coming of death, which would have appeared as a gift to you, something you've been deprived of unjustly at birth, after you've grown weary of the world through the immeasurable passage of time spent living, overpowered by the thought that you cannot escape from your own self, condemned to be as you are for evermore. Marty wasn't the only person I've known who didn't want to be what he was — I think it's quite a common trait of us, humans — but he was the only one who despised that "inability" of human beings so openly that when he spoke, I saw him naked but terrifyingly unable to tear the burning skin off his bare bones, to shed it like reptiles do.

"'She's like my Mary," he coughed up at length, with a gasp of torment.

'He meant your mum of course,' Mr Kubla explained, looking watchfully at Derick. 'He was so close to her; he loved her like his own child. I don't know whether he secretly desired her, but probably yes, he did. On that day he confessed to me that he'd always been obsessed over having a daughter, a gift Maggie had never been willing to give him as she didn't want to have more children after Nathan's birth because it was so painful to her that she nearly gave up her ghost to him at birth. She was too scared to live and suffer through it all ever again — the pain and fear for her life had burnt and left an unhealable scar on her young mind. Marty told me once that on that day when he saw his wife nearly dying from pain in front of his eyes, he decided to set off to wage a war on pain, which he was determined to win by getting rid of it from his life forever and then eradicate that most undesirable feeling of all feelings from the world. The more he tried, the more pain was coming through his body and dispersing in the air until he'd lost control even over his own actions.

'He blamed himself for the death of your father and the subsequent departure of Mary from his life, despite the fact that it was her idea to go to the mountains that summer when it happened. He just couldn't bear it within himself that he was unable to dissuade them from going. On the contrary, it was his own voice of encouragement that tipped the balance in favour of the mountain trip and broke Nathan's stubborn reluctance to go, who himself wasn't born mountaineer at all, unlike Mary and your grandad. Mary has never forgiven him for that, it was just too bitter for her still growing body and mind to lose her beloved one at such a young age — she shut her heart for him and she's never revealed she was pregnant with Nathan. Henceforth, he lived on — bearing the ever so painful and heavy burden of eternal blame, although not fully justified as you can see. I truly believe that if your grandad had never found out that you're his grandson, you would have never met him. Was it all serendipity or ill-fate? I think you may already know the answer.

'The simple fact that this young girl, Mirandelle evoked in Marty such strong feelings and memories of Mary was nothing short of eye-opening, to say the least, but the way he tried to get to her heart was an absolute game-changer. It wasn't until that one very cold day under the mountains when I found out about your grandad's second son as he began to divulge his life's hidden secrets, feeling like falling to pieces.'

'So, you know about Shean?!' asked Derick, breaking in, agitated by the return of still fresh memories of Windchain.

'Yes, I know about him,' said Mr Kubla.

'Why has he been jailed for so long then? Maybe you can tell me more?'

'Please, let me carry on with my story, and we will get there,' answered Mr Kubla, steadily yet with caution.

'But I want to know why he's still there and, why no one seems to do anything to get him out,' Derick insisted.

'Didn't he tell you?' asked Mr Kubla.

'Wow! I heard from him that my grandad tried to kill Simon, but he's failed in doing so because it was like... like killing a better image of him I think, but he didn't tell me why he wanted to kill him in the first place.'

He paused as he said this. Few droplets of cold sweat appeared on his brow. He was staring at Mr Kubla with his strained eyes that seemed to forget how to blink.

'Wait a minute! Were you not just trying to tell me my grandad was calling himself Simon?'

'Yes, that's right' said Mr Kubla, calm and sedate as usual.

'I'm confused now,' returned Derick, somewhat irked with himself. 'Have I missed the point?'

'I don't think so,' replied Mr Kubla, 'because we haven't reached it yet, but you must comprehend now that Simon Redeldrag and Maarten Burdent is the same person.'

Derick went grave-silent, struck by lightning he was, caving in his armchair, he had no words to describe his state. Only he knew what was going through his mind at this precise moment when the revelation came to light and hit the bloodstream hard and fast. The key had always been flowing in his bloodstream. Mr Kubla paused at this moment to take a breather. He took a long look at the photo Derick brought with him, waiting for him to collect his thoughts and bring his mind up for the rest, but when the silence grew deep and vociferous, he decided to speak first, seeing Derick was still lost for words.

'Look, that photo was taken the day after I met that girl, Mirandelle, and ended up in your grandad's office to witness him having a monstrous breakdown I've never seen before. Do you know what is written under that photo, right? It was the last official photo of Maarteen Burdent indeed. It was one of the very rare occasions when they let us out, only because nearly all the equipment was dysfunctional due to the severely low temperature inside, and everyone had a break. We went out, outside of our mountain base and took a few pictures together. A short time after that photo was taken, Maarteen Burdent disappeared, but the truth is that he hasn't, ever. You saw him, didn't you?'

'Didn't you?!' shouted Mr Kubla and smote his hand fiercely against the table in one fell blow, making the glass clink and crack, the baking tin made a clank and fell on the floor upside down. Mr Kubla hewed his hand down so quickly and vehemently that Derick didn't even have time to blink, his head only swagged in a slight nod of silent, uncomfortable, heavy avowal.

'Sit now and listen,' said Mr Kubla with downward brusqueness in his voice that sounded strict and unforgiving. 'Your grandad never happened to take his time to look around himself, always been so bent forward and inside as if he had a black hole in his belly button, sitting happily behind the curtain of his own event horizon, but you will, you will take your time.'

'But what has it all to do with me?'

'Everything. Everything because you're just like your granddad. I can see it in your eyes; Simon could see it too from the beginning.'

'What do you mean by that?'

'He's always known you're Marty's grandson, most likely from your stepfather. He's been keeping tabs on you with every breath you've been taking since your childhood. I know how you're probably feeling like right now — like a player, a shooting star in a blockbuster movie, the scenario to which someone has written for you and slipped it under your pillow at night while all of you were asleep, more than two decades ago. It's in your blood now, the life you've lived, the air you've breathed, and the moves you've made. I know you're feeling like sliding off but lie down instead and hearken carefully.

'Your grandfather has sacrificed his love — then he flew to Xuva. He was like a mountainside there — he was high, but low he was too and lonely. When that young girl came down there, he went berserk. Perhaps, she was just a trigger to unleash what had always been lurking deep inside of him. Maybe Maarten knew it all from the start, he just wanted to make sure? Perhaps, even more so Marty was under his spell, he was impressed by his ego, then he's created "Simon" in his mind, in Maarten's image and deceived himself into believing he could merge his own and Maarten's personality into one being.

'He could only do so by deceiving others. His escapism from himself had only dragged him down and down into the deepest, darkest corners of his soul where the trap had already been set and hidden from him. I truly believe it was Maarten's device to allow Marty to confabulate his life to the point of no return. Thus, I have learnt about his "perfect" alter ego — Simon, whose only existence bore any signs of traceability in the minds of people deceived by Marty, like Mirandelle, whom he subjected to the glare of his new persona with an aim to seduce her I deem, with a striking accuracy. She fell for his supposedly flawless, straightforward, misanthropic superiority, a disposition of a man that has overcome himself with the power and charm of his beautiful mind. Only a fluky matter of coincidence has stalled him in his actions — when upon responding to the knock on the door in the cold he saw my face instead of hers. Marty himself claimed he was never aware of his undoings unless imploded, pushed back to the wall. Perhaps, he was right about his unawareness, although I was always sceptical to believe him — things have just fallen too quickly since that day even for me to find my own bearings.

'I was too engulfed with the unplotting of Marty's mythomania, too exasperated, but at the same time too enticed by his revelations about the birth of Shean, Marty's bitter disappointment he wasn't the female offspring he'd always desired to have, his inability to find even a spark of love for him that bordered with nefariousness, and his obsessive fear of Maggie, should she ever find out... He was compulsively pedantic in covering it all up with spider webs of lies, his scrupulous attention to separate both worlds of his life that invariably and, alas, irrevocably led to his light being snuffed out by his own shadow. He has never had enough courage to face the truth, he could only escape from it by creating the alternative "truths" about his life. What he thought was his greatest ability and a gift from the gods was in truth his worst curse since he could never leave the form — he could only go from one to another. His spirit of creativity eventually overpowered him: a runaway form himself, from all the pain and the cross of blame he bore on his shoulders for missing the mark, getting unceasingly heavier and heavier, with an ever so shrinking margin for error brought him here, deep under the cold mountain slopes where he could repent his sins and plot his second coming as a redeemer of fates, bringing forth a salvation from pain. "Simon" was his answer — a ruthless, relentless, outspoken, and seductive visionary who led a "secret group of scientists" on a crusade for eternal happiness, whose esoteric chemistry would in time work magic for all humankind. He went for broke at it, losing himself completely in the pursuit of that "holy grail" of his.

'No wonder he had Mirandelle like a canary in the cage, ready to take her deep into the mines of his ravishing mind where he could praise her delights unbound, hearing only their own echoes reverberating against the stone silent, impermeable granites. She was just like Mary to him indeed, but younger and more attractive, he simply couldn't resist her. He nearly ran after her when brought to tears after images from his past had become so revealing he couldn't bear them anymore. I had no strength to stop him, the pain inside of him was too strong. I remember, I only said, "She would cause you more pain than you could ever imagine."

'This has stopped him right by the door. His hand was on the knob when it got suddenly numb, and he stalled on his way out. I watched his head moving slowly to the left, then again to the right like a pendulum while his mouth and eyes were opening wide gradually; his complexion was getting paler as if he was being filled with an outburst of strong, flashing light. I understood then he had an insight. He grabbed me by my hand and threw me out of the office. His grip was too strong; he ran, and I ran after him. He wasn't in hot pursuit after Mirandelle, far from it, he was off to the main lab, two zones ahead of us. I saw his craziness like the palms of my hands. He was changing moods like socks and completely enslaving himself in them as if he was a fast-acting amnesiac. I couldn't chase him all the way as my sore, frostbitten nose had finally got the better of me when I felt something running out of it. It was my blood. I went to seek a medic instead.

'When I finally made it to the lab, it was so late I didn't expect anyone to be there, but your grandad was still present, only he was fast asleep. All his limbs were hanging loosely from the sides of his chair, his head dropped over his left shoulder — for a moment, I felt chills up and down my body, thinking he'd frozen up, but when I approached him and smelled alcohol, I saw the bottle of spirit on the desktop. It was almost empty. He needed that just to keep his body warm and alive. Marty was snoozing gracefully like a bear, covered in a furry coat. I noticed a few spreadsheets of paper on the desk, over the main control panel of the computer and on the floor, right beneath his hand. It looked like he had suddenly lost his balance and slumped on the top of his chair when the alcohol was too much for his tired, spent spirit and body. I quickly gathered all the paperwork and skimmed through it. On something that looked like the last page, he wrote: *"Pain is only imagined"*.

'I still have that paper with me,' said Mr Kubla. 'It's over there, above the doorframe, planted onto the wall inside that white cabinet. The key is on the top of the cabinet. Please, feel free to take it out.

'Do you see those vials on the top of the filing cabinet on your right?' Mr Kubla continued his monologue as Derick was reaching for the key to the cabinet. 'They are prepared according to the formula your grandad invented more than twenty years ago. It fools your brain into thinking pain is a simple by-product of the thinking process, not a concrete but a very abstract one, such as —'

'Imagination!' Derick interrupted.

'Yes, that's right. Put them down here on the table and start reading. The problem with it is that when the active compound is unavailable, the pain caused by the same stimuli cannot be alleviated by anything else, which causes a potent issue of dependence. Thereby it has never been patented, but I like to use it because even that old formula alters my thinking of pain as an obsolete phenomenon and works in tandem with burning pain receptors in the body so well that after years of subsequent use I won't even feel a great deal if I have a heart attack or when my body rolls on the floor during a seizure. I simply don't wanna feel I am here when I'm dying.

'The only issue we thought we had back in the days of the advent of the new ways of dealing with pain was its genetic underpinning. As much as I had some ideas what mechanisms were responsible for the arousal of that feeling, and I am sure others had too, including Marty, we had no idea how to alter them in a nanoscale so that the changes in the probability of the occurrence of any particular event could be passed on through generations, the very golden dream of your grandad. I understood we had no technology developed high enough to tackle the problem back then, but now…'

'Are you suggesting that someone…' said Derick.

'All I'm going to say is that even stranger things ensued. I studied Marty's papers all night long. When I woke up, I still felt drunk. Yes, I drunk too that night, just to keep warm, mind you. Early in the morning when I felt it was still the night, I heard the knock on the door. It was no other than Mirandelle. Seeing her snow-white face and golden hair with pearls embedded and cocooned in it was like a bucket of ice-cold water for me — I woke up instantly! She greeted me with her stately, dignified, little curtsy, then she announced that I was in demand because everyone had to go outside today. I saw Marteen Burdent everywhere, he'd just sprung to life from the ashes, rematerialised himself out of the dusty cloud of magic powder — a truly strange specimen; he was dogging Marty everywhere too, as usual really. When I came out of the mountain, the first thing that went through my head was that it wasn't even half as cold as it was yesterday, but everyone was clad in much thicker winter clothes than me. As far as I could see, I was the only one without a protective shawl, although the sun was already shining from above the mountain peaks. I thought it must be the alcohol I drunk yesterday that was still giving me warmth; I wasn't really used to drinking much these days.

'I saw that girl, Mirandelle screaming and waving at me as

though she'd just caught sight of her nearest and dearest. Her camera was ready. They were ready too. It was her who took that very picture you've brought with you. Sadly, I had to be back down inside the mountain fairly quickly after I'd barely got the sun as my nose was literally falling off again, and I had to undergo a mini operation. I tell you, I hated doctors, but I had no choice, the nose is not like the fingers. By the evening I was having dessert, recovering and scouring through Marty's papers, not looking for particularly anything, just wondering when something suddenly crossed my mind — I'd completely forgotten to ask if Marty's reactions were reversible — and they were as I later found out, which meant that the same compounds could alter the probability of the occurrence of pain in both ways, resulting in either assuaging or aggravating it.

'I ran out of my office like a wild boar, charging through the "worm tubes", still feeling pretty deflated, like the pieces on the wind, having my nose in tatters. The doc told me not to move a lot at least for a day to let it settle, but who bothers listening to doctors? I thought it wouldn't last like a sun, but it has. My nose feels shattered and in pieces to this day, the scar is still there.'

Mr Kubla then pointed at his nose, which still looked crooked to the left side and dismembered, with a tiny scar right above the left nostril. One part of it was slightly smaller than the other and mildly elevated, giving it the impression it had wings and was about to fly off.

'Believe me or not, it was the only injury I've ever had in my life,' he took up his story again. 'Lucky, wasn't I? Well, I wasn't feeling so lucky after I'd come back,' he cursed, writhing his mouth like a squeezed lemon, swallowing grotty grains of acrimony in his abruptly shifting voice.

'As I arrived before the door to Marty's office, I quickly realized I was at the scene of a bitter argument. What I witnessed that day has changed my life forever. The door was shut; I couldn't hear anything since all doors were fitted with noise cancelling sheets. Fortunately, I had a little ace up my sleeve, and more precisely, down my pocket. It was a jammy, elfin eavesdropping device, remarkably ingenious and simple. It was made with an extremely malleable alloy of light metals, carbon, and plastic, so it could be bent nearly to the right angle and looked like the elongated bell of a trumpet. It worked a bit like a stethoscope, but was much more sensitive, allowing to amplify the sounds more than ten times in their magnitude. I tucked the earpiece into my left ear, bent the other, obtuse end and planted it on the door so that I could peek through the tiny, square window at an acute angle to avoid being seen. That window had mesh wiring passed through it, but it didn't affect visibility so badly. It was situated close to the top frame of the door, above the plates with the names of your grandad and Maarten. Luckily, the light was on, so I could see what I heard.

'Marty was sitting on his chair on the right. He looked miserable with both of his hands smothering his skull as if he had two octopuses sucked into his brain, his fingers resembled tentacles, creeping and crawling at the back of his head, trying to reach the spinal cord. He was swinging his torso compulsively back and forth, screaming loud without uttering a single word. His agony was a struggle to retain what's been left of his identity for himself. The grim figure of tall stature towered above him, encased in a long, beige cape, wearing huge stockman hat that was casting its shadow on the whole place, covering Marty's bulging, sinewy face with darkness. It couldn't be Maarten Burdent, he was too bulky, too pythonic to be him. His voice was different too: it was hissy, jabbing but prodigious and anfractuous, getting under the skin through all bodily channels, then gripping to the heart and soul only in a sly attempt to avulse them from inside with one, sharp, wringing thrust. He had his back turned towards the door, so I couldn't see his face as he was speaking.

'"All you've created was a myth. No one would ever believe you. You are a liar and a cheat, unloving as a father, neglecting as a lover. You don't want to allow the world to see what you truly are, how right you are, like a superstar, yeah, right you are — not worth a broken shelong. I've taken what has been rightfully mine, the world is mine, but don't you worry, I will take your torch, the burden of saving your fellow humans from hurting one another.

I will reap what you've sown and bestow the riches upon them. They need a real hero, like me. Now you go home and learn how to love again. Without you, would I have ever discovered what I've been capable of? You've brought the best out of me, I've got the better of you."

"'Simon! You've stolen my personality!"

"'I've only borrowed it. I've given it substance. Your lies were shallow and legless, you hollow man."

'He twisted his head, canting it down against the neck, which thickened like a wet rope, allowing winding folds to crop up on its serpentine surface. Spineless it appeared, like spiral stairs in a tower as his head turned right slightly, letting the smugly smirks unfold the distinctive lineaments of his profile. I saw the face of Simon Redeldrag as you know it for the first time. It appeared as Marteen's own face had been skinned off, assimilated and reproduced anew — it was so alike yet different. He'd become a chameleon, he'd hidden Maarten's overt, unmasking obnoxiousness, his malevolence, his scornful hatred of humankind under the deep skin of a very righteous, wise, charmingly well-spoken, silver-tongued, conscience-breaking persona. I saw his right eye crawled to the side, closed and reopen shiftingly reptilian, with its slitty pupil on fire. His open smile was lengthened to the touching distance with the ear.

'I took my eyes off the window. It was too much for me. The more I heard Marty's laments, the more pity and compassion I felt for... Simon. He was right — I understood it then that I too had been under his appeasingly tantalizing influence. My heart was thumping in fear, I wished I had never witnessed it, but I was simply powerless to unplug myself from the stunning reality behind the closed door. It was too ensnaring for me. I had to listen — no matter what.

"'You've betrayed me! You've used me. You've never told me you have a split personality, that you can dissociate."

"'You've never told me you were a mythomaniac. Tell me, what were you going to do with that poor Mirandelle, how much your black heart was eager to corrupt her silver and gold? You're weak; now I've taken control over your creations."

'"So it was you…"

'"You're learning too quickly."

'Then, there was a moment of silence, very disconcerting silence. I let my head roll on my right cheek. I saw Marty's hand find and grab a pointy, well-sharpened pencil that was lying idle on the pile of paperwork. He jumped to his throat, swinging and clenching his right fist sharply, but he faltered as Simon spoke, pointing his long, bony, and tapered index finger at him from above, almost touching his skull.

'"Sit down," he commanded. Marty fawned, then he slumped helplessly on his chair.

'"Of course, it was me. Life is only a set-up."

'He burst into loud, gaudy, and sinister laughter, then he left the room like the wind. The bottom of his cape, which was nearly down to his ankles, fluttered in the air, spreading out like a peacock's tail, then tumbling down with a force of a mountain avalanche it blew all the papers up in the air as he made way towards the door. I just managed to escape and take shelter in the toilet that was next to Marty's office. He stopped after making a few, long strides as the office door shut behind him and turned his head towards me, grinning contentedly complacent and self-assured as if he knew I was there, behind the wall. He knew he'd overborne us all. He looked just like him from the face, but it wasn't Marteen Burdent. His character was now different. He was — his "reversed alter ego".

'My poor nose had suffered enough at that precise moment when I fell under a shadow imminent encounter. A few stitches had already busted, and small droplets of blood were dripping on my boots, one by one as my heart was pounding wilder and wilder. Then he was gone — out of my sight, treading off with long steps in a matter of urgency. The window on the door to Marty's office had its blind drawn when I finally found the courage to leave my precarious hideaway and come close to it after what I'd just seen. Shouting his name repeatedly in a fearfully muffled voice and a heavy barrage of knocks on the door was of no avail — all had fallen on deaf ears. The silence was total, prevailing, and pervasive. I feared the worst but thought that Marty had simply locked himself in and barricaded the door in case of Simon's return. I couldn't afford to perch there any longer, I cursed my nose, which was falling apart again, and disappeared, leaving it all to chance.

'The next day, I rushed to Marty's office as soon as I could, but it was already way past midday when I got there because of the pathetically dire state of my face. The door was locked, and the blind was still pulled down, even as I saw it yesterday upon leaving the scene, but the plate with his name had already been removed, so had Maarten's. No one knew where they'd gone. Asking a lot was point-blank ridiculous — as far as I could gather, I was the only person in the know about what had really happened; everyone else had been living a dream, hooked on a blissful unconsciousness. I felt like a confounded idiot even to think about telling anyone the truth. A few days later, I received the telegram that informed me that I'd been asked to retire, offering me a "good care", really kindly forcing me to go out to grass. In a matter of days, everyone had been laid off, with the only known, circulating information that the "Tree under the mountain project had been conclusively aborted". I thought I had control over what was going on under the mountains, but I was blind and had failed to see, even as your grandad had — fooled by an illusive sense of self-importance. You see, life is a patchwork — you only see small fragments of what happens to you every day. It has all been set up indeed.'

Mr Kubla stopped his monologue and sighed. He looked up at the top of his TV where the brown, wooden clock was standing. It had the shape of a rectangle tilted at ninety degrees, with a round, white face embedded in the middle and sticking out a bit beyond the frame from the top. He signalled to Derik, who was still in a daze, sitting deep in the armchair, that he needed another dose of his special concoction from the top of the filing cabinet. It was getting really late; he knew that his story wasn't any more conclusive than his own life had been to himself, than life was now to Derick — more and more surprising by the day. Nonetheless, he carried on as usual after receiving his potion, calm but steadfast, playing the last fiddle, singing his last octave.

'I had a long time to ponder over my life and over the past,' he began again, 'but my health has strangely deteriorated right away after all has collapsed. It must have been my age and the fact that I've spent so many years in isolation. When I could no longer fend for myself, when the pain of moving my old, frail bones was too much for me, the government gave me this wheelchair and put me right here. I spent the last nine years inside this building, between these walls, under scrutiny and supervision, but at least I'm still alive, still able to reflect upon what's been going on — my age warrants it, and my memories — memories of your grandad, memories of life. Marty loved life. "Life is like planet Earth to humans," he used to say. And do you know what Simon's been doing with that planet? — He's been throwing it in the air as if it was a coin. His greatest trickery is his mastery over the opposing forces. You see, his influence has already been making you feel pity and compassion for him, you can't deny that, while in reality, the opposite is true about him. He's had more than enough time to get rid of you, but he hasn't done it; only he knows why, and perhaps your grandad too.

'The scenes from that day haven't stopped daunting me even for a moment. I see it every day as a dark mare overcasting the sky. If only I'd known it was the very last time I was to see his face in my life. It was all one impossible, remarkable coincidence; and "coincidence" is the word you must pay attention to because it is what has brought you here, isn't it? It was what has sealed your grandad's fate, it's the fine, horizon line you've been treading on all your life. Now the world is requiring your war. The world I have trodden on far and wide, contemplating, studying deep and hard what a "coincidence" it was. I learned that some people "dissociate", they leave their own mind and live as someone else in their bodies, without being aware of their actions, triggered by something purely coincidental, such as "déjà vu". That's why it's called "coincidental dissociation". Extremely rarely, it is possible they "join" with personalities, especially with those belonging to their close ones, usurping their identity, seemingly stemming from the fear of inferiority, benevolently — trying to put the "inferiority-superiority" balance right — in their favour. They are "joincidental dissociates", whereby their own persona transmutes into a new being. And this is exactly what I believe I have witnessed, but I fear it wasn't Marteen's feeling of inferiority that caused him to "take over" and become Simon, it was Marty's. As much as an improbable event of extreme ill-fate it may seem, Marty's mania brought him to create Simon as an alternative ego of himself in Maarten's image at the same time as Maarten's "joincidental dissociation" sparked to life. Maarten somehow must have been aware of Marty's malady beforehand, but perhaps not so much of his own... "capability" — as he was gloating over the carven, bowed, and distraught silhouette of your grandad, crowed and glorified.

'My worst fear is that he's gained full control over his new characteristics and discovered how to shift them at will thanks to Marty's mythomania, unless... he's always been able to. Remember, Simon says everything as mirror images of the truth only in order to make you believe his lies are true. Marty's created an empty vessel, a matrix he couldn't personify, so he founded it on his lies and filled it with myths, confabulations. Maarten took the chance and "borrowed" it from him, splitting himself in two, "filling Simon's shoes". I dare not think how much of Marty's own personality he was able to acquire, how deep inside of him he was able to see, and how much more wicked he's become from inside, having the ability to hide himself under the umbrella of salvation and dignified righteousness.'

Mr Kubla stopped there. He took a look at Derick's still exaggerated but slowly deflating physiognomy, knowing the fear factor had gone, that the smoke was going down, and he would rather go now, adding, 'You're the living proof he's not taken everything he wanted. Perhaps, Marty's somehow concealed something important he's been so desperate but unable to take from him, no matter how beguiling and coercing he was. You still live because Simon still needs you for something, knowing you may be holding the key in your bloodstream as you are Marty's bloodline. Whatever it is, use it to your advantage. Simon is rightful, he does his wicked utmost to appear as honourable, as redeeming as the world allows him to be, he wants to be world's ultimate saviour; he wouldn't burn or destroy unless something or someone poses a direct threat to him. He takes pleasure from deceiving, corrupting, enslaving and ruling, and he needs others to participate in his evils and dance to his mysterious tune.'

'I wish I had known all this before,' Derick sighed. 'I only came here to find him. Instead, I found his past. Maybe you know where he could be now, but I don't suppose you've heard a great deal from him for the last twenty years.'

Mr Kubla's sight fell on Derick's face — cold and stern. Perhaps, he was getting tired; the implied peevishness and bitterly palpable strain in his voice suggested that. When their eyes met, he saw the same impartial doggedness he used to see in Marty's eyes, casting a blind eye on the world around him, interested only in the venture of his own, looking inside-out.

'I told you, Marty is a tragic character, nevertheless, he's one of the smartest people I've ever known. You'd all have thought he'd gone to another planet, traversed through galaxies to spent the rest of his miserable life in the darkest corners of the universe, but nothing could be more deceptive than the thought of distance being the best denominator for the one who's got away — and he knows it, most probably he's taken great advantage of it and has gone nowhere. Look for him in his hideout, just outside of Belgar. Near to the banks of the Leyron River on the other side of the falls of the River Brook and a bit to the north, there is a marshy fenland, full or reeds, willows, and wild animals. He used to take me there with his wife, so many years ago, but I still only remember it because I nearly drowned there once in a swamp, having the swimming skills of a giraffe. He used to have a hut there, built by himself for the purposes of bird watching as far as I can remember, which looked like a fusion of a mini shed and a ground bunker because some of it was actually below ground level. If you cannot find him there, you will have to decide what to do next yourself as I've told you everything I knew. I was surprised, but at the same time glad to find out Marty is still alive.'

'Thank you,' muttered Derick, still partially stunned by Mr Kubla's latest revelation because Belgar was the settlement that was nearest to Willowood where he'd spent most of his life. Both villages were only separated by the mighty falls of River Brook and slow, humming waters of River Leyron, linked together by two bridges. Belgar, being much less populated, hardly making a "village" status, was situated less than three miles to the northeast from Willowood. Derick knew the surrounding area quite well, but he was still grappling with the bizarre idea of having to seek his grandfather by the means of scouring and scouting through local marshland that was now classified as a landscape of natural beauty. As he was coming to terms with himself upon deciding his next move, Mr Kubla spoke.

'He has vanished off the face of the earth, he's gone off the grid, traceless he's become — like a ghost since that calamitous attempt of putting Simon to death, once and for all, and the subsequent detention of his son. I haven't had even a single sign of life from him for over twenty years until now. I had only scraps of information about him for the period after his return from Xuva until his imposed disappearance. I knew he'd been trying to chase Simon, but no one stood on his side, finally when he was telling the pure truth, but only known to himself — no one believed him. He was even accused of Maarteen Burdent's murder. When Simon reappeared, he began usurping his life and his family. No wonder that Marty, the most benevolent, the gentlest person I've ever known decided to assassinate him. He hated him and "the world's silent plaudit for the forging of his evil empire". The rest is history. I don't know what Simon's intentions were, whether he's achieved his goals, but I wouldn't be surprised if he just wants to have the whole world at his feet and want that world to be thankful to him for being there.

'What an irony! — Marty's life is a perfect example of the might of irony and the majestic power of probability, especially ever since he met Maarten Burdent. How ironic it's been — to live life alongside someone who believed that the only probable thing in the whole universe is that nothing is improbable. Then he's fallen a victim of his only god — probability — when a pure coincidence has decided his fate as his unconscious mythomania met with very much more conscious dissociation of Maarten Burdent. A chance of such an event occurring again is probably more or less likely as a chance that a monkey would learn how to write a book. And do you know what your grandad would probably have said about it all? He would have said that if anything is probable to happen, it will happen. As simple as that.'

Having finished the sentence he burst into loud, wild laughter. He was laughing long and hard. It sounded so chaotically absurd that Derick had to cover his ears with his hands, seeing Mr Kubla's eyes closed and his cheeks puffed up. He had no chance to hear the first gentle, timid taps on the door. Only when the subtle knocks turned into a cannonade of whacks followed by a few hailing rams, did Derick rise from his armchair. Mr Kubla's preposterous, haphazard outbursts seemed to be somewhat taming when his delirious laughter turned into a no less hysteric, snivelling voice.

'No one believes me! Do you? Do you believe me?!'

'I do,' muttered Derick, sounding hollow and impersonating, marooned on an isle beneath his feet, stranded in the middle of the corridor in the foreign land of Xuva, watching as the very door he went through ages ago to meet with old Alexander Kubla — standing alone like a silent dam of concrete, was being breached and letting the ocean of human heads pour in. Before long, he was surrounded and besieged by a squadron of bearlike humans, all wearing wintry army uniforms: leathern, dark brown, opaque jackets with ornate shoulder straps, faux, coonskin hats, and black, planky combat boots. Their faces — audacious and stout, stemming from stocky necks, carved in coarse mountain rock were all pointed at him like spiky, sharp arrows from flexed, taut bows. When they chained Derick from every direction, one of them, the tallest one who looked like a rare specimen, a descendant of indigenous Xuvans, with a huge flab of tissue protruding from the bottom of the forehead and diamond-shaped, hooked eyes, embedded deep and aslant against the thick walls of his nose, stepped forward and spoke to Derick.

'What is your name, mister? Can I see your documents, please?'

'Derick McCrafty.'

'Oh, Derick! Very well. Welcome to Xuva,' said the tall man and smiled at Derick, handing his papers back to him. Then he took his black, furry hat off in a welcoming gesture, and all of his companions saluted him at once. As they moved on to the living room where Mr Kubla was still choking on crashing waves of his sudden humour, now firmly meeting the land, Derick still couldn't take his eyes off the front door, in the frame of which voluptuous curves of a young female appeared as a white star out of the dark in her shining, scrimpy uniform, wearing chunky, triangle spectacles in ebony frame, holding a black clipboard in her right arm like a newborn baby. Her mahogany complexion and full, round eyes ignited a sudden fire inside Derick's strayed body as she crossed the threshold to the apartment.

'Hi, I'm Doctor Blair,' she introduced herself. 'I hope you are enjoying your stay. I came to collect my patient.' The scent of musk and lily of the valley was emanating from her breast, inviting him to shift his head athwart as she was passing him by, adjacent to his body, whispering in his ear and leering at him sideways.

'Who? Mr Kubla? I thought he's residing here,' said Derick, disoriented and still pinned to the spot, twisting his head towards the living room and the back of Dr Blair's figure, quickly being captured by the sight of her prominent, buxom gifts of God, distracted from the whole scene of hiving commotion, where her "assistants" were busy helping Mr Kubla dress up and stuffing his portmanteau valises in front of her, now standing diligently by the metal filing cabinet and making notes, glancing only sparingly at them.

'He was an army man,' said she. 'He wants to rest together with them, where his heart truly belongs. They just came to take him there — to his final resting place.'

'I beg your pardon, but it looks to me like a soft act of

abduction.'

'He's terminally ill,' Dr Blair explained. 'He hasn't got more than a month left now. In fact, he may pass away at any time now.'

'He may sometimes go on hallucinating for hours and hours,' she added after a short pause, 'talking nonsense about global addiction, total enslaving, and the end of the world, but with such a tantalizingly vivid credibility that you just find it hardly believable it's all lies, like a dream, a projection of the mind made up.'

'What do you mean?!' asked Derick, startled by that fantastic yet horrifying remark.

'That I hope you've enjoyed the conversation,' she said in a mellow voice, full of suppleness, giving him a full-on, sidelong smile.

As Mr Kubla was passing them by and into the corridor, being pushed in his wheelchair by one of the troops, he stopped next to Derick. Then he propped himself up by grabbing a firm hold of his hanging out shirt, and gazing deep into his eyes from close range, he spoke with these words: 'When you meet with Marty again, choose the right moment to tell him right in his face that he's been used all his life, but don't tell him it was the message from me — it would tear him asunder even more.'

He lost hold of Derick's shirt as well as his eyesight as he uttered the last word. He slouched in the seat of his wheelchair and relaxed all his muscles with a few weighty, poignant gasps before speaking again, this time without looking at Derick at all.

'I have failed to forget the image of your grandad when I saw him for the last time through all those years.'

He sighed and was gone from Derick's sight after waving his slender hand in the faintest of farewells. Derick reflexively turned his head to Dr Blair, who was still making notes on her big spreadsheet, asking, 'But what am I gonna do now?'

She answered, 'You're in the free state of the People's Republic of Xuva. You can do whatever you want.'

He gave her one measured, mischievous look, scanning her pleasing body from head to toe with his flaring eyes. Everyone else had gone. They were here alone, face to face, but then, suddenly, he heard the tannoy again. 'Doctor Davis, Doctor Blair, Doctor Davis, Doctor Blair,' was the sequence — the same he heard throughout the evening, spoken by the same exotic, female voice with a strong Xuvan accent. Dr Blair turned on her heels and disappeared through the doorframe into the dark, wherefrom she came, without saying anything. She'd left Derick alone, in the middle of the corridor of the freshly abandoned apartment in the city of Thargau in the distant, foreign land of Xuva, feeling empty as a barn in the spring.

11
ENCOUNTERS

After Natalie had left, Dorian and his father sat long in deep silence. Somber it grew and formidable like a shadow of a mountain tall, dividing these two solitary figures, sitting back on the opposite slopes of a valley of gloom, slowly slipping along the ridges into a misty feel of their inner thoughts. The mansion stuffed with dozens of bedrooms was lit with lavish darkness, casting a cold shroud of falling summer brights onto the grandeur and opulence amassed by Dorian father's life of success and splendour, whose granite face signified a growing degree of offence he was taking at Derick's innuendoes. On the other side was his son — a man of valour and intrepidity — Derick's best friend.

'What do you make of it?' asked Dorian at length, seeing his father in no mood for a talk.

'I don't know,' replied he, touching his forehead nervously, 'I'm not feeling very well now.'

'What's the matter, Dad? You look like you're troubled so hard.'

'I shall be fine, just need to sit back and rest for a while.'

'I'm gonna call for mama,' Dorian insisted.

'No, please don't!' Dorian's father screamed out, flailing his open hand in front of his son's face like a sabre, rushing out from his armchair to stop him in his madness, with his eyes suddenly imbrued in red mist.

'Wow! Dad, you've scared me! What's happened to you?'

'She must not get involved in it!' Dorian's father barked out. 'Promise me this, please if you're my son.'

'But you always seek her wisdom if you're in this way,' said Dorian, trying to calm the uprising drama.

'She's been hurt far too many times because of me,' Dorian's father suddenly confessed, coming right out of the dark. 'Leave her alone now; do it for me, please.'

'But why? I can't recognize you, Dad! It's not your usual billing to be a beggar in your own kingdom, not in the face of anyone, let alone your son's. What's clouding your mind, Dad? Tell me, please.'

'Me and your mum — we are so different yet we are so alike. We've remained the same for each other for years, so let it be this way if there is any kind of justice under the sky.'

'Like fractals?'

'Like what?'

'So different but so alike! Dad — you've hit it on the head!'

'I beg your pardon?'

'I've got to try to find James Niggle. I will talk to mam later.'

'Don't tell her about Simon, please,' said Dorian's father as if he was pleading.

'Why are you covering for him? What has he done to you?' asked Dorian.

'You must promise me first! Why James?'

'The card, Dad! The card!' said Dorian, who then quickly arose from his seat, grabbed the jacket from the sofa and was about to go out when his father barred the way out, literally throwing his body in line with Dorian's.

'You must know that I'm only taking care of the good name of our family,' he said in a grating, surly voice, glaring deep into his son's eyes. It was a grim encounter, right when Dorian's mind was glowing like a light bulb.

'Step out of my way, I gotta go,' he said to his father, whose unwavering obstinacy and lurking fear didn't allow him to move even an inch. Deaf as an adder he stood before his son, snuffing his light out like a wall impregnable to the sky, knowing his virtues of fatherhood were untouchable.

Dorian shoved the obstacle hindering his way aside, ramming against his dad's chest with those bulky arms of his, blowing his untouchability like the wind blows a house of cards. He fell heavily on the sofa, exactly in the same place where Dorian's jacket was before he took it. He watched his son walking out beyond his reach, leaving him shattered and pulverised. The silence grew indomitable again, only snakes were laughing.

Dorian knew he must flee from home as quickly as he could, even if that meant evading the shadow of his father at all cost. The top of his head was still illuminating like the back end of a glow-worm. It was something special even for him, a man of exceptional insight and inquisitiveness. Momently, he felt his head was on fire, he just had to go, it was too dark inside, but inside of him it was another world, contrasting with what he saw with his eyes: the shadows of a few early falling leaves were just not real enough for a sight of boiling over and evaporating tips of cypress trees, standing tall at attention on both sides of the avenue like a battalion of troops, serving a guard of honour to the outside gate of his manor for a "once-in-a-lifetime" fantastic achievement of toppling the one he's been looking up to all his life.

He was disbelieving how hot it was outside; his jacket was just a needless acquisition for the paltry days of fall. Intrigued how things were not adding up around him — his hot breath, cold sweats accompanied with beams of scorching southern sun surfing on breezy waves of northern winds, he relished the moment of true freedom, without the repugnant smell of the frowsty air of his house no one wanted to breathe anymore. Wondering whether this was how freedom from control felt like, he was still moving along like a doll of controlled freedom as he rushed towards the gate of golden spikes, shut and electrified. Even his dad's vulgar protests from the intercom speaker were much too hollow for his stubborn, steadfast spirit and embrighted mind, which had yet another troublesome riddle ahead of him as there was no way out now the fifteen feet tall gate and all-encompassing fence were under deadly electric current. He needed just a miracle of insight from his ingenious mind now or else he was at risk of being on the wrong end of his dad's glorious fury.

He knew he could try to smash the control panel on the side of the gate's round post or even set fire to the nearby bunker shed where a mini power plant powering the gates, two swimming pools, and numerous fountains was hidden, not to mention dozens of lampposts. It was not in his style, though; it didn't suit the mood he was in, for it was one violent conduct too far for him, even if it gave him a rotten, forbidden taste of falling free.

When the low sun broke through the blanket of rising clouds and its waning warmth met with his high forehead, it became plain to him it was the quote of his father that brought about this avalanche of heat and luminosity inside him. For a moment he could peek through the "rabbit hole" and comprehend with a sublime lucidity that... when science meets evolution, people become like fractals — they are so different yet so are they the same — when you're on the outside, looking in.

'I think I'm an outsider on the wrong side of the rainbow,' he said slowly to himself, 'and thanks God for that!' Then, as he was immersed in his own subversive contemplation, he was dazzled with high beams fired in short bursts from the headlights of a car approaching the gate like thunder from the sky as he was standing right behind it. He managed to open them slowly after a while, still hardly being able to withstand the piercing pain. Squinting tight one of them, he peered through the gate to see his mum's red, sporty cabrio taking a turn from the main boulevard to the private drive in front of the promenade garden that resembled more a forest in its size and density of abundant growth. Dorian had to move quickly out of the way to avoid being wiped out as the outside gate could open inwards only, but it was exactly the thing he wanted to see happen now. He was standing motionless next to the right wing of the gate, looking like a caddy on a golf course as his mum whizzed past him, giving him a rather curious face, simply because it was obviously odd for her to see her son by the gate acting like a trespasser, especially when she knew full well that he never walked to the gate, always drove there and out — it was almost half a mile from there to the front of the house.

Dorian knew his father would find himself occupied for quite some time now, so he had to take his chance and run. He was without his car, though, and without any idea where to find James; the only place he could think of was East Point University. He heard stories that James hardly ever left the university, that it was his home now. He could only hope those were true stories, not just rumours. He simply had to find him — by hook or by crook — yet the thought of taking the subway was filling him with dread and exasperation, and he almost puked as he bolted to the nearest station. He detested travelling by tube: it was always a loathsome experience to smell people's armpits from under the pressurised slabs of intense antiperspirant fats curling around the jungles of hair, sticking out like stalactites or icicles, inside immovably overcrowded compartments where he was just one of the freshly slaughtered sardines maturing in their own juices, immune to outside forces, squeezed up into an inert, hurtling tin, observing the silence of an immeasurable sea of matches' heads, precariously rubbing against striking strips of imagined frontiers of personal spaces. People were like ghosts there — desensitized and impalpable, wearing blinders of diffused responsibility, happy on their own, pretending nothing really bothered them. On the flip side, the tube was extremely fast, so the distance of over fifteen miles that was between his house and the university was covered within a matter of minutes; it was all that counted — all the rest was bullshit.

East Point University was the acquainted backbone of wisdom in the city of snakes and ravaging hornets. Mounted on the rubble of the medieval castle, haunted yet revered with devotion and dread, a resting place for the kings of old, it boasted hundreds of years of history down its pipeline into the bare bones of still boiling cauldron, containing within its means the oldest soup of bones without bones. A place of witchcraft and wizardry for many — where the chemistry of time bygone had been mixing in the present with futuristic visions of myriads of lost dream catchers about the times that hadn't yet come to pass. For others, though, it was just a place of utter feudal bigotry, rotten and slimy from its bloody foundations, where the outspoken hypocrisy of innovation and inclusivity was only a dazzling, distracting shroud over the coffin of the traditions of chivalry, which might as well have never existed in the first place, aside from being a poignant reminder of lost magic for a few longing hearts, inside dusted over covers of lays and legends. For Dorian, it was unquestionably the latter, but above all, it was the place where his old man met the dame of his dreams and where they had spent so many luscious, romantic nights together by the banks of the round and shallow Lake Elborn, the serene waters of which were reflecting full moonshine perfectly into lovers' faces, roosting close to each other in the girdle of love in or under the rustling elm trees, some of which were probably as old as the university itself.

The legend goes that the flocks of white swans, which hardly ever leave the confines of the lake, grounded to its flat surface by some magic spell, are the reincarnated souls of doomed and forsaken princesses who have been imprisoned and left to die in the dungeons of the castle because of their devout love for a foreign prince. They can return to their former shape only if a lone man declares love to one of them while they're spreading their wings, bathed in the gleaming light of the full moon. Many have tried, but no one knows if anyone has ever succeeded. Dorian was most certainly an arch-pessimist when it came to such ludicrous behaviours; it was just a fantasy for him, a fairy tale for those brokenhearted who were too sorry for themselves to mount a straight rebound — after all, the relationship with his fiancee was a "byproduct" of a cheeky one-night stand, one of the many he had in his youth, when both partiers were more often than not just too intoxicated to remember each other's names the day after, given they introduced themselves properly to begin with.

Now it all felt like yesteryear for him as he was walking along the lakeside, poignantly reminded that even himself used to be going to the shores of Lake Elborn in search of white swans under the spell of black magic, attempting to break it and find the love of his life. Embarrassing as it was, it felt all too remote now and probably he wouldn't have remembered it right now if he wasn't at the scene of swan feeding, with the only difference being the surface of the lake, which was bleak and lacklustre as the low-life, diminutive sun was putting its shamed face to sleep beyond a vast armada of depressing clouds. Like his father, he was there alone in his teenagehood, plain as salt and bread, before all the parties started, before he started scoring, and before the spell was broken. He was too streetwise nowadays and knew that princesses did not come that easy.

The main buildings of the university came into sight as he emerged from the lakeshore grove. Most of them were elevated on and around the massive hill-like structure, which was a natural hill itself, where the castle used to be. The castle had been the home and the guarding place for the Olwick family, which came to the country from overseas, namely the north, with the waves of sea warriors, hacking and smashing its way to the top of the hill to rule the land from there for hundreds of years before the castle was razed to the ground in the wake of industrial revolution, its resources traded to build roads, towers and, last but not least, the university, which had its main building raised on the foundations of the old castle. This place was full of hidden secrets — starting with the dungeons, which now served as basements; the hill itself, which at the time of its prime looked like a lonely mountain before it was re-levelled, was the place of geographic significance due to its situation by the old route towards the sea that was coming along the River Brook, linking the lowlands of the south and east with the elevated plateau of Eastern Highlands, being the very last of the ancient Barrow Hills and the site of pagan cults, as old as the seven seas.

Barrow Hills were outstretching over fifty miles south-north from the northernmost parts of Clarksdowne, specifically the Hill of Olwick where the East Point University was situated now, owing its name to the Olwick family, which renamed the Hill in its honour, up trough Hillbarrow and then past Kirkwood where the Hills crumbled into a plain in the valley of the River Leyron. They formed a natural gate in the wall of Eastern Highlands whence all cold winds were blowing. The Hill of Olwick overlooked the last miles of the River Brook until its falls, nearly ten miles beyond the borders of the city of Clarksdowne. The land to the east and south of the River Leyron was low and flat for some good two hundred miles before reaching the end and falling off the cliffs to the warm, azure sea of the south.

ENCOUNTERS

Darkness was creeping into every nook as Dorian went through the revolving backdoor to the Department of Biological Sciences. The main entrance was already closed at this time in the evening when the faces of people walking past were all turning sable and numb. The path leading to the door was only rarely used these days; not many people seemed to have remembered where it led to, neither where it came from — only the door, still being kept as one of the official emergency exits, never used, though, even during terrorist attack drills because of the dense and impenetrable evergreen hedgerow growing right in front of it, secluding it from the rest of the complex and the outside world so that it was always in its shade, was the point where the past met the future. The prodigious hedgerow itself was so old that it probably remembered the reigns of the kings of old when they were building tombs for their forefathers greater than the houses for the living, but it was maintained and well-groomed at all times by the local wicker men.

The offices of the PhD students were on the uppermost tier of the building for some unknown reason. Maybe their spongy brains were banking on the closeness of the sun and the moon and their universal impact on everything. This time, there was no one sticking out of the window on the lookout to spot Dorian as he was closing in. Inside, the lifts were next to the entrance, on the right, as opposed to the main entrance where the lifts were on the left as you came in. When the lift door opened with its signature, old-fashioned tink, Dorian slipped in through the narrow jaw, which shut immediately behind him before he made his choice, just the way the outmoded machines did — designed to behave with the spirit of the times when the technology of "space for everyone" or "all-inclusive" was simply an unthinkable offence, a witchcraft, for the practising of which burning at the stake was a trendy punishment or at least a severe flagellation if you were lucky enough. The control panel was an unpolished chunk of bulged aluminium mass that was warped concave along the rounded edges, probably because far too many of the primordial users were thinking of it as a handle, at the time when "user manuals" were things unheard of, with gross and livid buttons rammed in with the precision of a sledgehammer.

Out of curiosity, he pressed the red "arrow down" button instead of the green "arrow up", indicating the direction of travel before choosing one number from zero to eight. Everyone knew that the button he pressed never worked, it was there for no reason; only for students, academics, and visitors to wonder what happens if… pressing it over and over — by mistake, of course, tempting the fate, making a laughing stock of themselves in the face of some botched contraption. Yet there was no mistaking he was going down when the butterflies had arisen in his stomach and nearly flew out of his mouth, being thwarted only where the end of the throat was and pegged back right where they came from. It was the first time he saw that button alight, but flickering weakly as if it knew with its dispirited soul of its makers it was reaching the netherworld where nothing was carved in stone.

As he came out of the lift in the wall, instead of seeing a rat-infested, bedraggled, slimy dungeon, the way he ever imagined this place could look like, a spacious, neat auditorium emerged in front of him. The lights above his head were so unpleasantly dimmed, he could only navigate through that new land he was swept to by the presence of emergency lights above the "fire exit" signs. He saw a compact, rectangular set of benches tidily situated in rows, systematically divided with open spaces between them, forming one long column that was taking a dip towards something that looked like a stretch of the glass wall. As Dorian was approaching the wall, passing row by row, he noticed the black devices resembling ridiculously thick, convex glasses lying in the middle of every seat. He picked up one of them, and to his surprise, they turned out to be virtual reality headsets with audio and video receivers. None of them worked, though, they had no buttons, knobs or switches on them; they looked like remotely controlled devices, and they were still slightly warm to the touch.

It was all too bizarre for him, his cautiousness of the mind and iron plausibility of logic kicked in, the increased conductance of his tightened skin and muscles was sending him alert signals to remain vigilant on this trailblazing venture. If only he'd known he found himself inside the same underground theatre his best friend had explored nearly two weeks ago, but in the opposite wing to that where Derick was. Both wings were mirror images of each other, both located on the sides of the vast hall with the stage, which was now empty. The stage he was looking at from above through the one-way mirror, standing in the corner of a raised platform, was the only place in the whole darkening vastness some light was still focused on. He looked left and down: he saw the signs leading to the emergency exit below; he looked right and up: he saw the safety railings of the uppermost platform and the stairs, but just a few yards behind him he spotted some furniture — crude, chunky pieces of wood put together in a makeshift way, having very geometrical smooth surfaces with very sharp edges. There was something weird about it as the desk was screwed down to the floor and the chair was insanely heavy, even for such a brawny athlete like Dorian. Yet the strangest thing about it was the shredder inserted in a massive, rectangular hole in the desk with a large bin attached to the desktop from underneath it. The bin was empty, but Dorian could see the keyhole on the metal plate right next to the insertions. It was fixed very securely as it hasn't budged an inch, even when Dorian exerted all his pure strength of a henchman to remove it.

Resigned but not dejected, he straightened his arched back and made his way downstairs towards the "fire exit" signs, treading steadily but carefully, looking around in nothing but wonder, keeping the fast multiplying, pressing questions of the mind in check, trying to pay as much attention as he could to what was unrolling before his eyes. He found the door quite easily, in the place where it should be, right below the "fire exit" sign. On the other side, it was slightly warmer but still very cold; the air was even more stifling and itchy yet surprisingly viscous, as though it still contained the heavy, breathed out mouthfuls of those who were occupying those seats last time around. Dorian climbed the stage quickly and as quietly as he could master. He stood still in the spotlight for a while — unseen, unheard, unnoticed, fearless as a warrior of an ancient world, ready to face whatever was lurking behind the curtains.

Behind the scenes, the curtains were drawn, complete darkness fell there — where two last lost souls of the day were still undecided about the fate of the world, pondering what to do next. That peculiar conversation he was an unexpected witness of felt like hearing a rehearsal to some cheap tragicomedy of some unusual sort for Dorian, who crept closer to find out who those voices, which sounded familiar but somewhat strange in their tones, belonged to.

'I will give you billions over billions in gold,' declared the first and harsher voice, sounding old and haughty.

'Give me a billion hearts,' mused the other voice, much lighter and more pleasant to the ear than the first one.

'Mr righteous, ehh?' hissed the first voice. Surely, that must have been Simon Redeldrag himself, thought Dorian, and mustering his courage he poked his nose out of the shadows to see the back of the man he so highly suspected to see, speaking to the one he had high hopes to find — James Niggle.

'Still running over the same old ground? Decade after decade, like the one little man without whom we most probably would have nothing to do with each other now, but yes, I shall put the hearts of all special people in bags for you. They'll be fearless — going forward.'

'You're so outward with your obtuseness, everyone would see it as a riddle unguessable, a metaphor within a metaphor, while in reality, the stroke of genius lays within the purity of your literalness. Magic stuff!'

'You couldn't have put it any simpler than that!' Simon crowed. 'You need to build the tree, so I shall give you the leaves.'

'They are like sombreros in your mind, aren't they? Why did you go for sombreros?'

'They are like umbrellas but for sunny days. The allusion to the toxicity and murkiness of the world is left out while its protective aspect stays the same. We need that exotic, esoteric aura of positivity around us.'

'Indeed, Mr Redeldrag. For the better world!'

'Yes,' he hissed stridently, then left James alone, reassuring him he'd be back once he'd checked something upstairs as he was walking down the stairs from the stage.

James, in the meantime, produced his organiser from somewhere and began to murmur something to himself in a very unintelligible voice, probably checking a set-up for the new world order. He was leaning against the top of the old, ponderous, bricky piano, his left hand, bent at the elbow, was propping his big head that was shaped like an egg turned upside-down, and his legs were crossed just below the knees. The keyboard of the piano was opened and after a while, James simply couldn't resist plucking a few strings. The notes reverberated in the grandness of the hall, turning the nocturnal silence into a concert of the colours of the rainbow — such a copious joyfulness was flowing through James's fingers. Dorian, who himself had been taking piano lessons throughout his childhood, listened in awe how dexterous James was. He imagined glimmers of light flying to and fro onstage, free like butterflies, transforming the place into a living theatre of dreams. Then he remembered the card, and his visions suddenly became clear. It was all so painfully, impudently simple! He wished Derick had been with him now when the secrets of his card were being revealed. 'If people are like leaves and leaves are like fractals, why do they need sombreros like umbrellas? What do they need to be protected from?'

Suddenly, the music stopped, and the lights went out completely. A dark, grave, and smothering silence fell from all directions. Dorian stopped talking all at once, but he pinched his tongue too little too late.

'From themselves,' James's hollow voice broke through. 'Can you reveal yourself now, please? You know I have heard you.'

Dorian, having no choice, stepped up immediately, as befitted a man of honour that he was. He gazed into James's eyes with unflinching gallantry.

'Dorian Rose,' said James in an acclaiming tone, appearing only half-surprised, 'I don't think Simon would be happy to see your flat, owlish face here. Do you see in the dark as good as you can hear?'

'I can't say nay to that,' replied Dorian, 'but how can you fawn so low before such a traducent person as Simon?'

'How dare you to be so judgemental of me without knowing me and my intentions?'

'Because from what I could gather you act like Simon's bitch. He may just be using you for his own purposes.'

'Now you've only managed to insult my intellect, Mr clever riddle breaker. You must be so excited for yourself, aren't you?

'By no means, I am,' Dorian answered. 'If you were so kind and could tell me why those sombreros from your card form an octagon when you draw lines between them.'

'Pff — I have no idea what you are talking about,' James dismissed.

'But you gave the card to Derick when he first met you and Natalie, didn't you?'

James's attention sharpened promptly after Dorian had mentioned Natalie's name. He gave his face a few curious glances, clearly weighing up words in his mouth, then he answered, with an artificial unceremoniousness, hardly able to hide his agitation.

'Derick is a dreamer, but Simon knows that the spirit of his grandfather and those who were before him is permeating through him. Occasionally, without even being conscious about it, he let it slip through his fingers, literally.'

'Wow, I thought you barely know each other,' said Dorian in amazement.

'That is absolutely true, but Simon is a friend of the family. What do you think of Natalie then?'

'She's like the wind.'

'You don't need to tell me that. I've known her since we were two little kids in a sandbox. Are you interested in her?'

Before Dorian could answer that, they both got distracted by the noise of loud steps close by. It was clear Simon was coming back. Dorian was told to hide again and stay out of sight. 'Under no circumstances can you show your face. I shall not stitch you up,' said James in a hurry and picked up his organiser from the top of the piano whilst Dorian quickly ensconced himself in thick, maroon curtains. He stood there as though nothing had ever happened, trying his best to poise himself before the arrival of his boss, but as the waiting prolonged, he noticed, much to his befuddlement, that the sound of the steps became gradually fainter. James was under the impression that somebody was walking back and forth under the stage at an irregular, messy pace that was too clicky-clacky for Simon's liking, making far too much commotion, unlike Simon, whose stride was stealthy and direct, always right to the core. He went onstage, spurred by his own curiosity, but could hardly see a thing through that dense thicket of blackness as he forgot to switch the lights back on.

'Who's there?!' he shouted aloud, intending to appear scary and dissuasive.

'James?' said the voice from under the stage, but it sounded too womanly to be Simon's.

James answered nothing; he only ran backstage and turned the lights on. When he was back, he saw his friend of old, a grown-up tomboy, with whom he'd spent more time than with any other woman in his lifetime, scrambling the stage clumsily.

'Natalie! I can't tell you how much I've missed having you around, but what on earth are you doing here?! It wasn't you I was expecting to find here.'

'And who the hell were you expecting?! Virgin Mary?' asked Natalie, rolling her eyes together with the head and catching a sudden dizziness — nearly falling offstage. 'Oh, no my sweetie. I don't think it's quite your time yet,' she added after her sense of balance was restored.

'Don't you even start it,' grouched James. 'I know that talking to you is like hammering wooden nails into a wall of hard concrete, but this is not the best place to be for a person like you. We'd better go offstage.'

'What do you mean?!' retorted Natalie, 'I'm loving it! You may be treating it as your new home, but I'm a journalist — I'm used to walking my own walk.'

'I'm not denying that,' said James, 'but I'm worried about

you.'

'You'd better tell me about the card,' requested Natalie, with her usual corky lightheartedness, appearing unconcerned with James's stance.

'The card?' said he, far more surprised than when he saw Dorian coming out of the gloom. When Dorian heard that Natalie too mentioned the card, he twitched like reeds in the breeze and, holding his breath, he was all ears even more so — he knew he wasn't the only one who had a keen interest in the card.

'Yeaa —' drawled Natalie, trying to draw out the answers from James, 'the card. You know, the one you gave to my boyfriend, I mean, Derick when we first met.'

'Your boyfriend,' repeated James, but with a double cheesiness added on, 'aww, how sweet!'

'Stop it or else I'll kick you in the balls,' warned Natalie, in no mood for mawkishness.

'Why is everyone suddenly so interested in it?!' blasted James, snapping out of the drama. 'Simon gave it to me to give it out to Derick when I eventually met him, so I did. I had no idea it was so precious.'

'What?! Simon gave it to you?'

'He wanted us to appear professional and appealing, so he's made one for me. I was about to order the first batch for myself, but I was still undecided about the design.'

'This is bonkers!' Natalie belted out. 'Why didn't you tell me before that card was special?'

'What do you mean?' asked James, confounded by Natalie's remark. 'I don't get you.' Then he stopped and went all silent, tilting his head down awkwardly as if he was trying to listen carefully to something.

'What are you straining your ears for?' asked Natalie. 'I can't hear anything.'

James only raised his hand towards her mouth and kept on listening intently.

'Quick, hide,' he said abruptly in a half-subdued voice. 'Simon is back,' he whispered when Natalie was nearly perfectly veiled in the curtain.

James didn't have time to bother about how knotty the situation had become, he had to compose himself to appear as genuine as the first kiss, although inside he was like a cat on hot bricks. He picked up his organiser from the top of the piano and began fiddling with it, pretending to be busy. When Simon came back, he didn't want to open his mouth too soon, he didn't want to raise any suspicions. Quite unaware of how irrational his thoughts had become, he only managed to crack half a smile, a very nervy smile.

'What are you grinning at?' Simon snapped. 'We've got work to do.'

'Nothing, nothing at all really,' replied James. 'I was just wondering about that card you gave me the other day. Can I have more of those?'

'Are you organising a happening?'

'No, not at all. I'm just missing my title.'

'Next time I'll call you "the king of hearts,"' said Simon and returning him a derisive half-smile, he stepped up towards him, then put his right arm on the top of the piano and looked down at his organiser. James was playing good old Tetris, but the game was now paused.

'Is everything ready for tomorrow?'

'Are we not waiting for Derick?'

'He will join us in his own time,' smirked Simon. 'Tell me now, what will you do with your dear friend if she digs too deep? She's a hot snoophead and a very nosy lark. You don't want to see her feathers ruffled a lot, do you?'

'Mr Redeldrag,' gasped James, 'you scare me sometimes.'

'Scared ones are easy to be commanded,' jeered Simon, 'but she doesn't obey anyone, including herself. She will be commanded too.'

'Mmmm —' mumbled James, unsure how to reply, afraid to appear dubious, afraid to touch upon Simon's thoughts amongst a growing sense of humanitarian duty.

'Mother nature will bend her knees. She's just a woman, that is the fate of all of them. Sooner or later they all got to give...'

Behind the curtain, Natalie was seething at that venomous slew of insults. It was difficult to tell who spotted who first, but when her and Dorian's eyes met, it was a pure miracle none of them uttered a sound. Perhaps they were petrified too. Their faces resembled question marks, they were all over them, appearing suddenly, in pairs, with driblets of cold sweat. Dorian fidgeted clumsily, feeling like something was sliding from under his dapper shirt. He had more reasons to remain hidden, despite jiggling about nervously. Simon or James didn't seem to notice the unusual rustling of the curtain, neither of them even looked that way; they weren't prepared to leave, perhaps, they were waiting for someone or for something to happen. Natalie though — she wouldn't be herself if she wasn't gonna do anything about the situation; she simply despised that sort of chauvinistic behaviour. She revealed herself, appearing within kicking distance of Simon's manfulness, right in front of his face.

'Well, well, well,' said Simon, completely unfazed by Natalie's unexpected emergence. 'It appears, we don't need no crumbs for our lovebird.'

'I'd rather be a naive bird than a backstabbing, slanderous swine.'

'Hold on a minute, sweetheart,' said Simon, staying provokingly calm. 'Who do you call swine? We are academics and serious businessmen, not livestock.'

'Do academics work hidden in a burrow beneath the face of the earth?'

'That depends on the purpose,' replied Simon, still mockingly unmoved. 'Do damsels spy on friends like two-faced rats?' Saying this he grasped Natalie by her pointy chin and squeezed her lower jaw, trying to open the mouth in demand for a swift answer, directing her sight at James.

'Or perhaps, you're not lady-like at all,' he carried on, curling her long blonde hair with his index finger, 'but just one hell of a hot bitch, lost in shadow, desperate for your fifteen minutes of fame. I'm sorry to disappoint you, but you've landed badly. Your man has already deserted you. You're alone, bitter, facing the night of your day, betraying your friends, when all the life had gone beyond the shrunken walls of your heart.'

'Where is Derick?' breathed Natalie, wriggling her face from Simon's grip.

'I couldn't care less about him,' said Simon, pretending to be walking off.

'Or maybe you're not,' he continued, stopping exactly next to the place where Dorian was hidden, and sweeping the curtain aside with one fell swoop, he caught him with his hands in the cookie jar — more specifically, under his shirt, trying to pull something up around his chest.

'I knew she couldn't have ventured here alone,' gloated Simon, looking at Dorian the way a hungry wolf looks at a sheep lost in the woods, towering before him like Goliath.

'What a surprise! Another Rose in the way,' fleered Simon. 'You're as sly as your crippled father.'

'Leave my father alone,' growled Dorian.

'Arthur Donald Rose,' declaimed Simon, 'a great man who has got everything small. I bet he's got his little fingers deep in this side of the pie too. Is it his invisible hand you're hiding under your shirt?'

Then Simon plunged with his arms forward, as swiftly as he could, intending to pull Dorian by the shirt, but as he barely laid hands on him, Dorian twisted on his heels to the right, and before Simon managed to get a firm grip on his chest, he deflected his hands with a raw, chopping movement of his left hand.

'I have learnt to deal with scumbags like you in school. You're cooked,' said Dorian as Simon backed off, having received a hardy blow to his hands.

'I wonder if they taught you how to deal with this,' said Simon, and in response, he pulled out a short, silver revolver from behind his belt and aimed it at Dorian's chest.

'Simon, no!' screamed James, who was a mere spectator since Simon's arrival.

'Shut it, James!' Simon retorted.

It shut him indeed. Everyone else was shut, except Simon,

who was smiling at Dorian, having regained full control of the situation.

'Now, Mr braveheart, drop your spying gadgets on the floor, but slowly.'

'You may kill me, but I will never bow to you.'

'No? What about killing your fellow partner in crime then,' said Simon, now aiming the gun at Natalie's head, 'or even better, letting one friend kill another?' he ended and handed the gun to James.

'James, don't listen to him!' said Natalie. 'You don't have to do anything; you have the choice.'

'A man must always have a choice,' said James, still keeping the muzzle straight at Natalie, 'and here is what I have chosen.'

He took the gun away from Natalie's head and put the cold barrel between Dorian's brows.

'Do what Simon said,' he commanded, gazing deep into Dorian's eyes, pressing the barrel of the gun even stronger against Dorian's forehead, forcing him to submission, 'and drop your stuff on the floor.'

Dorian slowly put one hand under his shirt. Next moment, a heavy, old-school tape recorder with a large microphone attached to it by a wire plunked on the floor. James picked it up and, holding it high above his head, he asked Simon, 'What shall I do with it?'

'Smash it!'

James let it drop on the floor again and then crushed his foot into it, breaking the plastic recorder into pieces.

'What should we do with them now?' asked James, eagerly, still keeping the gun firmly pointed at Dorian's head. Strangely, he winked at him before finishing the sentence.

'James, you're such a snake!' cried Natalie.

'Let them go,' Simon said.

'But why?'

'Do not question the orders whilst executing them,' was Simon's plain response.

'You two, you're free. You know where the door is,' said James, brandishing the revolver in front of their faces, pointing the direction with it.

'When you come back home, don't forget to tell your lovely mummy that I'm sorry not to send her cards anymore, but I'm just too busy at the moment,' Simon said to Dorian as he was walking away.

When Dorian and Natalie finally left the stage, Simon took the gun from James's hand. The first thing he said to him was to admit that he'd put only blanks inside the cylinder. Then he went on saying that he went upstairs only to take his revolver. That news had thrown James into real consternation. Everything was acted out superbly, even the scenery was so appropriate.

'Mind you, I've never killed any people in my life,' said Simon. 'People have always killed themselves for me.'

When Dorian and Natalie went outside, they were both deep in their thoughts, ruminating over the recent events; more so Dorian than Natalie, who was always keen to forget the past quickly as long as she's immediately got something else she could look forward to looming over the horizon. Dorian was completely different. He now let his all too analytical mind loose, trying to match the newly unearthed pieces of the puzzle to the bigger picture, trying too hard, as it seemed, taking it all too much to heart — thinking about his mum. Why did Simon say that? Why had James winked at him? He looked at Natalie, a bit bashfully, as he wasn't accustomed to asking people he didn't know very well to give him their opinion about his private matters. Her face appeared lightened and unfussed, translucent like the wings of butterflies in the crimson glints of the lowly sun, suddenly piercing through the narrow gap in the dark, garnet-blue clouds. She seemed to be adoring the last reflections of the sun on the undisturbed waters of Lake Elborn, but inside she was missing someone, and the swans were no more. She could hear the name — but it was of the person, the images of whom she wanted to avoid.

'Simon — my father doesn't want to talk about him for some reason,' said Dorian, looking at Natalie's face with tension. 'I think it has got something to do with my mum. I better ask her.'

'Better not,' said Natalie.

'Why? Why you, women, always have something to hide?'

'Because you, men, cannot be trusted.'

'But... Are you convinced about Simon, now you've seen it with your own eyes?'

She gave him one stinging look that was more telling than a hundred words. They spent the rest of the time on their way out in silence before parting by the tube station nearest to the university. They went in opposite directions. Natalie was in no mood to offer Dorian a lift. She hadn't heard anything from Derick since the morning. It saddened her badly; her thoughts were getting cloudier. She didn't know Derick was putting his feet on the ground in the foreign land of Xuva as she was leaving the multi-storey university car park. She left her phone on the passenger seat, hoping it would buzz again today. It didn't. If only she'd known — this morning was the first and the last time she was to hear from him for the whole week, but her hope was high, it was going to die last.

* * *

It was very early Sunday, by the end of the week, a week after his trip to Windchain was over, when Derick arrived back in the country. His overnight flight from Xuva had wearied him much, his face was a bleary sight to look upon, but still — driven by nothing but urgency, and ever-present, nagging curiosity, he wasted no time looking for a resting place around the airport. He knew it's gonna take him some time to get to Willowood today as Sunday buses were not too frequent these days. The airport was on a plain, south to the slowing waters of the River Brook, which were gradually losing speed after falling through the southern drops of the plateau of Eastern Highlands before reaching the city of Clarksdowne as a tame, lethargic waterway, split into many drowsy channels, which at night were turning hazy, attracting hosts of crepuscular creatures. Derick's destination was about twenty-six miles from his standpoint; he was pinned to the metal post, painted yellow-green,

238

standing on the recently laid on asphalt, smelling its tarry fumes in the morning, looking out for the bus. It was one of the magic moments reminding him that he lived in the culture of layers and cover-ups, in the age of wonderment over rapid transformations, where the shallowness was the only measure of depth. He was less than a mile from Clarksdowne beltway, the busiest freeway around the city, but there was no point in venturing there on foot as no one would ever pull off, no matter what.

His last stop was only the next after the one that was the closest to his former place where he grew up. He could see the trees of the orchard belonging to his stepfather as he was passing by the bus stop that was only a stone's throw away from his old home. The long, brown bench he found that white feather on, earlier this summer, only flashed before his eyes. Where is it now? What is its destiny? — he thought. Is it still floating through the air? He felt suddenly tired of his recent escapades. He needed vacations, now more than ever. But he was on vacation, he'd just forgotten its chastening purpose, sucked in and engulfed by the river of lies, beleaguered by faces, all alone, dreaming.

A well-trodden trackway passing through the two narrow footbridges over the rivers Brook and Leyron respectively was the only way to Belgar from Willowood. It was inaccessible by motor vehicles, except for certain motorbikes as it led through the marshy fields on the edge of the small forest, wedged between the rivers. The bus stopped less than ten yards away from the first bridge, next to the point where the trackway appeared from under the grass blades. It drove off south-east, leaving Derick behind, on the provincial, tarmac road that was joining with another provincial road, a few miles on, being one of the only two roads cars could drive on, leading to the small village of Belgar that was surrounded from the north by dense coniferous forest.

Derick couldn't escape from falling under the impression he was going back in time as he crossed over the roaring waters of River Brook that came to life once more before joining forces with River Leyron in the tumult of its rapids. He was fortunate it hadn't been raining too heavily recently, as the marshy, woody area between the rivers normally turned into a boggy lake when it rained for more than two days straight, being squeezed into a slight depression from both sides by the flanking rivers like a sponge that has to soak up an excess of water. The landscape had changed only marginally since he was here last time, alone, but on the eastern side of Leyron — he was trying his hardest to evoke memories of being there, but a complete emptiness of space surrounded him as he lost himself in summoning the spirits of this place.

A vast, flat, open fenland spread far and wide under his feet as he stepped down from the last bridge. He noticed sticky, black and brown sludges of mud around his boots; he knew he had to be careful not to fall into a bog. It was so flat he could see some dwellings far under the horizon. It was the village of Belgar, a small settlement of woodmen, fishermen, and hunters, living at the gate of one of the largest forests in the country — the Lamrack Forest. Derick could clearly distinguish the dark line of tall trees, miles away, stretching from west to east on his left. All the visible area, although lying low over its full length, was abundant with great expanses of soaring reeds, growing compact and thick, forming smooth, rustling blankets, alongside the edges of which the paths were laid down. Occasionally, tiny patches of green and yellow ferns were popping out here and there. Derick had no clue how he could possibly find his grandad here.

Slowly advancing with tiptoe steps, he set forth on another adventure, seemingly being weary of them. He put out his phone and set up the interactive compass on its screen. He felt he couldn't afford to get lost in a place he only so vaguely remembered now, unsure why, but he couldn't think about it too much now, he had to plough on. Holding his mobile reminded him of his friends, especially of Natalie — but they would be too curious about everything, too nosy, too… blameful for everything to face them today. He felt too derelict, too run-down for it, he just wanted to find Marty, that's all.

Perhaps he was too deep in thoughts about his dear friends that he didn't at first notice how his right foot was disappearing in the bog until he was up to his knee in it and started losing balance. He lifted his leg out of it with a sharp, forceful swing back of his torso as soon as he felt the murky slime pouring over the upper of his boot. His bottom landed on the muddy ground with a splat: his legs were free, and his hands were free, but his phone — it took a dive in the bog, and it was sinking, sinking deep. Derick could only watch in horror how the last civilized part of him was ebbing away.

He was lost, in the middle of wasteland, sitting in the soil by the side of the massive bog devouring his phone, dowsed in mud, disarmed and lonely as always, in search of his crazy elusive grandfather. He'd still got time to turn back before it was too late, but no strength to move. He swung back his body once more and spread out his arms. The sun was shining bright directly above his head. The day was in full bloom.

'At least it's a nice day,' said Derick, closing his eyes.

There was no answer; he expected none anyway. The wind was humming among the reeds, birds were chirping around, and the cloudless sky was standing still. Derick felt like the whole of eternity was passing through him, he was reminiscent of his ancestors — only ever driven by their survival instincts. Suddenly, he pulled up his body, sniffing out the smell of burning grass. That odour — of smoking dragon fern, infused him, filling his head with light. It wasn't from the sun, it came from within. His mind flashed; he was going back in time indeed. The gate was open: once forgotten, now found again.

He saw himself, crying, sitting by the strand of a reedy lake. The lowly reeds were sparse and bowing to the wind. Near the edge of a forest, there was a shed, partially underground, made of a mixture of peat, boughs and smaller twigs of nearby trees, covered mainly with ferns. A bonfire was next to it, it was just smouldering, about to burn out, when a man of shadowy, scrunched down stature emerged from the bushes. It was Marty. He was over twenty years younger than now. He came over to crying baby Derick, only a few years old. He was holding some undergrowth in his hands, which he promptly released into the fire. It sparked into flames again. The earthy, spicy scent of dragon fern saturated the air, filling hearts with joy. Derick stopped crying as Marty took him closer to the fire, and crouching next to him, they put forth their open hands to get warm. Suddenly, a figure of a young woman appeared through the short, arched hole in the shed, resembling a doorframe, covered by the light sheet of brown leather. It was Mary. A rare smile was holding to her face. It faded away as soon as she looked at Marty. She was followed out by a man who now came into sight, towering over her. It was Simon. He came up to Derick and caressed his hair briskly. He smiled at him and looked into his eyes. It was the first time Derick gazed into Simon's glistening eyes.

Derick stood up at once, feeling momently aroused. He went around the edge of the bog, chasing the smell down to its source. Reeds were giving way to small shrubs and little trees. He'd just realized how close to the forest he found himself. He started running slowly but clumsily. The land was drying up. The transpiring smell was becoming more pungent with every step he took. It fluttered in the air like the wings of humming birds. As he turned the corner, the images from his dream materialized. A small, round area of smooth, cut grass opened out before him. It was a partly enclosed recess, by the neck of the woods, before the finite lines of the trees of Lamrack Forest. He saw the same large, reedy lake, the shore of which was now heavily assaulted by overgrowth, turning it into a shallow pond. The same peaty shed was standing there too, looking only a bit more moth-eaten and decomposed, but still defying the passage of time. The same fire was burning slowly and giving off a lovely, transcending scent of dragon fern. Suddenly, the sound of rustling and crackling reeds stirred the air. Derick, disoriented where that sound was coming from, skimmed through the wall of reeds with his eyes, going left to right and right to left. He didn't see the arched figure of a man coming out until he opened his mouth wide, as wide as he could. It was his grandad, still holding the same undergrowth in his hands, more than twenty years on.

He dropped the underwood on the grass immediately as he saw him. Looking at Derick with those dreamy, bright blue eyes, smiling at him bizarrely, he might as well have been reminiscent of the lost time that he was looking upon his face here before.

'Derick, my dear,' Marty sighed at length, shedding a tear. 'Is that you I'm seeing, or am I dreaming?'

Derick said nothing but came up to him and hugged the old man. Marty felt now he wasn't hallucinating, and that everything he ate this morning was perfectly fine. He pressed Derick's face against his chest tightly and clawed his palm into his lush, dark hair. He smelled really foul from living in woods and marshes, but that didn't bother Derick at all. He's found what he was looking for. It was back to the starting point for him.

'How did you find me? I was getting really worried about you. Where have you been? Your home is empty like a ghost house.'

'It's a long story,' Derick mused, sobbing through the tears.

'Did you find Walter?'

'No, but I found someone else,' said Derick, and tilting his head backwards, he looked at Marty's drabbed face, struggling to suppress the tears. He found the same, inextricable curiosity permeating him through and emanating out. His eyes were shining like blue stars in the sky.

Marty didn't say anything at first, only showed Derick a hand towards the shed. It was much more spacious than it looked from the outside since only its top, slightly arching part was overground, with nearly all the surface of the roof openable from inside, so that it could be adapted as a window when the weather allowed it. A large, steep staircase was right behind the entrance. The room was perfectly round and resembled "the room of thousand clocks" from Marty's old house, except, instead of the clocks and watches, there were jars of different sizes and shapes everywhere, with various plants and herbs stuck inside. In the centre of the room, a huge, wicked cauldron was suspended on a metal railing between two thick, black posts made of a hardy, jet-black material. It looked so witchy, Derick couldn't resist himself remarking it must have been stolen from a local coven. Marty smiled but only slightly. Slabs of coal and peat glowed orange and yellow from underneath it. It wasn't just a shed he found himself in, it was a plants and herbs pantry and biochemistry lab in one. It was unusually warm and dry inside. The mixture of coal and peat was keeping the unwanted moisture out, insulating the whole place at the same time.

'You know, I spend much time in the forest now,' began Marty. 'I found that talking to trees can be much more self-gratifying than talking to fellow humans.'

'I didn't know trees had voices,' said Derick.

'Oh yes, they have — if you listen very hard, and when you are one with them and one is all, but it takes an awful lot of time to say anything in their speech. They speak only if they have to, undisturbed by time, unlike humans who are in a constant hurry to build bigger and bigger towers of words, and in the end, they get entangled in their pursuit of the kingdom of heaven.'

They both sat by the fire on the seats made of dry peat. Marty took one of the jars from the shelf above his head and poured the content into two large bowls made of black clay, then he left them on the side of the cauldron to heat up. The vibrant smell of wild mushrooms, summer berries, and fresh nuts filled the room. All windows were shut at this time, which allowed the warm, pervading scent to intensify and prevented it from escaping, but sitting in semi-darkness, around softly glowing coals, although warm and cosy, somehow kept Derick from opening up. He saw Marty peering at him intensively, slowly sipping his hot broth, occasionally blowing on it. The colours on his face, they were fluctuating between dark and light. He was weary of silence.

'Are you not eating? It's hot enough.'

'I'm not hungry,'

'You have changed. What's happened?'

'I don't know where to start. There's so much to remember.'

'When you tell the truth, you don't have to remember anything because the truth is universal. Only a lie has to take forms. Truth is formless, shapeless, like water. It's infinite.'

'But you said that even infinity is repeatable.'

Marty shrugged and stirred in his seat. He took up Derick's bowl and stood up, bringing it to him, to the other side of the fire. Derick took a sup. It was so heartily tasty and warming, he desired to down it all at once, but he would have burnt himself in doing so, it was that hot. Marty hunkered down by his side and fondled his hair gently, then pinched his cheek — the way he liked, the way he used to do it, smiling at him fondly. He took Derick's hand and put it forth close to the fire, together with his.

'I would do everything for you if I could,' he said with a sigh. 'I know, I should have done much better for you. You're the only one I've got.'

Derick's hand slipped down through Marty's fingers, flopping lifelessly as soon as he said this. He took the bowl down from his mouth and put it on the floor, on the other side of the seat. His smile had faded away as he looked at Marty again.

'Why are you lying to me?' he asked. 'I've met your son at Windchain,' he added after a moment.

Marty rose up and slowly went back to his resting place, leaving Derick on his seat, without saying a word to him. He sank deep in his seat, submerging himself in thoughts, his head down on the chest, his palms covering the brow, with only thumbs on the outside as if he was trying to hide something from the world in every possible way. He was making one desperate, last-ditch effort to separate himself from the past that devastated his life, haunting him like an inseparable shadow of his own statue of greatness, now lying in ruins. It took Derick a while to notice Marty was weeping.

'Simon has twisted him beyond control,' he said at length, in a shattered voice.

'Why is everyone blaming Simon for everything?!'

At this time, Marty's concoction inside the cauldron started giving off loud, bubbling noises. Thin, white vapours arose above the brim. Marty sprang to his feet quickly and cast a glance down his magic pot. Derick, stirred up by his grandad's weird behaviour, stood up too and had a look inside. There was hardly any liquid there, for such a massive cauldron, being nearly up to his chest in height. What was left was boiling and seething profusely on the bottom. Suddenly, a fine line of white condensation became visible, just above the line of that watery solution. Marty made a dash for the stairs like fire in the reeds as soon as he saw that.

'What is more important, your herbs or me!?' shouted Derick, at the top of his lungs, in a frenzied outpour of anger as Marty disappeared through the hole, taking no heed of Derick's voice. Derick stood there, next to the cauldron, boiling mad but so curious at the same time.

When Marty reappeared at the top of the staircase, he was holding the same bunch of undergrowth he dropped by the reeds. He ran down the stairs and quickly threw it into the cauldron. The same vivid, earthy, insightful scent of dragon fern, burning in sudden flames, filled the room. Marty produced a long, white ladle from somewhere. It was so long it could get to the bottom of the cauldron with ease. There was a narrow spatula on one end, with a tiny hole above it, and a small, shallow, sharp-edged cup on the other end. Marty lowered the cup end in the cauldron with both his arms, his head was gone too; he fiddled and jiggled with it for a bit before bobbing up.

He was holding the ladle carefully by its cup end, examining what he'd just gathered. A black, tarry, odourless substance was setting quickly inside the cup. He hung the ladle above the cauldron and turned to a narrow, horizontal fissure in the wall, lined with silver tinsel, from where he took a small precision syringe with an impossibly thin needle on the top of it, which Derick couldn't see in that nocturnal light. Marty cautiously filled the syringe with the black liquid sitting in the cup of the ladle, and then injected the content into the bloodstream, just above the wrist, much to Derick's shock. He flung the empty syringe into the fire, then he lodged the narrow end of the ladle between two large, burning coals, before finally slumping back down in his seat.

Derick couldn't believe his eyes. He'd just witnessed how his grandad, perfectly casually, drugged himself with something. He'd even forgotten why he came here: his mind went blank, his eyes were blind, he didn't remember what he said. He was just standing like a pillar of salt, observing in horror how Marty's furrowed face was turning mellow.

'Can you give me that ladle from the fire, please?' asked Marty's dozy voice, after a long while. 'But be careful, it's super hot.'

ENCOUNTERS

Derick was so terrified he didn't respond to Marty's question at first, thinking he was dying or something, but as he saw his desiccated, veiny limb swinging towards the fire, he took the ladle from it. It was inhumanly hot, even on the end that wasn't in the fire. Derick couldn't hold it for longer than a few seconds before getting skin burns, so he propped it clumsily against Marty's seat. Marty managed to catch it mid-air as it was falling free. He pressed the hottest, glowing spatula end against the place on the skin he'd just pinned. Derick watched in dismay and terror how the skin started to melt and lather. The foul, disgusting smell of burnt fat devoured the heartiness of dragon fern. Everything happened so quickly that profound silence, which dominated that dreadful scenery, had gone completely unnoticed. Marty hadn't uttered even a single whimper, despite maiming himself.

'May I call myself indestructible now?' asked Marty, lifting his wounded, bleeding hand. 'I feel not a great deal indeed.'

'What have you done to yourself?!' cried Derick.

'What I have taken was only a very crude and potentially poisonous form of the substance that is being administered to hundreds of kind-hearted, good-willed people, misled and deceived by your "sorry, persecuted" Simon and his minions, even as we speak. I had to know what he's up to. That's why I have turned to you for help, to get you involved. You must know a lot more than me now, I presume, probably more than you should, but only the truth can shield you from Simon. Haven't you noticed yet?! He tries to take you away from everyone and take control of your life.'

'I don't know,' said Derick. 'Marty, you're bleeding! Do you really not feel anything?'

'You must understand that my pain receptors are gone for now,' replied Marty, wrapping a thick piece of garment around his hand.'

'I know, but I thought it was all just a fantasy all the time, that... it wasn't for real.'

'Imagine now thousands and thousands of people taking this substance, but in a more refined and much more potent form, that alters their perception of pain, one of the very underpinning of

247

being human, without their awareness, thinking they're doing it for their children, but not knowing how dependent on it they become. If Simon figures out how to pass it on, he's a winner.'

Suddenly, Derick remembered his last trip to Mowhaken, how he met Maarten Burdent, and what he saw. He'd realized he'd been watching a movie he'd played the main role in without suspecting it, without feeling anything. But what if Marty didn't know Maarten was at work too? He took out the old, crumpled piece of paper he'd got from Dorian's father, containing the photo of Marty, Maarten, and Mr Kubla, taken in Xuva, more than twenty years ago, and threw it before his face.

Marty took it from the ground and unfolded it slowly in his hands. He knew the message now, he knew what was coming, the real purpose of his grandson's "magical" appearance. He didn't come here to bring him news about Walter, no, he was there to bring him greetings from the dead — or so he thought. Marty found with surprise he didn't feel pain or any discomfort when looking at the old picture of himself and his lost companions. He wanted to express what was inside of him, but he was losing sight of it with every passing moment. He was just on a verge of a new remarkably horrific discovery that the unfeeling of pain may run deeper than he previously thought. He stared at his grandson, standing by his side, with a strange sensation of comforting numbness in his tongue, a fluent speechlessness.

'I know what you wanna say,' began Derick, growing somewhat impatient of Marty's inability to speak, 'but you don't have to say anything; I know it's not your fault. "You become what you hate the most as long as you fight against it — that's the biggest dilemma of all warriors". Do you remember the day when you told me that tale about a lonely warrior fighting the wind? I don't know why I've got reminded of it now, but I really liked the fact that he eventually turned into the wind himself and was everywhere, lonely no more. — "Not everyone who's lost faith in paradise begins to believe in hell," my old man, so don't worry, I don't believe in Simon, I believe in myself. I will take your torch and finish what you have started.'

ENCOUNTERS

Marty was staring at Derick, knowing that he'd failed him. His only hope was in Derick not failing himself. He couldn't resist smiling at him, in spite of his powerlessness. At the back of his mind, he was curious about Derick's sudden leaps of confidence. He couldn't do much more about it. His strengths were leaving him. He could just carry on.

'I suspect Walter found a secret, underground passage leading to a place where that new "cure for pain" is made,' he said at length, still pushing on. 'I think he may know about a few more of them. I just never got hold of him. Simon has his hands on all enforcement and security services. It's now impossible for me to come out.'

'I will find that out for you,' said Derick, fond of himself, and helped Marty to stand up.

They both came outside and parted in peace after a long while spent on talking about the weather, food in the wild, and the directions of the world. The fire had burned out. The wind from the east was picking up. Unusual, but it always meant a change of seasons. Marty told Derick to move along the line of trees, always making sure to have the sun in front of him, thus being certain to be heading westward. Sticking to those two simple tips would ensure that sooner or later he would meet the River Leyron on his path, leaving Lamrack Forest behind him. Then, moving away from the forest, he would follow the riverbank until he found the first bridge. Marty gave him his blessing, no matter whatever it meant for him. Derick was in a surprisingly good mood. He felt like singing — even though his road seemed to go ever on and on.

12
FALL

Derick spent the night in Clarksdowne. He didn't feel particularly safe in Willowood anymore, thinking Marty looked so dire he could haunt him at night. Everybody had disappeared; the streets were empty, so was his house. Bruce must have moved out to Clarksdowne, he thought at once. He was fortunate enough to catch the last bus to the city. There, he caught an eye of a certain taxi driver, starting it all over again, taking it slow upon his return from holidays, once again, looking out for a fare. He'd rescued Derick from falling on his face just in time. It was his "lucky day" in the end: he found his grandad at the first attempt, he was picked up from the street when he was just about to lose his last leg and offered a place to stay overnight when he had no money left even for a shelter. He'd left his life in Hillbarrow; he just didn't feel like coming back there yet. For now, life was good for Derick.

Good old captain Jim, his favourite cabman, didn't ask much, seeing Derick's dead tired face. He was content Derick was spending his time actively. He lived on the tenth floor of an old, concrete apartment house, one of the very many cheap places in this part of southern Clarksdowne, the area of the city known for its stark contrasts between people who lived there, swarmed into high, skyscraper-like apartment buildings, and those below, who worked in small but spacious, air-conditioned, modern buildings of public services, such as courts, libraries, and hospitals. Jim, like many other residents, was an immigrant, a product of chance and necessity, commonly blamed for the highest crime rate in the whole agglomeration. Gang wars were a common sight in these parts, it was a way of life, an opportunity to be seen and recognized more than a curse — the only way back down to the life of splendour and affluence, where the free access to hospitals, jails, and courts of law laid open.

Being so close to the roof was sickening for Derick, even though he wasn't afraid of heights. It was the feeling of being exposed when you lay down in bed, bare and naked, elevated above everyone else, staring at the stars, trying to reach them when they are just too far. Jim fell fast asleep, probably by mistake, leaving the beer business unfinished by his side. He was snoring heartily, plonked deep in his armchair. A set of darts and a small pocket knife was still on the glass top table, next to opened beer cans, letting the dartboard down. Derick found him in exactly the same position in the morning, still deep in slumber. It may be his day off-duty, he thought. He took the cans from the table and went out.

Outside, he was waiting for a bus again. It was time to go north again. He waited, but the buses were nowhere in sight. The luck had deserted him. Then he remembered it was Monday — a national state holiday, but that meant there was no one to take him to Hillbarrow today. He dismissed the thought of coming back and begging Jim for a ride; the old man had already done too many unreturned favours for him, and probably he was still asleep. It was too far to his apartment anyway. Derick left the bus stop, and while loitering along the streets, he was thinking about the next steps. As he was going past a large, locked door of a shopping mall, he thought he stumbled across a face of someone he was used to seeing much more frequently than nowadays, even though there was no one around him. He halted and stared… at the wanted notice of Mrs Dauntwraith.

'Jim was absolutely right,' he muttered under his breath, 'society is a mousetrap, it's like flypaper. I hope she's not got busted yet.'

Suddenly, even as he was reflecting upon the sight of the black and white wanted poster of Mrs Dauntwraight, he thought he heard voices.

'Hey, mister! Over here!' a male voice shouted.

'I'm so glad I could find someone on the street today!' he gasped, running at Derick from behind.

Derick turned his face towards the man, but was immediately

in shock to find it was his stepfather crossing the street on a red light. He could only wonder why he saw him just today.

'Derick?!'

'Bruce?!'

'I — what are you doing here?'

'I could ask you the same,' replied Derick.

Bruce was dressed very smartly; his startling, glossed up attire dazzled Derick in the eyes, but it was somehow togged up: he had a thick, long, purple and black gown with ornate, golden fringes thrown over his shoulder, and on his head there was a grey wig, sitting precariously.

'I — I'm sorry for everything. If only I'd known...'

Bruce's tattered and unintelligible speech struck Derick with wonder, but he let him continue, still startled by his portentous array.

'Everyone had left me.'

'What are you saying?'

'Can you bring me your mother back, please. I can't live without her.'

'I don't know where she is, maybe you tell me?' asked Derick, unmoved, but now slightly surprised by his own bluntness. Bruce nodded his head sideways and down, then he spoke, letting that burdensome weight slide off on the sidewalk — his gown fell off his shoulder.

'I know Simon fabricated your studies. He told me today, right in my face, just when the proceedings were about to commence.'

'I've always believed I was a law student,' said Derick, cold as stone.

'You've followed your dreams; now my whole career hangs by a thread, and he's just laughing. I hate him! He treats people as if he could own everybody.'

Why is everyone blaming Simon for everything, even Bruce? thought Derick, but he listened on, captured by Bruce's sudden change of heart. After all, he'd not made his mind up yet about where to go.

'Suddenly, one of the jurors got seriously sick and had to be driven to Greenfields,' Bruce carried on. 'We're one juror down. If I can't take this case to its conclusion today, I'm finished. It's the most important day of my life.'

Hearing about Bruce's apparent plight, Derick lent him an even more eager ear. He knew next to nothing about court proceedings, despite the fact that his stepfather was a head judge and that his own name was still in the directory of law students at East Point University, but it appeared strange even for him that such an important institution was not secured against as likely an occurrence as sickness.

'Are there any replacements?' asked Derick.

'For the cases of the highest importance, no replacements are considered,' explained Bruce. 'The jurors must stand from start to finish. Only death can relieve them from their duty. The problem is that one juror has just had a heart attack and died.'

'What has it got to do with you? Why are you working anyway? It's the state holiday; even politicians stay at home.'

'Exactly. But courts always work on state holidays. I thought you knew about that. Everyone else watches the proceedings remotely at home and learns how the most important decisions are made. I am accountable for the whole case as a head judge, but I'm running out of time. If I do run out, I'm rid of and replaced. Today the streets are nearly empty, and the court hall is empty. We do that to avoid the bias, we must avoid it at all cost. I have to find a juror now, I cannot adjourn anymore.'

Derick listened with his head down, admiring how his feet swept him off under the very doorstep of another adventure. There were times he wished he'd never gone out his room on that day where it all started. Now leaves were falling on his feet from the rusty sky, seeds of fall were in his mind. He was just as shadows of those falling leaves, subject to the ever-changing feelings of the wind, a net force of chances, twitching along the line of mediocrity, but the seeds of change were already planted within him before. Finally, he understood that twitching along the line of mediocrity wasn't for him.

'What's your case about?' asked Derick, lifting his head up.

'I must not tell you anything,' said Bruce. 'I have sworn under the oath that under no circumstances will I influence the jury; therefore, I can't intervene.'

Bruce tapped Derick's shoulder, signalling him it was time to go. Derick followed in his stride. He mustn't know anything about the case until he's met with other members of the jury. No names were given, nothing unnecessary that could lead to bias, just 'pure facts and the deeds' as Bruce tried to explain. 'The letter of law must always be governed by the iron, all-else-defying logic, and it is the purity of logic that defines the purity of law,' he said to Derick upon their parting on the long, flat stairs of the High Court in Clarksdowne. He went through the door on the left and told Derick to go through the door on the right.

The room Derick entered was muggy and claustrophobic, filled with sweat and the repulsive odour of butts from cigars and cigarettes, even though all windows were open. They must have opened them right now, thought Derick, who was hit by the malodorous wave of draught as he opened the door. All was black or white inside: the people, numbering seven, excluding Derick, the furniture, and the walls. He was under an impression he'd entered an old movie scene. Quickly he noticed he was definitely the youngest of them all. They all looked so different but so alike at the same time: black polished shoes, black fitted trousers, white tailored shirts and black ties or no ties; their scrawny faces were smooth and clean shaven — it was a living assemblage of corpses before they were all fitted into the coffins and put on biers for display. Derick found they had no names but numbers only. He was juror number eight. They all sat on black chairs by the sides of the black table. What really struck him was the shape of the table. It was octagonal, the same as the shape of the court's building, which was only a few storeys high but immense in its flatness. He learnt that day that an octagon was the symbol of law, order, and undivided unanimity.

The case was of a person who happened to be in the wrong place at the wrong time, and this was exactly what the "indicted one", as the person in question was called in the legal jargon, was accused of. Derick couldn't believe his ears that the High Court was dealing with such a petty "crime" as being in the wrong place at the wrong time. One of the jurors, number seven, the oldest and the most outspoken one, argued that they were all guilty of that crime at times in their lives, but that was fine as long as the crime had gone unnoticed. 'It only comes to light,' he deduced 'when another event occurs that allows the crime to be noticed.' In this case, that was exactly what happened with the "indicted one", who was caught red-handed as a witness of a fire, which was proved to be an arson. The directory of the firm he was employed in stated clearly that the "indicted one" was supposed to be on vacation in the exotic island, the name of which was withheld, likewise any other names and descriptions of any kind that 'could lead to bias' as Bruce said, at the time the event happened. That was the main piece of evidence against the "indicted one". It was undeniable, logical, and prevailing without a shadow of a doubt.

Then there was the arson. Derick was terrified to find out that it was a completely unrelated event in the eyes of the law, pending investigation, as the fingerprints found there belonged to "no one alive", not to the "indicted one", who was only found at the scene.

'What does it mean?' asked Derick, puzzled by the ambivalence of the argot they were using.

'It means that the fingerprints must have belonged to someone who's already died,' juror number three answered patiently. He was the tallest and the second youngest by the look of his face. He was the only one without a tie. He was also the one who'd got the most truthful eyes — bright blue and serene as if they belonged to someone else.

'But that's an absolute nonsense!' cried Derick.

'Not at all!' a few jurors protested in rabid response to Derick's dissonant voice.

'That only tells us that the "indicted one" was not an arsonist' number three said again, giving Derick a respectful glance over his face.

'Yes, yes! Indeed!' more voices joined in, giving consent to number three.

'Of course, he wasn't!' retorted Derick. 'Just look again at the video. Can someone zoom the image, please?'

There was also a very unclear video recording capturing the back of the "indicted one" watching as the fire was spreading. It also captured a very dim silhouette or a "caricature of a person" in the tempest of fire as it suddenly blew out of proportion. It emerged out of the fire, running as if from within as the fire appeared out of nowhere through the floor before taking on the wall, scrunched, moving quickly and stealthily, swinging its head, with dangling arms almost to the floor. Then it ran into the wall and disappeared. It was a mysterious event, even so Derick thought he had a hunch about who that might have been, but he was told that it was another matter altogether by not one but all of the jurors. Unanimity had prevailed.

'What about the sentence?' asked Derick.

'Only the head judge can give the sentence. We're only here to plead,' said another juror, number one, who was keeping hold of the remote control.

'What are we pleading then, fellows?' asked number seven, standing up from the chair. 'Is the "indicted one" guilty of the crime of being in the wrong place at the wrong time or not guilty?'

'Guilty!' they pleaded, one by one. Derick conformed, for his own sake. He thought his good name mustn't be marred in that farce; after all, the case was a no-brainer. They were all probably right about it. What kind of sentence could one get for pleading guilty of being in the wrong place at the wrong time anyway?

'I've got to go to the toilet,' he only said.

No one objected. No one went with him either. He was escorted there by two male guards standing outside the room, but the real surprise awaited him when he came out once he finished.

Two female guards stood at attention by both sides of the door to the female toilet. Then the third woman appeared through the door. She wore black and white, striped pyjamas, hanging loosely on her skeleton. Both her hands and legs were restrained in super tight, thick manacles. She looked at Derick with her morbid face; she resembled the woman he'd known for many years in nothing but voice — still so daunting and perfectly patronising.

'Derick! What are you doing here?! You should be taking care of your mother,' said Mrs Dauntwraith, standing in the void between the mighty posts of the doorcase.

The door of the room where the rest of the jurors was sitting patiently, waiting for Derick's comeback was now open, even as he was terrorised by the macabre state of being he found Mrs Dauntwraith in, and they poured out, one by one, treading unanimously in single file as an aboriginal tribe — bonded by blood.

'Where are you all going?' asked Derick.

'It's time to go.'

'But I don't…'

They wouldn't listen, they left for the court hall, united by silence of one mind, as befitted — the procession of justice. Derick followed after number seven. Mrs Dauntwraith was in the lead after receiving jabs in the ribs from the female guards. Male guards joined in behind Derick, who'd now realized what a gruesome spectacle he'd found himself to be a part of.

They entered the court hall: a huge chamber that was almost empty, except for the head judge, elevated on the highest pedestal behind an enormous desk between two towers of files, two other people who looked like the prosecutor and the defendant attorney, standing below on the court floor, and the "indicted one" who was boxed on the podium to the left of the head judge's desk, only slightly less upraised. There was a door right behind that box, guarded by two armed men.

A sudden tremor of fear possessed Derick's body, and his head was pierced by a momentous terror of light as his eyes were fastened on the podium. His worst forebodings had just sprung to life. At last, he'd found him, but not in circumstances he'd ever wished for. The "indicted one" was no other than Walter Dauntwraith himself. Why had he taken no heed of his own deep, inner feelings? Now, he'd driven the final nail in his coffin.

He observed how Mrs Dauntwraith sat on the first of the many benches for the audience. She was the only one to witness it. The door they entered the court hall through was shut; now guarded by the same men who had followed Derick's footsteps since he left the room. He noticed that the two female guards who were around Mrs Dautwraith all the time were still standing at attention, likewise the rest of them. Maybe they were forming a figure, a secret symbol of something? Then, as the sunlight came through the arched, stained glass windows, thus making everything that tiny bit more lightsome, Derick noticed that the female guards were twins; they looked exactly the same, they were so alike. Their uniforms, they were so skimpy, so cropped, so tight to the body, making everything more blithesome. How to stay unbiased? he thought. He was just too young for that, then he thought he heard whispers: Mr Dauntwraith hadn't taken his eyes off him even for a moment since he entered the court hall, now he was trying to speak as Bruce was preparing himself to read the sentence, as he finally recognized Derick for himself, calling his grandad's name, waking him up from the stare.

'Do my eyes deceive me, or am I not looking at old Marty's grandson's twin?!'

One stare led to another — Derick's eyes turned, all other eyes were on Mr Dauntwraith too.

'You are a godsend in the hour of need!' he said to Derick — in words that prompted him to think that he must have heard them somewhere before.

'Tell your old man that Mowhaken was only a set-up to get him out, but Simon — he is interested only in you.'

'Silence, please!' shouted Bruce, and his voice was heard everywhere through the tannoys.

'We are all being used.'

'Silence!!'

Mr Dauntwraight spoke no more. Derick, sitting furthest from him of all the jurors, as number eight, said nothing either, thus letting Bruce read the sentence.

'By means of the independent and unbiased jury that has sworn under oath, I, the head judge of the High Court rule that the "indicted one" is pled guilty of the crime of being in the wrong place at the wrong time, and hereby I sentence him to death by means of lethal injection as capital punishment. Henceforth, the case is closed.'

Having announced the sentence, Bruce thumped the gavel against the block and made his way towards the door behind Mr Dauntwraith. The guards took Mr Dauntwraith aside and disappeared right away after Bruce. Derick was as pale as dead; he thought that couldn't be real, he just wanted to wake up now more than ever. He saw Mrs Dauntwraith's unspeakable face gaping at him. She was in denial, wishing it were a dream too. Then he remembered his old, wounded and persecuted grandad. How would he explain this to him? — Perhaps he wouldn't. Why would he? Was he really destined to share his fate? He stood up for himself and ran outside the court hall. He couldn't stand Mrs Dauntwraith anymore.

He ran, ran through the long corridor after the fast-moving shadow of his stepfather until he trampled on its head. He was slowing down. Portraits of his predecessors were mounted on the wall, on both sides. Twisting double candleholders with tiny electric candles were placed between them. All the portraits were on scarlet background, fitted in golden and ornamental winding frame depicting various kinds of climbing plants. The last portrait was of Bruce himself.

'Why did you sentence him?!' asked Derick, finally catching up.

'I just followed the unanimous order from the jury.'

'But you ordered the death penalty!' screamed Derick.

'We cannot take risks in our modern society where the integrity and safety of all of our citizens are at stake. Think of the circumstances.'

'How is that unbiased?'

'Bias has got nothing to do with circumstances,' said Bruce, more phlegmatically.

Derick said nothing. Bruce's latest statement left him lost for words.

'Look. I'm tired of all that. If you want, then go ahead and ask him why he's chosen Mowhaken of all wrong places.'

'I know why.'

'Do you really?' asked Bruce and looked at Derick for the first time. 'Tell me then, enlight my way.'

They stopped by Bruce's portrait. He looked in it more than a decade younger than now. Next to them, there was the door to his office. He looked for the key. When he found it and set in the keyhole, it wouldn't move — the door was already unlocked. He gave it a gentle push and sneaked in. Derick followed him inside. They had no idea they were shadowed.

'Simon?' asked Bruce, seeing the back of his own swivel chair revolving slightly to the left, then to the right.

'Probably not,' said the voice, and the chair rotated.

That voice belonged to Maarten Burdent. He was holding a small, black pistol with a long silencer attached to it in his spidery hand. He pulled the trigger, and a single shot was fired. Bruce fell on the floor, shot in the heart. It was a swift and silent death. The bullet whizzed through the air and pierced the chest impeccably, leaving only his black shirt stained with blood. Derick's eyes bulged out as he looked down at the puddle of blood oozing from beneath Bruce's body. He thought it was his turn now, but then — he was still standing. Maarten Burdent's hand put the gun down on the desk carefully so that it made no sound and returned to its former position, joining with the other hand, all fingers crossed, pointing outwards. Only now Derick noticed that he was wearing black gloves and he was smiling at him.

'Close the door,' he said in a low voice.

'You killed him!'

'He knew too much about you.'

'So it was my fault?!'

'Let me tell you something as a fellow scientist,' said Maarten Burdent. 'Do you know why scientists don't take the most unpredictable factors into account? Because they are unpredictable. They call them "outliers" and cast them away, out and beyond their set universe where they exist in nonexistence. Now close that door and sit down.'

Before the door was closed it opened even further. A female

guard appeared through. She looked down briefly at Bruce's lifeless body, then at Maarten and Derick, but there was something odd about her outfit. Her face, although well concealed behind the black, opaque sunglasses and the shade of the firm outback hat, still divulged signs of age, atypical for the guards of the High Court who must be in their prime. It was plain it wasn't the first time she was at the raw scene of murder as she didn't give even the slightest of trembles to the sight of the still warm, dead body close to her feet, except a cast of the cold eye. She took the glasses off and carefully placed it in the small, side pocket whilst sliding the hat behind her neck on the piece of string attached to it. She looked at least fifteen years younger in that uniform, her thought-provoking makeup only exaggerated the effect. There she stood again before Derick's life, tall and proud — his own gran. She reached out for Derick — upholding her open hand in the air, she spoke to him, defiant of what happened.

'At last, I've found you. Please, come with me.' Her green eyes were shining bright as emerald stars.

'Well, well, well. What an unexpected turn of events,' said Maarten Burdent, in a much harsher voice, still smiling sinisterly. 'Nina Deeprow, the secret agent, stands in my way, thinking she can upset the applecart. What an audacity — what a fallacy.'

Mrs Deeprow's hand was shot down in the air as Marteen Burdent spoke. She brought it back down to her body and looked at him with new eyes.

'Who are you?'

'Derick, maybe you tell her.'

Derick, being totally confused, internally torn apart, couldn't say a word as they were all stuck in his dried throat. There he was in the situation where he couldn't move away; there were no escape routes, no safe havens — only Bruce's dead body spread under his feet at the end of the nightmare, right before waking up, but he was between two strangers — people for whom his life was a battlefield overcast with fog.

'Your face — you look like… It cannot be, it's impossible.'

'At last! One of the best super recognizers in the country is finally able to tell the head from the tail. Dangerous business an infatuation is — when you know not the name who you think you desire.'

'You are lying!'

'Derick, tell her if I'm lying, or maybe I should call your comrade of old — Mr Kubla if he's still alive. Since when were you two secretly in touch again?!' he growled.

Mrs Deeprow looked down at the black pistol on the desk. She was the closest to it, but Maarteen saw how her eyes wandered and embraced the new object of desire. She had to act quickly, but she had one crucial advantage — his hands were joined. She lashed her right hand to seize the gun but was intercepted halfway through by Derick's hand. He clutched and constricted her hand just above the wrist. Maarten Burdent didn't move a muscle; he was motionless as he was so far, but he pounced and grabbed the gun as Derick constrained Mrs Deeprow. Now he was holding it in the same hand as before. Mrs Deeprow gazed into Derick's cold, dark brown eyes.

'He's killed your dad!' she screamed.

'He's never been my dad!'

Her eyes glowed with fire as she wrestled her hand from Derick's and ran away, leaving the door wide open. Maarten Burdent put the gun down gently on the desk, then he joined his hands in exactly the same position as before — all fingers crossed, pointing outwards. He was still smiling at Derick, then he looked down at the gun.

'Now it's your turn. Kill her! She must not tell anyone what she's witnessed.'

13
THE CROSSROADS

Maarten said that the truth was like light. Both could be distorted. Distorted light was still light. Distorted truth was a lie. He thought he couldn't agree more. The only thing he thought he couldn't agree was that he was predictable.

Let's show him some predictability, he thought in his mind. We will all see.

He remembered Marty. He couldn't tell him about Marty. He knew everything about him anyway, didn't he? The most important thing was to remain himself, truthful to his own cause.

On his way out, he met those mysterious guards again. The same females, the twins he saw in the court hall passed him by, taking absolutely no notice of him. Their full, round eyes were beautiful, so cold and so out of reach, but he thought they opened sideways.

Maarten told him he was safe. He would have predicted that, wouldn't he? Maybe he was unrecognizable, even to himself or… because he chose life. He looked back at them, but they didn't — only silent faces from portraits had their eyes wide open. They were the only ones alive; otherwise, the place was abandoned.

Outside, here and there, groups of stray people appeared, flocking from lights to lights. The sky was grey and heavy, it was even muggier than before. It seemed as the day just broke, the night fell upon its shoulders. The early signs of a brewing storm were written on the wall of the heavens. The falling leaves could fall no more, trammelled in gliding pockets of air, unable to fulfil their destiny, they rose up to the sky in massive whirlpools before getting dispersed in every direction of the world.

Why is it that day breaks but night falls? thought Derick, feeling a sudden onrush of sentiment overflowing his mind. Then there was a flash and a sound resembling a crack of a bullwhip tore the sky apart. The sultry smell of petrichor oozed out from the pores in the ground. It diffused Derick's attention and probably prevented him from sulking into a torpor. Instead, he was nearly caught up in a panic attack, thinking he was surrounded by invisible, ubiquitous forces, eying to suffocate him with its vapoury tentacles. Only nightfall could come to the rescue. Fortunately for him, it was coming down now, much earlier than on other sunny days that gloom has taken over by storm. It was a good omen the valley of River Brook was drawing near as he was moving north through the dying, soaking wet streets of southern Clarksdowne. The area surrounding the valley and the Old Market was dark and hazy, just perfect as a hideout through the night.

Moths are attracted to light, but sooner or later that proves lethal for them, he brooded as the sky darkened even more. The same force that gives you life, kills you in the end, but if one seeks darkness, does it mean one is afraid of light, fearing for one's life?

One swift glance over his head told him that the clouds were no wimps, they were there to stay, but that was actually a welcoming and relieving sight as above all else he desired not to be seen, heard or followed after, but as he was looking over the peaks of skyscraping tenement houses, he realized he walked into déjà vu. The same fire stairs he was perching on with Natalie the other week, embraced by the tears of falling rain, even as he was now, emerged out of the torrent, right above him. The images of their first kiss under the beams of police spotlights crossing over in the sky turned him maudlin and woeful for a moment as he stopped by the bottom of the staircase, hankering. The haunted sounds of melancholy brought him back to that day when they were so crazy and young, when he felt he had the whole world at his disposal. Yet he thought he still had it all — that only depended on how he looked at it now — he just apprehended how badly he'd missed her, but the time of reunion was still tantalizingly beyond his reach, in the land of shadows.

He drooped his head and sighed. The rain was falling so heavily it was bouncing off the broad slabs of concrete and pouring into his shoes. He remembered how ironic it was he never happened to have an umbrella with him when he needed it the most, even if that mattered nothing at all. He was already soaked to the skin, but that didn't matter either; his melancholic trip back in time took him to better days. He knew that the finest days were still ahead of him, he just had to move on, but then he shuddered suddenly — from getting that tingling sensation when you suspect you are being watched, as the shrill sound of meowing abruptly disturbed his blue adventure. Only yards away from him, he spotted a black cat peering at him with its gleaming eyes. Seeing a black cat, stalking, was already strange enough, but seeing a black cat stalking in the rain was just like discovering a new wonder of the world. He thought he saw that cat someplace before, but he just couldn't remember anything on the spot. Then the cat shook its fur off the rain, jumped onto the trash bin, and disappeared. Derick couldn't afford to stand there forever, wondering; after all, it was raining cats and dogs. He followed the suit and disappeared too.

He was closer to the canals than he thought, but he was heading towards a small, lonely island in the river that was sandwiched between two canals. He could have a little breathing space there among the low-hanging trees in the grove. He hoped to be alone there, and it was raining, so he had a good shot at reaching his destination unoccupied. There was only one way in and out of the island: through the narrow, arched footbridge made of wooden planks and having the skeleton of steel. There were a few benches and short, globe lampposts along the pathway that was encircling the island by the riverside. The centre of the island was slightly more elevated, the terrain was overgrown with a dense copse of shrubs and small trees, but there was one tree, the oldest of them all, right in the middle of the island, which probably still remembered the times when the island was the part of dry land, that had grown beyond the canopy of other trees. It was the only climbable tree over there, with branches long and thick as the girth of an adult human, and this was where Derick intended to stay — out of sight and out of light.

'You cannot separate evil from good,' he said to himself as he settled on one of the lowest branches after clambering the trunk of the tree, still being high enough not to get noticed readily. 'What did he mean by this?' Then he sighed. 'Always not enough time to ask questions. I feel like I want to stay here forever; people are just too painful to experience.'

He took out a small, glass phial from his pocket and began to examine it carefully, turning it in his wet, slippery fingers. It contained a tiny amount of pitch black, solidified yet quite crumbly powder; the top was sealed by a slightly tapered, wooden cork. It was the last gift from Marty, a truly gifted man who turned out to be his "lost" grandfather. How could he believe him now when he was sitting on the branch of some random tree in the middle of some lonely island, close to the city's downtown after a couple of weeks of searching for the man whom he'd just accidentally sent to certain death? He didn't have to — it was enough that he had it with himself; curiosity would do the rest.

Marty told him to take it only if he had to, only in time of real "moral quandary" when he felt so divorced from the whole world and himself; it would clear his mind, it would let the pain go, whatever the decision, in spite of whatever end he would meet. Was he too predicting something? Perhaps he was, but how could he speak of morality after all that he'd done? Bet he still feels like the world's only saviour. He is the very epidemy of that undying, stupid drive of humanity to make everything more complex and intricate. Why? Why wondering whether evil must be only a lack of goodness insomuch as dark is a lack of light or cold a lack of warmth, or it is something more primal — that exists by itself, in its own right? But what if there is no good or evil? What if… they're the same thing?

His eyes flashed in the dark as this unexpected realization came to his mind, which shone bright with the light visible only to him, the light that has always been within him. Time slowed down in a split second as his head turned from left to right and back as if in an acknowledgement that everything that is once was.

When the emotions of the moment went down as dust after a great battle, he felt sad as loneliness had surrounded and ensnared him. He wondered why the biggest dreams were dreamt, the greatest ideas were born, the most revealing thoughts conceived only when we were alone. He leaned back against the tree trunk with one of his legs hanging loosely from the branch and looked up to the sky, breathing heavily. The other leg, bent firmly in the knee, was supporting the hand that was holding the phial. He was thinking about Natalie — he wanted to get back to her, but first, he had to go somewhere else.

Why does getting to know yourself seem to be the most difficult thing in life? he mused, looking at the phial for the last time before putting it back into his pocket and taking a well-deserved, forgiving rest after another troublesome day to forget.

*　*　*

As he came back to his senses, tickled by the golden rays of the early sun, piercing through the foliage above his head, the first thing he did was to check his back pocket in a sudden, reflexive swing of his right arm. He nearly fell off the tree while doing that, but the pocket was empty. For a moment, he was just staring at the rustling leaves, some of which were already turning orange and yellow, in confusion, blinking with his eyes as if he was trying to remember if yesterday really happened. Maybe it was a dream, he thought, but then how would he know about the phial? His face saddened, but as he looked around in wonder how bright the grove was in the morning, getting used to the sun again, he spotted two little, furry squirrels running up and down the adjoining tree. They were after doing some mischief, he thought. He saw them playing in the undergrowth, probably collecting as many acorns as they could at this time of the year, but as he was looking down, watching the frisky animals, he thought he saw something glimmering momently next to one of them. It was his phial. Fortunately, it was unbroken, all content was still there. Suddenly, he realized how curious he became about this little, precious thing he had in his hand, virtually overnight. It's just remarkable how much one turn of the curtain can change, he thought, picking it up from the ground. He knew now that he was gonna need it.

As he straightened up, stretching his benumbed arms, he became aware of many hearty, yip-yapping barks flying around him. For a moment, again, he thought he was being surrounded, but even then he came forth without hesitation, cautiously treading over damp brushwood. A few people walking the dogs couldn't be bothered to take their eyes off their lovely pets even for a second to look at him as he emerged out of the grove. So typical, he thought. Even if an army of bloodthirsty zombies came out of there, they just wouldn't give a shit about them until their fluffy, treasured puppies were in their bloody mouths. On the other hand, the fact he could still be inconspicuous among them was so tampering for his weary mind. Their meaningless voices suddenly sounded soft and inviting as the notes of a harp entwined with a poetic declamation of heroic deeds when they were fluttering in the air — they all had a purpose, and so he had the purpose.

Even though it was really early, the city was already teeming with life; the last preparations for the morning rat race were well underway, the chase was about to commence, the breaths of all the people were being held until a sneaky, turdy fart from the timid crowd announced that the goldrush hour was on.

Derick felt hellishly peckish all at once; fortunately, he had more than enough money from Maarten. Speaking of the devil, he thought. It was about the right time to put his resolve to the test. He moved away from the island, and after crossing the river, he made for downtown to the nearest tube station, grabbing some tasty morsels along the way. Once full, he left for Mowhaken.

* * *

Exactly as predicted, the library, the oldest and the largest in the city, was bursting at the seams at that time. Although it wasn't the official university unit, it was a go-to place for all those early birds who were looking to kick-start their endless journey to quench the thirst for wisdom because it was situated only less than a mile from East Point University. The hunger for knowledge was incessant among them — it rallied their hearts and souls and raised their minds from the dead; summer death by stagnation was finally over, and now it was back to the sources, adding flavours to the ever-boiling cauldron of curiosity, trying to pinch a carrot from a stick. So, what place could be better to begin that noble quest, which was both a pilgrimage and a crusade at the same time, than Mowhaken, where the art of resourcing was rooted in antiquity?

Halls and passages were multitudinous with faces: spellcasters, truthseekers, globetrotters, dreamcatchers, all of them blundering under a strange incantation of assumed belongingness, freedom-glorifying libertines whose only freedom of choice was slavery itself. Running all around the clock with a head full of mixed ideas, a boiling over hodgepodge, didn't seem to bode well for all those whose restraint belts were all too loose to get buckled up on time. Those "free electrons" who were either too languid or too undecided to find their own space in time were destined for limbo, straddled beyond manifestation in a simple code of rights and wrongs. People who, for reasons only known to themselves — if lucky, did not take part in the analyses of the means were as fascinating as they were unpredictable, and according to Derick, they were the ones that in the end would be left out to be blamed for bringing another wave of societal destitution, a marking line for the rise and fall of civilizations. After all, all that a society needs to live and thrive is a fine-tuned, specialist, professional organism made from finely ground, techy adjectives hanging off branded and copyright-protected nouns, signifying a pedigree of belongingness. He knew full well, as he was walking through the silent aisles full of purposeful people, that their multifarious minds would ultimately end up as dust clouds coming from under the screeching wheels of a dump-bearing truck leaving a local landfill site. He knew that the purpose was systemic too.

He knew — too what to do as he ran into the wall between two blocks containing ancients texts, none of which he could read with any degree of comprehension, simply because it wasn't his field, although the command of his mother tongue should allow him to because of memory: a fine web of channels evolved to serve a common purpose of extricating the system into smaller, perfectly manageable chunks, such as knowing that tipping his head too much, too full of earthbound crap would be of no avail when he slid underground. Making sure he wasn't seen by any of stranded souls was another reason he needed to rely on his memory — to stave off any ill-begotten thoughts and keep his cool as he wanted to be as alive as he was unrestrained when he came back up, even as some tiny nudges at the back of his head were whispering that he should be doing quite something else at this time of the year.

Armed with the knowledge that Mowaken ran deeper than he previously thought, he set about bringing its hidden secrets to light. On the face of it, everything looked the same: the dim and cold emergency lights, the dusty smell of scorched plastic was still in the air, but nothing new was added to the scenery — it was copied and pasted into reality from his last memory of being there, only Maarten was missing. He found the file of the case of Mr Dauntwraith still there, untouched, left on the glass top of the UV light scanner, only now it was all useless. His desire was to go into the unknown, only then the poignancy of staring at the blank again pages of the case could turn into something fulfilling.

The problem he had was of a usual, very humane sort: searching for something without knowing it ever existed or still exists, but was it not the way almost all discoveries were made? How curious that coincidence is the true ruler of the world? Is there anything more certain in life than death? he thought, still staring at the case of Mr Daunthraith as he felt the piece of metal concealed under his belt getting colder and colder in that unheated environment. He just couldn't take his eyes off the file at the moment as if it was there where the answers to all his questions laid buried. But what if his grandad was wrong, and there was no purpose in re-exploring this place? He was, however, beyond doubt right about Derick — being just like him. Derick thought about the stairs Maarten used to get here, but instead, he opened the file again.

He thought he had all the time in the world as Natalie must be at work today. It wasn't until the evening or night he wanted to go there, somehow his fright of the sun was growing deeper with every waking hour; he noticed he took a new kind of fondness for subterranean spaces. It catered for his needs of being internally closed within himself, it pandered his senses with encompassing minimality of experience. Oh, how he relished the moment of pure perfection as he was leafing through the pages of that opus magnum of creation that brought all insights into one and then — the all consumating feeling of fulfilment came down on him as he gloated over the realization that being everywhere at the same time wasn't just an impossible dream but reality, and he felt so proud of being the vital part of it. He imagined how all people in the world could feel the same — nothing but absolute happiness.

He failed to hear furtive steps on the staircase he wished to explore later as he was so consumed in reading the indulgently genius prose of Maarten Burdent once again as if he was the one who had an eye for details to lay directly on the line what he wanted, which was so appealing for Derick, who for once could cling to something concrete, even if that meant crossing the boundaries of his occupation. But the meaning, he realized, everything that he was, was only ascribed to him and in essence, everything was so meaningless unless a meaning was brought to it. The simple fact he could read someone else's words was meaningful in itself as without the meaning they would be as empty as outermost space. It appeared as a new religion to him, the words he wanted to preach, feeling he had the privilege to know, but as he heard someone's body stumbling into the lab, he hastily closed the file and turned the ultraviolet light off, just as much he loathed the possibility of having to share his resources with anyone.

At first glance, he thought it was Maarten as the outline closely resembled his own hunched and lurching stature, yet of all people he would have least expected him to be there again, thinking he should be busy elsewhere at this point in time, but his down-to-the-ground, spindly limbs suggested anyone but him as he moved within touching distance of Derick, allowing the specks of light to fall on his face. As he came closer, it became apparent it was the bright, blue eyes of his grandad that shone as he noticed Derick, who was still confoundingly impressed how alike were the two images of two different people he had in his mind. Marty, without saying anything, laid his hands on the file of the case of Mr Dauntwraith, probably having figured out it was not what it seemed to be after the latest visit of his grandson, and tucked it under his arm, but somewhat ineptly as if the sensation of touch was dramatically reduced to an awkward guesswork. Derick, who even now was unsure whether to trust his own judgement, didn't pay much attention to that brazen but audacious act of theft at first as he was stupefied by a sudden entanglement of his mind, playing tricks on what he saw, telling him to make himself believe he'd been seeing only one and the same person all the time.

'Derick, my dear. It's such a fluke of luck I have found you here. I've risked it all to find you.'

'Grandad?! But you told me it was impossible for you to leave the valley.'

'I was worried too much about you. You were too sure of things, too... collected as we spoke last time. I noticed that after you'd left, that something else must have happened to you.'

At that moment, Derick saw how tightly Marty was holding to the file of the case of Mr Dauntwraith. Either he was really so afraid of losing it or had no trust in his grip whatsoever. He desired to snatch it from him right away, but at the same time, he was confident it wasn't the file that was the reason for his visit since he knew him now better — beyond a treacherous, fallacious value of first impressions, which was simply not applicable to him the way it applied to the rest of the world, for which it was so commonly applauded, and the skill of making the right impression at the right time had grown into a dark art in modern times of momentary judgement. He composed himself instead and let Marty, who was clearly struggling to keep hold of the file under his armpit as if he was hurting too badly from something, do the talking.

'I just couldn't leave you on your own, I had to act.'

THE CROSSROADS

'You're the bravest man I've ever known.'

Marty didn't reply to Derick's remark; he didn't even return him half a smile. He didn't like the way he spoke: it was so flattering, so measured, so well-judged, exactly the way he knew someone else had ever conducted himself. It really worried him inside; he was clinging to the file with growing misgivings.

'Do you still have it?' he asked at length, sensing Derick would say no more.

'Are you addicted?'

'No. Destroy it, please. I was wrong to give it to you.'

'Why? You wouldn't be saying this without a reason.'

'Exactly,' said a faint voice from an unknown location. It was thin and dull as if it was coming from a remote place, but clearly discernible and salient.

The lights directly above their heads went on suddenly, then they saw the silvery, metallic door of the tall, reinforced closet situated on the far back wall of the lab opening outwards, with huge, black "X" warning signs on triangular, yellow background disappearing on both sides as the door opened. Derick and Marty turned their heads as it happened to notice the passage into another chamber right behind the closet and a dark figure of a human in the middle of it.

'That must be the one who just spoke,' said Marty as the shadowy face moved down and stepped into the light. There he beheld his "comrade" of old, a person deemed dead by many but himself. It was a grim meeting, none of them looked especially enthused by the sight of each other — Marty looking markedly more dismayed.

'Exactly as predicted,' sneered Maarten. 'In madness, madness itself is the most predictable, the most pleasurable thing that can happen a madman.'

'Who the hell are you talking to?! I cannot see any madmen over here!' bellowed Marty, swinging his head and arm around.

'Poor old Marty — there is no end to your sanity. All your life everyone's been after you, but you never knew where to draw the line between determination and resignation.'

'You have been exposed. You've been walking on thin ice for far too long, but your time has come now. Derick be my witness.'

His grandson looked at him suspiciously as he spoke, but he wasn't wondering what kind of new mad idea had just possessed him; the desire to take the file from him was burning bright from within.

'Indeed, you may be right about me,' snapped Maarten, 'but unlike you, I have come out prepared, and Derick is my witness too.'

Marty saw Derick's stern, stony face in that new opulent light shining from above, full of once hidden, now apparent details: his eyes wandering down, fixating, his brows widened and darkened — only his forehead relaxed with preimposed selflessness, giving him a smile of penultimate compassion. The world was turning around and against him as he felt the ground being lost under his feet.

'Marty, the file,' said Derick, slowly bringing forth his open hand to release the old man.

'Even you, my son?'

'You must face the truth,' said Maarten, who now closed in on Marty, leaving the door behind him wide open. 'Once and for all, you must realize that all your life only yourself have been after you. You're still so entangled within that you cannot see the gates of tomorrow even as they are gaping at you.'

Marty, being poor, had only one last dying nod of hope to bestow upon Derick whom he loved beyond resolve of his sickening mind.

'Shall we?' asked he as his eyes shot forth.

'Marty, the file first,' said Derick, still smiling with compassion — the ultimate sign of ignorance — his eyes, being fixated solely on the file.

'Since when did you act as his stalwart?'

'He's the only person who's never lied to me, the only one who's always been truthful to his words.'

That was one sting in the heart too many for Marty, who slumped to the ground, feeling hurt beyond measure — on his knees, letting the file go from his grip. He was clinging to his left arm above the elbow, holding it straight against the body, cringing in pain; his blackened, grainy veins protruded as rivers bursting their banks, carrying too much filth. A small, white envelope was sticking out of his pocket. Derick lifted his body up from the floor and sat him on the glass top of the UV light scanner. Marty was still conscious but breathing heavily. Derick took the envelope from his back pocket and read the words on the front of it, holding it behind Marty's neck. It was addressed to his wife, but the address itself was missing. Without saying anything to Marty, he swung his left arm and tucked the letter into his pocket.

'I love you, Grandad, but your time has come too,' said Derick, as softly as he could.

'He's twisted you beyond recognition,' replied Marty, staring into Derick's eyes, raising and pointing his hand at Maarten, but he wasn't there anymore. Whilst Derick was dealing with Marty's collapse, he sneaked in behind and took the file from the floor. Now he was standing again, next to Derick.

'He's not gonna hang on for much longer in such a dire state,' said Maarten, looking at Marty's infected arm.

'I shall be fine,' retorted Marty, springing back to life upon hearing Maarten's foul voice again. 'Pain is only imagined! You both should already know about that.'

'Certainly. You have by far the strongest imagination of us all,' gibed Maarten.

'Save your jibes to yourself and tell me what's behind that bloody door,' returned Marty. 'Where did you come from?'

'The future.'

'Grandad, he's right,' said Derick, 'your arm is fading away. I must take you to a hospital.'

'I see he's always right in your eyes!'

'Indeed,' Maarten broke in. 'If he wishes so, I could show him inside and let die — seeing a glimpse of heaven. It's his choice.'

'You see, he's cruel.'

'He wants to help. He's not like Simon.'

'He is Simon!'

'We don't need him anymore,' said Maarten. 'He's gone, as he has always been — existing only inside your head — a perfect creation of your sickened mind. He was only a myth, a myth you've believed in so much it has become a reality.'

'Derick, no! Don't believe him — you saw him. You saw him with your own eyes! He only trades you fiction for reality.'

'Fiction differs from reality only in the presentation of facts, not in facts themselves,' said Maarten, and then he burst into loud, wild laughter. He snatched the file of the case of Mr Dauntwraith and turned back on his heels.

'Derick, for Lord's sake! Can't you open your eyes at last!? He's playing with us. He's predicted that we're both gonna come here today. It's not a coincidence!'

'I heard that,' said Maarten.

'Marty, stop agitating! Your arm's gonna bleed.'

'I don't care if I die here. Just listen to me if you're my grandson! If we wipe out all "evil", all pain from our souls, how do we then know if there is any goodness left inside of us? Can you tell me how? Can your new partner in crime tell you how? I bet he knows.'

'Leave him alone. He is delirious,' said Maarten, now standing by the door.

'No? So let me tell you that we can't know because goodness loses its identity and then it can be substituted by anything — called goodness.'

'I know,' said Derick, 'but now I must get you out of here. Your arm is really bad.'

It wasn't long before Marty passed out, but ere it happened he remembered the envelope he had in his pocket. Thinking he'd lost it, brought him to the edge of his wits, and his arm started to bleed. Derick had to act quickly; he cast Maarten one last parting yet profound glance, then waved the envelope in front of Marty's hazy eyes. Maarten Burdent was gone whence he came, the door was shut after his shadow, leaving Derick with his spent grandad. His last wish was to bring the envelope to his wife's attention.

THE CROSSROADS

* * *

'Marty will live; his will to live is stronger than his will to create, his will to lie,' said Derick under his breath upon leaving the room Marty was in, tied down to the impeccably white bed, sparing him the last, remote glance, putting his fate in the trusty hands of specialists.

It wasn't unwelcome, but a calamity of a state Derick's grandad was in left him with little choice but to take that shrivelled up body to the nearest hospital with an intensive care facility. It frustrated his progress, chaining him to the old's man side, but it might have saved his arm. Haste, as it often turns out to be the worst enemy, a devil's pointy tail, sometimes is a blessing — when only seconds can fall from a brink of death.

Leaving the frail bones of his grandad behind wasn't an easy choice for Derick, but at this stage he'd been simply stripped off sentiments; a rare but autonomous blend of blindness and predestination had crept up upon him, skewing the sun and the moon along with the horizon line towards him, thus making him the focal point of the whole world.

Marty's sacrifice, his frayed mind must not go into the shadows of forgetfulness, heedless and headless as a phantom of an ancient knight galloping through the dark of the woods on a black horse.

Derick's thoughts about his grandad, about the reality he saw were granite, diamond-hard and grafted — the days of freedom from knowing, a stellar sign of childishness and free-spiritedness were gone away from his cooling bloodstream, pumping the very mature, very calculative blood of belongingness, ruled by the virtue of an alibi. Suddenly, miraculously, a thought-unwinding partiality came down upon his mind, making the life for sidedness a simple matter of choices he'd made. Everything was explained, everything he thought he was not he had a reason to hate. It was cool — to do as one chooses and wishes because it was making the very fabric of what he was.

Marty was, on the other hand, on the other side, against the world but not against life. Derick was the world, but did he chose life as he thought he did? Did he not, by accident, exchange the melodic chirrup of singing birds in the frames of the breezy windows of his old house for the humming honks of ever hungry, fuel-powered vultures?

Marty's demise was in Derick's eyes his hideous dissociation from others, being on no one's side, but always on his own. He chose life with no one, now he was dying without everybody. To carry his torch, as he said, was to be somehow, sometime for people — without them taking too much notice of that happening, but the problem he felt he had in his body was that in spite of getting rid of a slew of belongings, including a permanent place to stay gave him, with time, a scaly mail of belongings growing around him: on his neck, in his pockets, behind his belt, nearly tipping his normally straight gait sideways.

He had to cast away every single one of them, sensibly, one by one, just like the trees around him were losing their leaves as the summer suddenly moved on, letting the fall slip in, allowing the day to die in the arms of the night.

*   *   *

Barrow Hills's well-rounded, sandy shape was gone from Derick's sight as the night fell. Unfortunately for him, he was unaware of the clouds gathering above his head in vast enormities, forming a layer of blackness, capable of dimming even the brightest starlight. Natalie's house was only a short walk uphill from the bus stop, but that didn't prevent him from getting scared that he would get soaked again before he reached Natalie's house, but more disconcerting was the thought that the letter he had in his pocket would get washed out and become too blurry to be read.

He wanted to avoid her mother at all cost because she was always so snoopy every time she saw him coming. He simply had too much on him to afford a close encounter of any kind now. In fact, he wasn't so keen to see Natalie either after his visit to Mowhaken, but carrying the mystery envelope from his grandad was yet another reason he was more eager to find his wife, and Natalie was the only person he suspected of knowing her whereabouts. He had no idea where his mom was, but Natalie might know that one too. He saw his family break apart as if there had never been any sense of togetherness and belongingness; he saw himself running up and down the hills, but to attribute every mishap to his own actions was simply a bias, or so he thought — that everything might as well have been a well-conceived roleplay.

Still, there was no playing around, no time for an onset of some capricious unwindings of his own tattered, mashed-up, bejumbled affairs as the rain began to take its toll on his clothes. He was at the bottom of the last and the tallest hill in the Hillbarrow, going past the church, the only one in the village. It was always a busy place, one of the best-lit venues around, with the small park in front of it, usually full of old, prudish bigots and young drunkards at this time of the late, falling evening.

He heard voices, high cries of solemnity, bells of devotion coming his way from inside as he was going past the church. A kind of ceremony, a nocturnal mass was being serviced to the faithful. He hadn't been to the churches for... well, a long time — since he didn't remember the last time. Somehow, the light, the occult sounds enticed him, probing, prickling his slippery skin with its indulgent smell of burnt incense. He felt he could go in and pray for an umbrella — the one thing he never had when he really needed as if it was his curse, or a just simple act of ignorance.

He decided not to side with a devil at length. Walking away, he knew he couldn't fill his heart with false remedies and promises of a promised land when his body was dying of sadness, changing moods in swings and bouts. Everything, satisfactions were working by inversion: the gratifying worldly side of desires only left you bare and prone to attacks from spiritual beings, even if they might only be creations of imagination, fears, or simple justifications of actions taken in life. But it was those carnal meanings he needed now, he'd missed by a long way, even though his feelings were making him irrational in the face of the world — he had no choice but to cave in as he was only a human being — not to be blamed after all.

Natalie's house had the elevation made of old, wooden siding panels, which in Derick's case encouraged climbing as there was no way he could just appear through the front door as a lame duck asking for a piggyback. He went around the back of the house where the window to her bedroom was, on the first floor. Luckily for him, a built-in, one storey tall garage was on the side of the house, with its roof considerably aslope to the outer wall of the house, allowing melting snow to slide down during winter months. It was a piece of cake to get there and then hope to reach the bedroom's window, but he had to decide now whether to risk bringing the gun inside with him. This was his chance: the sliding window above his head was open, the rain was drooling from the gutter, washing away spews and dirt of the day from the face of the earth, but his back was getting battered by the water as he was weighing up his way up. Then he bowed down as he stumbled upon something solid, probably bruising his toe. He crouched and felt the protrusion from the ground with his fingers. After sweeping aside the mossy vegetation with stalks of some climbing plants, he discovered the wooden door of the old and forgotten coal chute, with a badly corroded locking plate and a padlock. He put the gun down carefully in the corner between the wall of the house and the stodgy, concrete curb protecting the door of the chute from all sides, projecting only a few inches above the ground, and covered it meticulously with moss and stalks. He knew no one was gonna look for anything over there as the era of coal-powered hearths was on the wane — nowadays almost all modern fireplaces were electric.

After climbing and throwing his body through the window, he observed how unthrilling it was to stand again in the complete dark of Natalie's bedroom, in spite of a magnificent stroke of fortune to be able to smuggle himself so seamlessly into her house. Despite all his misadventures, all his near misses, everything was somehow coming along; his "stupid luck" was his hidden armour, normally leaving him on his own with day-to-day errands, even those weirdest and the most unpredictable ones, but at the same time, always showing him the way through the eye of the storm, the path studded with thorns as if he was a kind of protected species, destined for something else but a death by accident.

Even as he was about to make a move to switch the light on, he heard that short command from the dark: 'If you move any further, I will shoot your wretched, trespassing ass to kingdom come!'

Derick froze to the spot instantly; he didn't expect any welcoming committee.

'Now, put your hands over your head and step back to the window, but slowly,' said the voice.

As Derick felt the windowsill by his backside, the lights went on and he beheld Natalie's mum in her wheelchair inside the doorframe, wielding a massive double barrel shotgun in her hands.

'Derick?! Is that you?'

'Mrs Maine, yes it's me, in flesh and bones,' said Derick, 'but I would feel much better if you could point your shotgun elsewhere.'

'Oh, I'm sorry my darling; I didn't want to scare you! It's not mine anyway; it belonged to my dead husband, you know — he was a soldier.'

'Thank goodness those shells didn't fire. It's huge!'

'I saw someone stalking around the house through the kitchen window, so I took precautions,' said Mrs Maine, nodding at the shotgun. 'Then I remembered I left the window open in Natalie's bedroom, and lo and behold, you've used it to break in.'

'I'm so sorry,' said Derick, trying to come across as apologetic, 'but Mrs Maine, how did you get upstairs in your wheelchair?'

'Come outside and see it for yourself. The staircase has got a revamp!'

Derick left the bedroom to see that the staircase had been completely overhauled: it had been widened, and the lift on steel railing had been fixed to it permanently, allowing Mrs Maine to travel up and down.

'Is it your custom to use windows for doors like a bloody

scoundrel?' remarked Mrs Maine as Derick was checking out the staircase. 'I nearly blasted your ass off!'

'I just wanted to make a surprise!' replied Derick, quite casually, still absorbed by the new device, pretending to be interested in its inner workings.

'Mmm — surprise, you're saying?' said Mrs Maine. 'You're full of surprises. Where have you been? You look completely different. Something has changed?'

'Here we go again,' Derick mumbled under his nose, then turning his face towards Mrs Maine, 'It's been a long way away, but it's still me.' He gave her a wide, uncompromising, reassuring smile — something he just had to do at that point.

'Heh, I can hear you now. You nearly got my own daughter depressed.'

'Where is she? I thought —'

'The church! She's praying for your soul. We thought you're lost or even dead. Personally, I thought they'd detained you at Windchain, but knowing you, I wouldn't put my money on it.'

Derick was cursing within at this moment — he should have gone to church for once. Again, his gut feeling was right, but again it was ignored.

'Come down with me,' said Mrs Maine, 'I've got to phone her to announce the good news — her angel of love has gracefully appeared.' She gave Derick little evils, shaking her head mildly, but went aboard of the stair lift. Once she secured herself on the platform, she went sliding down after pushing some buttons. Derick wanted to try the lift too, but, in the end, he used the stairs, having no time to waste figuring out how it worked.

In the kitchen, he found Mrs Maine hanging on the phone to Natalie — undoubtedly, as when her voice was heard through the loudspeaker he shivered, letting his neck bones crack.

'Don't you tell me I mustn't call you!' cried Mrs Maine, taking the handset off her ear. 'Why did you then take it with you, to play games?! He's here, little rogue. I nearly stuffed his arse with a whole lotta buckshot, mind you, as he mistook your window for a door, poor soul — he looks so tired.'

THE CROSSROADS

When Natalie spoke, Mrs Maine didn't make attempts to listen; she knew she's gonna go berserk and leave the church in a frenzy. Instead, she added even more fuel to the fire by saying: 'You'd better come quickly before he runs away again,' then she hung up.

'That's her sorted my lovey; she'll be here in a crack of a whip. Do you like some tea?'

'Yes, please,' said Derick, just to snuff out her curiosity for a while, to keep her mind occupied as he felt somehow dragged and all at sea.

When Natalie came, it was her turn to look like she'd been chased by all the restless spirits of the Hillbarrow Cemetery all the way up here, Derick thought as seeing her posing at the door in all the cheekiness was one drop short of a rainfall to hide she'd been through a cloudburst.

'Thank you, O Shepherd, for bringing me amongst the sheep!' she gasped as she looked upon Derick's bushy eyebrows for the first time in nearly two weeks.

Soon they were lying on the sofa — one of them having the cheeks on both sides changing their colours rather remarkably: from baby pink, through scarlet, to deep carmine as Mrs Maine brought in the tea.

'Your wish was granted — at last,' said Mrs Maine.

'Yes,' said Natalie, through the tears, 'but why was your phone always out of reach? Why didn't you call us saying you're coming home?'

'I lost it in a bog.'

'Lost in a bog?!' both Natalie and her mum reacted, almost standing from their seats.

'It was an accident.'

'Was breaking into her bedroom an accident too?' asked Mrs Maine.

Luckily for Derick, Natalie wasn't gonna take any prisoners; stardust was in her eyes, and she knew her mum too well to allow her tongue to unwind too much as she was exactly the same. Again, Derick was dragged upstairs unceremoniously as an animal of prey fallen into a trap, with the only difference being his intentions — this time it felt like salvation to be salvaged from the sharp, prying teeth and penetrating, hawk-like eyes of Natalie's mum.

'What about the tea?' cried out Mrs Maine.

'Maybe later!' returned Natalie.

'And the cakes?'

She waited, but when there was no answer to her question, she only shook her head and cleaned off the table. She knew the feeling of being so headstrong, as her daughter was, very well. She couldn't yet share her misgivings with her as even if she could, her daughter wouldn't listen — she was too awakened for it, walking on the air, upstairs, listening to the stories of his life to the beat of his heart, lying on his bare chest.

'If at least half of what you said isn't less than half-true, then we've got a winner,' said Natalie.

'Are you taking the mick?'

'I saw him a few days ago and it was horrible! He almost made James kill me! I need to get him out of this before something worse happens to him.'

'He's no more; he won't come back,' said Derick.

'Then who's behind all of it? Of course, it was Simon. Don't try to pull the wool over my eyes now and tell me he was only your grandad's sick alter ego that has ever existed only in his mind.'

'I don't know.'

'How can I believe it when I saw him only bloody last week?!'

'Well, if you don't, if you think I don't make too much sense, that's because… maybe I'm broken minded.'

'Don't say that!' retorted Natalie. 'Give me that letter. Let's see if your grandad didn't leave any more surprises, shall we?'

'I don't know.'

She rolled to the side of her bed and snapped the letter from under the night lamp, which she just switched on. Carefully she unsealed the envelope and took out a clean, white piece of paper, trifolded precisely to the measure. The empty envelope was put back by the lamp, on top of the small commode. Derick rolled by her side immediately and, once spooned to her body, he had a gander too. They dared to read only a few sentences from it, but they didn't need any more. It was a farewell love letter to Marty's "love of his life" — sweet and poignant yet sunk in haplessness, given the life he chose to live. Natalie snuggled it back into the envelope, then turned the light off.

'So, do you know where my grandma live now?'

Natalie bit Derick's earlobe in response, then she kissed it before whispering something into his ear. When she finished, he turned his head towards her and stared into her eyes for a little while.

'Kirkwood? That's miles away,' he said. 'And my mum?'

'They live together, you silly man.'

Derick smiled at her. He could go to sleep now, free to say goodbye to another day.

* * *

When Natalie was wakened from sleep, it was still early in the morning, the day was only dawning, but Derick was no more — her bed was empty as she arose from it. The window was shut, and the door was shut. She ran into the corridor and to the bathroom because she needed it, but he wasn't there either. As she was about to close the door, she spotted rather a peculiar object to be found in the bathroom — a tablespoon. It was left next to her toothbrush on the shelf between the sink and the mirror. She realized it must have been taken from the kitchen because it was exactly the same as one of her mother's cutlery sets. She alarmed her mother, nearly throwing her off the bed. Soon they were both sitting in the kitchen, both still wearing their bathrobes and flip-flops. Mrs Maine, who knew her tableware to the last fork, confirmed that one spoon was missing.

'Let me tell you something my love,' said Mrs Maine, holding the spoon. 'In my youth I've seen spoons in many different places other than kitchens and living rooms, such as bathrooms and toilets, not least bathrooms and toilets. I knew what was going on right off the bat — we were children of the sun, we were flower people, and everyone was pinning. I've never been, but your dad has been, although it wasn't the dragon that killed him, but a fellow human being.'

Tears appeared in Natalie's eyes. It was another dagger in the heart for her, another bitter pill to swallow, but she just took the spoon from her mother and put it back where it belonged without saying anything. It was another storm she just had to ride through.

'We used to be jokin' that there was no spoon when we saw one in a place like you did, but let's not beat around the bush, you've got to watch him. I'm not sure if you noticed, but he's changed. I can't really describe it, but he's not himself; he was so cool with everything as if he always knew that what was right was right, you know.'

'He asked about his grandma first,' said Natalie.

'Hmm... He looked like he had a bullet in his head, like there was some madness in his heart.'

'Where has he gone?'

'Where you told him to.'

Natalie hopped out of her flip-flops and ran upstairs. She was back in a crack and ready to go, but her mum stopped her immediately.

'How far are you prepared to go for him? Tell me the truth,' she said, looking into her daughter's pulsating eyes, but Natalie wouldn't answer, she wouldn't hold back — enough had been said.

'Please, be careful. I have a very bad feeling about this,' said Mrs Maine.

'You always have bad feelings about something; you watch far too much TV.'

'It's not like that, babe. Life is the art of choice, but love is the art of lasting. Remember, even if your problems seem like mountains that are about to crumble on you, thank your lucky star that you're not deaf or blind.'

'I will keep that in mind,' said Natalie, then she left home.

The day was rising bright, the sky was pure blue and clear after last night's antics, leaving the path of the sun open to beholders, igniting hopes, filling spirits with light — such was the power of revealing when no shadow was going to be passed by. Still, it wasn't cloudless enough for Natalie, who forgot the remote, and was blinking stupidly at the garage door. Luckily, yesterday she forgot to lock it too, so she only needed to find a crank to lever it up.

As she was staring at the sun, looking for God to give her a hand, Derick arrived in the pilgrimage town of Kirkwood, the place where a wind rose culminated in one point, the place of the crossroads between the south and the west, the north and the east, with a huge, monumental cathedral in the northern fringes of the town, overlooking the picturesque meeting of the Barrow Hills and the valley of River Leyron. Somnolent and sacred it was — the whole vicinity, a home for many saints, populated largely by God-fearing habitants of goodwill. Clandestine piety could be smelt in the air everywhere around: dorms for thirsty pilgrims and wayfarers from all walks of life were strewn across the town and neighbouring villages, reeking of alcohol, and at night the lights in the windows — all turned red and pink — people walking only straight ahead, hands in one another's pockets of brotherhood love.

Derick set his foot on the clean, polished piece of basalt pavement: very mature and atoned, making him feel more revered and purposeful, except for the gutter in the gap he had to mind constantly, otherwise risking falling into the abyss of many storm drains, now blocked by the foliage falling from the paradise. The house he had the address for was only several blocks up the avenue, quite close to the cathedral, the bell towers of which he could catch a glimpse of as he strolled along the glossy, measured tablets of stone. Somehow he felt he belonged there, that he could blend in very well, walking the way of a chameleon along the opaqueness and greyishness of streets and houses, seeing virtually no one. A few dwellers only emerged out of their residences as the bells rang for the early morning rites. Everyone was bowing low, greeting and then walking in silence, yielding to the subduing reverberance of the bourdon giants.

INSIDE-INSIDE

He stopped by a small, grey, wooden gate, made of old and arching, chunky planks, having round vertical railings. The gate was hinged on two thick posts made of the same kind of grey wood as the rest, attached and standing alongside taller, up to Derick's chin, concrete posts with flat tops, on which vessels resembling ancient water jugs were carved out of the grey rock. Everything was grey: the roof of the house, the door and the large, rectangle lattice windows. Only the house's elevation that was of the colour of red burnt bricks was out of the picture, likewise the green hedge, forming a natural fence on both sides of the gate that opened inwards when pushed gently, which was in itself very welcoming. Derick's mood was greying too as the life he sensed seemed so laid-back, so ambient, neither black nor white, just grey and confused into one formless, nameless entity. Only now he noticed he was in that way since leaving Natalie's house.

Everything felt like riding luck to him: if they had escaped to the cathedral for the service, he would have to go there — he didn't fancy... another trip, as if only he'd had another chance, another time, but still hanging on the door handle he couldn't get away from the impression of being timeless as the handle was getting cold and indifferent in his hands he knew that life would take care of itself because he felt it in his veins as the door opened suddenly, he lost the grip on it — his mother was standing before him — his eyes rolling sideways, now refocused, as she took the center stage she was crying, her face in her hands. Then she threw herself into his arms.

'I just can't believe it's you! You were standing outside motionless for five minutes, staring at the door, then I recognized you.'

Derick said nothing, still staring at the door and into the house, not showing her his lustrous eyes.

'You're very cold. I can't feel your heartbeat,' his mum noticed, touching his hand. 'Come inside.'

'Where is gran? Is she with you?' asked he, peering into the living room and kitchen. Then their eyes met. They were the only remnants of his mother in his body — now even they were turning unrecognizable as she looked at him, standing by the door — white and thin like the air.

'She is in the bathroom, getting ready to go out. We were going to mass,' said she and closed the door but without locking it.

'I will wait.'

He went straight to the kitchen and took a seat by a small, rhomb-shaped table, covered with a red and white, checked oilcloth. Leftovers from an unfinished breakfast were scattered haphazardly on it: a glass of yellow juice, a red, plastic egg cup with half-eaten, soft-boiled egg stuck into the form, an open carton of milk and a white plate with two nibbled, drying toasts. His mum peeked through the frame into the kitchen to see him sitting in silence: spine straightened up, hands on knees, completely ice-cooled and composed as if it was just another ordinary day of an ordinary life.

'Does she know you're coming?'

'Perhaps,' said he without paying much attention.

'How did you find us?' asked she, sitting down by the opposite side of the table.

'From Natalie,' said Derick. Then their eyes met for the second time. Their weathered, withered bond plunged into a coma as he — turned wanderer was feeding upon her fluctuating helplessness to fend for herself, quietly gathering wits among growing sufferance.

Mrs Deeprow, only yards away, locked in the bathroom, aware of the changing complexion of breathing air, wavered — on the door handle, even as Derick did, except he was getting cold, unlike his grandma, who knew what happened two days ago. She had little choice; she had to come to the rescue. Derick didn't budge, nor did he look at her as she came out and strode into the kitchen, taking a seat between him and his mother. He only produced the envelope and placed it neatly on the table, right before himself, resting his palms on both sides of it in a pedantic gesture of measured precision.

The women's eyes were drawn towards it immediately as Derick smiled mildly, saying: 'Do you recognize this style?'

'Marty —' breathed Mrs Deeprow, seeing her own name

written on it.

'It's yours. Take it,' said Derick.

Mrs Deeprow hesitated at first, but then she slipped and laid her hand on the envelope, fueled by her own curiosity. As she began to read the letter, it became apparent she was deeply moved by the content when tears appeared to roll down her cheeks. Derick's mum looked at her son, who was unstirred, sitting motionless with his palms flat on the table, staring at Mrs Deeprow, paying his mother little attention as she brought herself closer to his gran, but still observing his static stature with intense tension as if she expected something else to happen.

'What is he saying?' asked Derick's mum when Mrs Deeprow took her eyes off the letter.

'He's saying farewell,' said Mrs Deeprow and wept. Her tears were falling on black letters, moistening the most difficult words on the slightly crumpled piece of paper.

'No reason to cry, Nina,' said Derick. 'He's in good hands and quite content about what he's done in life.'

As he said that he put out the pistol he'd carried with himself all the way up here and rested it exactly in the same place in front of himself, replacing the envelope with the gun, filling the empty space between his palms. Derick's mother brought Mrs Deeprow's shaken body even closer to herself, even further from him as the real reason of his visit was about to be revealed.

'He must have seriously impressed you indeed to make you come out searching for me,' said Mrs Deeprow with tart bitterness.

'Of all the people I've met, he's the only one who's always been telling me the truth. Even you have been lying to me, all my life, in fact. Now, I demand answers.'

He took up the pistol from the table and aimed it precisely at Mr Deeprow's chest, holding it low and close to his ribcage. He didn't know it was the same weapon by the use of which Marty wanted to kill Simon many years ago. Perhaps, he didn't know that history, as befits the mother of all ironies, seemingly likes to repeat itself too. Maarten, of course, didn't tell him any of that.

'What do you want? Share the same fate as Marty?'

THE CROSSROADS

'"Old flames never die," as they say,' Derick sneered at Mrs Deeporw. 'I am sick of all your covert affairs and all of you at once.'

'I pity you, Derick. You can't see beyond the tip of your nose. He was talking about Simon, not Alexander, you fool. But you won't believe me; you're too wrapped up, I'm afraid.'

Upon hearing Simon's name yet again, he burst into wild, gloating laughter. It didn't matter whether it was him, Mr Kubla, Marty, or someone else. They were all illusioned by his existence. Only he was spared from that lunacy; he could now question anyone and anything, believing no one but himself. His own mother couldn't recognize her son anymore — she waited, harrowed from inside by his sight.

'He's no more as he never was real,' crowed Derick, 'but you all have been deceived.'

'It's too late now, but from all of us you're the only one that has,' said Mrs Deeprow. 'You're my grandson, and it breaks my heart to see what you're doing to us.' She touched herself in the chest as she said that.

'Prove it!' snapped he, then aroused from his seat, fully extending his arm, ready to pull the trigger.

The heart-shaped necklace, having escaped from the embraces of his partly unbuttoned shirt as he stood up, shone purple-crimson on his chest when the first beams of the morning sun came dazzling through the windows. Mary thundered from her seat, pushing the table his way, and before he could readjust, she landed a red, hot slap to his face. Now her heart was between him and Mrs Deeprow.

'I've sensed you weren't yourself since I first looked upon you today,' shouted Mary, 'but to claim in this manner that you're not your grandma's grandson is beyond heavenly absolution!'

She snatched the necklace from Derick's neck and lifted it before his eyes, even as he was holding his gun before hers.

'Look! Have you forgotten who you got this necklace from? Have you forgotten whom it belonged to before? If you have, then you will have to kill me first!'

She put the necklace back around her neck where it truly

belonged. Derick gazed deep into her unflinching, dark brown eyes, now hot and radiant like a thousand suns. They were exactly the same as his in every single detail, still bearing flames of love deep inside — long lost but not forgotten. His world appeared warped, his heart was twitching and thumping hard, something was happening, losing ground, then he heard the hit and felt the pang: Mrs Deeprow — "miraculously" fell on the floor without him firing a single shot. Her body was seized by twinges, rolling from side to side behind Mary's legs, she was breathing heavily, suffocating. Mary dropped by her side immediately, fearing for the worst.

'Derick! Can you call for help, please!? I think she's having a heart attack.'

He looked down at them: Mary was holding Mrs Deeprow in her arms, trying to communicate with her, petrified as her world had shrunk suddenly. She looked up at Derick, who was still holding them at gunpoint, but shaking and dwindling gradually as if he was weighing up his luck, staring numb and cold at them.

'What are you waiting for?! The telephone is in the living room, on the mantelpiece.'

He didn't respond; he let his pistol flop by his thigh with a sigh of resignation, looking more dejected than terrified. Then he turned back and ran away, leaving the door open behind him. Outside, the sun was shining on the pavement's polished slabs, rising above the line of a few short trees. He left the gate open too, but then, suddenly, he bumped into Natalie.

'Derick? Where are you going?!' asked she.

'I'm going to live without pain.'

*   *   *

The day was at its fullest, the sun was at its highest as Derick arrived in the city of Clarksdowne. He got off the bus near to the High Court in the southern sprawls. He felt dull and distraught, he was there to look for someone, someone who could reignite his own meaning. He'd lost the gun in transit, he couldn't quite remember where, probably thrown into mud in some remote ditch by the end of some random road. It was a crying shame as it could have become a major family trophy in years to come, but it was exactly the aim of his life — to get rid of everything that restricted, to set himself free.

As he approached the white, flat stairs of the High Court, he felt cold chills and sweats all over his body — he just remembered the pistol wasn't the last item he wanted so desperately to dispose of. He found with a surprise that he'd still got James's card in his back pocket. As he produced it, he made a remark that the card had replaced the necklace. He looked astounded to see another sombrero alight as he was standing by the bottom of the stairs. The stairs were like a pyramid: long and wide by the base, tapering gradually towards the top before giving way to the flatness of its cropped pinnacle. Light winds were slowly shuffling masses of rapidly warming air among the sparse, discoloured faces of silence, all walking far from him.

He looked up to the top of the stairs where the white house of the court building was set. A tall, shadowy figure of a man was standing on the very last step, peering down at him. The sun was towering right above him, dazzling Derick's eyes, blurring his vision. His shadow crept all the way down, spreading itself upon Derick's feet. He trod up over its unreal surface until he could see the man's face. He thought it was Simon at first since he was really tall, but then he recognized Shean as he stopped on one of the last steps.

'Come,' said he, opening his right arm, inviting Derick to follow him around the building.

When Shean stopped by the outer back wall of the building, a huge lea of cut grass with yellowish pathways of hardened sand and crushed stone crossing it over appeared at the bottom of the hill. Right in front of them, only several yards down, there was a rectangle-shaped pond of clear, shallow water. Suddenly, the holographic images of many school benches materialised before their eyes, levitating all over and above the undisturbed surface of the pond as though they were conjured up by magic. Then even more realistic images of human beings, all standing at attention by the benches, emerged from obscurity.

'Look down,' said Shean, 'it has all been done solely for you. These are the holograms of the people we've tested. These are the hollow men, and they will obey.'

'So it has all been true…'

'You've lived the true dream called life.'

'Indeed. Life is only a dream,' hissed Derick.

14
THE HOPE

When Natalie arrived in Kirkwood, her heart was in her throat. She left her car by the curb, near to the Mrs Deeprow's house of residence. She didn't even look whether she had to pay a parking fee; she ran along the polished slabs of pavement, zigzagging through masses of people, all greeting her politely, all slowly heading for the cathedral. As she turned the corner, suddenly, she bumped into Derick. He was running in the opposite direction. She stopped once she recognized him.

'Derick? Where are you going?!' asked Natalie.

'I'm going to live without pain,' he answered, running away from her. Their eyes never met.

She saw as he was gone from her sight, disappearing around the corner. Then she looked towards the gate of Mrs Deeprow's property — it was left open. She knew now where he was running from. As she came through the gate, she noticed that the front door was left open too. She stepped up her pace but walked into the house cautiously, listening with rising blood pressure. The living room and corridor were empty, but as she went inside, she became aware of thin wailing and laments coming from the kitchen. There, on the floor, she saw Mary with Mrs Deeprow in her arms. She was trying her hardest to resuscitate her but was failing badly on her own and her heart was falling into despair. When she saw Natalie, her eyes widened. Natalie immediately took her phone out and called for an ambulance, dropping to her knees by Mrs Deeprow's side.

Luckily, they didn't have to wait long because the hospital was only about a mile away from the house. It seemed that fortune was on their side in the end, despite all the setbacks and suffering, despite being denied to accompany the paramedics on their way back to the hospital because of the small size of the ambulance. They were reassured that she would live, leaving them somewhat uplifted from the gloom, gazing into each other's eyes. Mrs Deeprow suddenly grabbed Natalie's hand as she was being carefully placed on the stretcher. Natalie felt a surge of an electric current coming from her body and travelling up and down her spine as Mrs Deeprow's eyes flashed like dying stars. Then she breathed out and closed her eyes before being taken away.

'What's happened here?' asked Natalie as paramedics left the house. Her voice was shaking.

Mary prepared the glasses and poured still water into each of them, then she sat with her by the table in the kitchen. Natalie mentioned a strange, tingling sensation she had when Mrs Deeprow touched her hand. Mary smiled at her, saying that she'd always been a great mystery to her. Then she began unwinding today's story — from the moment they woke up until the time of Natalie's coming into the house. Natalie listened with growing terror as horrifying images of Derick's deeds entering her mind only confirmed her worst fears. She dropped to the floor again, holding herself tight by the stomach, suffering convulsions, unbelieving that her beloved one had just attempted to murder his own gran.

'Don't despair, my lovely. You must believe. You must live for the love you have inside of you.'

'How can I still believe when I'm on my knees?'

'Because love is the greatest power in this universe. We are made of stars.'

'I can't,' said Natalie, 'I'm feeling an extreme pain — the pain of living and being alive.'

'What's the matter, my love?'

'I'm pregnant with him.'

Mary slowly took the necklace off her chest, then she fastened it carefully around Natalie's neck.

'Every hope is born in pain,' said she, gazing deep into Natalie's eyes.